SURPRISE TOUCH

His jaw clenched. "I'm not a mercenary. And I'm not a snake."

Talia tried not to laugh. "That offends you? Tough guy like yourself? I imagine you've been called much worse."

"Oh, I've been called many things, sweetheart. But snake?" Archer shook his head. "I really must be losing my touch."

Now she cocked a hand on her hip. "You have a touch?"

Adrenaline pumped through her, along with something else. She wasn't actually enjoying this little heated interchange. Was she?

"Did you really think you'd just pop into my life, drop this amazing little fairy tale in my lap, and expect me to go dancing off behind you, all because you twinkled those eyes and showed off that little cleft in your chin?"

Oops. Bad strategy. She'd been doing fine up to that last part. What had been the vaguest suspicion of a smile quirking his lips now became one in full.

"You noticed the cleft, huh?"

Gone completely was the impatient, frustrated mercenary. In his place was . . . well, she didn't even want to think about what was going on behind those heated eyes.

Then he stepped closer . . .

The Royal Hunter

Donna Kauffman

Bantam Books

This is a work of fiction. Names, places, characters, and incidents are either the product of the author's imagination or are used fictitiously. Any resemblance to actual persons, living or dead, or locales is entirely coincidental.

THE ROYAL HUNTER

A Bantam Book

PUBLISHING HISTORY
Bantam paperback edition / October 2001

ISBN 0-553-58242-9

Published simultaneously in the United States and Canada

Bantam Books are published by Bantam Books, a division of Random house, Inc. Its trademark, consisting of the words "Bantam Books" and the portrayal of a rooster, is Registered in U.S. Patent and Trademark Office and in other countries. Marca Registrada. Bantam Books, 1540 Broadway, New York, New York 10036.

PRINTED IN THE UNITED STATES OF AMERICA

OPM 10 9 8 7 6 5 4 3 2 1

For Jill & David

Two people who understand the true power of love

Acknowledgments

I need to thank several people who were instrumental in helping me with this book. First, Kara Cesare, my editor, whose support for my doing things "a bit different" is unflagging and invaluable. Also to my mom, Jean Hobday, for the same unflagging support and for reading under a tight deadline. To Karen Solem for coming in at a difficult time and jumping right in with her help. Thanks to Jill Shalvis for being there for me every day and reading . . . and reading. Thanks again to the reliable creative mind of Michael Cretu for providing the sound track that I work by.

To Mitchell, Spencer, and Brandon, thank you for respecting summer work hours so well and for being proud of what your mom does. Lastly and always to my husband Mark, who defines the meaning of love and support. The quest continues . . .

Prologue

She must be found and brought to me."

Queen Catriona was dying. No one would have guessed from her imperious tone. Even propped up in bed, her skin as pale as the white satin robe buttoned tightly at her neck, she radiated royalty.

Archer wasn't concerned with royal heirs or vacated thrones. He was a businessman. "It has been more than a quarter century since the healer's disappearance. Many have tried to find her. All have failed." In fact, they'd stopped looking long before the king's brutal murder three years earlier, when the queen was only twenty-two. Long before she lay dying with the successor to the Welsh throne of Llanfair slumbering peacefully in her belly.

"Finding her is my only hope. You have your orders."

He wasn't much for commands, nor did he hold out much hope of success in this case. But if she was willing to pay him to try and save her life, who was he to say no? Devin Archer, savior. He supposed if he really thought about it, he had saved a number of people. But not for anything as ephemeral and unrewarding as honor. Honor didn't pay the bills or put fuel in the tank. He'd been called many things; renegade, rogue, pirate, spy. All accurate, if lacking imagination. Professional savior. He rather liked that one. He'd have to make sure that one got around. Might be good for business.

"I realize you could give a good goddamn whether I live or die," the queen said abruptly.

"I beg your pardon?"

"You beg nothing of me. Which is precisely why I selected you. I understand why you have no dedication or allegiance to a country that has never given you anything without asking your sacrifice first."

Archer frowned. He'd never denied his Australian heritage, but every other detail of his life, including his nomadic childhood as a slave and other less than savory details, had been deeply buried. Notoriety only went so far in business and he preferred to keep his past private. Anyone looking for information about one Devin Archer would only discover details from the time he'd arrived in the troubled kingdom of Llanfair. The queen's knowledge did not amuse him. But he respected anyone with better contacts than his own.

"And yet you wish to hire me nonetheless?"

"I believe you understand the machinations at hand better than most. You've likely worked for any number of those involved."

Archer's estimation of the young queen rose several notches. "We're not mates or anything, if that's what you're suggesting. As for my clientele . . ." He shrugged. "I'm not a political sort. Tends to limit a man's business opportunities."

"Exactly my point. A mercenary is loyal only to the one who pays him."

"I prefer *merchant*," he said quietly, returning her direct gaze. "I just follow the law of supply and demand. They demand, I supply." Thank God for free enterprise. "As for my allegiance, I have found that relying only on myself means I am less often disappointed."

The queen nodded, as if she understood the sentiment. And given her circumstances, it was likely that she did. "Succeed and you will be rewarded beyond your wildest imagination."

Archer smiled. "I have a fairly avid imagination."

She smiled as well. "I have a fairly deep purse."

"You'll need it if I succeed."

The smile vanished and the implacable face of a ruler once again emerged. "There is no *if*, Mr. Archer. Only *when*. You will use whatever means necessary to find Eleri Trahaern and return her to my protection. The child I carry must be brought safely into this world before I depart it. The Dalwyn line must continue."

If she sounded nothing like a dewy-eyed mother-to-be and more like a monarch engaged in a strategic campaign, Archer understood. Besides, what did he know about maternal instincts? His mother certainly hadn't had any. She'd sold him at the age of five. He'd long ago decided to view that as a good business decision on her part. She'd gotten the money she so desperately needed and he'd discovered the world of commerce. Twenty-five years later, he was a master of it. When he thought about it, and he rarely did anymore, he probably owed it all to her.

"What of the child if you die?" Archer asked baldly. "Who will care for it?"

"Not that it is any of your concern, but I have made the proper arrangements with those loyal to the House of Dalwyn. Chamberlain will not dare try to usurp the throne as long as the Dalwyn lineage remains intact." She eyed him. "But remain intact it will, or there will be chaos in this land." She folded her arms over her swollen belly. "Of course, you no doubt see that as a potential upswing in employment opportunity."

He managed not to appear surprised by the summation. Maternal she may not be, but she was a survivor. He respected that above all else. "I operate on one principal," Archer said, his accent amplified by irritation. "You don't question how I do my job and I won't question why you need it done." He took a step closer to the bedside. "But when you hire me, if it can *be* done, it will *get* done."

"That is the only reason you are standing before me. Bring her to me, Archer, and you will never want for anything, ever again."

And that was, after all, his entire goal in life. He nodded once—as close to a bow as he would ever make to anyone—then turned on his heel.

Catriona stopped him at the door. "There is one other thing."

Archer turned but said nothing.

"She must come willingly, or she will be no more able to heal me of this cursed affliction than any of the parade of incompetents that have come before her."

Archer frowned. "You wait until now to tell me this?"

Now it was the queen's turn to smile. For the first time, Archer was treated to the full force of the magnetism that had captivated the people of his adopted country.

"It should make little difference to you. I am certain that your broad range of skills, which I understand extend rather heavily into areas dealing with members of the opposite sex, will hold you in good stead in this matter." She let her head sink more deeply into the pillows. "I will not question how you convince her to return to my side. Just see that she does so. Willingly."

Archer's responding nod was curt to the point of rudeness, but he was not summoned back again.

Chapter 1

*B*loody hell and damn." Archer switched off his datatran and threw it across the room. The resulting crash wasn't satisfying, but then nothing else had satisfied him today, so why should that be any different? He'd spent hours making contacts, and contacts of contacts, even going so far as to talk to people he'd had no use for in years. He knew how to dig up information. This time had been different. He was no closer to finding a link to Eleri Trahaern than when he left the castle this morning.

He pressed a button on the com arm and a transmitter dropped down from the ceiling to hover in front of him. "Data on," he said wearily. He'd already read over the old reports from every other person who'd attempted to find Eleri Trahaern. "Page three," he ordered, skimming once again the first report, filed days after her disappearance. There was one bit of information that nagged at him. "The Old One," he murmured. The reclusive mystic was the only person connected to the royal healer who had never been found or interrogated. "Probably dead by now."

A sleek black cat undulated around the corner of the living area and leaped into his lap. "A cat, huh? Well, I suppose we are on the prowl."

Ringer studiously washed his paws, ignoring his master entirely, but making himself quite at home in his lap.

"Beastie," he muttered, but scratched him behind the ears as he reread the report. "Find visual of the Old One," he ordered. "Search logs dated thirty years or before."

"No visual available," purred the audiotrak.

"Yeah, yeah. Locate contacts of the Old One. Any contact." It wasn't a promising lead, but it was better than nothing.

"No available information."

Just then a loud burst of static sputtered from across the room where the datatran lay in several pieces. "Jesus, Joseph, and Elvis." Covering his ears, Archer pushed Ringer off his thighs and crossed the room, intent on stomping the damn thing to death.

The air flickered in front of him, stopping him in his tracks. The squeal died as the air shifted and transformed into the image of an old man in a white robe.

"I believe you are looking for me."

Even though it was obviously a hologram, Archer palmed the gaz he always wore and looked from floor to ceiling, wall to wall, wondering where in the hell it was transmitting from. He had no such expensive apparatus here. Had the queen sent someone in to have him watched? He didn't think anyone could breach his security rig, but then she'd found out about his past. Maybe he'd underestimated her far too much.

"Your field is secure," the old man said quietly. "I suggest you ask the questions you wish and do it quickly if you intend to succeed in your mission. Trust that I am not making contact because I enjoy the company."

"Who the hell are you?"

"I am Baleweg. I believe you know me as the Old One. Meet me in one hour. Your datatran contains the address." Then the image blinked away, the air still and clear.

"Why not answer my questions right n—" He was gone. Archer dragged over a chair and spent a few minutes scanning the metal-beamed ceiling, but knew it was no use. Whatever had made that transmission wouldn't be obvious. A real inspection would take time. Time the Old One was correct in stating he didn't have.

He pocketed his gun and scooped up the abused datatran. The cover had broken off and the ear wire was bent, but . . . He pressed his thumb to the identapad on the back, and after another patch of static and a brief ear-piercing squeal, it hummed to life. "Screen on." The screen glowed blue . . . and an address typed itself out. "How in the hell did he do that?"

The Old One was the clue, the one man who'd claimed to have seen Eleri before she disappeared. Then he'd vanished as well. Until now. Archer wondered why and intended to have that answered along with everything else.

Ringer trotted after him as he headed for the door. "I don't suppose you'll stay here?" The cat merely stared at him. "Fine, fine, but no wise-guy stuff today. Got it?"

Ringer blinked up at him.

"Why do I even bother?" he muttered.

They arrived at the small row house over an hour later. Traffic through the capital city had been a bitch. Getting to the east side this late in the day was roughly the equivalent of a suicide mission. Archer shoved the violation disc he'd gotten for reckless endangerment under the seat with all the others and sealed the vehicle.

Ringer rubbed against his legs as he stood in front of the door. "Third floor," he said to the monitor. He looked down. "And don't think all this sudden affection will earn you any bonus points." He ignored the deep purr vibrating against his calf. "You had to go and embarrass me like that with those City Transport Agents, right? Oh, they thought you were hilarious. A real joker." Shifters enjoyed the ability to select an image that made a statement about their particular feelings at the moment. Archer was rarely amused. "How did you learn what a platypus looked like anyway?"

He turned his attention back to the building, but the doors to the air lift refused to slide open. "Come on. And keep up with me or I might leave you down here." He shoved open the door to the stairs and took them two at a time, Ringer right on his heels.

He palmed the gaz out of his waistband, but his instincts weren't screaming trap. Still, no point in taking chances. He rounded the landing and started up the next flight, grumbling under his breath. They could build entire colonies in space, he thought, but they couldn't make an air lift that didn't break down every other day. One of the many reasons he lived in a one-floor warehouse.

It was warm and humid on the third floor, meaning air control was also out of whack. Archer wouldn't have been surprised to find mold growing on the baseboards, but the place was surprisingly clean. The pale green carpet was worn, but not dirty. Sheer yellow curtains covered the tall window at the far end of the hall, keeping the light to a dim shadow and contributing to the overall greenhouse feel of the place. There were three doors. One they'd just come out of, the other two were painted white, one on each side of the hall. Neither had numbers on them.

Archer banged his fist on the nearest one. "Baleweg?"

Ringer grumbled and sat, staring out the window, tail twitching.

"You want to chase pigeons? Taking this cat deal a bit far, aren't you, mate?" Ringer meowed, his tail twitching faster. Archer followed his gaze outside then looked back at him. He swore the beastie was smiling, and smugly at that. "Think you're hot shit, do you now?" He shoved the window until it moved grudgingly upward. Ringer leaped out onto the rooftop in a flash of black with Archer right behind him. They both reached the prostrate form of the old man at the same time.

How in the hell had someone gotten to him? The old man had stayed safely hidden for almost three decades. "Shit."

Ringer gave the old man's feathery cheek a long swipe with his tongue. The man emitted a snore, then smiled. "Nadja, you minx," he mumbled.

"Jesus." Archer nudged him with his toe. "Baleweg, you got company."

The man shifted to his side, frowned and rubbed at his nose, then slowly blinked his eyes open. He focused first on Ringer and smiled, then frowned as he looked at Archer. "Ah. The royal hunter. Sorry. I doze when I can. You took your time."

"Have you tried to cross town lately?"

"I don't avail myself of public transportation when I can avoid it."

"Speaking of which, how did you transmit your image—"

"We must not waste any more time." He gathered his robes and moved surprisingly gracefully into a cross-legged position. He motioned Archer to sit.

Archer looked around instead. The rooftop had been transformed into a lavish tropical paradise.

But the leafy fronds and dense foliage made it diffi-cult to see beyond and therefore not secure. "Can we speak inside?"

"I assure you this location is perfectly adequate. My private sanctuary. Lovely spot, don't you think?"

"I'd rather speak inside, if you don't mind."

Baleweg seemed unaffected by Archer's most un-compromising stare, but he sighed and stood. "Young people. Always so melodramatic."

"These are melodramatic times," Archer said.

Baleweg merely sighed. "Might I offer you some refreshment?"

"You said yourself we're short on time. I just need some information."

The old man reached into the folds of his robe and came out with a small treat, which he tossed to Ringer. "Just because your human companion lacks in the social graces, doesn't mean you should suffer for it, does it now, my little soldier?"

"Ringer," Archer warned. Not that it did a bit of good. The cat snatched the snack and made off for the bushes in the far corner with his treasure.

Archer swore under his breath, but turned back to the old man. "I want to know what you know about—"

"Eleri Trahaern. Yes, I know."

Royal hunter. Now he understood the reference. "I was unaware my recent job offering had become public knowledge."

"It hasn't," Baleweg answered, maintaining steady eye contact.

"Reports say you were the last one to see her."

"Yes, I did speak to her on the afternoon that she disappeared."

"You've been impossible to locate since that day. I suspect most people think you are dead."

"Perfectly acceptable to me. Allows me more time

to enjoy the pursuit of knowledge. Never had patience for politics or the abuse of power. Especially powers that are misunderstood."

"Why surface now?"

"It is time," he said simply.

And yet Archer was fully aware there was nothing simple about this. "Then you know where she is?"

Baleweg nodded.

Archer felt the initial buzz of excitement, but it was tempered by wariness. "Why haven't you offered this information to the queen?"

"I had other allegiances. I believe you might understand the predicament."

Archer ignored that. "And now?"

"Now it is time," he repeated.

"We'd all have had a hell of a lot more time if you'd come forward sooner."

"Ah, but then you wouldn't be in the position to earn such a handsome paycheck."

Now he understood. It always came down to money. So much for the mystical mumbo jumbo. "You want to know what your piece of the action will be if this works, right? Well, mate, I have a standard—"

"I do not wish recompense of any sort."

Archer sat back on his heels, surprised into silence. It was beyond him why anyone would willingly turn down money. It made him suspicious. "But you will help me? Why?"

"All things happen as they do for a reason, young Archer. You needn't know those reasons to benefit from them, aye?" Baleweg rearranged his flowing robes over his legs. His hair was white and sparse on his tanned head, but his face was almost baby smooth, the skin translucent. Add in those eyes and he was a rather unique-looking character. Part gnome, part sorcerer, part mental patient. "The human mind is a supremely stubborn thing, thwarting its own ability to expand and encompass ideas not easily explained." Baleweg tilted his head and gave Archer a probing look, real interest in his eyes now. "Are you willing to expand your mind?"

Archer had no idea what the hell he was talking about. "I just want to find Eleri Trahaern."

"Then you must accept that not all things lie on a scientific plane."

Like that transmission you made into my home earlier? he wanted to ask, but didn't. Instead he shrugged. "I've learned not to question the existence of things just because I don't understand them. I operate on instinct. Saved my backside many times."

"Then let your instinct guide you now. Eleri is no longer here in this time."

"Excuse me?"

Baleweg stared at him, his eyes sparking a blue so sharp and clear it almost hurt to look at them. "She is no longer in this time," he repeated calmly. "Meaning she is in another."

"Time travel." Archer swore silently. "Right." He pushed to a stand. "Sorry to have taken up your time." Though he was only really sorry at having been suckered in by this quack. No wonder the report had been so short.

Baleweg didn't rise. "Did you not just state that you don't dismiss things you don't understand?"

"Scientists have tried to bend time for centuries. No one's ever done it."

Baleweg smiled. "As I said, not all things exist on a scientific plane."

"Okay, then, tell me how to get to where she is and I'll leave you to your business."

"This is nothing so simple. You do not enter a time that is not your own, nor disturb the life of another, without good reason."

"Saving the queen's life isn't a good reason?"

"I did not say it must be good for another. What good is in it for the one whose life will be disturbed?"

The man was more frustrating than Ringer. "I will gladly pay her and pay her well for her help."

"Ah, but not all things can be solved with money." He lifted a finger to stall Archer's response. "Nor is money the reward all men, or women, seek."

"Then tell me what she wants and I'll bloody well give it to her." In Archer's extensive experience, everyone had something they wanted, and were willing to barter to get. "It's not like she can't go back to her old life once she's healed the queen."

"Lives, once dabbled in, never return to their former sameness. Like a rock thrown in a pond. Even after the surface ripples smooth, the landscape beneath is forever altered."

"Fine. I don't mean her any harm and neither does the queen."

"Yes, but have you stopped to consider that others will want to prevent her from helping the queen? Can you keep her safe from this harm?"

"Me? I'm just the deliveryman. The queen will handle protection."

"The royal court tried to protect her once before and she almost lost her life. Why should she trust them again?"

"That was almost thirty years ago. Security is far more advanced."

"As are those who strive to get around it. Did it occur to you that there is a reason she has not returned? She did not depart this time with an easy heart. It was her duty from birth to attend the royal family and she was the first ever in her line to disobey and put her own needs over those she was born to help."

"If her heart was so heavy at the thought of

leaving, hearing of the queen's predicament would make her want to return, wouldn't it?"

"She never knew the young queen," Baleweg announced. "Eleri was in service during the time of King Cynan."

Archer leaned forward. "So, tell me how to find her. I assume you know how to get me there?"

Baleweg studied Archer. "Your impatience will cost you things you can ill afford to lose if you are not careful."

"I haven't had too much trouble up to this point."

Baleweg merely sighed. "Time is an ongoing continuum. Rushing toward it does not make it advance any faster."

Archer took a deep breath and tried to smile without clenching his jaw. "How do we find her, then?"

"The heart will be your guide."

"Wonderful." He had no heart. He'd given the only one he had to his mother . . . and she'd sold it. *C'est la vie.*

"Trust me."

Archer stared at the old man. "Like I said."

Baleweg sighed, then rose to his feet. "You will see."

Archer whistled for Ringer. "I guess I need you to show me how to get back once I find her." Not that he really believed he was going anywhere.

"There will be no need. I will be coming with you."

Archer laughed. "I work alone. Nonnegotiable."

Baleweg turned. "I go with you, or you stay right here in the twenty-third century. Nonnegotiable."

Archer stared him down.

"Do you wish to trust *your* heart? Or mine?"

Score one for the old man. Archer swore under his breath. "There are going to be some ground rules. I am in charge. We go where I want, when I want, no questions asked. If you don't keep up, you get left behind. And if it comes to a choice between my skin and yours guess which one I'm going to save? You still in?"

Baleweg smiled. "If you don't keep track of my skin, as you call it, you will be forever stuck in the past. Are *you* still in?"

"The past?" Somehow he'd assumed the old man had been talking about the future. For the first time, the skin on the back of Archer's neck prickled. Not a good sign.

"Yes, the past. And be aware, we cannot return to this precise moment. I cannot move you backward in your own life's span. The time we spend there will also be spent here." Ringer meowed and rubbed against Baleweg's legs.

"Traitor," Archer muttered. Could this guy really know what he was doing? Could he risk not finding out? "Okay, fine, fine, we're both in. What do we do next?"

Baleweg turned and focused on a point somewhere in front of him. He began to chant beneath his breath. A chill that Archer couldn't define, or control, chased over his skin. The hair on the back of his neck stood straight out, his instincts all but shrieking that he was about to take an irreversible step. He was a heartbeat away from stepping back and telling the old man to stop, when Baleweg turned to him and said, "Step through it."

Archer looked in front of him and, amid the jungle of plants and flowers, he saw a small triangle emerge in the air. It grew larger, the air inside it wavy, like liquid, as if it had trapped all the heat and contained it. Only it hadn't. Archer was sweating, his palms damp, but his skin was oddly chilled. *What in the hell was happening? Was this really possible?*

He stared at Baleweg. He hardly knew this bloke and here he was, about to follow him into God knew what.

"The doorway will not remain open forever," Baleweg replied, his features looking somewhat strained. "Go or stay. Choose now."

"Shit." Archer slapped his thigh and Ringer jumped into his arms. "Until we figure out where in the hell we are, just stay a cat, dammit, hear me?" Ringer merely purred and butted his head against Archer's hand.

Archer held him tightly, then stepped into the watery air in front of them. Baleweg followed.

A moment later Archer found himself standing on a busy downtown thoroughfare. He turned and looked behind him just as the triangle doorway to Baleweg's jungle garden shrank to almost nothing, then evaporated. In a blink it was as if it never existed.

He swallowed hard, urging his heart to slow to a rate that would keep it from exploding out of his chest. He'd faced the unknown many times. *This is merely another adventure, mate.*

The buildings didn't tower nearly so tall. In fact, he could see the tops of every one of them. And sky traffic was nonexistent. Also, the building materials were more raw and crude-looking. The busy intersection was filled as usual with bumper-to-bumper traffic. Then he noticed all the cars rested directly on the ground. He coughed as one sped by. And they belched smoke.

"Great." He waved a hand in front of his face. Whatever time they were in, air purification hadn't been mandated yet. Ringer squirmed in his arms. He looked down. "Jesus, didn't I tell you— Never mind." He tucked him under one arm. "Just stay quiet, for God's sake."

Clusters of people pushed by them, apparently oblivious to the sudden arrival of two men . . . and a big white duck. "What year is it, anyway?"

"It is the beginning of the second millennium. The year two thousand one, to be exact."

"What part of Britain is this? This isn't Llanfair."

"No, it isn't. Britain was still somewhat united in those days, with only one monarchy, I believe, not three. But we are not in Britain. We are in America."

Archer swung his gaze back to the old man. "America? We hopped time *and* continents? Are you sure we're even in the right place?"

"Close enough. We are in the right state. Connecticut."

"How in the hell can you tell?"

Baleweg gestured at a metal plate on one of the vehicles parked curbside.

Archer ignored the smile. "She's here, then? Eleri is here?"

Baleweg laid his hand on Archer's heart. "The one you seek is close." Then he turned, white robes flowing, and whistled sharply for a taxi.

Chapter 2

"Talia, can you come here? Something's wrong with this puppy."

Talia Trahaern crossed the day room and helped her new employee with the wriggling pile of fluff he was trying to handle. "What happened?"

The young man looked to her, eyes overbright. "The colonel was playing tug with his blanket and he caught his teeth in the threads and—I'm sorry, Talia."

"It's okay." Talia felt a bit like squirming herself under Jimmy's imploring stare. There was something about him that bothered her, but she couldn't put her finger on it. Something about the focused way he watched her. But he was always polite, extremely loyal, and good with the animals. He was probably just trying too hard, she told herself. That was rare enough these days and dedicated kennel help was difficult to find. Still, her smile was a bit forced. "I can take it from here. Why don't you go help Miss Helen over there? She'll have cat hair from head to toe if she lets Marble rub all over her like that."

"I think she just likes the lint roller afterward," Jimmy said with a roll of his eyes, then hurried off, leaving Talia choking on a surprised laugh. Maybe he was just going through that awkward teenage phase, she told herself.

She knelt by the colonel's chair. Furry Friends Day at the Lodge was her favorite day of the month, but there was always a crisis or two to keep things interesting.

"Young fella here seems to have his tooth stuck," the older man said, trying to calm the puppy down, his spotted hands a bit shaky.

Talia smiled reassuringly, but swallowed as she prepared herself for the onslaught that would hit her as soon as she made the connection. Keeping her voice soft, she put her hands over the colonel's and nudged his aside so she could hold the little one. Pain instantly shot through her gums, but she managed not to flinch or give anything away. "What did you do you little rascal," she managed through gritted teeth. As carefully as she could, hoping the fine trembling in her own hands wasn't too noticeable, she gently worked the fine strands of yarn loose from two of the puppy's teeth. He'd pulled so hard that the yarn had shredded and cut into his gums. "Steady, there you go," she murmured, using her sleeve to dab at the blood as the last thread slipped free.

The throb in her own gums dulled immediately and she smiled as the puppy wriggled and licked her all over, happy once again. "You little imp." She tried to get another look at the puppy's gums, but it was hard. There didn't seem to be any fresh blood. She looked up at the colonel. "He'll be okay, but we can't let him chew on your blanket. Use the rawhide or the squeaky toy." She placed both in his lap, then carefully handed the dog back to him.

"Orders received," the colonel said with a salute. At the age of eighty-eight, his body was beginning to

fail him, but his booming voice could still easily
command an army.

Talia saluted him, then stood and looked around
at the seniors presently nuzzling the animals from
her private shelter. The unconditional love shared
in this room was in many cases the only affection
some of the Lodge residents ever received. And all
of her orphaned animals needed as much love as
possible.

Still smiling, she turned in time to see a man with
a long white flowing beard and equally white flowing
robes enter the room. He beamed her a smile and
an odd shiver ran down her spine. It was as if she
recognized him somehow, but she knew she'd never
laid eyes on the man before.

The sensation was quickly forgotten when she
spied the man who entered just behind him. He was
closer to her own age, tall, rangy, and dressed in
dark pants, black boots, and a leather jacket. The
clothes looked different somehow, but she couldn't
quite figure out why. She also couldn't imagine what
connection he had with the older man; they couldn't
be more different. Where the older man was almost
glowing with pure white, the younger man had dark
hair and even darker eyes. His stern expression only
served to enhance the hard lines that shaped his face.
He was definitely a bit wild, made somehow more so
by the small scruffy dog he cradled in his arms.

She relaxed at once, realizing the reason for his
intensity and the surprise intrusion. Obviously he'd
found a stray, or his dog had been hurt and someone had steered him here. She wasn't quite sure what
to do with him; he was unsettling in a way she
couldn't put her finger on. But she knew what to do
with the dog.

She crossed the room reluctantly. If she hadn't
been so focused on the way he filled the doorway,

she'd have picked up more quickly on the fact that the dog wasn't communicating anything to her. Usually she knew what an animal was feeling even before she looked at it. Not this one. She stopped a few feet short as confusion settled in. "Can I help you?" she asked. "Is this about your dog?"

His gaze locked on hers and she was aware that he didn't seem all that concerned about his pet. In fact, his attention seemed completely focused on her. She was on the verge of taking a step back when the older gentleman stepped forward.

"We've come looking for you, Miss Trahaern."

So they knew her name, not all that odd if someone had indeed steered them her way. "About the dog?" The old man was looking at her—into her—in a way that made her even more uncomfortable. For a moment she wondered if he knew about her special . . . ability. But that couldn't be.

The younger man, obviously impatient, butted in. "Eleri? You are Eleri Trahaern, are you not?"

Talia froze, only peripherally aware of the older man shaking his head. Hearing her mother's name for the first time in over twenty years left her speechless.

"Archer, we can't simply leap—"

"We have little time to waste," he stated flatly. "You *are* Eleri Trahaern, aren't you?"

Talia began backing away, her skin prickling in alarm. Years of working with animals had taught her much in reading the signals they gave off. Especially those between predator and prey.

He pulled a folded piece of paper from his back pocket. "I just want to talk to you." He unfolded the paper and flashed a picture at her.

It was her mother, there was no doubt about that. Talia felt her knees give a little. She didn't have a picture of her. As far as she knew there was no one alive who had ever known her mother. If there had been, she wouldn't have been left to the sisters at St. Evangeline's when she was six years old.

Her head began to swim. She looked just like her mother. The powerful punch-in-the-gut connection she'd wanted so badly for so many years had finally been made. Distant memories of her mother swam to the surface of her mind. For years she'd carefully pulled out the few she had, but they were like worn storybooks with pictures faded from too many readings.

"Eleri, we must talk."

It was hearing her mother's name again that yanked Talia from her nearly trancelike state. She jerked her gaze to the man called Archer. *This* man had known her mother. "I'm . . . I'm not—How did you know—?"

Archer scanned the room behind her. "We need to talk, but not here. Is there somewhere more private?"

She realized she had to act before he made a scene. She turned toward the residents, pasting a smile on her face even as her mind was reeling. "I'll be right back," she said, hoping she sounded reassuring. She sure didn't feel it at the moment.

Colonel Rosewall started to stand, obviously ready to put his forty-seven years of military experience to use if she needed his aid. He couldn't move faster than a snail and had less strength than a puppy, but the gesture warmed her heart. "It's fine, Colonel. I'll be right back."

But it wasn't fine. Talia turned to the two men, a million questions filling her mind, but her tongue hopelessly tangled. She started to lead them into the lobby, when all of a sudden Archer froze and yelled, "You!"

She whirled around just in time to see Jimmy

leaping toward her. Before she had time to think, Jimmy grabbed her, and with a strength she hadn't thought he was capable of, he spun her around and locked his arm around her neck, twisting her other arm behind her back for leverage. Her heart was drumming, her mind spinning, unable to comprehend what was happening.

"You're too late. She's mine, Archer. I got here first."

"Too bad you weren't the last, Dideon." Archer launched himself over the chair between them.

Talia instinctively closed her eyes and flinched against the expected impact, but instead Jimmy stumbled back away from Archer, tripping over someone's walker, sending them all sprawling. His grip relaxed slightly and Talia immediately fought her way free. But Jimmy was already rolling to his feet and racing for the door, shoving through the chairs, knocking several of the residents aside in his haste. Archer was fast on his heels.

Talia crawled to her feet as the melee erupted in full. Dideon? He'd called Jimmy Dideon. "But Jimmy's last name is Mason," she mumbled, to no one in particular. She spied the old man in the flowing robes, who now had the scruffy dog tucked under his arm, being carried out with the crowd, and headed after him.

It was complete chaos. Canes were waving, there was swearing and shouting, dogs barked, Marble screeched, walkers banged into each other. The scene was topped off by a wheelchair logjam in the doorway as Archer raced out, hot on Jimmy's heels.

The whole group spilled into the foyer. Talia managed to shout to the desk manager as she raced by to please help calm everyone down. But those who were mobile were all giving chase—at varying speeds, of course. The entire scene came to a tangled halt just past the courtyard at the edge of the parking lot, when Jimmy made it over the rear wall and disappeared into the wooded area behind the main building.

Archer was walking back toward her, breathing hard and cursing quietly.

The mob of residents moved closer, ready to rescue her. If she hadn't been so dumbfounded by the whole situation, she would have laughed. If they could only see themselves. This was the most animated they'd been since that morning Mr. Lambert had been found dead, with a smile on his face, in Mrs. Zambini's bed.

"It's okay, everyone," she called to them. Had Jimmy really tried to hurt her? Or had he just been scared and she'd been a convenient target? *I found her first.* She shivered at the memory of his words, the look in his eyes. But it made no sense. "Show's over," she called out, trying to sound confident.

"He chased that sweet Jimmy," Miss Helen cried, cat hair sticking straight out all over her sweater. She pounded her cane on the sidewalk and waved her sticky roller in the air. "I say let's get him!"

"Your 'sweet Jimmy' tried to choke our Talia," the colonel barked. "I say we call the police!"

"It's okay, Miss Helen, Colonel. I'll find out what's going on. Please, could you all go back inside and help Tom round up the animals for me?"

Worry for their furry friends all left behind in the stampede immediately filled their faces, as Talia had hoped it would. She knew the desk manager had likely rounded them all up at this point, but they wouldn't have thought of that. They all shuffled back toward the building. All except for Colonel Rosewall.

"Young man, I'll have it from you now." He rapped Archer smartly on the chest with the handle of his cane, as if he were running inspection and Archer had failed it. Miserably. "Why in blazes did you come in here like the fourth cavalry charging a hill when a simple question or two would have sufficed? I'm certain whatever the situation is with young James, it could have been handled more discreetly."

Archer nudged the cane handle aside. "Sorry, Commander, this really doesn't—"

"That's *colonel,* soldier!" Rosewall straightened his thin shoulders, looking amazingly authoritarian in his navy blue bathrobe. "And if it concerns young Miss Trahaern here, then it most certainly—"

Talia intervened and placed a gentle hand on the colonel's arm. "It's okay, Colonel. I need to have a discussion with Mr. Archer here. Would you do me a favor and go back inside and help the others? I know they look to you for guidance." She leaned closer. "And if I'm not inside in ten minutes, call the cops, okay?"

The colonel harrumphed, but finally saluted her, gave Archer a brief once-over that likely would have left his troops trembling but made no obvious impact on Archer, then walked toward the lobby door. "Ten minutes," he repeated. "Not a second longer."

Talia nodded, waiting until he was inside before turning around. "Just what in the hell is going on here? Who are you? Some kind of cop or something?" He didn't look like a cop. And the old man hardly looked like a cop's partner. It might not be wise to remain outside alone with him, but he knew something about her mother. She shuddered again and rubbed gently at her neck. "How did you know my mother? And what does that have to do with Jimmy?"

"Mother?"

"You said you were looking for Eleri Trahaern."

Archer swore. "Where is she?"

"I— She's dead."

Just then the older man materialized behind her, seemingly out of nowhere. Archer took the dog from its happy perch in the old man's arms. "You didn't take us far enough back. This is her daughter. We need Eleri."

"We are precisely where we need to be," he said calmly. "Eleri was pregnant with young Talia here, you see. That is why she left."

"*Now* you tell me?"

"Now is when it matters," he said simply. "Going back to her lifetime would have yielded us nothing. We wouldn't have convinced her to return with a young child."

Talia's attention flickered between them. She had no idea what they were talking about. "My mother died when I was six."

Pain flickered over Baleweg's smooth face. "I know, my dear, and you have my deepest condolences. I tried to help, but she was a stubborn one. However, now your time has come. Only you can help us."

Talia felt as if she'd been dropped into Oz. "Help you with what? Wait a minute, *you* knew my mother?"

He nodded and smiled gently. "I did. And I'm sorry to barge in on you like this." He sent a baleful look toward Archer, then turned his sublime countenance back to her. "What we have to tell you, Miss Trahaern, will seem fantastical, but I'm asking that you open both your mind and your young heart and hear us out. Lives are at stake."

He took her hand and what felt like a mild electrical current smoothed up and down her arm. She would have pulled away, but the sensation felt so incredibly good she didn't seem to have the will-power to end the contact. His eyes were so blue, she realized absently, you could stare at them forever.

She shook her head then and blinked a couple of times, frowning as she pulled her arm free. The pleasurable sensations lingered, however. "I don't know how I can be of any help to you. I remember very little about my mother."

"What do you remember?" the old man asked.

For all that Talia was enthralled with the idea that she had finally met someone with clues to her past, this was just too strange. She folded her arms. "I think perhaps you should explain yourself first."

Archer sighed in disgust, drawing her attention back to him.

"What is your problem?" The tension finally snapped her control. "And why were you after Jimmy? What did he mean, 'I found her first'?"

"You mean Dideon? I'm guessing he was sent here to kill you." He said this as smoothly as if he'd been discussing the weather. "I thought you'd appreciate me stopping him." He turned to Baleweg. "I get no gratitude."

Talia's mouth dropped open. So he *was* a cop. But their accents . . . they were both Brits. That made a strange sort of sense, as her mother had been Welsh. So what kind of cops could they be? Some sort of secret agents? Like James Bond or something? This was all too surreal. Maybe he wasn't a secret agent, just deranged. They'd both escaped from some mental institution and they'd just thought they'd known Jimmy. Except . . . Jimmy had definitely recognized Archer. And they both knew Eleri. They had her picture. A headache of mammoth proportions spang to life inside her head.

Baleweg sighed the sigh of the eternally weary and

folded his hands together. "If you'd allow me to conduct this in the manner in which we'd agreed—"

"No, mate, you instructed, I never agreed."

"And they wonder why I don't get involved in the affairs of the court," Baleweg muttered.

The court? "Is Jimmy in some kind of legal trouble? What did he do?" She knew something was weird about that guy. But how in the hell it involved her mother . . . Her head throbbed.

Baleweg turned to them both, his serene countenance now shored up with a goodly amount of steel. "Miss Trahaern, I apologize for the manner in which this situation has been brought to your attention. However, I cannot reverse what has been done." He looked at Archer. "Much as I would like to. Once a life is entered, I can only go forward in it." He gestured behind them. "I see there is a gazebo down near the gardens. Why don't we head there and I will endeavor to answer all your questions."

A life entered? Again, she had no idea what he was talking about. She did know that the gazebo was another hundred yards father away from the Lodge. Not a good idea. "We'll have our little talk right here." She eyed first Archer, then Baleweg. "You'll answer my questions, then I'll decide what, if anything, I'll do to help you."

Archer stared at the woman who was worth a queen's ransom to him. Unfortunately, this wasn't a dead-or-alive mission. He turned to Baleweg. "Catriona wants Eleri Trahaern. How do you know her daughter will be able to help?"

Baleweg didn't look away from Talia. "The gift is passed from mother to daughter."

If Archer had shifted his gaze to Talia's even a moment later, he would have missed the split-second flash of . . . what had it been? Fear? Understanding?

It was the latter that propelled him forward. If she was a healer like her mother, then she would do. "What do you remember about your mother?"

"I believe I said I would ask the questions." There was heat in her voice. Her eyes had edged away from the wildness he'd seen earlier. Perhaps she was made of stronger stuff than her willowy frame and fine halo of dark hair would lead one to believe. But it was those ethereal gray eyes that held his attention. "How do you know my mother?" She looked to them both.

"I never knew her," Archer replied. "But I knew of her. She held a rather prominent position in court."

"Court? I don't remember her ever mentioning she was involved in the legal system."

"The House of Dalwyn."

Baleweg stepped between them both. "He is speaking of the royal court."

Talia looked confused. "Royal? But isn't Queen Elizabeth a Windsor or something?"

"The House of Dalwyn comes after the Windsors. Much after, in fact." Baleweg reached out a hand. "This is confusing, but I assure you we can explain everything."

Talia backed away from his touch. "Just tell me how you know my mother and how you tracked me down." She left Jimmy's role out of it for now. She glanced at her watch, then darted a look to the lobby door.

Archer knew their time was growing short. Baleweg was handling this all wrong. Looking into her eyes, Archer realized what it was he'd seen earlier, beyond the fear, the understanding. Curiosity. She was terrified, but she still wanted to know. She'd been six when Eleri died and apparently knew nothing about her mother's role in a future kingdom. He could change that.

"We come from a future time. As did your mother." He gauged her reaction. Stunned confusion. She didn't know anything about this. Archer swore under his breath. Nothing was ever easy. "Our ruler, Queen Catriona Dalwyn, is very ill. Your mother served her father, King Cynan." A flicker of recognition. He leaped on it. "You recognize the name?"

She shook her head, but she was lying.

"Your mother, what did she tell you about him?" he insisted.

"Nothing. It was . . . it was a bedtime story. A fairy tale." Real fear flickered in her eyes.

"It's no fairy tale, Talia. Your mother was telling you where she was from. That was her home. Now the queen needs your help."

Talia's expression clearly said that she felt as if she were placating the insane. Archer sympathized. He was beginning to think this whole mission was insane. How in the hell was he going to convince her they spoke the truth?

He turned to Baleweg for help, but the older man merely motioned for him to continue. *Thanks, mate.* "Your mother was born into service for the House of Dalwyn. She was the royal healer. But there was trouble, an attempt was made on her life, and she escaped. She found a doorway . . . to the past." He motioned to Baleweg. "He helped her to come here."

Talia simply stared at him, looking mostly numb now.

"Baleweg says your mother passed her skills to you." He noticed she glanced immediately at Ringer, then back at him. He wasn't sure what that signaled, but apparently Baleweg did.

The old man stepped forward. "Ah, you're an empath, aren't you, my dear?"

The wild edge immediately returned to her eyes.

"It is fairly common in our time. And certainly among your kind."

"My kind?" she whispered. Her face was losing color, except for two bright pink splotches high in her cheeks.

"You are a healer, as well, Talia," Baleweg said kindly. "Your mother came here, to this time, to protect you, but it seems as though she was taken from you before she could explain your destiny. She said nothing at all to you?"

Talia's mouth opened, then shut again. She blinked a few times, as if seeing something inside her mind, then shook her head. "No. No, she didn't."

"You're lying again." Archer knew it, just as he knew they'd run out of time.

Her eyes flew to him, the bright spots in her cheeks heightening further, her eyes growing glassy. "No! I don't know anything about what you're telling me."

"You recalled something, just now. What?" He took her arm. "Tell me."

"They were just a bunch of fairy tales! They didn't mean anything."

Baleweg shook his head and smoothly relieved her arm from Archer's grasp. "Archer, really. Not all things can be solved with your bullying ways. And here I had heard stories of your prowess with the fairer sex. Propaganda I'm beginning to disbelieve."

Archer tossed him a look. "This isn't a seduction, old man."

"I should hope not. You'd be going about it all wrong."

"This is why I always work alone," he muttered.

Baleweg turned his gaze to Talia. "I don't know about the bedtime tales your mother told you, but I imagine a goodly part of them were based on her life in court. Perhaps she'd have explained that in time. We'll never know. But that can't be helped. The queen needs your help. It is time for you to return and take your rightful place."

"I'm not a . . . I can't—this is crazy." Her voice was a strangled whisper.

"Yes, you can," Archer said firmly. "I will pay you very well. Riches beyond your imagination. And as soon as you help the queen, I'll make sure you're brought back to this very spot." He carefully averted his gaze from Baleweg. He had no idea if Catriona would let her leave, but that wasn't his problem at the moment. "Do we have a deal?"

Her gaze bounced almost frantically between Archer and Baleweg. Her throat worked, but she said nothing.

"Really, Archer," Baleweg implored, "money is not the solution here—"

"Money is always the solution," he shot back.

Whatever Talia might have said was drowned by the sudden wail of sirens. Two vehicles spun into the side lot. Men in blue uniforms poured out of the doors before the rolling vehicles had come to a complete stop, all of them shouting commands.

"Come, Archer," Baleweg commanded. "Our time is up for now." He closed his eyes and Archer saw the triangle begin to open behind him amid the hedgerow.

• Archer pulled Talia around to face him. Her dazed gray eyes finally locked on his. "You will help us, Talia Trahaern. We will be back."

With great reluctance, he released her. Just as the first man in blue planted himself and pulled what must have been some kind of weapon, Archer turned and stepped into the bushes and through the triangle after Baleweg and Ringer.

Chapter 3

Talia awoke with a start, then slapped a hand on her chest to keep the book from falling off. She swung a leg to the porch to keep from dumping herself out of the hammock she'd been reading in. Or napping in, apparently.

She blew out a long breath and lay back, giving a little push before tucking her foot into the hammock again. She stared at the porch roof as she swung gently, the early evening air filled with the sounds of frogs and crickets. But she didn't hear them, nor did she see the peeling paint above her. She saw Archer, his black eyes flashing, commanding. She heard his dark voice, with that beguiling accent, ordering her to return with him. Aussie, she realized now. Not Welsh like her mum.

Images of her mother bombarded her again, followed by images of Archer. She closed her eyes against them, but it only served to intensify them. If only it *had* been a dream, she thought. One from which she'd awake trembling, but shake off and put behind her in the morning. But it wasn't a bad dream. More like a waking nightmare.

Less than forty-eight hours ago Archer and Baleweg had destroyed the nice, peaceful little world she'd so painstakingly built. A world she'd naïvely believed to be safe. Forty-eight hours of jumping at every little sound, of seeing shadows where none existed, of waiting, wondering. Of remembering bits and pieces of her mother, of her own childhood, not knowing what was fact and what was fancy, produced by a brain on overdrive.

She'd tried to escape it. She'd spent yesterday immersed in work. Two of her kennel help had called in sick, and with Jimmy gone, there was plenty to do. She sighed as she thought about her discussions with the police. They hadn't been able to find him and she'd opted not to press an assault charge, since the last thing she wanted was for them to find him and involve her in any way with him again. Not that she really thought they'd locate him anyway. His address had turned out to be bogus and she knew nothing else about him except he'd always been on time for work and did whatever she asked him to. *She's mine. I found her first.* She shuddered and tried to forget that part.

You're going to have to deal with this, you know.

Talia frowned and looked over at the huge cat sprawled on the railing next to her. She knew Marblehead hadn't really spoken to her, even telepathically. She simply felt what he was feeling. The verbal translation was her own, a small fancy she'd given in to as a young girl. Back when she used to have conversations out loud with any and all creatures who crossed her path. Before she'd learned that wasn't always such a good idea.

She smiled a bit wistfully as she recalled the first time she'd been caught doing her Dr. Dolittle routine. She'd been around three or four. They'd just moved in and Talia had been playing in the backyard when she'd felt a sudden surge of terror. She'd started to call out to her mum, but then she'd spied her neighbor's little tiger-stripe kitty up the tree. Talia very distinctly remembered understanding exactly what the kitten was feeling. As if she were feeling the same thing herself. But as her fear grew, the kitten's lessened. Somehow she'd understood she was taking on the kitten's terror, thereby alleviating it from the poor thing. It had been instinctive, and despite being a bit shaken, she'd been quite proud of her accomplishment.

Talia had stood beneath the tree until the kitten had come down safely. She thought the cat was a marvel, the way he was able to transmit his emotions to humans like that. Then old Mrs. Wickerly—or Mrs. Whackerly as she'd come to think of her—had come out and overheard her talking to the cat. Talia remembered excitedly asking the older woman how her cat had learned to talk to people. Apparently the cat didn't talk to Mrs. Whackerly the way it talked to Talia. Or the old woman was simply too stubborn to listen, was more like it, Talia remembered thinking.

The old woman had snatched the kitty up and warned her away, from both the cat and her property. At age four Talia hadn't understood what the woman was really saying. That she was different. Odd. But it hadn't taken long to learn.

Talia had asked endless questions when she'd figured out it wasn't the kitty who had special abilities, but her. And that not everyone shared her little knack. Her beautiful mother had always smiled and gently explained that other people couldn't be faulted for disparaging what they didn't understand.

Talia felt tears spring to her eyes now. Her beautiful mother. She couldn't remember the last time she'd so clearly pictured her face. Maybe it was because of having seen that picture of her. The memory now was as vivid as if it had happened yesterday. The back porch door swinging open and her mother leaning out, smiling, beckoning her gently to come inside for an afternoon sweet. Talia saw the smile she'd extended beyond her daughter to old Whackerly, but only now did her mind's eye zero in on the tension at the corners of her mouth, the tight focus of her gray eyes. Eyes like Talia's.

Her mother had encouraged Talia to be herself and delighted in her differences, but only when they'd been alone, she realized now. She'd promised that when Talia got older she'd tell her a wonderful story and teach her just how special her gifts were. But for now, she was to simply enjoy being a child.

Talia had listened to her mother and she'd tried to keep her gift to herself, really she had. But somehow, people always seemed to find out. She never meant to let them know, but she often couldn't help it. An animal in need always seemed to stray into her path at the most inopportune moment. And she could never find it in her heart to turn her back to their pain. She remembered hating when that hunted look would enter her mother's eyes, knowing it meant they would have to move again, and quickly.

Talia steadied the hammock and swung her legs over the side. What had her mother been running from? How had she forgotten all this? Or perhaps she'd purposely repressed it, as a way of coping. Talia jerked as another remembrance pushed forward, startling Marble into rousing his head to stare balefully at her. But her mind was turned firmly inward . . . and backward. She was six years old and so confused about how to make her mother happy. They'd moved once again, to Connecticut this time. It was summer and so hot, but their tiny apartment had no air conditioner. The memory was so vivid she could feel the sticky air clinging to her skin, could feel her mother gently stroking her forehead, soothing her to sleep with magical stories about a kingdom far away with a brave king who thought it was marvelous that little girls could talk to animals.

Talia blinked and the image was gone. Replaced by another one. A cold bed in the orphanage. It wasn't until her mother died, shortly after that hot night, that it occurred to Talia to wonder who her father was. No one knew. She'd never known any family but her mother and had long ago given up trying to find any ties to her past. And she'd never found that magical world her mother had spoken of. But she had quickly become far more adept at hiding her gift. She'd also gotten smart. No one had wanted to adopt the odd little girl who talked to animals and foster homes had been more like slave-labor camps for her.

She remembered lying awake at night, retelling her mother's stories to herself over and over, wishing her mother had taken her with her, wherever she'd gone. Maybe heaven was the magical kingdom she'd spoken about. If that was true, then one day Talia would see her mum again. As a child, that was the truth she'd eventually clung to.

But growing up meant letting go of dreams and taking hold of harsh realities. And the reality was, there was no one else who understood her, much less who was like her. Animals were the only creatures who seemed to offer her unconditional love and support. Animals and old people.

Old Whackerly being the exception, obviously. Talia felt her mouth quirk up into a dry smile, even as she tasted the salt of the tears that slowly coursed down her face.

She had never forgotten the day she'd turned eighteen and had become an emancipated adult, free forever of trying to fit in with people who had no desire to fit in with her. She knew if she was to make her way in this world and overcome the constant feeling of being a misfit, she needed to find a way to make her special talents work for her. Then she could find happiness and a kind of peace and put her inner sense of disquiet at ease.

Talia smiled now and wiped her cheeks with her sleeves. That is precisely what she'd done. She'd stopped believing in fairy tales and found her place in the real world. "And no one is going to take that away from me."

She shoved to her feet and went down the wide steps that fronted the old Victorian house. It was three stories of blue siding and white gingerbread trim with a wildly enthusiastic garden fronting the whole thing. The trim needed painting and the garden was overstepping its generous bounds. She mentally rearranged the next day's chores to fit in a couple of hours of playing in the dirt. Beatrice had loved her flowers, and although Talia had never been drawn to the pleasures of gardening, she did her best to wrestle the various beds into submission on a semiregular basis as a tribute to her late benefactress.

She wondered what Beatrice would have made of Archer and Baleweg. Talia's lips quirked at the thought. She'd have probably invited them in for lemonade and her famous tea cookies. Beatrice was as Victorian as her house, a pragmatic woman who'd had no trouble speaking her mind, but always seeming to find an oh-so-proper way of doing so. Talia couldn't imagine how Beatrice would have managed a polite response to their claims of being from the future. But she would have loved to see her try.

Her smile faded as she wandered down the front path toward the large pond and marshes that lay between her property and the Lodge. This was her favorite time of year. Warm enough to enjoy a walk in the evening, but not so humid and hot as to stir up all the mosquitoes and gnats that would make this same stroll all but untenable a month or so from now.

She snagged her walking stick from the side of the garden shed and slipped Beatrice's old fishing bonnet—only Beatrice could come up with such a creation—off the handle and dropped it on her head. She considered taking a pole with her, but decided against it. Shading her eyes against the setting sun, she looked across the backyard toward the long, low kennel building.

As always, a sense of pride filled her. Beatrice would have approved of the haven Talia had built. In addition to the stables and two small paddocks that had been here in Beatrice's time, Talia had added the kennel building with an office inside. The building was temperature controlled and had runs that went indoors and out. Behind the building was a large field that ran all the way to the trees. She'd thought about fencing some of the area in and taking on more larger animals. She made a note to run figures again.

She ran her gaze over the outdoor runs, satisfied that Stella had finished hosing them down before leaving. She didn't have as many animals in residence right now, which was always a blessing as it meant she'd been successful at finding good homes for her odd assortment of strays. When colder months returned, however, the indoor facilities would fill up again. There were always orphans to tend to.

She looked to the paddock and saw Old Sam plodding toward the new mare she'd brought home a few weeks ago. The appaloosa was skittish—and who wouldn't be, mistreated as she'd been—but while other horses would have only antagonized her, Old Sam was a calming influence. Talia was counting on that, counting on Sam to do some of the work, so Talia could take over when the mare was ready to finally accept human help. She made another mental note to call the vet and schedule a visit.

She smiled again. Ken was a nice guy. So immersed in his practice that he didn't notice much beyond it. Talia relaxed around him in a way she did with very few others. He was a whiz with animals, but people were anomalies to him. To the point that he'd never noticed Talia's "gift" with animals was anything more than someone with a soft heart who had a modest inheritance to indulge that heart with. Yep, good old Ken was safe.

Safe life. Safe friends. Safe four-legged pals.

Archer wasn't safe.

As if she'd summoned him, he materialized in front of her, emerging from the tall reeds a dozen or so yards ahead. He was dressed in the same plain dark pants, boots, and shirt, yet he still managed to look like some sort of exotic woodland creature. Maybe it was those eyes, the way they commanded without realizing it. Or maybe he fully realized it. Probably he did. Maybe it was that accent of his.

Or maybe it was because he claimed to be from the future.

Whatever the reason, she stopped dead, immediately looking behind him for the old man. Somehow, even though Baleweg spooked her plenty, she felt safer with him.

There was that word again. *Safe.* Had she really felt so threatened by the rest of the world? Yes. The answer was immediate. And true.

She'd always felt she was a misfit, but she'd never associated her inherent discomfort around most people with actual fear. She'd attributed it to her years in the orphanage. And her "gift." Who wouldn't feel like an outcast with that combo? And it wasn't as if she hadn't gotten over it, found her niche.

But now she realized a certain fear had been there, creeping beneath the surface of all her decisions. Had her mother fed that fear? Talia would have said no if asked a week ago. But now she wouldn't be so quick to deny it. What had her mother been running from? Whatever the threat had been . . . did it still exist?

He was sent here to kill you.

Her gaze flew to Archer's, as if he'd spoken the words again. Whatever threats might have hovered about her young life, Talia had no doubt she was facing a real one now. "What do you want?" It came out sharp, but with at least as much temper as fear.

"G'day to you, too, Ms. Trahaern," he said, tipping his fingers to his brow. Then the light disappeared from his eyes and the dark intensity returned. "I believe you know exactly what I want."

"I thought lives were in danger. You certainly took long enough to come back." Talia snapped her mouth shut. She'd sounded for all the world like she was whining that he'd left her alone so long. And maybe she was. Dealing with Archer and getting this over with had to be better than what she'd been putting herself through. She didn't bother asking how he'd found her here.

"There were things to be taken care of first."

Jimmy's face flashed through her mind. She tried not to think about that. "Where is Baleweg?"

"I came alone."

"Does he know you're here?"

"He's not my keeper."

He was too defensive. Meaning the old man ran the show. Interesting. "Speaking of keepers, where is your dog?"

"My dog?" He looked at her blankly. "Oh, you mean Ringer. With Baleweg."

Talia frowned. He'd forgotten he owned a dog? Maybe the little mutt had just been a prop of sorts, to get close to her. Her opinion of him lowered further.

"I assume you've thought about what we told you."

I haven't been thinking about anything else, she wanted to shout. Instead she eyed him evenly. "Some."

He propped both hands on his hips now. "And?"

Something about his attitude just jerked her chain. Despite the fact that she was out here alone with him, and he was capable of God knew what, she just couldn't resist poking back at him. Maybe it was the blasted accent. She mimicked his posture. "And what? I'm just supposed to believe your fantastic tales and run off to the future with you? Save the queen, rescue the planet, and all that rot? Well, I'm sorry to disappoint you, but I'm no superhero. You'll have to find another solution to your problem."

He stalked toward her. "We have no other solution."

It took all of her willpower and courage to stand her ground. He stopped several feet in front of her, but what space was left between them fairly vibrated with the tension emanating from him. From them.

"You can't honestly expect me to just up and walk away from my life here to go with you on some insane journey to—" She couldn't say it out loud again. *To the future.* It was so absurd she should be laughing hysterically at the mere suggestion. Only when she looked into Archer's eyes, she didn't feel remotely like laughing. Somehow, looking into those dark eyes, the fantastic didn't seem so impossible.

"It's not forever. You would be able to return."

He looked away, only for a second, but it was a telling break.

"When? Exactly how long do you think this is going to take?" She felt no satisfaction when he didn't—or couldn't—answer her. "You said I was some sort of healer. I can tell you right now that I have no healing powers whatsoever."

He simply stared at her, in that aggravating Crocodile Dundee way of his.

She didn't give any ground, either.

Finally he blew out a breath and said, "You're an empath. I don't know that much about them myself, but they're common enough. Baleweg pegged you the moment he looked at you." She arched an eyebrow, and he sighed. "You understand the feelings of others. You have certain skills. Don't deny it."

Talia wanted to, vehemently. But she was so taken aback by his simple summation of her abilities that she was caught off guard by his nonchalance. His gaze remained unwavering and she heard herself say out loud what she had never said to anyone, just to see how he'd react.

"So, yeah, maybe I'm a . . . a . . . I have some skills, okay?" He didn't even blink. This both annoyed and entranced her. The very idea that someone was unfazed by what she could do stunned her. "But I'm no healer," she was quick to add. "I know when animals are hurting, and where they are hurting. But that's the extent of it. I call the vet out here to fix those hurts just like everyone else. I wouldn't be of the slightest use to you."

"Your mother was a healer."

"So *you* say. I never saw any evidence of that. And it doesn't matter, because anything my mother may or may not have known in that area she was never able to pass down to me. So even if I were willing—"

"Baleweg can help you learn."

"*He's* a healer? Then why can't he save your ruler, your . . . whatever?"

"Queen. Catriona Dalwyn. She inherited the throne three years ago when King Cynan, her father, was assassinated. She's fought a hard battle to keep her kingdom from chaos. Now she's fighting a battle for her life. If she loses this one, the kingdom will fall apart."

That stopped Talia. Just the way he said it. Not with reverence, but simply as fact. Perhaps it was the lack of reverence that caught her. He didn't sound like a fanatic. He sounded like a man frustrated with his role in this crazy mission. Which brought up another question.

"You're Australian, right?"

Now it was his turn to look wary. "I was born there."

"How did you end up a British subject?"

"I am no one's subject."

Talia wholly understood that feeling and wasn't at all keen that she shared something in common with the man. "Then what is in this for you?"

He didn't answer her. Instead, he said, "Baleweg is not a healer. You're the last in that line."

"How can he help me learn, then?"

"I don't know!" Archer exploded in frustration. "He can get inside your mind, help you discover the hidden talents you possess. Whatever."

"But—"

"You have doubts, I understand that. I know this sounds ludicrous. I didn't believe in time travel, either. Believe me, it's not an everyday occurrence in my time. In fact, until a few days ago, I didn't know it existed. But I trusted Baleweg to get me here and he did. He'll get you there and back. It's not so hard." When she continued to stare at him, he slapped at his thighs. "Why would I make something like this up?"

"I have no idea. I don't know you."

"If you're concerned about the travel itself, I can assure you that it is quite simple. Baleweg does all the work."

"What if I refuse to go? What happens then?"

He held her gaze for some time before finally saying, "I can't force you. However," he added quickly, "I'd like you to think long and hard about what is being asked of you. In the context of the rest of your life, the output for you is small. And yet the rewards for an entire kingdom of people will be immense."

He made it sound like a quick jaunt. Save the world and be home by dinner. "What about the risks? You have no idea what might be required of me." She couldn't believe she was even having this conversation.

"The risks exist whether you return or not. That much must be obvious to you."

Right at that moment, nothing was obvious to her, except this was too much to contemplate. "There is suffering all over the world. Always has been, always will be. I can't take the weight of the world—present or future—on my shoulders. No one person could. Why is it so hard to comprehend that I might not be willing to put myself up to that task?"

"Because no one is asking you to save the world."

"Sounds like it to me."

"You say there will always be suffering in the world. You would be right. That does not change. However, for all the suffering in the world, many could be called upon to champion the cause of those other victims. In the case of the queen, there is only you."

"No one else can help her?"

"All who could have helped have tried, and failed."

"I find it odd that you keep going on about how your beloved queen is in mortal danger, yet you don't seem to care overmuch for her."

That took him aback. "How would you know what I feel?" His gaze narrowed. "I thought you said your empathy dealt only with animals."

She couldn't get used to the way he talked so easily about her gift. It unnerved her. "Just answer my question."

"I am here at the queen's request."

"So this is what, a favor? A good deed? I asked you before what was in it for you and you didn't answer. I want an answer."

He looked her dead in the eye. "A pile of money."

She swallowed. So, there was what amounted to a bounty on her head. And she was looking at what was probably the future's best bounty hunter. Lovely, just lovely. "So you're basically kidnapping me. And I'm supposed to go along with this willingly, to boot."

"I am not a kidnapper." He seemed honestly affronted by the notion. "I'm a businessman. Of sorts."

"You're a mercenary, you mean. A professional bully. Of sorts."

He shrugged off the sarcasm, but there was an air of supreme confidence about him now. Okay, a bigger air than usual. "I don't bully. But I do have special skills of my own. Available for a price."

Talia wasn't used to people jerking her chain, not in her quiet, safe little existence. But her chain had been jerked now and she found it impossible to remain passive. Maybe she was too far down the Yellow Brick Road now to have any perspective left. Whatever the cause, she found herself running her gaze over him, documenting his serviceable clothing, his body's latent powerful stance, the calculating look that met hers when she came back to his eyes. "Yes, I can imagine you do."

His eyes widened a bit and for the first time a tiny spark of awareness shot into their dark depths. Sexual awareness. *Whoa*, she thought, backpedaling quickly. *We won't be going there again.* His mercenary skills apparently extended beyond kidnapping for his queen to . . . other things. Things she had little experience with and no business fooling around with. Not with him anyway.

She glanced away and caught her reflection in the pond. Baggy overalls, a T-shirt that was almost as old as she was, and Beatrice's fishing bonnet. Oh, yeah, she was just a seduction waiting to happen. She smiled wryly.

"I'm glad I amuse you," he said shortly. The spark—if it ever really existed—had died, replaced by the cool competence and impatience that were more typical of him.

She didn't tell him she was amused at herself, not him. She liked him better when he was on the defensive. He was still cocky and arrogant as hell, but he seemed more human somehow.

"You said there would always be risks, whether I went with you or not. What did you mean? Does it have something to do with Jimmy?"

"There are those who would like nothing better than for Wales to—"

She lifted her hand. "Hold up. Wales?"

"Of course. One of Britain's three kingdoms."

"Countries, you mean. Wales, Scotland, and England. But they are united under one monarchy."

He stared at her for a long moment, then said, "That changes."

"Oh." Talia wanted to ask him more, and at the

same time she didn't want to hear another damn thing. Right now she had goose bumps on her goose bumps. He was pretty damn good at this "I'm from the future" thing and she wasn't liking it.

"Lord Chamberlain, our High Parliamentarian, would like nothing better than for Llanfair to lose its ruler and heir to the throne in one tragic death."

She stilled. *Llanfair?* In her mother's fairy tales King Cynan's castle was set in the magical land of Llanfair. She'd thought it had been all make-believe. She desperately wanted to keep believing that. Then something else he'd said struck her. "Ruler *and* heir?"

"Queen Catriona is pregnant with a son. The heir to the throne."

Chapter 4

Pregnant. Talia's stomach tightened. She wanted to believe this was indeed some sort of elaborate fairy tale, a bizarre dream that she might still wake up from. But the idea that there was an unborn child at the center of it all made everything that much harder.

Archer didn't let up. "If she dies, and the heir with her, it will make those difficulties she inherited from her father look like a simple ripple of disturbance."

"Does she have enemies?" Why was she talking about this person as if she really existed? Only, technically she didn't actually exist. Not yet. Not for some unnamed number of years in the future. Talia's head began to throb.

"On the surface, things seem in line, but there is an undercurrent of corruption that I know to be fact. Chamberlain has organized his opposition well. They are simply waiting for word of her death to overthrow what would remain of the monarchy."

"And you know all this firsthand? High-level access for a businessman, wouldn't you say?"

He didn't so much as twitch a muscle. "There are all sorts of commodities one can broker in. Information being one of them." He held her gaze. "Baleweg, it appears, isn't the only one who has mastered time travel. Chamberlain had Dideon sent here to stop you from returning."

This was the part that Talia had the hardest time explaining away. Archer and Baleweg could be two flakes or con artists who happened to know her mother and somehow knew about her make-believe tales. However, Jimmy's threat and assault, and the fact that he knew Archer . . . that one was a bit harder. Too many people seemed to know all about this. And believe it. "How did you recognize Jimmy?"

"Dideon. His name is Dideon. I knew he worked for Chamberlain. Or he did."

Talia's eyes widened. "What does that mean?"

"It means he's no longer a threat to you."

"You—" She couldn't say it. All of a sudden this was no longer a joke or an elaborate charade. The man *was* a mercenary, after all. No matter what title he gave it. Didn't mercenaries kill people? "Is he . . . ?"

"Gone."

Talia swallowed hard. So that was the business he'd been taking care of. A shudder crawled down her spine.

"But trust me," Archer said, "there will be others. Better for you to come with us. We can get you to the queen, put you under her direct protection."

"Wait a minute. If Jimmy wanted me dead, why am I still alive? He certainly had ample opportunity." She thought of the long hours they'd spent alone in the kennels when she'd first trained him and shuddered again.

"We questioned him on that. Apparently, Dideon was originally sent here to observe you, find out if there was a way to subvert your powers, use them for their good against the queen. He was as much your warden as your hangman."

Talia was trying to sort it all out in her mind, but it was such an impossible thing to truly comprehend. One indisputable fact was that Jimmy *had* threatened her. "So if they send someone else, can you recognize him?"

"I know most of the players, but I don't intend to stick around here and find them all out. It is best if we move quickly. The faster we get you back, the faster this will come to an end, and you can return to your life here, safe and sound."

He was wrong. Safe was no longer an option. Her life was suddenly filled with insanity that she was supposed to accept. And she simply couldn't stand there one second longer. She'd hit maximum stress level. Without another word, she turned and began marching back to the house.

Archer immediately caught up to her and grabbed her arm. "We don't have time for this."

Talia yanked her arm free and poked a finger at his chest. "Correction, *you* don't have time for this. *I*, on the other hand, have as much time as I want. So why don't you just let me go and return to wherever you slithered out from."

His eyes widened with real surprise. "Slithered?"

"Isn't that what kidnapping mercenary snakes do? Slither?"

His jaw clenched. "I'm not a mercenary or a kidnapper. And I'm not a snake."

She almost laughed. "That offends you? Tough guy like yourself? I imagine you've been called much worse."

It didn't help matters that this close up, she noticed he had a tiny cleft in his chin. And that when he got angry, his accent was stronger, flatter. No, she shouldn't be noticing stuff like that. She had an escape to make.

"Oh, I've been called many things, sweetheart.

But snake? Slithered?" He shook his head. "I really must be losing my touch."

Now she cocked a hand on her hip. "You have a touch?"

His eyebrows lifted.

Talia caught herself wanting to smile. Adrenaline was pumping through her, along with something else that she couldn't quite put her finger on. She wasn't actually enjoying this little heated interchange. Was she? It was just some sort of weird stress transfer that suddenly had her hyperaware of him. "Did you really think you'd just pop into my life, drop this amazing little fairy tale of yours in my lap, and expect me to go dancing off behind you, all because you twinkled those eyes and showed off that little cleft in your chin?"

Oops. She'd been doing fine up to that last part. What had been the vaguest suspicion of a smile became a blinding grin. As it turned out, the man had touch. In spades.

"You noticed the cleft, huh?" Gone completely was the impatient, frustrated mercenary. In the short time she'd known him, she'd never have guessed him capable of anything resembling charm. She immediately decided he was safer when he was cold and mercenarylike.

"Okay," she managed, her throat tight and strangely achy. "So you might have a little . . . touch."

His smile widened. It exposed the fact that he had the smallest dimple on the right side of his mouth. Good God, the man was actually sexy when he grinned like that.

"Sweetheart, you don't know the half of it." He reached up a hand and took the hat off her head. "This is sort of a mood killer, though."

"I save homeless animals for a living," she managed, finding her own edge. "One generally doesn't dress in sequins and pearls in my occupation." She should be moving away from him.

"I'm not much into sequins and pearls, either," he said.

His voice was all deep and Down Under velvety. *Russell Crowe and Mel Gibson eat your hearts out,* she thought. Talia found herself sinking into the depths of his gleaming eyes. There was almost no distinction between pupil and iris. It was as if she could fall into their inky depths and never hit bottom. When he lifted a hand to push a wayward strand of hair off her face, she almost shuddered in anticipation of what his tough, hard hands would feel like on her skin.

But she never found out. Instead she all but jumped out of that skin at a sudden clearing of a throat behind her. It was only Archer's quick reflexes that kept her from falling ass-backward into the pond.

She wished he'd let her fall in. At least then she could disappear beneath the murky depths rather than face his knowing look. Or the considering expression on Baleweg's face when she turned to find the old man standing behind her.

Archer shifted his attention to Baleweg. No doubt the old man had seen the two of them standing close like that. *Lost my touch, eh mate?* Not bloody likely.

"I trust you have convinced Miss Trahaern to begin her studies?" Baleweg said mildly.

"I was getting to that."

"Studies?" Talia asked.

"We must begin your instruction, to help you bring forth your natural talents. So that you may return with us and help our queen."

Archer stepped between them. "Wait a minute.

What you mean is that she'll return with us, and *then* she'll begin whatever lessons she needs. I'm sure the queen can help you both with all that."

Baleweg shook his head. "She cannot return until she is ready. The queen's health is dwindling, yes, but she's not at death's door quite yet. Talia is of no use to her as she is now. Once we take her to Llanfair, things will move swiftly. Forces there will be ready to pounce upon her return. Even the queen would be hard-pressed to protect her in her current state. She must be able to act immediately. Everyone knows trust is a rapidly dwindling commodity at court these days."

"She's not exactly safe here, either," Archer argued.

"We have a more controlled position here," Baleweg responded. "We have only to weed out those few who have found their way here. It is easier for me to detect disturbances in the time continuum here than at home." His focus seemed to drift. "It is . . . quieter here. I have never felt such clarity." He didn't sound entirely comfortable with that, but his blue eyes sharpened once more as he looked back to Archer. "Your extensive knowledge of those likely to be involved should help us maintain security."

"Let me get this straight. You want me to play castle guard while you two play school?" Archer shook his head. "The deal was I find her, I convince her to come back. Something, I might remind you, I was about a second or two away from accomplishing before you so rudely interrupted."

Talia lifted an eyebrow. "Awfully sure of yourself, aren't you?"

Archer's mouth actually twitched. She surprised him. For all that she looked as if she'd break in a good stiff wind, she was a pretty tough sort. Her luminous eyes and elegantly shaped lips, framed between high cheekbones and a pair of delicate eyebrows, served to give her an ethereal, almost fragile air. Until she opened her mouth.

If Archer hadn't been so annoyed with the way this mission was going, he might have admired her adaptability. Lord knew, she was going to need that and a whole lot more before this was over. So, apparently, was he. "I think we should return and let the queen deal with this situation. I didn't hire on as baby-sitter."

Talia's mouth dropped open. Baleweg shook his head. "I do not have the energy to move us about through time on a whim. Taking our leave in such a rapid manner the other day has taxed me to a great degree. If I am to move all three of us forward, then I must conserve my strength."

Archer narrowed his gaze in doubt. Baleweg had seemed tired, but not overly taxed. "So which is the real concern? Your supposed fatigue or Talia's safety?"

"Both. But her safety is my foremost concern. I will be ready when she is."

Archer held his gaze, but Baleweg merely looked at him with such serenity that Archer knew there would be no point arguing with him. Archer sighed and looked out over the pond. His gaze narrowed further at the big white duck floating placidly amid the water lilies. Oh, great, that was all he needed.

"You two can argue all you want," Talia said, jerking his attention back to the matter at hand, "but you seem to have forgotten one key element in all your Machiavellian plans. My cooperation." She shot Archer a look. "Which you have not come close to securing."

"Machiavellian?" he said, for lack of a better comeback.

"I'm surprised you don't remember him from

school history. I'd think you'd have enjoyed his exploits."

"I'm not sure, but I think I've just been insulted." Archer turned to Baleweg, hoping to elicit a smile or at least some sign that he agreed she was being impossible. Nothing. Of course.

Baleweg merely motioned for him to continue. "You are doing such a fine job, after all."

"Fine, just fine." He was trapped in some archaic time period with a stubborn old man, a woman who refused to accept reality . . . and a duck. "I'd almost rather admit defeat now and go home," he muttered.

Home. He craned his neck and looked past the pond toward the bizarre structure Talia called home. It was so rustic it was made from tree-hewn planks and covered with some sort of blue polymer and white trim that resembled nothing so much as frosting on a decaying cake. He doubted she had bothered setting up a decent security seal for it. How in the hell was he supposed to keep her safe in this?

He turned back to Baleweg. "We can't stay here."

Talia crossed her arms. "You're damn right you can't."

He looked at her, resigned to the fact that they were stuck in her time, for at least the next couple of days. "I said *we,* sweetheart." He looked to Baleweg. "We have to find a place I can defend with whatever crude arsenal I can find here. Seeing as I was left with none of my personal equipment to defend us with. My skills are well honed, but I can only do so much with my bare hands."

He'd been quite unhappy to discover that his weapons hadn't made the journey back in time with him. He was never without armor of some sort. He was even more unhappy at the thought of his extensive collection lying about on Baleweg's roof.

Baleweg merely shrugged. "It is enough that we create a ripple in time by being here ourselves. We cannot risk introducing technology of our time, as well."

Archer fought to keep from looking at Ringer, floating on the pond. Talk about a ripple. "I don't see what one little gazzer would have hurt."

"We can't risk something that—"

"Excuse me," Talia interrupted in a tone that seemed excessively loud considering he was standing right beside her. "You both seem to be overlooking something here."

"We haven't overlooked you, sweetheart." As he looked in her eyes he had a sudden flash of that moment just before Baleweg's intrusion. Despite his comments to the contrary, he hadn't exactly been thinking mission strategy when he'd reached up to touch her. He hadn't been overlooking her then. He blinked the memory away. "We just have to agree on what to do with you."

She rolled her eyes. "I give up. You two can stand out here arguing all night for all I care. I have things to do early in the morning. I have a life, and my own obligations." She turned once more to leave.

Archer planted himself in front of her so fast that she ran right into him. She was soft, as well as hard. And in the most appealing places. That registered even as she was jumping away from him as though she'd been singed.

"We're here to stay, Talia."

She eyed him levelly as she yanked her arm free. "Then I hope you enjoy sleeping out under the stars. Good night."

Talia stalked off toward the house, trying hard not to give in to the fact that she was terrified. She was shaking. In fear, in anger, in frustration. And in awareness. Of Archer. Dammit. The man was completely insufferable. And he was too damn . . . real.

She tossed her walking stick toward the shed, only then remembering she'd left the fishing bonnet on the ground by the pond. Not wanting to think about that moment when Archer had been so close, looking as if he were about to—

Oh, no, she wasn't going there. She was going to bed. Where she would sleep the sleep of the innocent, wake up in the morning fully rested, and go back to the good work she was performing here. Work that had always been satisfying. Satisfying and . . . and enough.

Her steps faltered as she reached the porch. She sank to the top step, unable to balance her own weight on suddenly watery knees. It *was* enough, dammit. It had to be. She'd found her place. She hugged her knees, her gaze moving of its own volition back toward the path to the pond. "It is enough," she whispered. "I'm meant to do this."

Even saying the words made her shiver, made some part of her rebel, the part that now remembered her mother's fantastical tales . . . and wanted to believe the stories of castles and kings, of people who'd respect her, a place where she'd discover what she was meant to do.

She clutched her knees more tightly, thinking about this place she'd called home since the day Beatrice had found her sitting at a café in town, her heart and spirit irrevocably broken. It was the day she'd been forced to accept that her dream of becoming a veterinarian, a dream she'd slaved to pay for, sweat, blood and tears to achieve, was not going to come true. She'd known that in order to practice medicine, heal animals, she'd have to take on their pain. Her "gift" wasn't something she could switch off, but she'd naïvely thought she could somehow control it, make it work to her advantage. Until her first day in an operating room.

The dog had been mortally injured, hit by a car. He'd been rushed into emergency surgery at the clinic where she'd just signed on as a student assistant. The vet had yanked her in to help . . . then called for emergency assistance when she'd collapsed under the incredible onslaught of pain that had shoved its way through her entire body. They thought she'd had some kind of seizure. Only she knew what had really happened. Just as she knew she could never let it happen again. She wouldn't survive it . . . and certainly no animal in her care should have to risk her collapsing again like that.

She had been devastated, her only dream as crushed and beyond saving as that poor dog. She'd been so lost, having to give up the one place in the world she thought she'd fit in, helping the animals that called to her.

Then Beatrice had walked into her life, smiled knowingly, and offered Talia the path to her true calling. "Perhaps you weren't meant to heal them, my dear," she'd said, making it sound so simple. "Perhaps you were simply meant to rescue them."

And so it was that this place had become her castle. Beatrice, the animals they'd rescued, and the old people at the Lodge, those were her loyal subjects. Here was where she'd discovered what she was meant to do.

Baleweg emerged from the path and headed toward her. Archer followed several feet behind him. Talia tensed, telling herself to flee, to run inside the house and lock herself in tight until they finally gave up and went away. But she couldn't move. She could only look at them, watch them come closer. And know.

In the same way she'd known she could never be a vet . . . she knew her destiny was about to change again. She began trembling. In fear? In anticipation?

Baleweg stopped at the foot of the stairs. Slowly, he raised his hand to her.

"Come, Talia. It is time. You understand, don't you?"

Shaking so badly now she could hardly control it, she nodded jerkily. Her gaze shifted beyond the old man and found Archer's. What she expected to find there she didn't know. Strength? But strength to do what? Run?

Or accept the fate they'd come here to show her?

Archer held her gaze for what felt like an eternity. His eyes told her that he'd hold it as long as she needed him to. And she did find strength there.

She turned back to Baleweg, who stood waiting with endless patient wisdom glowing from his ethereal eyes . . . and lifted her hand to his.

Chapter 5

I can't do it." Talia turned stubbornly away from Baleweg and looked out the window at the setting sun. Instead she spied Archer leaning against the paddock fence talking to her kennel assistant, Stella. Great. She was stuck in here playing mind games and he was out there distracting her employees. Judging from the smile on Stella's young face, she wasn't minding a whole lot. Talia's scowl deepened.

"You can do it, Talia. Come, let us try again."

Talia sighed and wondered for at least the thousandth time why she'd let them barge into her life. Not that she'd had a hell of a lot of choice. Baleweg had promptly taken over the tower sewing room yesterday and had made it his own. Talia never used the room and had had no problem with the choice; it put him at a distance from her own room in the opposite tower. Until he'd made it clear that they were to begin their studies in this room. Immediately. She faced Baleweg squarely. "We've been at this since late yesterday almost nonstop. I have explained that my ability to feel emotions is limited to animals. And even if I could connect with people, I don't see how that will help me to heal them."

Baleweg's expression didn't so much as flicker. Talia sighed yet again.

"I realize this seems a rather overwhelming task," he said at length.

"That's an understatement," she said under her breath. To him she said, "You're not even a healer, so how can you teach me to be one anyway?"

"No one can teach you to be a healer. You are born to it. As is the case with you. Obviously your mother had little time to bring forth your natural ability. And it's apparent from what you've told me that you've done your best to suppress even your empathic skills." He tapped his wide forehead with his finger. "My skills lie in delving into the hidden powers of the mind. My hope is to help you delve into yours, help you free your natural abilities. In order to do that, I have to teach you how to focus, to stretch the boundaries of your empathic skills. Once you feel more comfortable with those skills you are aware of, those more deeply buried will surface."

Talia's breath hitched at the casual mention of her mother. She tried not to let him notice, but of course he did.

"Your mother would be proud of what you are doing, Talia. I am sorry you knew so little of this side of her."

"I didn't know any of it!"

He smiled kindly. "Perhaps you know more than you're aware of. She told you tales of her life. What do you remember of those nighttime stories?"

Just enough to frustrate her, Talia thought, and not enough to fully convince her that they were telling the truth. After all, it was a pretty damn fantastical truth. And there were no other explanations forthcoming. "They were just stories," she said stubbornly. But they both knew she was beginning to believe they had been much more than that.

He didn't push her. "Perhaps in return for all our

hard work," he said, "I can tell you some of what I knew of her."

He certainly knew the right carrot to dangle. "I would like that," she said honestly. In fact, it was learning about her mother as much as anything else that had prodded her to go along. "But I can't see where studying harder will change anything. Surely if I'd had any healing powers, they'd have surfaced by now."

"We've only been at this a day. Patience." But his eyes clouded ever so briefly, betraying his own anxiety. Wonderful.

"I am trying," she said quietly. "I just don't want to mislead you into believing I can actually help this . . . this—"

"Catriona."

Talia felt a little shiver along her spine. "Why are you doing this? I mean, I know Archer is doing it for the money. Are you doing it because you're close to the . . . the queen?" Just saying that felt strange . . . and yet . . .

"I'm doing this because I loved your mother. She was, perhaps, the daughter I never had." He shrugged, for the first time looking uncomfortable. "I suppose I was more mentor to her than father. We shared a great love for exploring the powers of the mind. She had an endless thirst for knowledge."

Talia had gone completely still. She had no doubt Baleweg spoke the truth. It was there in every note, every fiber of his very electric being. She asked the question that had been on her mind since she first realized he was close to Eleri. "Did she tell you who my father was?"

Baleweg looked even more sorrowful. "I'm so sorry. She didn't confide in me as a rule. Our relationship wasn't of that nature. When her life was threatened because of her alliance to the king, her power to help him, she knew the only way to protect you was to leave her own time. So she came to me and I helped her. I'm here now to prepare you for a task she never had the chance to."

"I don't want to disappoint you," Talia said honestly.

His expression cleared and he seemed relieved to return to his role as mentor. "I believe that if you can begin to connect with humans, your hidden talents should begin to surface."

"I've never once felt anything from another person. Only animals."

"It's all in the focus. I can teach you to shut out external stimulation and see with your mind's eye."

Everything inside her shied away from this. If she took on animals' pain as her own and found that draining and potentially destructive, she couldn't imagine taking on human pain and surviving with her own soul intact.

"It need not always be pain, Talia. Surely you connect with other emotions."

She paused, then nodded. "Usually only after I've known the animal, though. I generally don't have an animal long enough to have much experience with that." Just Marblehead, Beatrice's old tom. She connected with him effortlessly and usually it warmed her. But that was rare.

"Empaths, at least in our time . . ."

Our time. He did that, talked about them as if they were both of his time. As if she were little more than a visitor in her own. Oddly, if she thought about it, hadn't she always felt like that? A misfit, an outcast?

". . . must have some strong feeling about their subject to make the connection. Your connection with these unknown beasties is your empathizing with their suffering. For one as sensitive as you, this qualifies as a strong feeling. But the feeling can manifest itself in other ways. There might be depression, pain, even hate. But there can also be joy. Elation. Love."

There weren't many people who'd had the full measure of her love. Beatrice, her mother. Both beyond her reach now. If she'd connected with her mother, she hadn't recalled it. And she'd never thought to try with Beatrice. It had certainly never simply happened on its own.

Someday I'll show you a place where your powers are revered.

Her mother's words rang clearly in her mind, the memory obviously provoked by Baleweg's reminiscences. She wanted to clap her hands over her ears, drown out both Baleweg and her mother. Yet another part of her undeniably yearned to reach out and embrace that possible truth.

"Okay." She swore under her breath, then took another slow, steadying one. "Tell me again what to do. I'll try."

Baleweg turned to her and drifted his hand over her eyes. As always, his touch sent a ripple of odd, yet immensely pleasurable sensations over her. Her eyes shut as his hand passed over them.

"Clear your mind of all voices save mine."

She tried her best, then nodded.

"You must think of someone you feel strongly about."

She nodded again, though she had no one left to focus her thoughts on. She'd tried everyone she could think of already. Stella, her head kennel assistant. They weren't overly close—she wasn't overly close with anyone—but she did like the teenager. Nothing. She'd tried a few of the residents at the Lodge whom she was fond of. Nothing there, either.

She thought about the vet, Ken. He was a nice enough guy. What the hell. She focused on him, then nodded to signal her readiness.

"No noise, Talia. Block it out. Hear nothing. Smell nothing. See nothing. Focus your mind on the essence of this person, yet visualize no images."

Kindness. Distraction. Focus. Frustration. All these things were the essence of Ken. He was so bighearted, yet saw nothing beyond his desire to help animals, often frustrated by his own limitations. Talia took a deep breath, trying to keep her mind blank.

"Reach out and touch this essence, pull it inside yourself, make it your own. Feel what he feels."

Talia tried, ignoring how Baleweg knew it was a he. It was awkward and she felt inordinately clumsy. With animals there was no effort needed. Their feelings simply invaded her and took over. Originally it had happened so swiftly she'd had no control over it and had frequently been swamped with sudden raging pain. She'd learned over the years to build a defense, a warning system of sorts. She still couldn't keep the pain away, but she could brace herself. She wasn't often blindsided, but then, she rarely put herself in a position for nasty surprises.

But this . . . this reaching out into the blankness, seeking a connection rather than simply accepting one that was reaching for her . . . It was impossible.

"Do not give up. Remain in the darkness, yet open yourself."

Talia tried, really she did. Then she had a sudden vision of Obi Wan Kenobi intoning "Let the force be with you" over Luke Skywalker's ecstatic face and lost it altogether. She managed to not burst out laughing, but the moment was irretrievably lost. She opened her eyes and turned away, hoping he didn't see the lingering humor in her eyes. "I'm sorry. There's nothing there."

"This is no game we're playing, Talia."

For the first time she heard a sharp edge in his tone. She spun back, all images of Obi Wan gone. "I understand that. But I'm not feeling anything."

"Perhaps you need a different subject."

"I don't have a different subject!" She was yelling now. Suddenly and overwhelmingly, all the things that had happened in the last twenty-four hours came crashing down on her. "I've gone through everyone I know and it's a short list. I keep to myself, okay? I'm a loner, a recluse, a hermit, whatever term you want to use. Are you satisfied now?" She stormed to the door, but his voice stayed her.

"I'm sorry, Talia. For many things."

She didn't turn. "I don't want your pity. I am quite happy with my life. Or I was."

"Then I apologize for our intrusion into that happy life. But make no mistake, this is the life you were destined for. And it would have found you, one way or another. Trust that it is far better that I am your guide."

She turned around then. Something in his voice . . . "You know who sent Jimmy here, don't you?"

He nodded. "He is the only one more powerful than I. I don't know why he chose to find you, but then, his reasons are usually unfathomable to anyone other than himself."

"Does this all-powerful being have a name?"

Something indefinable flickered in the depths of Baleweg's eyes. Whatever it was, it was unsettling. "Emrys."

Talia shuddered without knowing quite why. "Why does he care about me?"

"I imagine it is another who cares about you."

Talia reached for the name Archer had mentioned earlier. "Chamberlain?"

Baleweg nodded.

"And Emrys?"

"Oh, I imagine he's more interested in besting me."

Talia's eyes narrowed. "Can he?"

Baleweg stroked his beard. "We will handle the others involved. What you need to concern yourself with is the queen. You are her only hope for survival."

"Then your queen is doomed." She left, and he didn't try to stop her.

&.

Archer leaned on the paddock fence and watched the horses munch on grass. He was supposed to be on perimeter recon, but he was already sick of the whole thing. He understood that there was a threat to Talia both here and in his own time. He even understood Baleweg's logic in keeping her here where there were fewer players in the game. He swatted at a monstrosity of a fly and swore under his breath. But he didn't have to like it.

One of the helpers—Stella?—came out of the kennel building and headed his way. He groaned silently. Talia had told her employees that he and Baleweg were friends of Beatrice's, the woman who'd left her that monstrosity of a house, as well as her livelihood as Patron Saint to Abandoned Beasties. He found a smile in that. So they were both paid saviors, of sorts.

"She's coming along great, isn't she?" Stella propped a boot up on the fence.

It took him a second to realize she was talking about the mare and not Talia. No one, including him, had been allowed access to her sessions with Baleweg. So he had no idea how she was coming along. Which had nothing whatsoever to do with his grotty mood. He couldn't care less what she was up to in there, or how she was faring. Honestly, he hardly even thought about her, except the way she had made his life a living, boring hell.

Stella was looking at him expectantly. He managed a noncommittal, "I suppose."

"Talia was right to put her in with Old Sam. She needs to be with her own kind for a while, you know?"

The perkier and more animated Stella became, the older and crankier he felt. He didn't belong in this pastoral setting where the only sound was the incessant buzzing of the flies. He wanted to be back in the city. At this point any city would do.

Stella leaned back against the fence, her attention moving from the horses to him, a speculative gleam in her eyes. Archer bit off the scowl, but kept his attention firmly on the horses. What was it about women, anyway? The more distant and uncommunicative a bloke got, the more interested they became in disturbing his peace. Talia being the main exception to that rule. Not that this annoyed him. Not a bit.

"She's really something, isn't she?" She waved to the grounds. "She built this herself, you know."

"I thought she inherited the whole gig from the old la—er, Beatrice."

Stella laughed, a high-pitched sound that grated on his already raw nerves. "Mrs. Fontaine took in strays, but she'd let them take over the house. I think at one time she had something like thirty cats and Lord knows what else living in there."

Archer shuddered.

"The stables were here, but that was for the few riding horses she kept. Talia was the one who turned this place into a real rescue operation." Stella smiled, but this time the warmth that filled her whole face was guileless and fully sincere. Archer wanted to tell her if she was interested in attracting boys, this was the smile she should hold on to.

Talia had chosen her help wisely. They held the same passions she did. But Talia was a puzzle. Passionate about her work, about the animals she saved, about the old people at the Lodge. But she lived alone. Other than the old cat he'd seen wandering about, she kept no animals in the house.

"She's really worked miracles here," Stella went on.

That caught his attention. "What kind of miracles?" Had Talia been holding out on him about her special skills?

"She finds good homes for all of her strays. They are never turned away or put down. It's almost spooky how successful she is."

"Spooky? In what way?"

Stella warmed to her subject. "Well, she works with rescue leagues and the Humane Society, even the pound. They send her their hopeless cases, animals they don't want to put down but know they can't find homes for."

"And she fixes them up herself?"

"No, the vet does that. Ken's a great guy, he helps her for cost." She studied him, considering. "I sort of thought he might have a thing for her, you know?"

Archer was still focused on the healing, and he was a bit slow on the uptake. "A thing?"

She stared at him meaningfully. "She is single, you know." Then she shrugged, the movement so calculated, Archer didn't know whether to laugh or pat her on the head and send her home. "But Ken is a workaholic who wouldn't know romance if it bit him on his butt." She sighed then. "And a nice butt it is."

Archer did smile now. "I'm sure," he said, wondering what Talia thought of Dr. Ken's butt. Not that it mattered one way or another. He managed to stop himself short of wondering what she might think of his own backside. He cleared his throat. "What did you mean about spooky?"

"Oh. Well, it's just that she saves so many of them. Even the hopelessly neurotic respond to her." She shrugged and Archer wisely kept silent. "It's the weirdest thing. It's like stray animals seem to find her. They just show up. They wander out of the fields and stuff, like there's some psychic animal network out there and they all know this is their mecca."

Archer just looked at her blankly, then she leaned closer, her expression animated. "She just shrugs it off. Still, it's odd. She's devoted her whole life to them. She spends more time with animals than with people. She needs more friends, y'know?"

More like the animals call out to her and she feels their distress, he thought. Obviously Talia kept her empathic gifts a secret from her staff. Archer understood that empaths weren't typical in this time. He looked around at what she'd done with her abilities and grudgingly admitted respect.

He knew how hard it was to be an outcast. He respected how hard it would have been for her to find her way, alone, with no one to guide her. He'd been alone longer than he could remember. And no one had ever stood by his side. Like Talia, he'd learned everything the hard way.

He thought Talia was doing okay. She'd sure earned Stella's respect and admiration. Yet, he couldn't stop thinking of her as a child, orphaned and alone in a time that didn't understand her. "Yeah, I guess I do know." He left Stella to her work, his thoughts all muddled as he approached the porch. Talia was supposed to be inside with Baleweg, but she was sitting on the swing, her gaze unseeing as she pushed her toe against the porch to make the swing rock.

Turn around and continue the recon assignment, Archer told himself. He wasn't one for entanglements or involving himself more than he had to. He should just leave and not push at things better left undisturbed. But Archer had long ago learned that he was biologically incapable of not pushing at boundaries.

He didn't go so far as to climb the steps. He moved near the end of the porch where the swing was and leaned against an old shade tree. "Evening."

She didn't startle, so she must have seen him approach. Perhaps she'd even watched him as he talked with young Stella. But if she was interested in his activities, she didn't show it. She nodded absently to his opening gambit.

Irritated without quite knowing why, he moved from the tree and drew closer to the railing. "Lessons all done for the day?"

She nodded again.

What had possessed him to try and be sociable with her, he had no idea. "Fine then, I'll go back to my rounds." He turned away. "Such as they are."

"Wait."

Archer didn't normally respond well to demands, but he wanted to respond to hers. He said nothing as she rose and moved down the porch stairs toward him.

He was not controlled enough to keep from noticing how gracefully she moved. Even the baggy getup she wore didn't disguise the innate elegance of her body. And he was fairly certain she was clueless about the graceful way she held herself, dignified and strong. As if she'd been born to serve at the feet of kings and queens.

Which, of course, she had.

"I'll go with you," she said. A command, not a request.

He fought a smile, wondering if she understood she had been born to serve royalty, not be royalty herself. "Will you, then?"

It was only when she drew closer that he noticed her expression was still distracted, that she wasn't focused on him as much as her own thoughts. He was surprised to discover he was curious about what she might be thinking. That bothered him. Entanglements and all that. But not enough to sway him from prodding her a bit.

"Tough day in healing school?"

That earned him a full-on glare. "I just want to take a walk, okay?"

Archer stopped and waved an arm in front of him. "By all means, walk on. Just tell me in what direction Your Healing Highness desires to go and I will make certain that my lowly presence doesn't cross her path and that danger doesn't befall her."

That finally seemed to snap her out of whatever state she was in. She stopped and put her hands on her hips. "Can you just walk and not talk at the same time?"

Maybe it was because she looked so damn contained and controlled when he felt anything but. Or maybe it was because he liked to stir things up, and Talia was available for the stirring. Whatever the case, he couldn't resist the urge to crumble her façade. "I can do a lot of things very quietly." When she didn't move, much less back down, he stepped closer. "But experience has taught me it's usually a lot more fun to be . . . expressive."

She didn't even blink. "Can you be . . . expressive silently?"

She didn't respond to him like most women. Normally he found it quite easy to be charming and affable with members of the opposite sex. Never around her, however. He'd told himself it was the situation, the mission. He wasn't here to be charming. But that didn't keep it from being damn frustrating. And okay, a little goading. He moved close enough that she was going to have to deal with him, one way or another.

"I can be amazingly silent." He reached out and lifted the heavy strap of her overalls, tucking a finger or two beneath the edge. Slowly, as he stared into those translucent gray eyes of hers, he slid the backs of his fingers down along the edge, stopping a breath away from brushing the outer swell of her breast with his fingertips.

Her eyes darkened. That was the sum total of her response. No pulse ticking away at her temple, no hard swallow, no nostrils flaring. In fact, it was almost as if she'd gone into a trance or something, she was so focused. He found himself impossibly aroused by her control. And wanting to slip his fingers further beneath her overalls to see just how affected she truly was. And she was affected. Because she wasn't pushing him away. His body hardened slowly and most pleasurably.

She held his gaze steadily, her gaze so intent he could feel it like an actual caress.

He moved closer, began leaning in, already imagining what those lips would taste like, when suddenly her eyes went wide and she stumbled away from him looking stricken. Archer glanced behind him, certain there was some immediate threat to her safety. Because no damn way was that reaction due to the kiss he'd almost taken from her. At least he couldn't imagine it. She was sheltered out here, but not that sheltered.

His hand went immediately to his hip and he swore—would it have killed Baleweg to give him one simple little gazzer?—even as he turned to find there was nothing behind them. He swung back to her.

Her cheeks were flushed, but the rest of her face was stone white. Her eyes were glassy, but not with desire. It looked more like shock. And perhaps a little awe.

"What in the hell happened?"

"It worked," she whispered, then covered her mouth. "Oh, my God," she said into her hand, then dropped it and said the words again. "I did it." She looked down at the ground, then at some point beyond him. "Jesus Christ, I actually did it!"

"What? What did you do?"

Then a sudden look of horror crossed her face as she looked at him. "Oh, my God. I did it with you!"

"What in the hell are you talking about? We didn't do a damn thing!" Maybe he'd been wrong and she had been that sheltered. No, no way. He'd seen the look in her eyes, she knew what was what. So what in hell had just happened? There was no doubt he was involved somehow. But how?

"You," she repeated, looking at him as if he'd just risen from hell or sprouted two heads. "Why in the world did it work with you? I've been trying for a dozen freaking hours with everyone under the sun and it ends up being *you*? Why?"

He had no idea what in the hell she was talking about, but he was pretty certain he was really insulted. "All I know is one second you're all but daring me to, to . . . you know damn well what you were daring me to do! Then the next you're leaping about like a cat on a hot sidewalk. What's wrong with you?"

The shock left her eyes as suddenly as if a shield had dropped over them. The glassiness remained, however. She looked straight at him. "Everything is wrong with me," she said flatly. Then without another word, she turned and walked back toward the house, leaving him behind without so much as a glance over her shoulder.

Jesus, Joseph, and Elvis, she was a royal pain in the arse. "What about our walk?"

She just waved a hand over her head. "You go on."

But he didn't want to go on. Not without her. Dammit, that wasn't what he'd meant to think at all. It was just that he wanted to know what in God's name had just happened. He'd been a participant in it, whatever it was, and somehow he'd managed to ruin whatever the hell it was she'd done, too.

"Hold up." He actually had to run after her. "Could you wait just a damn minute?"

She finally stopped at the base of the steps, but she didn't turn. When he tugged her around by the arm, she didn't meet his gaze. He cupped her chin and dragged her gaze to his. "What happened back there, Talia?"

"I . . . I can't explain. Not to you. I hardly understand it myself."

Leave her alone, you idiot.

And yet, for reasons he didn't quite understand, he couldn't do it. So he took her hand and turned back toward the pond, tugging her after him. "Come on."

She tugged back. "Archer, really, I don't want—"

He kept walking. "I promise, total silence. Just take a walk." He looked over at her. "For once I'll play bodyguard without getting all snakey about it, okay?"

She didn't smile. If anything she seemed irritated. That was how he knew he'd said the right thing. The hollow, haunted look was gone. This was the Talia he'd come to know, all prickly and edgy. He still didn't know what had happened, but somehow right then it didn't seem to matter. He'd find out in due time.

She managed to tug her hand free, but fell into step beside him.

He hid his smile and headed on down the path.

⠶

From above, Baleweg's eyes lit up as he watched the scene below from the tower window. He let the curtain flicker shut.

Chapter 6

Talia wouldn't call it a companionable silence—there was nothing truly companionable about Devin Archer—but he did remain mercifully quiet as they wandered down the path toward the pond. And while she was well aware of his big rangy body moving along beside her with that unlikely grace of his, her thoughts were a whirl that had little to do with him. At least directly.

Indirectly they had a hell of a lot to do with him.

She still felt the need to hyperventilate over what had happened back there. Baleweg had said she needed a strong emotion in order to connect. Her strong emotions for Archer were mostly along the lines of irritation. Mostly. She hadn't even planned on trying it, but then he was touching her, looking at her so intently, confusing her with the riot of emotions he was causing inside her. When he'd leaned in to kiss her, it had seemed like the most natural thing in the world to reach out, to figure out what was going on, why he wanted her. She hadn't even been aware of doing it really . . . until she'd connected. It had been like grabbing hold of a hot wire.

The second shock had been her reaction. A definite feeling of joy. It was as if she'd known she could do this all along, but had merely been waiting for someone to come along and teach her how to use it . . . and what to use it for.

She still wasn't too sure about that last part. Certainly she wasn't meant to use it to . . . well, to intercept feelings like the kind he'd been feeling. She darted a look at him, then quickly looked back to the path in front of her. The last thing she wanted at that moment was to encourage interaction of any kind. She'd interacted quite enough, thanks. In fact, she should really be back in the house, in her room, thinking about all the ramifications of what had happened today. Not walking next to the man who had, just moments ago, been wanting . . . what he wanted. Namely her.

And there it was. That zing of awareness. A bang really. It happened every time she allowed herself to think about what he had wanted. What he made her want. And dear God, had he made her want.

It was all she could do to keep putting one foot in front of the other as her mind took the perfectly logical leap to what it would feel like to be connected that way while he made love to her. The very idea of him being inside her while—

No, no, no. She shut that mental track down immediately. Just how in the hell was she supposed to deal with the man now? The magnitude of what she'd done by intruding into his feelings, the potential future complications, started to settle in. Would she *feel* things every time she looked at him? Or only when she tried? And how could she do one and not the other? She hadn't even been trying the first time, not really.

Baleweg. Her step faltered as she wondered what he'd make of this new breakthrough. If she could call it that. As they walked on, she was finally able to move past the hot-wired sexual element she'd initially tapped into and began to realize there had been something more there. It wasn't merely the sexual current that had reached out to her, into her. In fact, the more she thought about it, the more she realized that while that had been the initial jolt—and one hell of a jolt it had been—what had sent her stumbling away was that instant, that fraction of a second, when she'd reached beyond that surface level.

A shiver of dark, of cold, raced over her. Followed by a quick sensation of . . . of hollowness. Of . . . separateness. This she identified with as closely as anyone could. She'd felt it so many times in her life.

She risked another glance at him. Had it been more than their explosive sexual awareness and her intensified awareness, having just come from exhaustive attempts with Baleweg? Was it something else? Was there something inside him that called to her? What had she been about to touch? To feel? To discover?

She pushed a wayward strand off her forehead, surreptitiously rubbing at her temple. What had she done by allowing them to stay? By allowing Baleweg to fool with her mind? By allowing Archer to fool with . . . well, everything else? It was all too much.

"You know, this isn't a death march," he said, amused.

She slowed, tried not to stiffen. Just hearing his voice right now was too much. "You said you wouldn't talk."

He sighed, stopping. "Yeah, I know, I just—would you just wait a minute?"

She kept walking. If she were smart, she'd make an about-face and keep walking until she was back in the house, in her room, possibly under her bed or locked in her closet. She needed to search her thoughts, analyze them, categorize them, till she made some sense of what she'd allowed to happen to her . . . and what she was going to do about it now.

But turning around meant moving past him, possibly looking at him and—heaven forbid—touching him. Which was definitely not something she could deal with at the moment. So she kept walking.

She heard him jogging to catch up with her. "What, can't take a hint?" she muttered.

"I heard that." He fell into place beside her again.

She stopped suddenly and turned to him as the solution came to her. He managed to stop without slamming into her, but only barely.

"Why do you have to be here?"

He laughed in surprise. "I beg your pardon?"

"No, you don't. I'm doing the begging. Why can't you leave? Can you leave?"

"Not if you're walking around out here alone."

She sighed. "I don't mean right now, I mean permanently. As in adios, see ya, good-bye."

Understanding dawned on his too-damn-good-looking-for-his-own-damn-good face. He folded his arms across his chest. His too-damn-broad chest. And he had those too-damn-broad shoulders, too.

"And here I thought I was being a charming bloke."

She snorted. She didn't mean to, but it slipped out.

It got another surprised look from him; he even seemed a bit affronted, so she was glad she'd done it after all. In fact, she might do it again. Perhaps if people had done more snorting at Devin Archer earlier on, he wouldn't be so insufferable.

"I'm merely suggesting that your . . . services, such as they are, are no longer required. Baleweg is handling things by himself just fine." Boy, was he. She still didn't want to think about what the next step would be now that she'd made her first connection. If she were honest with herself, she'd admit that for the first time, she actually felt as if she were doing what she'd been put here to do. She'd felt it lying in bed at night, staring at the ceiling but seeing her past.

Which was why Baleweg was still in the tower room in her house, and why she'd given her kennel hands more responsibilities so she could spend time with him in that tower room. Exploring the possibilities, and discovering the realities. About her mother, about herself.

But Archer seemed to serve no purpose at all, other than to complicate an already complicated situation.

"I believe I am handling . . . things, as you call them, well," Archer said.

"Wandering around my property and ogling my kennel help? Who, by the way, is a bit too young for you, don't you think?"

He laughed right in her face. "So that's what this is? Female jealousy? I don't know why I'm surprised, but I guess I'd thought you were above all that." He held up a hand to stall her outraged response. And he was *so* off the mark. "Yes, even in my time, women still get their noses out of joint about men looking at and talking to other women."

"In your dreams, future man."

He was laughing again.

"Okay, fine," she said. "We won't talk about your penchant for teenagers. What I was saying was—"

Before she could see it coming, he clasped his hand around her wrist—and yanked her right in front of him. There was not a breath of air between them.

"Let me go."

There was no amused little gleam in his eyes now.

"For the record, I don't have a 'penchant for teenagers,'" he ground out. "Generally, I have no trouble finding grown women to occupy my time when I wish them to occupy it. I prefer a partner who knows her way about. I've never been one to understand the allure of initiating the untried."

The untried. Talia wondered if he had any clue how close to home that remark had hit. Not that she was a virgin, but her experiences had been discouraging enough she might as well have been untried. In fact, until a few moments ago, when she'd connected with Archer, she'd almost forgotten all about . . . trying.

"It might interest you to know," he went on, mercifully disrupting her thoughts, "that we were talking about you."

"Me?"

"Yeah. You. Your employees think you're the savior of all things fuzzy and homeless. The old people up on the hill probably think so, too, the way they all came to your rescue. I'm surprised they all don't drop to the ground when you pass to genuflect at your feet."

"Oh, please."

"But if you're worried about what I am attracted to, then let me set you straight." He moved in closer.

Don't think, she cautioned herself. *Don't think about him. Concentrate on something else, anything else.* She didn't want to know what he was feeling. She didn't even want to know what *she* was feeling.

"I like a woman with curves. Ample curves that fill a man's hands. And long hair, golden bright, like sunshine spilled across my pillow. I like dark eyes that have a look to them that tells a man she knows what is what, and makes it clear she wants it, too."

Wait a minute. Blond hair? Ample curves? Dark

eyes with that look? Talia had never known that look, much less delivered it. Not that it mattered. Archer had just described his ideal woman as being opposite in every way from her. Relief, she should be flooded with relief. But that wasn't at all what she was feeling. She was feeling . . . empowered. Because no matter what he told her about his preference in women, women she wasn't remotely like and could never hope to be, she had incontrovertible proof that he'd preferred her. At least momentarily. She'd *felt* it. Firsthand.

It was that knowledge that had her turning her gaze to his, a defiant smile on her face. And maybe, just maybe, the beginnings of that look he was describing. "Since I don't come close to fitting that description, why are you standing so close? Why aren't you letting me go?"

Archer's eyes widened in very satisfactory surprise. Yes, she could definitely get to enjoy this look business.

Then his surprise faded. Unfortunately, it didn't change to irritation or frustration. She knew how to deal with that. No, his surprise faded to a smile. A knowing smile, a smile that most certainly was part of that look, a smile that could only be described as, well . . . carnal.

She gulped. She wasn't even close to mastering *that* look. Perhaps it was time to cut her losses and run. Really fast.

She pulled free, moved around him, and headed toward the house at a speedy walk. Okay, a trot. She didn't even bother listening for his footsteps. She could well imagine the smirk on his handsome face. She wasn't even embarrassed. She should have known better than to try and play games with him. But one little peek into his head had left her feeling drunk with power.

She made it to the steps of the house, then remembered that Baleweg was still inside. No way could she deal with him right now. She spun around, thinking she'd go to her office in the kennel, but Stella was most likely still there, watering and feeding. She spun back around and spied her truck. A drive. That's what she needed. A drive through the countryside as the sun set. She'd roll her windows down so she could feel the night air, smell the heat of the day lift off the flowers and grasses, hear the trill of the crickets and the croaking of the frogs. She'd let the sounds of nature soothe her and help her sort out her thoughts.

Who was she kidding? She was going to drive like a bat out of hell, trying to outrun the chaos that her life had become.

She jumped in her truck, never more thankful that out here in the country a person could leave her keys in the ignition, and gunned the engine. She had a very satisfying vision of burning rubber and spraying gravel over Archer as he ran behind her, helpless to catch her.

That vision was ruined when he opened the passenger door and hopped in, his demeanor calm, as if they went for evening drives all the time. She resisted smacking the steering wheel, just as she resisted dropping her head to her hands and sobbing in frustration. She had her hand on the door handle, figuring she'd rather face Baleweg or Stella, but Archer's quiet words stopped her.

"I'm sorry."

Now it was her turn to look at him in surprise. "What did you say?"

He scowled. She was feeling better by the second.

"I said, I'm sorry. About back there. What I said. About women."

She leaned back and folded her arms on her chest. "Why?"

He raised his eyebrows. "Why what? Can't you just accept a man's apology, for Christ's sake?"

"I'm just curious. You seem exactly the sort who'd make comments like that about women. So what is it, exactly, you're apologizing for? I could care less what type of woman appeals to you. If anything, I suppose I should apologize to you for the crack about teenagers."

He swore under his breath, making Talia smile despite herself.

"I don't know why I bothered." He closed the door. "Where are we off to?"

Talia's smile fled with the clicking of the door. Suddenly the front seat of her truck felt immeasurably smaller and far more intimate. Which was silly, really, considering Archer was about as far from feeling intimate, judging from the look on his face, as a man could be. "I don't recall inviting you on this trip."

"And I don't recall telling you it was safe to leave the premises unescorted."

Safe. There was that word again. She was getting mightily sick and tired of it, too. "I'm a grown woman and if I want to risk life and limb by driving around the pond tonight, well, then, it's my risk to take." She threw the truck into gear. "Now, if you'll excuse me." She waited for him to exit the truck.

"Well, it's all fine and well for you to want to risk my future and that of a large number of men, women, and children in my kingdom, but frankly, I'm not willing to take that same risk. And since I'm responsible for delivering you back home, I can't—"

"*This* is my home."

"You know what I meant. Back to where you belong."

"I belong here." Even as she said it, she found herself not entirely believing it. What in the hell was happening to her? This was no lark into her past, doing some sort of genealogical search for her roots.

"As soon as you help the queen, you can come back here," he went on. "But until then, I'm in charge of making sure nothing happens to you. And that includes night drives around the pond." He shifted in his seat and looked at her. "Didn't you learn anything from how close you came with Dideon? He was here, on your property, in your kennels, in this truck. Do you still not comprehend the danger you are really in?"

A moment ago, she'd have said the only real danger she was in was making a complete fool of herself with Archer. Now, listening to him, seeing the absolute seriousness in his gaze, hearing the sincerity in his voice, she began, for the first time, to honestly assess her situation.

"You mean I really can't take a simple drive alone?"

As he shook his head, keeping his gaze steadily on hers, she had a sort of epiphany. A personal revelation. She'd believed she was *allowing* them in her life because she wanted to find out more about her mother, about her past, about her gifts. She hadn't thought it out, not really, but then she really didn't think she'd have to. She'd figured they'd realize she wasn't a healer at some point and move on. She'd been using them, their knowledge, to find some kind of peace within herself. To let herself believe that she was in control.

But she wasn't in control. She wasn't *allowing* them to do anything they wouldn't be doing anyway. She'd just made it a lot easier for them. And perhaps she'd made it easier for herself, although that was of little comfort at the moment.

In fact, she was a prisoner. On her own land, in her own house, in her own truck. And they were in control. As long as she was going along with their plan, they had allowed *her* to think she was in charge.

"But I'm not in charge," she voiced quietly. She turned and looked at him. "Am I?"

Archer stared at her. On the surface, Talia Trahaern seemed strong, smart, ready to deal with anything. And maybe she was all those things. Despite Archer's impatience to deliver her to the queen, he admitted a certain amount of admiration for how well she'd come to terms with the new direction her life had suddenly taken.

But she had also lied to herself about the full extent of her current predicament. *Just what the hell had she thought was happening?*

"I told you," he said quietly, sensing she needed calm and rationality right now. "As soon as you are finished, you'll be returned here. To this life." Though why in hell she'd want to was beyond him. If he had to spend one more night listening to the droning buzz of crickets and frogs, he'd go mad.

"There is one thing no one seems to have acknowledged," she said quietly.

"What is that?" he asked.

"Even if I go with you, I may not be able to help her." She shrugged helplessly. "Baleweg is helping me . . . discover some things about myself. But he is not a healer. And I still don't see any proof that I am one, either. My ability might allow me to zero in on an animal's problem more quickly, get specific help more quickly, but this is only remarkable because animals have no other means of directly communicating their needs or ills. The queen can certainly speak of what hurts her and where."

Archer had no direct argument for that. Nor could he explain the little hitch in his gut as he watched her valiant struggle to remain calm and rational when he knew he represented everything that was neither calm nor rational to her.

"Certainly medicine is more advanced in your time," she continued. "If that has failed, what in the world could *I* do?"

"I don't know. I'm not in charge of that." He reined in his impatience. "Maybe Baleweg could find someone knowledgeable in the healing arts to train you."

"Then why didn't you do that in the first place? Why did you choose Baleweg?"

"I didn't choose him, he found me. And I had no choice anyway. I needed him to get back here. To you."

"Are there others besides him and Emrys who can move through time?"

"Emrys?"

"He didn't tell you?"

Archer didn't like this at all, but there was no covering his ignorance. "You tell me."

"He said the one who moved Jimmy here was called Emrys. I don't know anything else. Just that, well, there is something between him and Baleweg. At least that's the impression he gave me." She rubbed at her arms. "I think Emrys is helping Chamberlain as a means of getting to Baleweg somehow."

Archer swore under his breath.

"He said he'd deal with him. It's just—"

"Just what?"

"Nothing really. Just that, well, something about the way he said his name led me to believe you should be lucky it was Baleweg and not Emrys who contacted you."

"Well, if this Emrys is working for Chamberlain, that would definitely hold true. Chamberlain's a conniving, manipulative bastard with his eye on the power of the throne. He'd sell his soul to the devil himself." He noticed her shiver. "You're thinking maybe Emrys is this devil?"

She shook her head, then shrugged. "I don't know what I think. You said time travel is not common in your time. That no one really knows they can do it. I wonder why they've come out now?"

"Baleweg has no love for court or politics—he only feels he has a commitment to your mother. I think he's remained hidden largely as a means to protect himself from those who want to subvert or abuse his skills. I can't say that I blame him. From what I gather, he sees himself as a scholar. He is only interested in discovery and learning the extent of what the mind can do."

"How did he know where I was? And this Emrys, he knew, too."

"I don't know. I didn't ask."

"It suited your needs, so why question it, right?"

It was a harsh judgment, but basically true. When he said nothing, she pressed on.

"Did Jimmy tell you anything else about what Chamberlain's plans are?"

"I didn't get that information from him."

Her composure slipped, just a little. "So is he . . . ? Did you . . . ?"

"He isn't dead, if that's what you're asking." She shot him a look of disbelief and he sighed. "What exactly is it I've done to give you the impression that I'm a murdering bastard? I'm not saying my chosen profession is an easy one with no risks, or that unfortunate things don't happen. But if it will soothe your sensibilities, I interrogated Dideon at length. He was under a form of mind control. Baleweg helped me with that. If he got any more out of him, he wasn't forthcoming to me."

"Where is Jimmy now?"

"Back in his own time. Whoever sent him will deal with his failure. But that doesn't mean they won't send another. And another."

"Why didn't you follow him back into your own time, see who he went to, or who came to claim him? Stop the threat directly at the source?"

Archer gave her a look. "Trust me, that was *my* plan."

The smallest of smiles quirked the corner of her mouth. "You were overruled by Baleweg. So he's in charge, then. I thought so."

He faced her squarely. "Baleweg is in no position to keep you safe. I'm needed here more." He smiled. "I don't suppose you feel the same way."

He'd expected another frown, a rolling of the eyes at best. What he hadn't expected was a smile. A real one. And it was a powerful thing.

Archer knew he'd enjoy the challenge of coaxing more smiles from her. Not those dry smiles when she was being sarcastic, either. He had the odd thought that earning an honest smile from her just now was even more rewarding than the seduction he'd almost begun earlier.

And that very notion stopped his musing cold. Since when had something as small, as easy, as a smile seemed a worthwhile victory? He really had been in the country too long.

He did realize that she'd relaxed some, her shoulders dropping, her posture far less defensive. He sensed that she was finally willing to believe in him, in what they were to do.

"Do you want to ask me questions about what it's like in my time Talia? It might ease some of your concerns."

The flare of awareness that lit her eyes when he'd spoken her name surprised him. Had he never said it before? Possibly not. Because he found he rather liked the sound of it.

She surprised him by yanking on the door handle and getting out of the truck. "Maybe some other time. I think I've had all the mind-expanding I can handle for one day. Perhaps for an entire week. Maybe more."

He jumped from the truck, unwilling to let their encounter end so abruptly. He told himself it was because he wanted to further her trust in him, but some part of him was forced to admit he simply didn't want her to leave yet.

He caught up to her at the base of the steps. "If I promise to resume my silent bodyguard routine, will you consider the drive? It might be good to take that break."

She stopped, but didn't turn to look at him. That stung him in a way he didn't fully comprehend. Oh, he was used to being shut out by people who were uncomfortable around him, which could be most anybody on any given day. And that was fine, as it suited his line of work more often than not. When he wanted attention, for whatever reason, he was fairly adept at using his charm to get it. And he did it without thinking twice about it. But he'd earned an honest smile from her . . . and suddenly playing the calculating charmer no longer suited him.

"I don't feel up to a drive anymore," she said simply, no censure or self-pity in the comment. "I have kennel rounds later and some paperwork that needs to get done. Despite everything, I still have important work to do here. I'm already doing my part to ease the suffering in the world." She gestured widely. "Here. Where I know I can make a difference."

"Talia—"

But it was too late. She was up the stairs and in the door. It wasn't until she shut him out, literally, that he realized he'd never found out what had really happened between them back by the pond earlier.

He turned, and surprisingly there was a smile on his face. He was still stuck here and he couldn't say he'd made much progress in convincing her to go back with him.

But he felt good. Pretty damn good, actually. Because something *had* happened down there by the pond, and in her truck, too. And he intended to figure out exactly what had happened and what it meant. And he was going to accompany Talia on her nightly kennel check, rather than watch her from a distance as he had the night before.

He didn't imagine she was going to be pleased with his revised schedule. All the more reason to enjoy himself, he thought, whistling as he made his way around the house for another perimeter check.

Chapter 7

Talia watched the two mixed breeds romp around the outdoor play area. The sun was so low she could barely make them out, but she could hear their playful growls as they chased each other. She was fortunate they had proved compatible. It was great for them, not to mention their future owners, to get this kind of workout. Both physically and emotionally.

She only had twelve dogs kenneled at the moment, the fewest she'd had in months. Four were puppies from an abandoned litter she'd found on the roadside a few weeks ago, barely old enough to have been weaned from the mother. She could only surmise that the mother had been killed in a road accident, or that the owners hadn't wanted to deal with the unwanted offspring. They weren't purebred. Part beagle, part terrier was her guess. She didn't think she'd have too much trouble placing them. They were adorable and had a good temperament for family dogs.

She looked back at the play yard. The older ones were always harder, but these two were openly loving and playful. One had been half-starved, full of worms, ticks, and fleas when he'd found his way onto her property. The other was a perfectly healthy death-row inmate the pound hadn't been able to find a home for. Everyone wanted a puppy, or at best a breed that was somewhat determinate. But these two would both make good family dogs. It just took time and time was the one commodity she afforded them.

She made a mental note to contact the Park Service about the upcoming family fair event they were sponsoring. She'd already put in a request to bring these two, and the puppies, who'd be old enough to adopt at that point. If she was lucky, she'd find suitable candidates for them all and perhaps a few more that day.

She made another note to contact Mr. Green about the kittens that Stella had brought in from the pound. They were feral and the county would have simply put them down. However, they would make wonderful barn cats, and she had a standing deal with the local agency to alert her to any tough cases they came across. Mr. Green ran a huge dairy farm and was always looking for barn cats to help him keep the mice and rat population down. These little hellions would be perfect.

There was another cat, a small, shy little tabby, who might be healthy enough to make the trip to the fair, as well. She mentally calculated how many crates she'd need. Stella would have to drive her pickup.

She took a deep breath and tried to keep from worrying. If she didn't place them this go-around, she would the next. She wouldn't think about Archer and his demands on her time . . . or her future. She'd made a pact with herself that for tonight she'd simply pretend all was normal. At least for a few, blessed hours.

Right now all she was looking forward to was heading into the house, stealing some of Baleweg's herb muffins—one high point of having him around

was he'd turned out to be a marvelous cook—and
sinking into bed with a book. A biography maybe, or
something on animal behavior. Definitely not fiction. She was getting enough of that in real life,
thank you.

She whistled for the two dogs, who were wrestling
over a stick. She shook the box of dog bones and
whistled again, laughing as they immediately
dropped the stick and trotted over to her. "Always
suckers for a treat, you two." She tossed them each a
small milk bone, then slapped her thigh and opened
the gate that led to the inside runs. "Come on."
She'd put them next to each other, which seemed to
be working out well.

Once they were safely in for the night, she made
the rest of her rounds, checking for tipped-over water and any other possible problems. Satisfied that
all was well, if not entirely peaceful, she let herself
out the end door.

"Do the rowdy blodgers ever all sleep at the same
time? A fella has a harder time sleeping out here in
the middle of nowhere than in the city."

Talia let out a little squeal, then swung around to
find Archer leaning against the fence.

"Didn't mean to startle you."

"How long have you been there?"

He effortlessly vaulted his rangy body over the
top. "Long enough," he said.

She didn't want to know long enough for what.
She did know she wasn't ready to be alone with him
again. She had no experience dealing with men like
him, not that she could imagine there were other
men like him. "Why are you out here?"

"You didn't think I was going to let you wander
out here in the dark unprotected, did you?"

He'd made his case for staying and she'd grudgingly admitted to herself, especially after their talk

about Dideon and Emrys, that he might be right. But just because she needed his protection, didn't mean she had to like it. "Well, I'm done now," she said shortly, "so you can punch the clock."

"I beg your pardon? Punch what?"

She looked to see if he was teasing her, but he appeared serious. "It's an expression. Means 'to clock out, punch your time card, stop working for the day.' "

He shrugged. "I don't punch a clock, as you say. I work as long as there is work to be done."

Lovely. A workaholic mercenary. Just what she needed. "Well, you can do what you want. I'm heading in for the night."

She glanced up to the house. The left tower-room window glowed. Baleweg was still up. And Archer had taken over the hammock on the porch. She'd offered him one of the other upstairs rooms that first night, when it became clear he was intending to stay along with Baleweg. But he'd told her that the hammock was the best place for him strategically. She'd shrugged and left him to it. Actually, she'd been relieved.

The idea of Archer under the same roof as herself, even though the house was enormous, was a little too unsettling. Not that knowing he was directly beneath her window had left her feeling all that settled.

"Don't you name the little battlers?" he asked.

"Excuse me?"

He nodded to the kennel, where the dogs were not so quietly settling in for the night. "The mongrels you so willingly give shelter to. You never call them by name."

She definitely didn't want to get into this discussion. Damn him for being so observant anyway. "I use general terms, like boy, girl, buddy, whatever."

"Don't they tell you their names, then?"

She looked sharply at him. "They don't 'tell' me anything."

He shrugged, not remotely abashed by her reaction. "I don't claim to understand your gift. Not really." ·

"Gift?" She wanted to laugh at that one. "It's an ability, nothing more. I thought empaths were commonplace in your time."

"Empaths exist, sure. But that doesn't mean I know all about them or how it works. I don't happen to know any personally. Until now."

Was he asking? She didn't know how she felt about explaining it to him. It was such a new experience, being treated so naturally. It made her feel oddly vulnerable, probably because he knew more about her, the real her, than anyone, and yet he was a total stranger to her.

He cocked his head to the side, a grin making his dimple wink at her. "A real battle going on in there."

"What?"

"You really want to believe we're making all this up." He took another step closer. "Only maybe, just maybe, the idea that it might be true thrills you a little. Doesn't it?" He took another step closer, and the air seemed to thicken, even though it was cooler now. "I think you want to believe there is a place where you fit in." He stopped a mere foot away. "You aren't all that well understood in this time, are you, Talia?"

Dear God, did he have to go and use her name like that? There was something about the way he said it, and it didn't have everything to do with that flat Aussie accent, either.

"I can understand that, you know," he went on. "I know what it is to be a misfit."

She had a sudden fleeting sensation of that dark hollowness she'd almost touched. No, they weren't remotely the same, no matter that they were both essentially loners in their respective worlds. She worked to put a sardonic edge to her tone. "I guess your line of work doesn't exactly come rife with pals and coworkers, huh?"

He smiled, that cockeyed half-smile that deepened the little cleft in his chin. "Not so you would notice, no. But I was a misfit long before I found my walk in life. I imagine the same could be said of you. In fact, we probably both found our callings because we didn't fit in, wouldn't you say?"

She wanted to tell him to stop comparing himself to her, stop saying they were anything alike. But he'd moved even closer, somehow robbing her of what little rational thought she had left. She could only nod in response.

"And what about you? What about those pals and coworkers? Is there no one you trust with your secret?"

"Secret?" she managed. He was far too close.

"You don't tell anyone, do you?" He didn't give her a chance to answer. "Is it because you fear they'll abandon you? Or simply think you're odd in the head?"

She smiled without thinking about it, then swallowed hard as she saw his eyes leap to life in response to it. She did try to move away, but he lifted his hand and gently brushed back a loose strand of hair that was dancing about in the night breeze.

"I do understand, Talia Trahaern. Everyone knows who we are as defined by our careers. We share that part of ourselves because it benefits us to do so. But we both have secrets, you and I, the things we keep locked in here." He let the tendril drop and grazed the back of his fingertips across her heart.

"And I think your heart is more tender than you are willing to admit."

He moved his hand away, and she had to catch herself from leaning forward.

He turned her hands palm up, cupped in his own. He was looking down at them as he spoke. "You don't give them names because you'll lose part of your heart to them if you do." He glanced up into her eyes, then dropped her hands. "And you can't risk your heart again, can you? Not ever."

The hollow look she'd seen in his eyes during that brief glance brought her directly back to that instant she'd connected with him. Some part of her heart tightened before she pulled loose, both physically and emotionally. So they both kept their hearts safely tucked away. That was certainly a good thing.

She put some space between them, but had to clear her throat to speak. "I don't give them names for the logical reason that naming a pet should be the right of the owner, a bond made between them. No point in confusing the poor thing by giving it something to recognize only to have someone come along and change it." He wasn't looking at her, which should have made her little speech easier, but it didn't. "You better than anyone understand I have a special attachment to every animal here, whether I wish to or not. So naming them is of little consequence when it comes to risking my emotions." Which was true, to a point.

That half-smile, the knowing one that made her feel naked and exposed, returned. But mercifully, he kept his hands to himself. "So defensive."

She had to stop herself from crossing her arms over her chest. "You were the one poking and prodding. I was merely trying to answer you."

"Why don't you keep more of them for your own?"

The question caught her off guard. "What?"

He waved a hand to the land surrounding the house and the house itself. "Since you have all this space and feel as you do about rescuing the unwanted, I figured you'd have adopted a gaggle of them yourself."

"Why all this concern about my life habits?"

He shrugged, but the intensity had returned. "I have to be alert to anything out of the ordinary. To understand that, I have to understand what ordinary is." He said it matter-of-factly, but his eyes told a different story. He wasn't merely making conversation. "Studying you and your setup here has left me with questions."

She took a different tack. Let *him* answer some questions. "Speaking of animals, what happened to your dog?"

He looked totally blank for a second. "My dog?" Then his expression cleared. "You mean Ringer."

"Yes, I believe that is what you called him once before. What was he? Some sort of convenient prop you used to meet me? And now that you've accomplished your invasion into my life, he is of no further use to you? What did you do to him, send him back to the future to fend for himself?"

"Send Ringer back to fend for himself?" He said it as though he couldn't believe he'd heard her right. "I wouldn't do that." His shock was so sincere she had to believe him.

Her soft heart swelled. Just a little. "What did you expect me to think? I haven't seen him since that day at the Lodge." Why was *she* on the defensive again?

"I didn't think it was your concern. You have enough mongrels to deal with, don't you, now?"

Rather than being stung by his brush-off, she was intrigued. He seemed a bit . . . disconcerted.

Evasive even. Interesting. "You had no problem sticking your nose in my affairs. Where is he?"

Archer actually shifted his weight ever so slightly. He waved a hand, striving for a casualness she now knew he didn't entirely feel. "Round and about. Likes to go on walkabout that one does."

"He's running loose?"

Archer propped his hands on his hips. "Well, he's not exactly a threat to the wildlife or the population in general. And it's not like you don't have room for him to roam a bit. He doesn't get much chance to run like this at home. I thought it would do him good."

"I'm not worried what trouble he'll make, I'm worried about the trouble that might find him, you idiot." Archer's eyebrows lifted at that one, but she continued on. "I don't know how they handle pet ownership in Australia, or in Britain, or . . . or wherever you're from, but here we are required to keep a handle on our pets. So they don't end up needing my services. Or worse. There are natural predators out there, ones he might not be familiar with."

"Trust me, Ringer can fend for himself quite well." He folded his arms, no longer seeming off balance. "Where I come from," he said, almost mockingly, "predators are a part of daily living. If he can make it there, I'm certain he can handle anything here. Ringer has a well-developed instinct for self-preservation."

She shook her head in disgust. "When was the last time you saw him? How is he being fed? Are you sure he's okay?"

Laughing, Archer stepped forward and lightly grasped her hands. He tugged her closer to him. It seemed an entirely natural gesture, as did the way she sort of fell against him, their body parts all aligning so perfectly. It actually took her breath away.

"I think I just figured out why you don't have animals in the house."

There was nowhere to look but up into his dancing black eyes. Her breath caught in her chest. "I have a cat. Marble," she managed.

"That's not a real pet."

"You want to tell him that? All twenty-eight pounds of him?"

"The way I hear it, he was Beatrice's beast and, from the looks of him, quite able to take care of himself. I imagine he'd do just fine without you." He moved even closer, tipping her head farther back. "But he chooses to stay with you." He leaned down. "Wise choice, I'd say."

Her breath caught the instant before his mouth covered hers. She'd known his intent, had seen it clearly in his dark eyes. But she hadn't shoved him away, she hadn't done any of the smart things some part of her mind should have screamed at her to do.

She swiftly realized that she didn't need to worry about connecting to his feelings again. She was too busy wallowing in her own. The incredible warmth of his lips on hers, how firm they were, how well they matched hers, how they seemed to know her, as if he'd kissed her a thousand times before. It was glorious, intoxicating, wondrous. And extremely dangerous.

That last part was what made her pull away. Still, she wanted to reach up and touch her mouth. It felt like something foreign, strangely alive when she hadn't even known it had been lying dormant all this time.

"They take it from you, don't they, Tali?" he asked quietly, his gaze steady on hers. She felt as if he were the one looking into her soul. When she looked away, he drew the tip of his finger along the side of her cheek, then along the lips he'd just thoroughly imprinted with his own. "You can't have them under your own roof all the time because you feel too much of them, and it drains you. They tug at your strength, your heart, all the time." He tipped up her chin and she chided herself for the glassy surface she knew he'd find in her eyes. "I didn't mean to upset you. I only wanted to understand you. I think maybe I do. A little bit more at any rate."

Her senses reeled. "Archer, I—"

"Time to finish my rounds."

"But—"

He dropped his mouth to hers for one last hard kiss. "I want you to head in." He left her, moving back to the fence, which he leaped over as effortlessly as he'd done earlier.

She wanted to be angry that he'd come to understand her so clearly. Especially the part of her she'd kept locked away the farthest. She did good work here, satisfying and important. Yet there was a part of her that had always felt some lingering guilt. That she hadn't been strong enough to put her abilities to use more directly.

Archer was the first one to make her feel like it was okay. The first one to truly understand why she'd chosen the path she had. And accept it.

She stared at his retreating back as she ran her fingers over her lips. He said he'd only intruded because he'd been curious about her. Well, damn it, she was curious about him now, too. There had been secrets in his eyes, secrets she wanted to uncover, just as he had hers.

Chapter 8

*A*rcher resisted the urge to slam his fist through the wall. Just barely. "What do you mean you don't know where the hell she is? She's supposed to be in here with you."

Baleweg didn't so much as flinch. As always, he was maddeningly serene. "She chose to skip our lesson this afternoon, and considering how badly distracted she was this morning, I thought it best to allow her time to herself." Baleweg studied Archer closely. "You wouldn't, perhaps, know the cause of her distraction?"

Archer opened his mouth to tell him he had no idea what was going through Talia's mind since she hadn't seen fit to speak to him since he'd kissed her last night. But he wasn't ready to discuss that with Baleweg. That is, if the old codger didn't already know it. He wondered if Talia had told him . . . or if he'd figured it out for himself. Either way, he wasn't about to go there at the moment.

"Didn't you think it best to inform me? You're the one who insisted I stay for protection." He shoved a kitchen chair so it clattered against the table. "I can hardly be expected to do that when the people I'm supposed to protect go wandering off without warning, now can I?" He was angry at Baleweg, but most of his anger was self-directed. He shouldn't have gone off looking for Ringer. But he'd thought Talia was safe with Baleweg in the tower.

And no matter what she said, he wasn't cavalier about maintaining his pet ownership. He'd never really thought about it that way anyway. He and Ringer were simply mates who happened to be stuck with each other for a time. He was truly happy Ringer was having such a grand time here. He had his freedom and could change at will if threatened. He certainly never felt any little twinges when he wondered if the beastie might be better off here than back in his own time.

All of this did little to explain his alarm this morning when he'd had no luck finding the little bugger in his usual haunts about the pond and in the marshes. It did even less to explain his total lack of professionalism in leaving his post to pursue the matter. That he still hadn't located Ringer didn't help, either.

He drew in a deep breath. "Did she say where she went off to?" Her truck was out front, so she couldn't have gone far. But he still didn't like having her out of his sight.

"I believe she went to the kennels to see after some business, then catch up with paperwork. There are other workers out there and someone would have signaled if anything was amiss."

"I've just come from the kennels. She's not there, or in her office."

Baleweg's bushy white brows furrowed, but there was no real concern in his eyes. "Perhaps she took a stroll around the pond. It's a pleasant enough day for it. And I daresay she could use the space."

Archer's eyes nearly popped out of his head. "Space? We're here to help her find her healing powers, or you are, and I'm here supposedly to keep her safe while you do it, which means containing her within boundaries I can monitor. And you *daresay* she could use some space?"

Baleweg's fleeting concern vanished, replaced by an annoyingly contemplative expression. "You have crowded her a bit of late."

Archer ground his back teeth. "We've been here too long already. With Dideon's return, Chamberlain now knows we're here. He has to be planning something else to thwart us. Every second that ticks away puts the queen in greater jeopardy, therefore upping the odds against Talia. I'm merely doing the job you insist I do."

Baleweg nodded, then looked away for a moment, but it was a telling one.

"What aren't you telling me?" Archer demanded. "I know about Emrys, if that's what's bothering you."

"Talia told you."

"I'd have rather had it from you. He's the one aiding Chamblerlain, right? Any other surprises I might nccd to know about?"

Baleweg shook his head, but didn't look remotely abashed.

"Let me go back and deal with him."

Baleweg merely shook his head. "You will not be dealing with the likes of him. Leave that to me." He lifted his hand to stall Archer's rebuttal. "I will not discuss him with you other than to say that I can feel the continuum quite clearly here and there has been no disturbance in it of late."

"I say we both go back. You can deal with this Emrys directly and I will deliver Talia safely to the queen. Then we'll wash our hands of it.". Even as he said it, he realized he couldn't imagine walking away from her now. Everything was far more complicated than when he'd stepped through that damned triangle on Baleweg's roof. He hated complications.

"Talia isn't ready to return. And for now it is best that you deal with any threat Emrys might provoke from here."

"Then you should be holed up in the tower with her right now, preparing her, not giving her the day off to wander to God knows where!"

Baleweg smiled pleasantly now. "Then perhaps rather than standing here haranguing me, you should set out about the pond and look for her, hmm?"

Archer's fingers curled inward, and he ruthlessly bit off several epithets as he walked to the door. He paused there long enough to point a finger toward Baleweg. "If anything has happened to her, it will be on your head, old man."

He was out the door when he heard the satisfied tone in Baleweg's voice as he said, "How very interesting."

Archer crossed the drive and took off down the path, trying hard to block out the old man's parting shot. He was doing his job. Nothing more, nothing less. A queen's ransom was riding on this and he'd be damned if some black-hearted Parliamentarian's mystic lackey was going to screw him out of it. Baleweg was being awfully closed-mouthed about this Emrys, but Archer knew the old man well enough to know that badgering him would yield nothing until he was ready to talk. He flexed his fingers. Fine. Let Emrys send another mark through time, he thought. He'd handle them all, do whatever he had to in order to buy Talia enough time to be fully prepared for what lay in store for her with the queen.

He was jogging by the time he got to the shed. The odd hat she'd been wearing that first day he'd met her out here was gone, as was the walking stick. Of course he was worried about her, he thought as he picked up speed, but he was being paid to worry. If he'd been a bit tighter in his surveillance, it had nothing whatsoever to do with that fact that he'd tasted her now. Or that he'd dreamed of tasting her again.

Of course, it had been a while since he'd dallied. That was likely the reason for his preoccupation. After all, she was the only woman above twenty-one and below seventy in these parts; naturally a man's mind would turn to that if he spent enough time in her presence. He continued around the curve of the pond, ducking and swatting at the scrub brush that was beginning to stretch its late-spring growth across the path. His thoughts continued just as doggedly.

It wasn't as if she did anything to draw a eye man's. Her clothes could, at best, be described as baggy and serviceable. He knew firsthand there were feminine curves beneath it, yet you'd never know to look at her. Her dark hair was as often as not stuffed up beneath a hat or yanked into a messy ponytail. Her face was forever clean of anything smacking of female artifice—she didn't even darken her lashes or smear color on her lips. He stumbled and cursed as a thorny swatch caught him on the cheek.

Okay, okay, so she didn't need painting up. Especially those lips. And perhaps she could maintain a pretty decent level of conversation, that is, assuming she kept her tongue civil. But he'd observed her with Stella enough to know she had a fair bit of wit tucked in with all that intelligence. Of course, he wasn't the least bit put out that she didn't often, if ever, care to share that smiling wit with him. No, far too often he earned the sharper side of her tongue.

And God help the man who wanted to wind his way past all that to try and steal a kiss. How he'd managed such a thing he now had no idea. She seemed more distant to him than ever. Which angered him all over again. Space. She needed space, did she? Well, wasn't that all she'd goddamn had for the past twenty-eight years of her life? Was it honestly all that much to ask for her to tolerate his existence for a few days? It wasn't as if he were sniffing about her, trying to paw her or anything.

No, he saved that for the night, after his eyes had finally shut. Damn the woman for those hot, twitching dreams, too.

He'd worked up a fairly good head of steam as he ducked around a tree, danced between its thick roots at the same time; then he almost fell facefirst into the pond when he spied her. He managed to cling to a thick branch overhead and avert certain disaster. Well, one disaster anyway.

She was sitting on a flat rock that jutted out into the pond, tossing stones at the glassy surface . . . and having a nice little chat. With Ringer.

Jesus, Joseph, and Elvis, this was all he needed to make the day complete. Relief that the little beast was safe, was brief, since there was a substantial chance that he'd wring the shifter's neck if he so much as changed a toenail in front of Talia. At least Ringer had the sense to be the same breed of dog he'd been the day they'd first met.

He was about to whistle for him when another idea came to him. Perhaps getting Ringer to pull one of his little shifting acts would be a good thing, after all. Prove to Talia that they were what they claimed to be. Maybe he should have just done that right off.

She laughed just then and reached out to pet Ringer's scruffy head. Beautiful music, that. He'd not heard her laugh like that before, without a thread of derision or surprise coloring it. This laugh had been filled with pure enjoyment. He scowled, feeling foolish for envying Ringer, even for a moment.

He pushed through the tangle of brush and climbed the path toward them. "I see you've finally made the little scrapper's acquaintance."

She looked up, obviously startled. Her smile remained, but a certain guardedness had crept into it. He felt a moment's remorse that he'd ruined her respite. Had she really wanted so badly to be rid of him? Was he such a bad sort? "Baleweg was concerned that you were off alone." A lie, but he'd also be damned if he'd let her know the emotions she'd wrung out of him this past hour.

"I heard a howl and tracked him," she said, the tiniest bit of defensiveness in her tone.

His brows narrowed as he shifted his attention to Ringer, who was shamelessly lying on his back for a belly rub now. Lucky little bastard. "He's okay, I take it?"

She nodded, but surprisingly there was no chastising in her expression. "He'd gotten himself into a tangle with some brambles, but other than a few scratches, he's fine." She scratched his belly. "Aren't ya, boy. That's a good fella." Ringer pumped his back legs in sheer ecstasy and groaned as she gave him a good scratch. She looked back at Archer, having to squint a bit as the sun suddenly peeked out from behind a cloud. "I guess I owe you an apology."

That surprised him. "For?"

She nodded at Ringer. "He's in good shape, his coat, scruffy as it is, is clean and untangled, and he doesn't miss many meals judging from this little belly." She grinned when Ringer shamelessly begged for more of her attention. Her obvious joy made his skin ripple in awareness.

"You've obviously kept an eye out for him. You were searching for him earlier."

No way did heat rise to his cheeks. "He takes care

of himself like a good mate. He doesn't need me panting about after his every move."

"I thought I saw you wandering down this way." She broke eye contact, turning her attention to Ringer. With a half-shrug she added, "I happened to glance out of the tower-room window."

Archer grinned. So, she'd been keeping watch over him, had she? Baleweg had said she'd been distracted and needed some space. But perhaps she'd seen him and come after him, hoping to share that space. The very idea, as well as the fact that they were, indeed, alone together made his body tighten. Surprising, considering that just moments ago he'd wanted to write her off as being entirely too much trouble.

But when she looked back up at him, with that hint of vulnerability in her eyes, he had a hard time remembering why he'd felt that way.

"Tell Baleweg I'm sorry for worrying him," she said.

He cleared his throat, feeling a bit bad now for the fib. "I'm sure he'll understand. You were simply heeding the call of the wild, right?"

"I guess you could say that." She stood up and brushed off the seat of her jeans shorts. He couldn't recall seeing her in shorts before. Her legs were exceedingly long and slender with a flair of calf muscle. Probably from all that walking. Probably had strong thighs, too, he imagined. Just as he imagined what those strong thighs would feel like, all tight and wrapped—

He cleared his throat and dragged his gaze to the pond. "Don't you have more lessons this afternoon?"

"I begged off."

He turned to her. "Baleweg said you were a bit unfocused. Something wrong?"

Rather than answer, she reached down to scratch Ringer between the ears. He stretched against her legs, then looked up at her adoringly.

"Looks like you've got a new mate there."

"He's a very affectionate little guy," she said. "I'm surprised he doesn't stay closer to the house. He seems to be a people person."

"He likes his space." Archer waited until she looked at him. "We all do from time to time, right?"

She shaded her eyes as the sun poked out again, so he couldn't see what was in them. But her voice reflected weariness. And wariness. "I suppose we do. Maybe I'm used to my solitude more than some."

"And we've taken a good deal of that away, haven't we?" She looked so surprised at his sympathy that he continued without thinking. "Am I such a callous blodger, then? You can't imagine that I might feel bad about the way we've invaded your life?"

That earned him a smile, a very dry one. "Honestly? No. I don't think it bothers you if it means getting the job done. Isn't that what matters most?"

"Yeah." But even as he said it, he realized it for the automatic response that it was. He refused to ponder that further. "It was what I hired on to do. I have no choice."

"Oh, we all have a choice." She looked him square in the eyes now. "Even me."

"What is that supposed to mean?"

"It means that despite what I'm getting out of this, which is a great deal more than you probably understand, I'm not at all sure I'm willing to pay you back in the way you'd like me to."

"Now, wait just a damn minute. I think the pixies have been wreaking havoc with your mind or you've baked in the sun here a bit too long. If you think that kiss last night meant I was looking for some kind of—" He broke off when her mouth dropped open, then closed again, but only so she could burst out laughing. Ringer began barking and running in circles, as if he too found this whole thing hilarious.

Archer propped his hands on his hips. "You obviously have a low opinion of me, and normally I don't care what anyone thinks, but I just want to make one thing clear."

She could hardly stop laughing long enough to listen to him. "And just what is that?"

He hopped up on the rock and took hold of her shoulders before he'd even thought the action through. She didn't struggle, but her laughter stopped now. He saw her throat work as she stared up into his eyes and it made his body even jumpier. "I'm not the sort that uses sex as some form of payment for services rendered." He wasn't shouting, but there was still temper in his tone, and in his eyes if her expression was any indication.

Not because she cowered or anything. Oh, no, not Talia. Whenever he got in a temper, she usually responded by following suit. This time was no exception. She didn't yank free of his hold, but her body tightened beneath his grip. "No, I don't suppose I should have to pay. The queen is doing that and quite well, I hear."

Her frosty tone should have roiled him further. And it did, but not in anger. Oh, the storm that brewed in those eyes of hers. He wondered if she was aware of the tempest he saw in them and how potent its promise was. He realized then she could wear sackcloth and smear ashes on her face. Appearances had nothing to do with what captivated him.

"I don't expect anything from you except that you follow the rules that allow me to keep you safe," he said heatedly. "That includes not running off on a wild-goose chase."

Her eyebrows lifted and the tempest stirred further. "I did not run off. I very deliberately left. And the animal I was trying to help was yours, not that I'd expect any gratitude."

Archer fought a grin. How did she do that? She had him hot under the collar one moment, and hot under the belt the next. "And you were just apologizing to me about the care and maintenance of my pet."

"Well, I take it back. He's probably fine *despite* you. And I no longer wonder why he spends his time out here in the wild. I was driven to do the very same after only two days of your hovering."

"Hovering?" He moved closer. "Hovering, is it?" He noticed her pupils shoot wide, the center of the storm taking control. Control of him. He lowered his mouth. "If there is any hovering to happen, it's here. My mouth above yours," he murmured. "What do you say to that?"

He felt the fine tremor of awareness shiver through her. "I say go ahead. But it won't change anything."

Now he pulled his head back. "Change anything?"

"When I said I wasn't prepared to make the payment you demanded, I didn't mean this." She actually threw back her shoulders as if about to enter the fray. "I meant that I'm not so sure I will go back with you. To your time. That is the payment I was referring to. Not . . . not this."

"Oh." He should feel like a cloddering fool, but she was in his arms and that drove all other thoughts from his mind. "And what of . . . this?"

"I . . . it won't change things, either."

His eyes widened. "You still think I mean to seduce you into going?"

She looked at him. "It hasn't crossed your mind?"

He couldn't help grinning. She just begged him to tweak that defiance of hers. "Would it work?"

"Whatever decision I end up making, I'll make alone."

"What if I told you that my wanting to kiss you has nothing whatever to do with my mission for the queen? And everything to do with finding out if your lips taste as good this time as they did the first time."

She blew out a very shaky breath. "I'd say you're really good at this seduction stuff and maybe I'd better step back and call it a day. I don't think I'm tough enough to play these games with you and come out unscathed."

"I think you're made of far tougher stuff than you credit yourself with."

"And I think you'd say just about anything right now to keep me from running."

"Is that right? So sure of your allure, are you?"

Surprisingly, that goaded a smile from her, a rather bold one. She pressed lightly against him, but it was enough. "Unless that's a fold-up walking stick in your pocket . . . yes."

He almost swallowed his own tongue in shock. "Well, then." And that was the best he could do.

She smiled and extricated herself from his grasp. "Maybe we should just keep things between us all business. Putting sexual involvement into the mix, even as light as this is, complicates everything."

Light? She thought his involvement a light thing? He couldn't think about the implications of why that shouldn't sting his pride because she'd started to turn away, and he knew he couldn't let her. "And you have so much experience with the mixing of business and pleasure, do you?"

She looked over her shoulder. "Enough to know I'm out of my league here. And not afraid to admit it. Just so you know, that was not a red flag meant to encourage the bull. I'm serious. Let's just let this one go."

"This," he repeated. "You mean this?" Without touching her he stepped up to her and lowered his mouth over hers. He expected a stinging slap, or a jerking away . . . was maybe even hoping for them. Then he could take the rejection, lick his wounds, and respect her wishes. But he got neither. Instead he got what, just perhaps, he'd really been wanting to find.

Her mouth softened under his, and he heard a moan. That it was his own only threw him off stride for a moment. She shifted, or maybe he did, but in the next instant they were tangled with one another, limbs and lips both. It was Ringer's incessant barking and running in circles around them that pulled him to the surface.

"Why did you do that?" she asked a bit breathlessly.

"I wanted to make sure this was just a light little thing that was easily dismissed. As you said it was. No worries, right?"

"Oh. Well. Right." She pulled away and jumped off the rock, then snatched her walking stick from a nearby tree and hit the path at a not-so-steady stride. Ringer, the traitor, jogged along at her side.

"Talia."

He wasn't sure she'd stop. But she did.

"Just so you know, you're not so far out of the league as you think."

Rather than smug triumph, there was a contemplative look on her face when she turned. "Isn't that double the reason to end this now, then? We both have jobs to do. Better for us both to do them with all our senses intact, don't you think?"

She left, not waiting for a response.

He jumped down from the rock and kept a steady pace just far enough back to give her the precious space she desired, but enabling him to keep a protective vigil.

The taste of her raged inside him. As did the warning bells. Warning bells telling him that she spoke the clear, certain truth.

"But I think we're going to have a hard time steering clear of this, Talia Trahaern. That's what I think."

Chapter 9

I still say this is a bad idea."

Talia loaded the puppies into their crate, then tucked them into the back of the truck. "Tell that to these little guys." She reached in and rubbed the noses of the four squirming pups. "I hope to find homes for them today." She smiled and reached in to scratch the two older dogs in the crates behind the puppies. "And yes, you guys, too. Just stay clean and you'll win a few hearts before the day is out." She shifted a few things around, making sure all was secure, and ignored Archer. Or tried to.

True to his word, since their interlude by the pond two days ago, he'd given her more space and she in turn had delved more deeply into her studies with Baleweg. Not that it had done much good. Baleweg knew about her connection with Archer and had implored her to try again, but Talia had put him off. She still wasn't seeing any signs of healing powers, and delving into Archer's emotions didn't seem a wise or particularly productive course of action. She had hoped her classes would at least provide a distraction from Archer, but that had not been the case. Every time Baleweg mentioned Archer's name, which was annoyingly often, she'd remember how his hands felt when he pulled her into his arms, how his mouth had felt when he'd kissed her.

Her time with Baleweg had produced one pro-
found change, however. Her empathic skills had
definitely grown sharper, which Baleweg found en-
couraging. She wasn't so sure. She'd initially realized it when she found Ringer. She'd been terrified
when she'd felt that first wave of pain. The dog
hadn't really howled as she'd told Archer, not out
loud anyway. But the pain she'd felt had been so
strong, she'd wanted to resist it, call the vet, let him
find the poor unfortunate creature and deal with it.
But she hadn't been able to do that. Steeling herself
against the pinpricks of pain stabbing at her, seemingly all over, she'd gone in search of whatever lay
out there.

Then she'd found the little mutt and discovered it
had only been some brambles stuck in his fur,
scratching his skin. As relieved as she'd been for
Ringer, she felt quite the opposite about her enhanced abilities. If she'd picked up so acutely on
what amounted to fairly minor discomfort, she
shuddered to think how sensitized she'd become
now to real distress.

There was no doubt that Baleweg had taught her
much about using the power of her mind, but what
if she couldn't learn to control it? Hell, she had
never really managed to control it up to now.

Archer moved in beside her as she shifted the last
few crates. She steeled herself against possible contact, thankful he hadn't touched her since that day
by the pond. She didn't want to think what connecting with him again might feel like. And yet, she'd
thought about it anyway. Often.

"If you're dead set on this," he said tersely, "then
send Stella."

"I can't," she said, busying herself checking crates
that didn't need any further checking.

"Talia?" Stella called out to her from the kennels.

Saved! "Be right there!" She barely glanced at Archer as she darted past him. He moved in and for a heart-stopping moment she thought he was going to touch her. That was the last thing she needed at the moment. He was far easier to deal with—if there was such a thing—when he was irritated. Which hadn't been a difficult task of late.

She moved quickly through the gate and closed it between them. "I'll be out in a minute." She ducked into the kennel, praying he wouldn't follow, and found Stella by the smallest run. "What do you need?"

"It's the little chihuahua-pom mix we just got in. Something's not right with him."

Talia stilled; she really couldn't handle this. Not now. At the same time she wondered why she hadn't felt the little guy's distress already. What was happening to her? Her connections were stronger and yet didn't seem to be as controlled or focused any longer. Had she been so focused on not letting Archer invade her mind and senses that she'd blocked out real suffering?

Maybe dabbling with Baleweg hadn't been such a good idea, after all. Maybe she'd really screwed herself up. She tried to clear her mind, reach out, but she still felt nothing. First her overreaction to Ringer, now this. She was overcome by the sudden feeling that everything was spiraling out of her control. She should have sent them away at the first. As if she'd had a choice! It had been hard enough dealing with her ability before. If she was losing what little control she had mastered over it . . . she didn't know if she could handle that. Or how to go back to the way things were before. She had a sick feeling that it wasn't possible.

"Talia? Is something wrong?"

Talia jerked her gaze to Stella. "Uh, no. No." She

took a deep breath. God, she badly wanted to just get the hell out of here and disappear on her own for a while. She just wanted some time to think, to figure out what in the hell was happening to her. But the trucks were loaded, people were waiting. Stella was waiting. The dog was waiting.

She took a deep breath and tried to ignore the nausea climbing from her stomach into her throat. "Let's see what the problem is," she told Stella, trying to cover the tremor in her voice with what she hoped was a reassuring smile. But when she looked inside the small run, a shiver of dread crawled through her. The puppy was curled up, its front left leg at an awkward angle, not moving.

This was the reason she'd left vet school. She waited for the overwhelming feeling to hit her, the waves of pain, the mental anguish the dog was suffering, wondering how she'd handle it now that everything seemed to be falling apart. Guilt overwhelmed her again, that sense of personal failure for not finding a way to handle this, to help the animals who always seemed to find her. Maybe she *was* supposed to be able to heal them all.

Stella clutched her arm. "Is he—"

Talia jerked at her touch. She'd opened a Pandora's box inside of herself, or maybe Archer and Baleweg had. It didn't matter. There was no going back now.

God help her.

Her sudden movement startled the dog, who thrashed around, his leg still stuck awkwardly near his face. Talia immediately spotted the problem. Light-headed with relief, she reached in and picked him up. Maybe her abilities hadn't spun that far out of control, after all. She laughed almost giddily. She hadn't felt the dog's pain because he hadn't been in any.

"He's okay?" Stella asked anxiously, leaning over her shoulder.

"He got his nail caught in his fur," she said, her voice still trembling. The dog squirmed and squeaked, covering the clumsiness of her wobbly fingers as she unwound the knotted fur from the tiny claw. "He has a little sliver peeling back here," she said to Stella, pointing to the claw. "Get me the trimmers."

Stella was back in a flash. "Thank God. I thought—" She shook her head, then blew out a large sigh of relief. "I'm just glad he's okay."

"I guess he kept digging, trying to get it free, making it worse." Talia checked his paws for other problems, then held the round ball of fluff up to her face. "Wore yourself out and fell asleep, did you?" The little dog shook his whole body, reaching out his tiny tongue to lick her face.

Stella laughed and reached out to stroke him. "You scared me, little guy." Grinning, she let the dog lick her cheek and chin. "Do I have time to hold him?"

Still weak with relief, Talia gladly agreed. She could use a few minutes to gather her wits. She'd come too close to losing it and that scared her. She was going to have to find a way to deal with all this, but right now she just wanted to regain her focus on the job at hand. "Be careful with that spot he dug at trying to get free. It might be a little tender. Five minutes, okay? Then we really have to get moving."

Stella nodded, all her attention on the dog. Talia did find a smile then. She'd been hoping to let the tiny mixed breed gain a bit more weight before placing him with an older person, someone without kids since the little one would likely not stand up to such rough play. But she recognized Stella's expression. Her heart was gone. Talia suspected it wouldn't be too much longer before her employee worked up the nerve to ask to adopt him.

She'd have to give that some thought. Stella was certainly mature enough for her age to handle the responsibility, but she would also likely settle down and marry during the dog's lifetime, with babies and all in her future. Talia was very specific about how she placed her animals and tried hard not to let wide eyes and overly soft hearts affect her judgment. But she had a feeling Stella would win this one.

She was still smiling when she stepped outside. The instant she saw Archer standing by her truck, her stomach knotted again. Dammit, she should have gone to her office, but it was too late to back-track now. One look at him and everything she'd felt standing in front of that run came rushing back at her. The pom mix's predicament was explained . . . but she still couldn't explain her overreaction to Ringer. *I've been around Baleweg too long,* she thought. *I just need to step back and get myself back under control. I can be on top of this.*

She quickly moved to her side of the truck, hoping Archer would stay on the other side and let her regain her composure. Of course, he didn't. He rounded the truck before she could even take a steadying breath

"Everything okay?"

"Fine, fine." Not so sharply, she schooled herself.

"For someone who claims everything is 'fine, fine,' you sure don't look it. Your face is white as a sheet." He looked closer. "And your pupils are like little pinpricks." He trapped her between the rearview mirror and the door. "What happened in there?"

"Nothing." *Everything. I feel as though I'm losing my mind.* "The little pom mix we just got in from the pound managed to get his nail stuck in a mat of hair. He's fine. Problem solved. Stella is with him." She was babbling. "I have things to do. Move." She looked up at him. "Please."

She knew she was lost the moment she looked at him. Archer's brow was furrowed in real concern. "You're trembling." He looked at the kennel, then back at her. Now he looked fierce. "Was anyone else in there besides Stella?" He shook her lightly. "Tell me what's wrong."

Oddly, it was the ferocity of his reaction that enabled her to find her own level of composure. "Nothing, Archer. I already told you. The dog is fine."

"No one was in there but you and Stella?"

"Just the dog."

He seemed to relax. Fractionally. "So what sent you running out here looking as if you'd seen a ghost?" Then his expression softened. Well, not softened exactly, but the hard line of his jaw wasn't quite as hard. "The little bloke's pain bothered you."

She'd just found a tiny bit of balance and he had to go and knock her off it. "Don't get all understanding on me, okay?"

Rather than look affronted, he looked amused. "Hey, I'm a sensitive guy."

She snorted. But she also took the out he was offering. Until she'd had time to think all this over, find her balance, she didn't want to talk about it. She wasn't certain she'd ever want to talk about it. Yet—and this made zero sense—she had an undeniable urge to just lean into him and tell him everything, to trust him. As if he really were an understanding and trustworthy guy. *Yeah, right.* Still, she ducked under his arm and moved away before she could do it anyway. "I've got to finish loading the truck."

He tugged her back and turned her face to his. Then he leaned down and kissed her lightly on the lips. Her eyes widened. He let her go and stepped back.

"What was that for?" she asked warily.

He grinned. "Just wanted to put some color back in your cheeks."

"Well." When she realized that was the best she could come up with, she gave up and turned tail for the kennel.

Archer watched Talia run away, and grinned despite himself. Christ but he was getting soft. And he thought he'd only been joking about being sensitive. She hadn't gotten to him, he told himself. Not really. It was just a momentary lapse. He was merely antsy about getting done with this thing.

And if that wasn't a crock of shit, he didn't know what was.

He thought about her all the time, and, truth be told, many a time it had nothing to do with the mission and everything to do with his growing . . . what? *Respect* was the word that had come to mind. *Admiration* was close behind it. And a balls-aching amount of plain healthy lust all the damn time. His fingers all but itched to touch her. How he'd kept from pulling her into his arms when she'd first come out of the kennel he had no idea. But Talia Trahaern was a strong one. She wasn't one to go bawling to a man with her troubles. Which just made him want her all the more.

Ringer chose that moment to show up. What was one more headache to deal with? He looked down at the mutt. "Best you stay that way today, mate." Ringer merely plopped down beside him, obviously without a care in the world. He should be so carefree. The sooner this day was over, the better, he thought. "And the sooner you get your head back on lookout, the better, too," he muttered.

The hairs on his neck had been at full alert all morning. Talia had assured him it was a simple trip to a local park area and she'd be in one spot the entire time with flocks of people about. What could possibly go wrong in the middle of a crowd like that? she'd asked him more than once. Archer grimaced at her naïveté. It might be a simple few hours and they'd return here where he could keep a closer watch. But he didn't think so. He rubbed a hand over his neck. He had a bad feeling about this.

Baleweg materialized beside him. "Under way, are we?" he asked calmly, reaching down to scratch Ringer between the ears.

Archer put a bit of distance between them. The man liked to crowd a person far too much for his liking. "She's loading the last of them up now." He looked over at him. "You know I'm not at all comfortable with this little trek today."

Baleweg surprised him by looking a bit troubled himself. "I can't say as I'm enthusiastic, either."

Oh, wonderful. Now Archer's instincts really clamored. "Well, why in the hell didn't you tell her that? She thinks I'm being an overprotective pain in the ass. A word from you would have gone a long way to making my job easier."

"I pondered that, as well." He turned a baleful eye on Archer. "I'd expected you to make more progress in earning her trust."

"And I'd expected you to make more progress teaching her."

Baleweg didn't react to the jab. "It would be best for her to succeed in placing these orphans of hers. It will help to ease her mind when we must leave."

Archer caught something in the old man's tone. "You know something I don't?"

"It will be soon, Devin." He looked at him fully.

He tried to ignore the weird feeling it gave him to have the old man call him by his birth name. It felt sort of . . . well, good. Jesus, he really was going wonky. "How soon?"

"Soon."

"And you're upset because you think she won't go?"

"That."

"And?"

Baleweg looked away, and for the first time, Archer was truly afraid that something was going to happen, something he wouldn't be able to control. "What's got you all snakey, mate?"

"She's going to need someone to count on, someone to be there for her." He left that statement to hover in Archer's mind as he turned and disappeared back toward the house.

"Aren't you coming with us?"

Baleweg shook his head. "I've done what I can. Now it's up to you." He paused long enough to look back at Archer. "Don't fail her. Or yourself."

Chapter 10

Talia waved good-bye to Mr. and Mrs. Hubert. They'd be a good match for the last pup.

Stella was beaming. "We done good."

"We sure did." It had been an outstanding day. She had prospects for all of the puppies, and the little tabby. Best of all, her two older dogs would likely be going to the same family. "It will be busy these next few days. We've got a bunch of people coming." She didn't release any of the animals to their new owners the first day. All of them had to agree to come to the kennels where she could observe them with the animal in a more relaxed setting and question them further. Plus, it gave the impulsive hearts a chance to have second thoughts. She didn't want anyone regretting their decision. But she had a good feeling about every match she'd made today.

"I'm going to go get a snow cone," Stella announced. "You want one?"

Talia started to say no, but then abruptly changed her mind. It had felt wonderful to get away from the house. It was a gorgeous day and she'd made a bunch of people and her animals very happy. And she'd spent eight merciful hours not thinking about what lay ahead for her. She should celebrate with some blueberry-flavored ice. She deserved it. Feeling lighter of heart and mind than she had for what seemed like forever, she linked her arm through Stella's. "Okay, but I'm buying."

"Buying what?"

Talia steeled herself against anything spoiling her mood. Including the wet blanket, otherwise known as Devin Archer. He'd been hovering all day. She'd tried to tune him out, but he was a hard guy to ignore. "Shaved ice. You want some?"

"You pay for ice? It's such a commodity, then?"

Talia darted a look at Stella, but the girl was too busy fluttering at Archer's accent to pay any attention to what he was saying.

"It's flavored ice," Talia clarified.

Stella nodded. "You've never had any? Don't they make them in Australia?"

Archer shook his head as if he still didn't get the appeal, but gestured with his hand. "Lead on."

"I thought you might stay here and watch the dogs," Talia said. "We'll be just across the way." She looked around. "Speaking of dogs, where is yours?"

"Here and about."

Talia sighed. "I told you, you can't just let him run loose in the park." With Stella standing there, she was limited as to what she could say. "We have laws."

"He's fine."

"Archer—"

"He's sacked out in the back of Stella's pickup, okay?" He winked at Stella, who all but swooned. "You can keep an eye on the dogs from there. They're in their pens."

Since he was unlikely to let her win this one, and Stella was moony-eyed, Talia didn't bother to argue. The event was close to over, most people were leaving, so there was no line and they ordered their cones right away. Stella took her lime-green one and went off to check out what was left of the fair. Talia ordered a blueberry one, then ended up ordering one for Archer when he would have refused. The vendor handed him the bloodred cherry ice and Archer took it gingerly.

Talia hid a private smile as they wandered toward the trees and strolled along the edges of the fair. He surreptitiously waited for her to bite into hers before tackling his own. "You really never had anything like this?" she asked.

He shook his head and analyzed his mound of ice as if looking for the best place to make a strategic attack.

She laughed. "Go ahead and bite it, Archer, it won't bite back."

He made a face at her.

She bit into hers, enjoying herself far more than she'd expected to. It tasted too sweet and the ice was so cold it hurt her teeth. Perfect. She took a few more bites, savoring each one, only to stop in mid-swallow when she caught Archer staring at her. She managed to choke down the rest. "What?"

"Nothing."

She turned her head and licked her lips, hoping she didn't have a blue ring around them. She looked back to find him still watching her. "You going to eat yours?"

He looked dubiously at the ice that was starting to drip over the side of the paper cup. She couldn't say what made her do it, but she stepped closer, covered his hand with hers and guided the cone to his mouth. "Just take a little off the top. It's easier once you make an edge."

His eyes widened, then darkened as he leaned over the cone and sank those perfectly white teeth deep into the lush red ice. All the while his gaze remained locked on hers. She didn't know who swallowed harder. Then he licked his lips and, when she went to pull her hand away, covered it with his other one, and took yet another bite, then another. All the while looking at her.

"You're right," he said, his accent dusky and rough. "It's quite good." He dropped his hand, then took the one of hers that held the cone. "Now you."

"That's o—" The word ended as blueberry ice covered her tongue and lips. Then she simply let herself sink into the sensation of looking into his hot eyes while feeling something so cold and sweet slide down her throat.

Talia was searching for something to say when Archer's expression suddenly went stone cold. "Shit!"

"What?" She swung around in time to see a man launch himself at her, his long black hair flying behind him, a deadly look in his eyes. Then Archer shoved her roughly to the ground, sending both their paper cups flying.

"Stay down!" he ordered as he propelled himself over her and tackled the man back into trees. They both hit the ground with a sickening thud, tumbling into the underbrush. Before Talia could react, Ringer raced in and she instinctively lunged and grabbed the little mutt, keeping him from entering the fray and getting himself hurt.

She looked wildly about, trying to hold the squirming dog in her arms, scanning the area for possible help, but everyone was packing up or leaving the park on the opposite side of the field. Archer swore, and she scrambled to her feet and started off into the woods after him. The attacker had managed to break free and was racing through the trees, deeper into the woods, Archer hot on his heels. Should she follow or stay back? What if the man were to circle around and come back for her? Ringer snarled in her arms, as if he'd read her thoughts. She held him more tightly and he stopped fighting to get down, his agitation seemingly more protective than defensive.

Then Archer came busting back out of the undergrowth, panting hard, his face scratched and dirty, his shirt torn in several places. "You okay?" He looked hard into her eyes, the intensity palpably leaping off him.

"Yeah. I'm fine."

She was still clutching Ringer, so he took her elbow in a firm grip and moved them both quickly back toward the trucks and animal pens. "Come on," he said, hauling her with him so she had to stumble to keep up. "We're packing up and leaving now."

She couldn't have agreed more, but a delayed reaction to what had almost happened to her, combined with the very visceral results of what he'd done to prevent it had her yanking them both to a halt. "Wait just a damn minute! What the hell happened back there? Who was that guy?"

Archer swung around on her, eyes blazing. "His name is Anteri. And I assume he wanted to stop you from coming back with me."

Talia tugged her arm from his grasp and let the wiggling dog leap into his master's arms. Archer grunted, but he stratched the dog's ears consolingly, which managed to calm both Ringer and Talia down. "He wanted to go after you," she said. "I didn't think that was a good idea."

"Thanks," Archer said, his breath slowing, but not his irritation. "Let's move."

Talia matched his stride, looking back at the woods as a shudder crept up her spine. "Where did he go? Is he still out there?"

"No. He went back home."

Home. Talia swallowed. To the future. Jesus. This was becoming way too real for her. She almost laughed. It was that or sob. It was already far too real for her, thank you very much. Now she had cold-blooded killers leaping out of the woods at her. And Archer had willingly, without hesitation, thrown himself at the guy. He wasn't armed, at least not like the other guy probably had been. She could tell herself that it was all about the money, that he'd only been protecting his paycheck . . . but the look in his eyes when he'd come back told her otherwise. He'd been angry and autocratic, nothing new there. But in that split second before he'd grabbed her elbow, when he'd demanded to know if she was okay . . . There was something there and she was quite certain he hadn't been thinking about the queen or his paycheck.

"Thank you," she said quietly. Something in her tone caught at him, and he stopped and looked back at her. She didn't know what else to say. She reached a hand up toward him, then let it drop away, not sure he wanted to be touched at the moment. "You didn't even blink."

She thought he might give her an arrogant smile, say something cocky. Maybe if he had, she'd have been able to brush the whole thing off, forget that she'd almost been attacked. But he didn't smile or say anything. He simply looked at her. Into her.

"You saved my life."

He managed a nod, then took her elbow, more gently this time. She looked over at him, wondering if she had actually embarrassed him. "Hasn't anyone ever thanked you before?"

He didn't slow down, only glanced at her. "Generally, there isn't much cause for thanks in my line of work." When he looked away, she knew the subject was closed.

But that didn't mean she'd stop thinking about it. Or what he'd done for her.

"I should have taken you more seriously," she said. "If anything had happened to Stella or the pups—"

"Yes, you should have and Anteri wasn't after Stella and the pups. But it is time to get the hell out of here. In case you haven't realized it, the stakes just went up. This guy wasn't sent here to baby-sit you, Talia."

She already knew that. Had known it the instant she looked into the killer's eyes. Still, a part of her wanted to cling to the fantasy that all this was happening to someone else. A childhood dream gone horribly awry that she'd awaken from at any moment. "But you said they just wanted to observe—"

"That was when they thought only they knew about you. And trust me, sweetheart, if they'd known we were on our way, Dideon would have likely kept you from ever being found."

She came to a dead stop. "Okay, that's it. I can't do this anymore."

He gaped at her. "Well, it's a bit late for that, sweetheart."

"I don't want to play these games of intrigue anymore. I don't want to have you hovering about all dark-eyed and mercenary or chasing after bad guys." She shivered. "It's not worth learning about my mother, my past, or even about myself. Maybe I already know too much. So, I've made my decision." She looked squarely at him. "I'm not going back with you. I'm sorry. I just can't do it. I can't heal anything anyway, so it's just as well we end this charade right now."

His expression flattened. "It's not that simple anymore."

"Maybe not for you, but I'm taking myself out of the game."

"You don't understand. It's too late for you to make that decision. There are others who will simply do it for you."

"Can't you just—" She flung one hand in the air in exasperation. And not a little fear. "I don't know, announce to the players on the field that I'm out of the game? I won't be going back to heal the queen, so I'm no longer a threat. Period, done, game over."

"It doesn't work that way. You were a player the day your mother conceived you. The only way I can protect you now is to take you to court, to the queen. They aren't going to stop. Class time is officially over."

Her trembling increased. "But if I make it clear I'm not going back, can't I just stay here? If I can't help Catriona, what threat am I to anyone?"

He shook his head. "I can't keep you safe in this time any longer. If Chamberlain sent Anteri, he's made it clear what he intends and he won't stop until he succeeds. Whatever Baleweg has taught you will have to be enough. We have to go back."

"Back." She laughed, only it sounded like a faint little chirp. "As in . . . forward. Really far. Forward." Her knees began to buckle.

Archer caught her before she hit the ground. "Come on, Talia," he said close to her ear. "I know you don't want a scene." But it was too late for that.

Heads turned as Stella rushed over. "What happened? Oh, my God, look at you! Were you in a fight or something? Talia! Is she okay?"

He tried a reassuring smile. "I think all that sugar went to her head. I was just helping some bloke with his, uh, truck," he improvised, "and the next thing I know her eyes are all glassy. She needs to eat more regularly." He turned his lips to her ear and whispered, "Come on, sweetheart. Open your eyes for me. Show Stella you're okay." Her eyelids fluttered once, then twice, and suddenly those fairy eyes were looking deeply into his. Stella and the rest of the concerned onlookers ceased to exist.

"Sorry," she murmured.

He smiled. "No worries. I have you now."

Her eyes clouded. "What's going to happen to me, Devin?"

He swore his heart stopped for several complete beats. If he'd thought hearing his given name on Baleweg's lips had been disconcerting, hearing it from hers was close to life-altering. "You'll be okay. But we have to get you out of here. You've created a bit of a looking on."

Stella stepped in. "Are you okay, Talia?"

Talia shifted to get out of his embrace, but Archer was suddenly unwilling to let her go. He tightened his hold almost instinctively, but when she cut her eyes sideways at Stella, he was forced to release her. He kept his hand on the small of her back. To steady her, in case her legs were still watery, he told himself.

Another crock of bull. The more he got his hands on her, the more he couldn't keep his hands off her.

"I'm fine, Stella," Talia said, her voice slightly wobbly. "Just a bit too much fair and not enough food, I think. I should be more careful." She looked at Archer then and deliberately moved away from his touch. "Why don't we load up the dogs and go back to the house?" She moved away, Stella at her side.

It stung him more than it should have, to be dismissed so easily. Her constant need to assert her independence from him was beginning to irritate him. No matter what she thought she'd decided, her entire world was about to go through some rapid changes and she'd need him to survive. And dammit, he wanted her to need him.

Christ, when had that happened?

Probably the moment he'd looked beyond Talia's blue-stained lips and found Anteri emerging from the woods. He'd thought his heart had stopped beating in that instant before he leaped into action. How could she capture all his attention, and to such a degree that his instincts—which he'd forged over a lifetime, enabling him to continue having a lifetime—simply shut down?

He looked over at Talia and Stella as they loaded the animals up. Ringer trotted over to him and butted his head against his leg. He knelt and scratched the beast behind the ears. "Thanks for staying with her, mate. I know she thought she was protecting you, but we know otherwise, right?" Ringer relished the attention, his soulful eyes as fathomless and unreadable as ever.

Archer stood and looked at Talia again. He had to stay sharp if he was going to keep them from going down the gurgler. He couldn't do that if he was mooning over her every other moment. Not that he mooned. He never mooned. Lust, that's what it was. And normally he was a man who lusted, slaked his lust, and moved on.

He watched as the wind caught her hair and danced it about her head. He wasted another moment wondering what it would be like to slake the lust he had building for her. He also wondered what it would be like to move on, to never see or touch her again. But he knew that would happen as soon as he delivered her to Catriona. So he'd better get used to it. And get over it.

He turned abruptly away and scanned the crowd

and the fringes of the woods that ringed the area. He was fairly certain Anteri had acted alone. But some-one—Emrys?—was keeping tabs on him, because no sooner had Archer been almost on top of him than he'd made it through one of those damn triangles and disappeared. Back to Llanfair and Chamberlain most likely, filing his report right now.

This latest threat to Talia would, he hoped, be enough to convince Baleweg that it was time for them all to go back. Back to the queen, who was waiting with his fortune.

And right then he was finally forced to admit that at some point he'd stopped thinking of this as a job. The mountain of money waiting for him when he delivered her was no longer his motivating factor. He hadn't even thought about it when he was chasing down Anteri. Which made no sense. It had been the only thing on his mind when he'd gone after Dideon. How had things changed so rapidly?

He shook his head clear. He had his goals and he'd be damned if he'd let her sidetrack him from accomplishing them. Alone and in control. That's how he got by. Responsible to no one's happiness but his own. Trusting no one to make him happy but himself. And dammit, that was how it would stay.

He stalked back over to Talia. It was obvious from her lighthearted banter with Stella that she'd managed to dismiss the entire situation. Well, he'd correct that as soon as Stella was no longer about. Then he'd have a talk with Baleweg. And then they'd go.

She turned and looked at him just then, and he saw that she hadn't dismissed anything. It was an act for Stella's sake. He had to know where to look, to see the fear, the dread. At times he wondered why no one but him saw past her strength to the vulnerability that lay beneath. Perhaps it was because no one could understand her in this time. He certainly wasn't special. Anyone from his time would see what he saw when looking into those fairy eyes of hers.

The thought was vaguely depressing.

But he could no longer let her suffering bother him. They all had jobs to do. She simply had to come to terms with hers. He told himself it wasn't his fault, that he hadn't done this to her. Chamberlain had. Catriona had. Her own mother had. Not him. Why it was imperative that he wasn't the one making her suffer, he didn't know. Just that, while he didn't want to be responsible for her happiness, he wouldn't stand for being responsible for her pain.

He swore beneath his breath and closed the remaining distance between them. "Almost ready?" His tone was more abrupt than he intended.

Her gaze shuttered, closing him out. She turned to her work. "We just have to secure the crates and fold the table and chairs up and we're all set."

And just like that, his resolve of only moments ago shattered. He couldn't stand it when she shut him out. He took hold of her arm. "Don't turn away from me."

"Excuse me?" She tried to pull her arm free, glancing over to where Stella was gathering the last few pieces of equipment.

Archer was past caring if Stella heard him. "I won't let anything happen to you, Talia. Not if I can help it."

Her mouth dropped open, but she said nothing. It had surprised the hell out of him, so it was no wonder it had shocked her, as well. But he didn't take his eyes from hers.

"We have to get the animals home," was all she said, and broke contact with him.

He felt her slipping away from him and it wasn't

merely physical. He found himself wishing he had her gift, wishing he could connect with her, in any way. Anything that would help him find a way to help her through this ordeal.

He, Devin Archer, the man who hated being responsible.

Well, one way or the other, they were heading back to the future. Together. And they'd stay together, at least until he was certain she'd be okay. After all, Devin Archer was also the man who never left a job half-done. It was good business.

He stalked around the truck, wishing like hell he could believe the emotions currently churning inside him had anything remotely to do with business.

Chapter 11

*T*alia was never so glad of anything in her life as she was to escape the close confines of her truck and distance herself from Archer. The drive home had been awful. Even Stella had eventually fallen quiet when the occupants of the front seat remained wrapped in their own thoughts.

"I'll start unloading," Stella said, apparently also relieved to make her escape.

"Just unstrap them," she said. "I'll help you unload."

Stella nodded, but before Talia could follow her, Archer stepped between them. Talia swallowed a sigh. And a healthy dose of trepidation. She was still shaky and her head was pounding. She did not feel up to dealing with one more thing today. Not even if it was a matter of life or death. Anyone's, even hers. "Please, I have a great deal to do tonight." She kept her gaze on some point past his shoulder. Of course he wouldn't accept that. She jerked her chin away from his touch, but kept her gaze on his, hoping it would be over faster this way. "What?"

"We have to talk. There is a lot to prepare you for."

"Isn't that what I've been doing every minute since you got here?"

"Not that. There are other things. I have to brief

you on what to expect in my time and who the players are. It will be a crash course on Dalwyn's court, but it must be done if you are to help yourself stay afloat. I probably should have done this sooner."

She felt the tremors run through her. It was finally happening. *It's all a fairy tale like the ones Mummy told you. Blink hard once or twice and you'll find yourself waking up in your hammock, all this a nasty dream.* If she were anywhere else, she might have convinced herself that was true. But when she looked at Archer . . . she knew. She knew she'd always known. Somewhere. Somehow. And she still wasn't ready.

"The dogs won't wait. So you're going to have to." She went to push past him, but he stopped her with his hand on her arm. There was such solid strength, such conviction in his touch, she didn't know whether to shrink from it . . . or lean into it. Things were going to change, she'd known it, felt it. Archer was the one constant. The one thing she knew she could count on. The one person she could trust.

That thought alone should have sent her screaming into the house, behind any number of locked doors.

Instead she looked into his eyes. Eyes that held hers with reliably steady strength. Eyes that looked at her and saw her for who she really was . . . and didn't turn away. Eyes that often looked at her with frustration and irritation, as well as desire. How had she come to trust him? Maybe it was because there was so much at stake for him, too, she knew he'd never risk failure. But that wasn't it. What she really thought was foolish. And dangerous. What she really thought was that he'd keep her safe because somewhere in that mercenary heart of his, he cared for her. She'd seen it in that moment he'd come out of the woods.

She blinked at a sudden moisture in her eyes, wishing she could laugh instead. Because it really was a ridiculous notion. "I know we have to deal with this. Please just let me handle the dogs and get Stella done and out of here. Surely we can wait that long."

He finally bent somewhat and nodded curtly. "By full dark, no later. And you don't leave my sight."

She wanted to argue, if for no other reason than it would give her a vent for all the screaming tension and fear building inside her. But time was moving on and she wasn't. So she nodded and went to work.

True to his word, for the next two and a half hours Archer never let her out of his sight, to the point where she swore his gaze alone felt like physical contact. But then it had always been that way around him. She'd thought the presence of the animals and Stella would act like a shield of sorts, but of course they hadn't.

In all honesty, as much as she dreaded what was to come later tonight, right now she was thankful for all his hovering. She might have been able to ignore the threat Jimmy had been to her . . . but there was no denying or forgetting the look in Anteri's eyes as he'd lunged for her. The idea that Anteri had been stalking her at the fair while she'd been blithely finding homes for her animals . . . She didn't want to think about what could have happened if Archer hadn't acted so quickly.

"They're all tucked in for the night," Stella announced, coming around the corner. "I checked the water and put the horses in."

Talia nodded. She finished administering medication to one of the strays she was still working with, then handed a tube of ointment to Stella. "Put this on the little spot where we had to pull the hair off that pom mix, okay?"

Stella's eyes lit up. "Sure." Then a furrow creased her brow and Talia knew she was working up her courage.

Not up to dealing with this tonight, she cut her off before she could speak. "I know how you feel about the little guy, Stella. But we'll talk about it later. Okay?"

Stella's face threatened to split from the force of her grin. An instant later Talia was enveloped in a hug. "You won't be sorry, Talia, I promise."

"Awful sure of yourself, aren't you?" she said, but there was no censure in it.

Stella beamed. "I'm meant for him, Tal. And he for me. You know how sometimes you just know it?"

Talia's smile faltered as Archer came into view at the far end of the kennel. Ringer came to sit beside his feet. A man and his dog. If only it were that simple.

"Yeah, I know," she said quietly. "Go on home and get some good rest. Tomorrow's going to be busy." This last she said with her eye on Archer. Somehow she had to convince him to let her stay another couple days. She had to see these guys safely away from here. Stella and her two part-time employees could deal with the horses and hold down the fort for the rest. She refused to think about the strays that could be turned away in her absence.

God, she thought. Was she really going to go? It wasn't as if she were going on a brief weekend jaunt to the shore, either. She couldn't truly wrap her mind around it. She smiled at Stella who nuzzled the sleepy little pom before shutting him back in his run for the night. "Good night, Stella."

She smiled, her eyes dreamy. "Night, Talia. And thank you so much. You won't be sorry."

"Tomorrow," Talia said. "We'll talk tomorrow."

And then she was alone with Archer and wondering why she'd been in such a hurry to see her young employee go. She walked to the kennel door that Stella had just floated through and scratched Ringer's scruffy head while Archer made sure it was locked and secure for the night.

"Now what?" she asked, knowing she sounded a bit snakey, as he would say.

"We talk. Care for a walk?"

"Do you really think that's wise?"

Archer stared at her for a long moment, as if debating an entirely different meaning than she'd intended. A shiver stole over her skin that had nothing to do with the sun setting. She was thinking about the last time they'd been down by the pond . . . and knew he was, too.

But then his expression changed, turned harder, and she knew he was in bodyguard mode again. Not that she wanted to reprise their little scene on that flat rock. Well, she *wanted* to, but she knew it would be better if they stayed in bodyguard mode from here on out. Dammit.

"Baleweg told me that moving through time isn't a precise thing. He can get the time right, but location is approximate. It's obvious Emrys is more skilled in that area. He moved Anteri in and out today and had the location pretty damn precise."

"Did you tell him? What did he say?"

"I haven't talked to him yet. I've been watching you."

"So, what do we do next? Where is Baleweg?" She'd been surprised that he hadn't appeared since they'd returned. "Don't you think we should all be together when you give your briefing, or whatever you call it?"

"Baleweg knows nothing about the court."

"On the contrary."

Both Talia and Archer turned to find Baleweg

standing just on the other side of the fence. Talia smiled. Something about Baleweg had always made her feel safe. Not in the way that Archer did. More in the way that, well, she supposed the way a child felt around a parent. That because they were older and acted wiser, somehow everything would always be okay if they were around. Another foolish notion. She, better than anyone, knew that having a parent guaranteed nothing.

"Why do you wish to discuss the House of Dalwyn, young Archer?"

"She must be told how it works, if she's to find her way through."

"You'll be there with me, won't you?" Talia asked Baleweg.

"I've taught you how to focus your mind in order to expand your connective feelings. There is not much more I can do." He paused, looking slightly troubled.

"What is it?"

"I had hoped your other inherited abilities would have surfaced by now."

Not for the first time, Talia wondered if Baleweg shared her doubts about her ability to be a healer. "I don't feel I know anything yet. And what I do know I'm not controlling very well."

"It will take practice," Baleweg said. "But I think you control things better than you assume. You've had years of experience in controlling your gifts so others don't surmise your hidden talents. In fact, I'd say you will fare far better when you learn to loosen your formidable control. Perhaps that will provide a path to awakening those other talents you were born to possess."

Talia glanced surreptitiously at Archer. The one time she'd loosened her control was the time she had connected with him. She hadn't attempted that again. "I'm still not sure I can help the queen." She looked to Baleweg and gave voice to the one thing they hadn't discussed. "What happens if I can't help her?"

Baleweg stepped closer and put his hand on her arm. She realized then that he rarely actually touched her. She wondered just what powers this man truly held.

"I'm afraid there is not much of a choice for you now, Talia. At least in terms of your safety."

"You knew about Anteri, didn't you?" The accusation came from Archer.

Baleweg held Archer's gaze steadily. "I sensed our time was dwindling. I believe you knew that, as well."

Archer stared. "Why didn't you warn me?"

Baleweg held up his hand. "Talia needed to place her animals. You were there with her and you felt the disturbance, as well, did you not?" He waited until Archer grudgingly nodded. "Your instincts are good ones, Devin."

Talia stepped forward. "There isn't anyone else to teach me? To pick up where we've left off?"

"Your mother was the only one," Baleweg said, turning back to her. "I only wish she'd had the time to work with you. But she made me promise to sever all contact with her. It was the only way she felt she could keep you safe."

"So she never intended to bring me back?"

"From what you tell me of the stories she told you as a child, I feel she did plan that very thing. Perhaps she wanted you to grow up first, in a place where she could teach you in relative safety, then bring you back as a grown woman, able to handle yourself."

"But how would she have brought me back if she had no contact with you?"

Baleweg smiled then. "Your mother was not without skills of her own. I have every faith she would have found a way to contact me had she been ready."

"She must have known someone was looking for her. We moved around a lot. Did she know about Emrys?"

Baleweg looked troubled then. "Yes, she did. But I thought she was being overly cautious. I honestly didn't think he'd have any interest in her, or you." He blinked several times, as if his eyes had grown glassy, then sighed. "I had no idea she lived with such fear and for that I am terribly sorry. I felt a disturbance when she died, but honored my promise to not interfere in your life. Perhaps I should have. Maybe this whole thing could have been avoided. But I stayed wrapped up in my studies." He looked to his hands, then to some point far beyond the two of them that only he could see. "Too wrapped up, it appears."

"Then why interfere now?" Talia asked gently.

His gaze sharpened as he brought it back to them. For the first time she saw anger edging those brilliant blue eyes of his. "Because Emrys does have an interest in you now, though why I cannot say. It can't only have to do with Chamberlain's wish to take on the power of the throne. He enjoys toying with the lives of others. If he's aiding Chamberlain, it is only because it serves some childish wish of his to entertain himself. And, as usual, his entertainment comes at a cost to others. I imagine my involvement with your mother is part of that amusement. He is using Chamberlain's desires to jab at me, draw me out."

"Then why didn't you step in sooner?" Archer asked. "You could have just come back and taken her to the queen yourself."

Baleweg turned on him, eyes snapping. "My

stepping into the game then, for the sole function of attempting to protect her, would have only served to heighten his amusement and shift the focus more sharply on her. As it was, the queen resolved the issue for me by taking up the search for Eleri herself. It had only been a matter of days by then that I had come to be aware that the plot with Dideon was afoot. As usual, I was fairly immersed in my studies, not in the latest political schemes. Then you were chosen. The royal hunter. And the path became clear to me. I knew you would be the one. And so you are."

Both Archer and Talia fell silent. Talia felt it the moment Archer shifted his gaze to her and wanted nothing more than to look into those eyes, take from his strength. But she needed to be strong herself. It was difficult enough to admit she trusted him, that she knew he'd risk his life to keep hers safe . . . but to simply give everything over to him . . . no, she couldn't do that. She had to know she could take care of herself.

Archer spoke then. "Tell us more about Emrys. We need to know who and what we're dealing with. He is more powerful than you are, isn't he?"

Baleweg looked to them both, remaining silent for so long neither thought he would speak, then finally, he said, "He is known as the Dark One. I assure you he deserves that moniker. His skills are, in some ways, more advanced than mine, but he has far less discipline." His expression turned baleful. "He's learned quickly, in far less time and with less effort. It is all a game to him and he bores easily. I'm certain this drama at court is a highly amusing little play to him, like a chess game, with Chamberlain as a rather entertaining pawn."

"So he's moving people about time at Chamberlain's whim for no reason but that it amuses him?" Archer snorted. "I find that hard to believe."

Baleweg looked to him. "It is difficult for someone like yourself, a man with long-held goals who is willing to work hard to achieve them, to understand the motivations of someone for whom obtaining things, material things, comes easily. When that is the case, goals shift. Security is not an issue and defeating boredom becomes the only challenge. When you have powers as strongly defined as Emrys's, your choice of entertainment can take on dire, even deadly, consequences. Especially for those with whom he chooses to play. Which, I imagine, is what draws him to the game in the first place. That and poking and prodding at me whenever the chance arises. This game with Chamberlain allows him to do both. He'd like nothing more than to draw me into this. He's never understood or accepted my chosen path of continued study. And I assure you he cares nothing about who gets hurt in the process."

Talia's throat tightened as the true consequences of her role in this sunk in. If she couldn't help the queen, far more was at stake than political chaos. "So if I fail . . . and the queen dies—"

Baleweg looked sharply at her. "You will have done what you can do. Fate will out. But you must see this through. I had hoped for more time, for us to make more tangible progress, but we must head back as soon as possible. If you remain here, you will be hunted. Anywhere you go, in this time or any other, you will be hunted, until the matter of the crown is dealt with. We must try to do what we can for Catriona. I believe this is what you mother would have wanted."

"What about Emrys?" Archer asked. "When the queen's fate is resolved, what will he do then?"

"That I cannot answer. But I will do what I must

when the time comes. Our first concern must be the queen's health. As to that, Talia should not be at court without someone whose interests are the same as my own. Make no mistake," he said, his voice quavering with emotion now, "I am not doing this for queen and kingdom. I am doing this because of a promise I made to a young woman who made a place for herself in my heart. I have honored Eleri's wishes, but now I must do what I can to protect her daughter, all that is left of her. The one to protect her must place her interests first, beyond those of the queen and court, beyond even his own." He turned and looked deeply into Archer's eyes. Even Talia shivered at the intensity. "I trust that you are the one who will fulfill this role."

Talia's first thought was that she didn't want anyone else's life placed in jeopardy, but she was stilled into silence by the look in his eyes. *I won't let anything happen to you, Talia. Not if I can help it.* The words he'd blurted out to her in the park earlier echoed through her.

He spoke to Baleweg, but his gaze continued to rest squarely on hers and she knew he was thinking about them, too. "You have nothing to fear on that quarter," he said, then turned and faced Baleweg. "I say we move swiftly. Tonight if possible."

Baleweg shook his head. "Despite the problems and threats facing us, patience in this matter is key. It is not so easy as dashing off." He stepped closer to her. "Talia, I think it best if you do what is necessary to square things away with your animals and their potential owners. Then explain to your employees that you will be making a short trip."

"Short?" Her voice was a croak.

"Whatever happens after your arrival will likely

happen quickly. Then it will be up to you to do what you wish from that point forward."

"Can't I return back here before I ever left?"

"No, it doesn't work that way. What time you spend in the future will also be spent here. I can only move you forward within the span of your natural life, never back."

She nodded as if she understood, when in fact she was totally overwhelmed. "When do we leave?"

"Soon." Baleweg shifted his attention back to Archer. "Until I am ready, I trust you will keep her safe, Devin. Stay close to her at all times." Then he looked down to Ringer, sitting obediently at his feet, and slapped at his robes. "Come, young soldier. Let us find something to eat."

Talia looked at Archer, but he was frowning at the retreating pair. "What next?" Her voice was rough, her throat still tight and achy from what had transpired between them. What *had* transpired between them?

She turned to find herself under Archer's steady regard. "I need to know something," he said quietly.

Surprised by his intensity, she said, "What?"

"What happened that day?" he asked abruptly. "The first day I almost kissed you, you jumped back as though something had bitten you. Can to tell me what happened?"

He'd taken her completely off guard. She'd supposed she'd known this was going to come out sooner or later. She'd been half-afraid Baleweg would tell him, but he'd honored her request not to. For what good it did her now. She rubbed at her arms, wanting to step back, put more space between them, but she could not. Did not. "Why?"

"I've wondered about it. A lot. I need to know."

Talia would have liked to evade this whole issue

any way she could. But she kept seeing the way he'd looked at her when he said he'd protect her. She owed him this, at the very least. "Well. Um. You know my empathic skills are limited to animals, right?" He didn't nod, he simply continued to stare at her. She cleared her throat. "Yes, well, Baleweg was teaching me how to try and connect with any mind, any feelings." She looked away for a moment, suddenly feeling wretched for what she'd done, even if it hadn't been intentional. It had been an invasion she'd had no right to make. "He was convinced my talent lay beyond the more simplistic animal mind. That maybe connecting with, you know . . . another person . . . would help me unlock my other supposed gifts."

"So you tried your skills on me?"

Now she did step back, but he caught at her arm. His touch was all the more alarming for its gentleness. "I—I didn't mean to. You were looking so intently at me, and it just happened. One second I was in my own skin, feeling my own . . . feelings, then like a thunderbolt I—" She faltered badly, but knew she had to finish, to confess. "I felt you. Felt . . . everything. Everything you felt. Even some things I didn't understand. I was so shocked I pulled back almost the moment I made the connection." She had no idea what he was thinking now. "I'm sorry."

"Then you ran."

"I didn't run, not exactly. I just thought—"

"Did it scare you, Talia? What I was feeling? Whatever other things inside me you connected with?"

Her mind was racing in a hundred directions. "I've never done it again. I swear."

"You didn't answer me. Did it scare you?"

"It surprised me. I didn't think . . . really didn't

imagine . . ." She looked down, gathered her courage, then looked back at him, almost defiantly. "Okay, it did scare me. A little. Okay, not a little. A lot."

"Because you could do it?"

She shook her head. "Oddly, that was more a relief. As if I had always known it. I felt, I don't know. Proud, I guess."

"So what scared you?"

She held his gaze. "That I was making you feel the same things you were making me feel. That there was something else inside you I connected with. I don't know, I can't explain it even to myself."

The light leapt into a flame. "Were you so surprised that a man might feel passion for you?"

"No. I've experienced passion before, Archer. I was just surprised I could make *you* feel that way. The deeper connection I felt . . . well, it went both ways."

He started to say something, then stopped.

"What? Now I've surprised you?" She smiled dryly. "Well, that's good, then. I shouldn't be the only one having her world turned upside down."

He muttered something that she couldn't quite catch.

"Shouldn't we be talking about the queen and her court?"

"You do surprise me, Talia," he said finally. "One moment shy, the next bold. I never know what to expect with you. Perhaps that's why I find myself unable to stop thinking about you." He stepped closer and her breath caught in her chest at the look in his eyes. "And that scares me," he said quietly. He moved closer still, until she had to tip her head back in order to maintain eye contact. "And if you were smart, it would scare you, too."

He lowered his mouth to hers, pausing just long

enough to whisper in her ear. "No fair peeking inside my head. If you want to know what I'm feeling,
just ask me. I'll show you."

"Right now I've got all I can handle feeling my
own feelings, thanks," she said faintly.

He laughed against her mouth. "Good. Then feel
this."

Chapter 12

*A*rcher only meant to indulge in his need to taste her before everything changed. He quickly realized he could not control his feelings, just as he realized he didn't give a damn. Not this one last time. He shut out Baleweg's dire warnings and predictions and did what he wanted, took what he wanted.

Gave her what *she* wanted.

He would stop, in just one more second. But right at that moment, she was making that soft moaning noise deep in her throat and he swore he felt every vibration of it throughout his entire body. He pulled her closer, groaning in satisfaction when she dug her long fingers into his hair. His hips found hers and his knees actually buckled slightly when she moved against him.

He gripped her tightly and made sure she understood exactly what she was moving toward.

"Archer—"

"Devin," he corrected. For whatever reason, he had a need to set this moment apart from every moment he'd ever shared with anyone else.

"Devin."

Damn, but just hearing her say it pushed him right to the edge. "I want more."

"So do I, but—"

He pulled her hard against him. "Sweet Christ, Talia, you have me inside out."

"I want you, too." She looked up at him. "What do we do with this, Devin? There is so much ahead of us, we can't . . . really shouldn't—"

"Must," he said, then his mouth was on hers again and she gave herself to him so sweetly, so gloriously, he was already planning where to take her when suddenly she managed to yank herself free.

"I can't think clearly like this." She looked at him, her hair dancing about her head in the night breeze like a wild fairy halo.

He felt empty with her gone from his arms. Surely if they'd take each other this aching need would dissipate, or at the very least become manageable enough that he could think straight again. "Then let's get this out of our systems. Perhaps we'll both be able to think more clearly then."

She looked away and he actually felt his heart catch a bit. There couldn't be more in this for her than he'd assumed, could there? *No more than there is in this for you,* his inner voice mocked him.

She looked back to him. "Baleweg is inside. I don't know where else we can go." She said it calmly, evenly, as if it were merely a physical matter, reducing their needs to animal lust, something a good rutting would take care of.

And suddenly he despised himself for making her admit she was willing to take that if it was all he had to offer. But hadn't that been exactly what attracted him to her? That she wanted the same thing, nothing more? So why did he suddenly want to create a bower for her, something filled with rose petals and feather down or some romantic shit like that? Jesus, this was getting way too complicated.

And yet he looked at her standing there, wanting him badly enough to take what little he offered, and his need for her almost drove him to his knees. He was willing to give her whatever it took to satisfy her. To make her smile up at him. To see the satisfied look in her eyes and know he'd been the one to put it there.

Goddamn, but his head hurt.

"We can't do this," he muttered.

"What?" She looked at him as if he'd lost his mind. And maybe he had. Because he was actually thinking about doing what he should have done ten minutes ago. Walk away, leave her be. Not . . . complicating everything. Despite the fact that they both wanted to complicate things so badly that the air all but pulsed with it.

She stepped close to him and he wasn't sure whether to laugh at the fierce determination in her eyes, or rip his hair out because he'd already decided that they couldn't do this. For both their sakes.

"What do you mean we can't do this?"

"We just shouldn't," he said, hating himself. "As you said, this will only complicate things. It's not because I don't want you. God knows I'm so hard with wanting you I can barely stand upright."

Her eyes widened and her throat worked and he almost caved in. Having a conscience was a pain in the ass. Probably why he'd never worked too hard on developing one. And hadn't he picked a fine time to start?

"If you think I'm going to go attaching all sorts of emotional obligations to this, you're wrong," she said.

Wasn't that what he wanted to hear? So why did it piss him off? "I think we need to focus on what lies ahead for you and not our raging hormones."

"Didn't you tell me that if we finished what we'd started, we could concentrate better? 'Get this out of our systems,' was how you put it."

He winced. Hearing the words tossed back at him only reinforced his decision. "Which is exactly why we can't do this."

She rubbed her temples. "Okay, I'm confused. I agree with you. No worries. So what's the big deal?"

Now she was really pissing him off. Because she was lying. She wanted more, just as he did.

Whoa, slow down there, mate.

"Fine then. Just damn fine," he said abruptly. Hell, he'd tried, hadn't he? He was no saint and had been a fool to pretend to be one. "If that's all it's to be, then why not, right?" His tone was a tad sharper than he meant it to be, but what the hell, right? "Why I was so worried about your delicate sensibilities when you seem to have none, I have no idea." She backed away, but her eyes were riveted to his and, dammit, it wasn't for fear of him he saw, it was anticipation of what he might do to her.

Damn her to hell. She'd well and truly done it.

She backed up against the fence and he came up against her. "I'm not so good at doing right by anyone but myself, Talia," he said, his own breathing labored now as his thundering heartbeat threatened to drown him out.

"So why are you starting now? Especially when I didn't ask for the favor?"

He blew out a deep breath, torn between shaking her and yanking her tightly against him. He ended up taking her into his arms, surprising even himself with his sudden gentleness. What was it about her anyway? The tougher she talked, the gentler he felt he needed to be with her. He pulled her close, tucking her against his chest and rested his chin on top of her head. "Damn if I know," he said, exhausted. "Damn if I know."

He felt her hand creep up to his cheek and the tenderness of the touch undid him.

"Come here, Devin."

He shifted and looked down into those wise gray eyes of hers. "I don't want to hurt you." The words just came out, before he even knew he'd thought them. And he realized he'd never meant anything more.

"I'm used to taking care of my own feelings," she said. "Don't worry about me."

And that was the crux of it right there. The realization hit him like a gazzer set on full blast. He did worry about her. He even liked being the one responsible for her.

Heaven help them both.

But then she was pulling his mouth to hers and he finally, blessedly, let the whole thing go. He did something he'd wanted to do all his life, only he hadn't known it until that very moment. He put his faith and trust in her hands. Trust that she knew what she was doing and that, somehow, they'd make this all okay afterward. Together. An amazingly freeing idea.

"Just enjoy this, Devin." She smiled up at him and it was so sweet and pure he swore he felt tears burning in his eyes. "I know I am," she added.

"Yeah," he said, was all he could say. "Show me what you're feeling."

And she did.

In fact, it was she who tore the shirt from the waistband of his pants. She who first ran her hands over bare skin. He'd thought he'd died and gone to heaven when her fingertips skated across his chest. She smoothed her hands along his sides, then stopped when her fingers brushed the leather hilt at the small of his back.

He swore at the distraction, wishing he'd had the foresight to disarm himself first. "A knife," he said. "I found it in the fishing shed and . . . borrowed it."

"I don't mind. It must be hard to be on protection duty with nothing to protect with."

He smiled. "Oh, you'd be amazed at what can be used as a weapon."

"I can only imagine." She raised a finger to his lips. "And I'd just as soon leave it at the imagination level, if you don't mind." She ran her hands along his sides, then looked him in the eyes as she boldly let them run over his backside and around his thighs. "Any other . . . armaments I should know about?"

He was torn between amazement and amusement. The sheer joy of her had him swinging her up into his arms. She spluttered and that just made it all the more enjoyable. "It's time to find that bower."

"What are you talking about?"

But he merely held her tighter when she struggled, humming a tune as he looked for the right place. There was no perfect place—something he swore he'd correct next time—but he wasn't about to take her up against a fence.

"I can walk, you know."

"So can I. Now hush, I'm thinking."

She rolled her eyes. "Yes, we all know how taxing that is for you."

That was another odd thing. The more biting and sarcastic she became, the more he wanted her. Then the answer came to him. It wasn't perfect, but it was right. "Do you have blankets somewhere around here?"

"What for?"

"Just answer the question."

She smiled sweetly at him. "Put me down and I will."

"Can't you just let me be in charge of anything for more than five minutes?"

"I'm not good at delegating," she said. Then she winked at him when he reluctantly set her on her feet. "But I promise to let you be in charge later."

He actually choked. "Yeah, I'll believe that when I see it." He tugged her against him and surprised her with another lingering kiss.

"What was that for?"

"You're more easily managed when you're breathless," he said.

She shot him an arch look, but couldn't maintain it. "You're probably right," she said, grinning unabashedly. "Wanna test that theory again?"

"As soon as you find those blankets."

"You drive a hard bargain."

"You don't know the half of it," he said under his breath.

She pulled free and turned toward her truck. He caught her hand. "Wait up."

"I'm just going to grab some blankets from my truck. I tossed some in the back seat in case I needed them at the fair, but I never used them."

"You're not going anywhere without me."

She stopped and looked at him, uncertainty in her eyes. "Do you really think there will be trouble tonight?"

He cursed himself. "Only if you don't hurry," he said with a grin, hoping to distract her. When it didn't work, he moved in close to her. "We'll be fine tonight, Tali. I won't leave your side."

"Good." Her eyes were shining in anticipation. She seemed to trust him to make it all okay. It would have terrified him if it hadn't made him feel so damn good.

All this trust was bound to lead to trouble. But the air was still warm, the sky was full of stars, and Talia was his for the night.

He flipped the blankets over his arm, took her hand in his, and headed for the path circling the pond. He felt her stiffen slightly and paused. "Is it okay?"

"Yes," she said softly. "It's very okay."

And he discovered then that the rewards for pleasing her were even better than he'd imagined. He vowed to find a way to do it again. As often as he could manage.

Talia's body was humming in anticipation, but her heart hitched when he took her hand in his. There was a different kind of intimacy in that palm-to-palm contact, a kind of implied trust. They were both in this together, equally, neither one leading the other. Her fingers tightened instinctively and he squeezed her hand in response.

Something inside her settled, then. She looked up to find him watching her. His smile was so natural and heartfelt, it warmed her heart, even as it seemed to warm his. They rounded the bend in the path and the large flat rock loomed ahead, bathed so perfectly in the moonlight it was as if the celestial gods had bestowed a gift on them.

She laughed at that. God, her mind was reeling.

"What's so funny?" He let go of her hand so she could help him spread the blanket. She missed the contact immediately and wondered if he'd hold her hand while making love to her.

"Nothing. Just silly notions." Very silly. This was about having sex, not getting all mushy. Best she remembered that, despite how the moonlight twinkled in his dark eyes, and how his voice slid over her skin like a warm night breeze, making her want . . . too much.

He pulled her up onto the rock and into his arms. "What sort of silly notions?"

She looked up into his eyes, eyes that were shining down into hers with surprising gentleness and fierce need. It was an electrifying combination and yet somehow reassuring. She felt fierce and gentle herself. And he'd laugh himself right off the rock if she started spouting stuff like that.

"Just that the moon seems so cooperative tonight, spotlighting our rock this way."

"Our rock." He leaned down and kissed her. Not satisfied with claiming only her mouth, he moved to her chin and along her jaw and down her neck until her knees simply refused to stay locked.

Our rock. She liked the way he'd said it, with a touch of wonder, but no mocking amusement. She suddenly didn't feel quite so silly after all.

He took her weight against him and sank down until he was sitting with her sprawled across his lap. He wrapped his arms around her and pulled her tightly into the cradle of his hips and they both groaned at the delicious contact.

She immediately reached for his open shirt, his waistband, anything that would get them out of the tangle of clothes and closer to fulfilling the need that was almost painful now.

His hands stopped hers. When she looked confused, he buried his face in her hair, then pulled back, dimple flashing in the moonlight. "I had a rather silly notion myself, I guess. Trying to be a romantic rather than the rutting stag you think me to be."

"I don't need romance, Devin." Which was such a lie. But she'd promised no emotional attachments and, no matter what she might feel afterward, it was a promise she had to keep.

He opened his mouth to respond, then apparently decided better of it.

"What? Tell me."

He stared at her for the longest time, his expression far too serious. "Don't you know what I'm feeling?"

She leaned farther back, offended. "I told you I'd never invade your privacy and I keep my word."

He pulled her back to him. "I didn't mean that way. Never mind. Come here." He smiled, but it didn't reach his eyes this time. "If it's not romance you want, then I guess you get the rutting stag."

"Wait a minute. What were you going to—" But she never got to complete the question because, true to his word, he took her. Fully, with no apologies. And none were necessary.

He unbuckled her overalls and they slid halfway down her legs, but she wasn't concerned with that tangle because finally, blessedly, his hands were beneath her tank top and covering her. Her nipples peaked so hard it was almost painful. Whatever she might have said came out as one long growl of pleasure. And then his mouth was on her breasts, suckling, nibbling, softly biting until she was a writhing mass of desire, bucking and arching beneath him and not caring how desperate she seemed.

He peeled the shirt over her head and pushed the rest down her legs until she kicked free from all of it and lay beneath him with nothing on but a scant pair of underwear. And even that felt like a dense, cumbersome barrier. She went to wriggle out of them, as well, but he was pulling his own shirt off at that moment and she found herself completely captivated by the look of Devin Archer's naked chest in the moonlight. *Dear God, but you're beautiful.*

It wasn't until he paused and looked down at her with that cocky grin of his that she realized she'd whispered the thought out loud.

She reached for him, but he stayed her hand, leaning down and pinning it over her head. He captured the other one just as easily and held them both in one hand. It was the oddest feeling, the sense of being a captive to him, and yet she was filled with the power of what she saw in his eyes as he looked at her, all of her. The naked want and desire made her feel like the captor, as well. It was delicious and wicked and she was anxious to explore it.

"You're the beautiful one, Talia." He leaned in close, keeping her hands above her head. "The way the moon dips down and touches you here." He kissed the very tip of one nipple. "And here." He kissed the other, then pulled it into his mouth. "You taste moon-kissed," he said and her heart sighed. Because he was giving her the romance anyway, whether he realized it or not.

He trailed lazy kisses down toward her navel. But his reach wouldn't extend farther as long as he held her hands. So she slid them free, silently begging him to continue.

And he did.

He dragged the tip of his tongue down the narrow line below her navel. Talia's breath caught and held as he hovered there. "Dear God" she managed, very close to pleading.

He looked up at her, desire so dark in his eyes she almost came right then. "I've just begun, sweetheart." He grinned and her hips lifted of their own volition. He skimmed her panties down her legs with one hand, bent his head to her, and with smooth fingers and a warm, wet tongue, proceeded to prove his point. He ripped her immediately over one edge, then dragged her almost screaming up the next. She came so hard the second time, she thought her body was breaking apart into little pieces of pure, saturated pleasure. And by the time he had her close to her third, he was climbing up her body, grinning like the conqueror he'd just proven himself to be.

Her legs moved up over his hips with no coercion from him. He slid out of his trousers so easily it was as if they melted off him, and probably had from the heat that leaped between them. He moved his hips so smoothly into hers it was as if they'd been created to fit there.

Cradling her cheek with one hand, he lowered his head as he began to press inside her. "Next time, we'll shoot for romance," he said, then pushed into her so hard she had to grab hold of his wide shoulders to keep from being shoved right off the blanket.

Her legs wrapped tightly to his hips as he sank deeply into her. It was a startling invasion, but her body welcomed it gleefully. Talia felt as if she'd stepped outside herself as her own body took to his, and took his, as if it had always known this was what it craved, what it needed. What it was born for.

Then she was back inside herself and feeling her own body's sensations. Oh God, was she feeling. He was a raging force inside her and she alone could master its fury. It was daunting and powerful, terrifyingly glorious and everything she'd ever wanted.

When he arched back and shouted through his release, pouring himself into her as if he meant to empty his very soul, she knew she'd never be able to give herself to anyone else, not like this. It made no sense, and it was no romanticized vision of their lovemaking. It hadn't been love, but a raw and powerful need that had been slaked. She knew that, understood it to her core. But that didn't negate the absolute knowledge that she'd found her mate. In the most primal sense of the word.

Archer slid from her and rolled to his back. They

both lay there, staring up at the sky as the night air cooled their bodies.

"Are you okay?" he finally asked.

She smiled up at the stars, still dazed and not a little shell-shocked. "I'm very okay."

"I was rough."

"You were perfect."

She didn't look at him, but she swore she felt him smile. Then his hand reached for hers and tears rose in her eyes, blurring the stars above. With his fingers tightly woven between hers she felt more intimately connected to him than ever before.

She had no idea how much time had passed, she might have even dozed off, when he tugged her to her side and pulled her into the shelter of his body. "Come here," he murmured.

She willingly let him wrap his heat around her. He tugged another blanket up and over them and she gladly burrowed into it, realizing for the first time how cool the night air had gotten.

The steady beat of his heart beneath her cheek had just begun to lull her to sleep when she felt his hand slide up her side and down along her back. All the sensations that had dimmed into a dull, pleasant buzz, hummed to life again.

"Time for that romance I promised you," he whispered.

She was going to correct him and save herself from the threat to her heart he'd inflict if he was gentle with her now, when she remembered the look on his face when he'd asked her before if she knew what he was feeling. And then it hit her. *He* was the one who needed the romance.

It was as shocking a realization as any she'd experienced since he'd walked into her life. Mr. Mercenary, a romantic? The idea made her smile as she looked up into his eyes and did what she knew was right, despite the risk to her heart. "I respect a man who keeps his promises."

And he was slow and wonderful, amazingly gentle, and perfect. And she realized she'd underestimated just how threatened her heart was. But she'd deal with that later. Much, much later.

Chapter 13

Archer brushed at the annoying gnats, then realized it was whiskers tickling his cheek as he
cracked one eye open.

Ringer.

It only took a heartbeat longer to realize that
Ringer was presently a cat, but it was a heartbeat too
long.

Talia opened her eyes and smiled in surprise.
"Where did you come from?"

Archer swore silently. This was not how he'd
planned this. But then he'd never planned this.

The cat butted his head against Talia's and rum-
bled as she scratched behind his ears. The sun was
just beginning to rise and the air was cool outside
the little cocoon they'd made inside their blankets.
Her hair was a mass of tangled curls and her face was
lined with pressure wrinkles from the blanket. Her
nose was pink from the cold, but her eyes were
sparkling and luminous. She smiled at him, then
laughed as the cat tried to wedge himself between
them. Lord, she was so beautiful it made his insides
hurt.

"Pushy sort," she said.

"Out of here, mate," he said. Archer scooped
Ringer up and deposited him outside their cocoon,
then pulled Talia back to his side.

"Wait, I should make sure he's okay. I've never seen him around here before." Archer held her against her wishes and she frowned up at him. "What?"

"He's fine."

"But—" She looked past him and stared at the cat, suddenly frowning. "That's odd."

"What?"

She looked back at him. "I didn't make any connection with him. Usually, unless I'm concentrating, the feelings sort of ambush me. And yet, he's not really signaling . . . anything." She pushed up on her elbow and stared at the cat again. "But there is this other feeling, like I know him."

"We can worry about the cat later," Archer said, tugging her back down against his chest, silently cursing Ringer to eternal hell.

She was still distracted, but at least she was distracted while nuzzling his chest. Distraction was a good thing. In fact, he intended to do a good deal more distracting, but just as he dipped his head to follow through on the thought, hers came up, delivering a good crack to his chin.

"Ow!"

She rubbed her head, then immediately rubbed at his chin. "I'm sorry. I just realized what bugged me."

Archer frowned and rubbed his chin. There would be no peace, or anything else, until she got it out. "What?"

"There's only one other animal I can never connect with. Ringer. But I figured it was because he was from the future or something." She shifted once again to the cat, who was sitting less than a foot away, studiously ignoring them both as he meticulously washed first one front paw, then the other. She looked back to Archer. "Nothing. Even when I try.

You know, I think my empathic skills are going haywire or something. That day Ringer was hurt, the signals were way stronger than his actual discomfort should have telegraphed. Almost as if he were intentionally trying to get my attention, now that I think about it." She looked at him and must have seen the guilt on his face, and her eyes narrowed in suspicion.

As he opened his mouth to confess, Ringer changed back to the scruffy mutt before Talia's wide, astonished gray eyes.

To her credit, she didn't scream or faint. A squeaking sort of sound came out, and she looked between the two of them wildly, then turned a rather unbecoming shade of gray before turning away altogether.

"Thanks, mate," he snarled at Ringer, who merely sat and wagged his tail as if to say, "No worries." Little shit.

"Talia—" He reached for her, but she stopped him by stiffening her shoulders. "It's cold, at least let me cover your shoulders up."

She said nothing, so he pulled the blanket over her and waited. He was really bad at waiting. "Say something," he prodded, at a loss as to how to handle her and hating feeling so helpless.

She turned her head slowly to his, her eyes unfocused, and, he noticed, purposely *not* looking at Ringer. "I—" Then she simply shook her head and tucked her chin.

Despite her resistance, he dragged her into his arms and held her against him. It was like hugging a marble statue, but he didn't care. She was trembling. It was hardly noticeable, but it made his chest hurt. And it was something he could do, hold her, give her his warmth, until she decided what she was ready to know.

"I should have told you," he said quietly, when, after what seemed like a lifetime, she still hadn't spoken. "But I didn't want to scare you off."

She laughed then, a semihysterical little wheeze. "Oh, well, thanks. Much appreciated. You come and tell me I'm some sort of royal healer and, by the way, I have to travel a couple hundred years into the future to save a queen I've never even heard of, but let's not scare Talia with the idea of some sort of . . . of . . ." She shuddered, unable to finish.

"He won't hurt you."

She looked up at him then. "I wasn't really in fear of my mortal life, thanks."

Archer grinned. He couldn't help it. She scowled. "I'm not having it on with you, really, but I can't help the smile. You make me do that a lot, Talia."

"Well, you're very welcome. Glad I could help."

Now it was all he could do not to laugh outright. She was scared within an inch of her life, but rather than cling and squeal, she was being sarcastic and pouty.

He tucked her rigid frame a bit closer, angling himself so Ringer was somewhat out of her direct line of vision if she were to look up at him. And he found he wanted that badly. He slowly stroked his fingertips up and down her back, then through her hair. Over and over again, until she slowly began to unwind. No, he wasn't a patient man, but somehow killing time this way, for the sake of her comfort, didn't seem to tax him too greatly.

When she finally relaxed, he shifted upward so she could pull herself more tightly into his chest. Perhaps it would go easier if she could listen without her reactions being viewed. "Want me to tell you about him?"

There was a long silence, then finally a tentative little nod against his chest. His smile was wide and his heart beat a bit steadier now that she'd given him another piece of trust. A valuable gift, and one he'd guard carefully.

"I was coming back from completing a difficult transaction. I'd been off-Earth for almost a month and all I wanted to do was get home, take a long hot steamer, and eat some food that didn't come from questionable sources."

Her breath caught and he paused, waiting to see if she had any questions. But he felt her breath skim out across his skin and she relaxed slightly back against him. So he continued.

"I had docked and was signing off on the space entry/exit forms when I heard a rustling behind the refuse transformers."

Talia's head came up. "The what?"

He bit back the smile. "Refuse transformers?"

"What exactly do you transform your refuse into?"

She didn't ask about off-Earth travel, but she wanted to know about recycling. He grinned. "I guess it's best described as a sort of liquid gas."

"And what do you do with that?"

"Reuse it in other ways."

"All of it?" She shook her head, then smiled a little. "I guess it's reassuring to know you all figured out some way to solve that problem."

He just stared at her until she looked up at him. "What?"

He shook his head. "I can't figure you out."

Her smile grew. "Well, some things haven't changed, then. Men have been trying to figure out women for eons. And vice versa. I guess you haven't solved all the world's mysteries, then."

"Not hardly."

She quieted then, her expression turning serious once more. "Tell me more," she said quietly.

"About Ringer?"

She shivered, just a little. "Are they—what do you call them anyway?"

"Shifters."

She managed a nod. "Are these . . . shifters . . . common?"

"Somewhat. They're the vagabond type, hitching rides around and about. A number of them have ended up here on Earth."

She was trembling, but pushed on. "So he followed you home?"

Archer laughed. "No, I found him in the transformer, hardly more than skin and ribs he was, but ready to fight me to the death over a moldy chicken bone." He sobered a bit as he recalled the rest of that night. "He tried to shift, into something large and threatening, but he got stuck between animals." He shuddered, as did Talia. "It wasn't pretty. I couldn't leave the little bloke like that. So I took him home, figuring he'd finish up after he'd warmed up a bit, and had some food."

"Does he have a basic shape? I've only seen him as a dog."

"Well, you've probably seen him as a few other things without knowing. But no, he's whatever he wants to be. There's no natural form as far as I know, but they each have their own preferences."

"And he's been with you ever since that night?"

Archer glanced at Ringer. "Yeah. We're mates, him and me. He can be a pain in the ass, but all in all, he's done all right by himself. And by me."

Ringer chose that moment to turn round and round on the corner of the blanket and plop himself down. Talia trembled and Archer looked concerned.

"It's okay. I just keep seeing him do that . . . thing . . . he did." She made a face. "Maybe we should stick with talking about trash and other developmental strides of humankind. Emphasis on the word *human*."

He smiled at that and decided that kissing her would be the most reasonable thing to do.

She was breathing a bit unevenly when he lifted his head. "Well."

"Yeah. Very well," he said. "Now, where were we?"

"I was sort of liking where we just were."

"You don't want to know any more? Have you asked Baleweg anything about our time?"

She shook her head. "I . . . I think I was afraid to ask anything more. I wasn't ready. He didn't push."

"And now?" He tilted her face to his. "Aren't you even a little curious where I come from, Talia?"

She stared at him for what seemed like forever, before asking, "Are you curious about *my* world?"

"I guess I've sort of figured out what I need to know to get by. After all, I'll only be here for a short time."

She nodded. "Exactly. I figure I'll go on a need-to-know basis, too."

Archer frowned. He didn't at all like that idea. *Why, for Christ's sake?* What made her situation any different from his? What did he want from her anyway? *Dangerous question, mate. You really want to answer that one?*

Ringer yawned and stretched, thankfully pulling Talia's attention away from . . . from wherever the hell they'd been going. She finally let herself look at the scruffy mutt and Archer remained silent while she came to terms with it.

Suddenly she grinned. "It just occurred to me that he must have scared the bejeebers out of the local animal population here, changing from one thing to the next." She turned to Archer, her soft heart in her eyes. "How did you name him?"

Her resilience never ceased to amaze him. It was

one of the things he loved— "Well," he said, clearing his throat, "he's able to change into any small mammal shape. A dead ringer. Which is exactly what he'd have been, too, if I hadn't forced him inside with me."

"Ah." Talia smiled. She continued to rub her arms and he tugged her close again.

"You keep getting away from me." He thought about what she was facing, wondering if he'd be as practical in dealing with it all as she'd been. Probably not. He rolled to his back and pulled her and the blanket across him. Ringer leaped up when his little blanket nest suddenly disappeared and grumbled as he jumped off the rock. Considering the problems he'd caused this morning, Archer didn't feel the least bit bad about it.

"What are you doing?" Talia grabbed at his shoulders for balance.

"Changing the subject."

"To what?"

"Sun's coming up and I thought how beautiful you'd look coming with the sky all streaked with bright colors behind you."

Her cheeks turned pink and he was pretty certain it had nothing to do with the cool morning air. "Pretty sure of yourself."

He grabbed her hips as if to lift her off him. "Well, if you don't think I can—"

She grabbed hold of his wrists and clamped her knees on his sides. "Did I say that?"

He looked into her eyes and grinned, but somehow his heart wasn't as light as his tone. "Have I ever not delivered on a promise made to you?"

She tilted her head, as if to ponder the question. He bumped his hips up and she gasped, then quickly shook her head. "I suppose not."

He pulled her down onto him and pushed deep.

His fingers tangled in her hair as she fell across his chest, their hips already locked in perfect rhythm. If he couldn't watch her when she climaxed, he'd feel it. And feeling her wrapped around him like this was surely more glorious than any sunrise God had ever created.

As he felt her come apart over him, he found himself making another vow. He'd make sure she remained safe, in his time and hers, and get her back here when it was all over so she could go on with her life.

Surely that was all he wanted. All he could want.

"I promise you," he whispered against the slick skin of her neck. Then he let go, shutting out the fact that he had just given far more to her than his body.

Chapter 14

Talia smiled as the first car pulled around the drive toward the kennel. Stella winked at her and went in to get the puppy the family had come to see and hopefully take home with them.

Talia recalled the talk she'd had with her young employee earlier this morning, about the pom mix. Tugger, she corrected herself. Stella had already named it. And it was probably good timing, since Stella was too wound up with her new baby to notice anything different about Talia today.

And there was no denying Talia felt different. As though her entire being had been altered. *It was just sex*, she reminded herself. Spectacular, mind-numbing, universe-altering sex, she amended, feeling her body heat just at the thought. Still, she tried hard to make herself believe it hadn't changed anything. Not really.

She was such a lousy liar.

One night with Archer had changed everything. The entire glorious time she'd been with him, she'd felt, well . . . right. As if she belonged in his arms. She hadn't worried about being different, about not being normal. Finally she'd been with someone she felt really knew her, understood her, and had wanted her, desired her. The real her.

Yep. One night had changed everything. She

spied Baleweg looking down from the tower window and waved to him, even as her stomach dropped. And it had changed nothing. She still had to deal with the future. Literally. And she still had no chance of having what could be described as a normal relationship with Devin. Whatever the hell that might be.

She turned to greet the family. Two children tumbled out of the car, squealing and scrambling to be the first to hold the puppy. She watched as the parents dealt with their enthusiasm with a gentle, but firm hand. They had seemed to be a good match at the fair and now she was certain of it. But she would go through with the formalities anyway, as usual.

Eight hours and too many interviews later, she was tired but extremely satisfied. She'd placed all but one of the puppies and the two older dogs had in fact ended up being adopted by the same couple. She'd also heard from Mr. Green about the kittens. He'd be picking them up tomorrow. She went to her office and dropped into her chair even as she scooped up the phone. She was hoping to push the remaining two interviews up to tomorrow morning. Once the tabby and the last puppy were gone, she could start getting ready.

Ready. What exactly did a person pack for the kind of trip she was about to take? She realized then that she'd never asked what year Baleweg and Archer were from. She laughed, but it was hollow and the tiniest bit on the hysterical side. *Gee, you might want to ask, oh, one or two questions before you go hopping off to the future, don't you think, Tal?*

She hung up the phone without dialing and buried her head in her arms instead. Maybe if she pretended she was, oh, an astronaut or something, going off to discover things for the good of mankind, it would be easier to deal with her predicament. She snorted.

And what had she been thinking to sleep with Archer? My God, he could have any number of diseases from places she couldn't even imagine, or . . . or . . . a history of heaven knew what. But had she cared? Had she even asked? Oh, no. She'd just run right off to be with him. She smiled against her arm, unable to help it. And damn, but it had been good.

At least it was the wrong time of the month for her. Please, God. Talk about altering the normal order of things. But then, hadn't her mother bringing her here already altered the normal order of things? Technically, then, she and Archer were actually from the same time and place. So they weren't so star-crossed after all, or time-crossed. Or . . . whatever! It didn't make what she'd done a smart move.

She lifted her head and raked her fingers through her hair. Her forehead was beginning to throb. There was no point in belaboring what she had already done. Or thinking about how much she'd like to do it again. And again. She should pack some condoms, though. Just to be safe. *Jesus, Talia.* But she couldn't stop thinking about Archer, about how he'd felt inside her, about how his hand had felt in hers, the way he'd so gently taken her— "Stop," she ordered herself. *Just stop.*

"Stop what?"

She jumped about a foot, but Archer settled her back in her chair with his big hands on her shoulders, rubbing her exactly where she needed to be rubbed. It felt wonderful, marvelous. And was going to lead her exactly where she'd just told herself she should never go again.

Then she made the critical mistake of looking up

at him and damn if her heart didn't just leap, happy as could be. If that wasn't warning enough, he leaned down and kissed her nose. Her nose, dammit. Could he be more sweet?

She stood quickly and his hands slid off her shoulders. Which she immediately regretted, but did nothing to remedy. Finally, a smart move. Too damn bad if her body hated her for it. Working to build on her success, scant though it was, she folded her arms and attempted to sound businesslike. Really hard to do when all she could think about was how he'd sounded just this morning, groaning in her ear as he came inside her. Had that just been this morning? How could she be this starved for him if she'd just had him a few hours ago?

"Have you talked with Baleweg?" She sounded shrill, even to her own ears. "I was just about to call the other two appointments and try to get them to come as early tomorrow as possible. They were the only ones who couldn't come today. Stella can handle Mr. Green. He's been here before and knows the drill. Then there are some questions I want to ask Baleweg before we—"

Her rapid-fire monologue was abruptly cut off when Archer leaned his head down and kissed her. Not that she stopped him, or even tried to. She couldn't even be angry at herself. She'd do the lecture later. Right now she had to finally admit she was scared out of her mind and it just felt too damn good to be in his strong, reassuring arms. She'd be independent and in total control later.

When the kiss ended, she laid her head against his chest, comforted to hear that his heart was pounding as hard as hers. God, her brain was cramping from analyzing overload, so she mercifully let go and just felt. And what she felt was fear.

His.

She looked up, already silently apologizing even as she asked, "What's wrong?"

He looked down into her eyes and said nothing.

"I'm sorry. My guard was down and I just . . . I felt your worry. I couldn't help it. Has something happened?" Her stomach knotted into a tight little ball of dread. "Has someone else found us?" She immediately tried to get out of his embrace. "Stella!"

He held tight. "She's fine. No one else has found us but Baleweg just told me the disturbances he's been feeling are building faster now."

"I . . . I don't know if I'm ready."

He looked into her eyes and smoothed her hair from her face. "I'll be with you, Tali. Every step of the way."

"But Baleweg said he wasn't sure what the queen would do regarding security and—"

"And I don't give a flying hang what she wants to do. She is paying me to deliver you. So she owes me a great deal and if I choose to take payment in the form of continuing to watch over you, then that is what I'll do. And what she'll agree to if she wants you there."

Talia felt she should be arguing with him, but in truth, she was so relieved she could have wept. She had no idea what she was going to face, only that it had to be easier with someone she could trust by her side. She smiled at that. Here she was, in the arms of a man who sold his loyalty to the highest bidder, and yet she was willing to trust him to remain loyal to her for . . . what? Great sex?

As if he had read her mind, he said, "You have to realize that you can trust no one."

"Except you. A mercenary who is being paid by the queen." She hadn't meant it as an accusation; she just wanted his reassurance.

He nodded, not remotely offended. In fact, there appeared to be increased respect in those fathomless eyes of his. "I may sell my services, Tali, but I decide where my loyalties lie and it doesn't always have to do with money."

"Or great sex?"

A surprised grin broke out on his face as understanding dawned. "Ah. So that's what prompted this concern?"

"I figured I didn't have much hope of enslaving you with my feminine wiles, not when I'm up against a queen's ransom." She'd said it jokingly, but his expression was serious when he responded.

"I answer only to myself. I'll never be a slave to anything or anyone, ever again."

She opened her mouth to ask him what he meant, but he took full advantage and kissed her.

"But I find myself not so bothered by wanting to protect you," he murmured. "I need you to understand that, other than myself, you must trust no one at court."

"And Baleweg?"

"I doubt he'll go to court with us. He has no use for politicians and their machinations, although they would love to capitalize on his formidable skills. He can't help the queen, and if what he says about Emrys is true, his presence there might actually create more problems than it would fix."

"But won't it be better to have him with us, in case we need his skills, if there's an emergency?" She felt a chill steal over her skin as fear bubbled up again.

"Baleweg has kept himself alive and prosperous by keeping to himself and following his own instincts. We won't be able to change his mind." Archer smiled then and traced a finger down the side of her face. "Does it bother you so much to be stuck alone with me?"

"I'm not sure."

Archer tipped his head back and laughed. "Ah, a woman after my own heart." He looked at her, still smiling. "You'll do well at court, Tali. Never stop questioning everything and you'll do just fine."

"Does it bother you that Baleweg all but thrust the job on you? Your job is done when you return with me. I don't want you risking—"

Archer cut her off. "I made that choice. Not him." His eyes burned into hers. "Tell me you know you can trust me. Honestly."

She swallowed hard then, knowing without knowing how that she'd gotten more from him than most, perhaps more than anyone. "I trust you." She reached for his face. "And thank you."

He closed his eyes at her touch and she could feel the muscles twitching in his cheek. He was as tense as she'd ever seen him and she tried not to let that frighten her further. Who was this man and how had she come to care for him so deeply? And want him to care for her the same way?

He opened his eyes and took her hand in his. "We have to hurry. You'll have no idea what is going on and I can't explain it all to you in the short time we have left."

She stilled as the finality of the moment began to sink in. "How short?"

"Now. Baleweg is waiting at the house."

She fought panic and barely maintained a edge. "I can't go now. I have to rearrange those appointments and . . . get things together and—"

"And nothing. We don't have any more time, Talia. Stella will have to handle things here. The worst that could happen is that she postpones the appointments, until . . ." His voice trailed off.

"Until what?"

He traced a tender finger down the side of her face. "Until I deliver you back here."

Talia looked into his eyes and found herself trying not to connect with his feelings. Would he be satisfied with bringing her back and going on his merry way? Or did he want . . . something else?

She shook free of those thoughts. Everything was confusing enough without bringing her disturbing feelings about Archer into it. If Archer wanted something more, he'd say so. He wasn't exactly a shy man.

What about her? If *she* wanted more? Would she say so?

Talia sighed. "Okay. I have to explain things to Stella. I'm certain enough about the two adoptions tomorrow—I'll let her handle them rather than make these people wait until . . . until I get back."

Devin took her hand then and it felt so natural, the sense of strength she got from it. A part of her thought it would be smarter if she could do this on her own, rely only on herself, as she'd always done. But he squeezed her hand just then and she knew she wouldn't turn away from what he had to offer. She pulled him toward the door, then had to jump back as it swung open and Stella came stumbling in.

"Hi, boss. Afternoon rounds are done." She smiled, then caught sight of Talia and Archer's joined hands. Her young brown eyes fairly danced as she looked back up at the two of them. "Cool."

Talia flushed, but her thoughts were on what she had to tell her. "Stella, listen. I—we—have to go out of town and I'll need you to take care of things here for a few days." She said it all in a rush, knowing from the speculative gleam in her employee's eyes what she was thinking this sudden trip was about. She was about to correct her, but a squeeze from

Archer stopped her. Letting Stella think what she thought was probably just as well.

"There are only two dogs getting medication at this point and I'm certain you can handle that. All the instructions are on the clipboard and you can follow what I've written in the past. Make sure you note the time and condition when you administer them. In case of emergency, contact Ken. The other two appointments for adoption are coming later tomorrow. I'm sure everything will be okay, and I trust you to handle the paperwork. You've done it with me often enough so it shouldn't be a problem."

Stella looked surprised, but willing and excited to take on the increased responsibilities. "Sure thing. I can handle it, you don't have to worry."

"Also, will you keep an eye on Marble for me? Not that he needs much monitoring, just keep some cat food and a water bowl on the porch, in case he deigns to eat here."

"No problem." For the first time, Stella looked concerned. "Will I be able to reach you? I mean, if I have a question or anything?"

"Um—"

Archer stepped in and with a smooth wink leaned down to Stella's ear and whispered, "I'm whisking her off for a bit. I'm not certain about the phone service. You understand. Certainly you and the others can get by, right?"

Stella nodded, totally mesmerized.

"You're a top sort, Stella." He squeezed her shoulder and Talia was surprised the girl didn't go into cardiac arrest right then.

"Thank you, Stella," Talia added. "I'm sorry to dump this on you. You can always call Karen and Sue in for extra hours if you need to. And you know Ken is just a call away. Don't worry about any overtime, I'll cover it." She smiled. "I know you're up to

the task and we're pretty low on guests at the moment anyway. Oh! If the county shelter calls or any
of the rescue leagues, well, use your judgment.
Don't take any extreme cases, or . . . or call Ken
and see if he can help. Damn." She looked up at
Archer. "How can I just go like this?" she asked quietly. "What if they need me?"

"You've trained your staff well."

"What about Mr. B?" Stella asked. "Is he staying?"

"Oh. Um. Well." Talia sputtered for a moment,
unsure how to explain why they'd be taking Baleweg
with them on a lover's holiday.

Archer came to the rescue again. "He'll be leaving
with us. We're dropping him off to visit some other
friends while we're gone."

"Oh. Cool." Stella beamed at them both. "Well,
have a great time." She impulsively leaned in and
hugged Talia. "Thank you for trusting me with this.
You won't be sorry. I'm glad you're taking some time
for yourself. You so deserve it, as hard as you work."
She glanced at Archer, then wiggled her perfectly
plucked brows at Talia. "Way to go, too. He's a total
hottie." Then she stepped back and smoothed her
T-shirt and shorts, striving to look professional and
mature. "Well. I guess I'll go check the charts and
make up my schedule for the next couple of days."

Talia smiled and sighed in relief as Stella all but
skipped off to the kennels. She was only eighteen,
but very responsible and not afraid to ask for help.
Talia would worry anyway, but Archer was right,
she'd trained her well. A certain pride filled her
then and she tried to ignore the little hitch that went
along with it. She was used to being needed, in fact,
she'd made certain she was needed here. It was what
her whole world revolved around. Or had.

"Baleweg is waiting," Archer said quietly.

"I know."

"She'll be fine."

Talia looked up at him. "I know that, too."

He opened his mouth to say something and she could see the understanding in his eyes. Instead he squeezed her hand, which said everything anyway. "Let's go."

The closer they got to the house, the harder she had to work not to throw up. The anxiety was too much. She worked to focus on one step, and then the next, and not think about what came after. Sort of like clacking up to the top of the first hill of a roller coaster. She'd just focus on surviving the climb . . . not the screaming descent that followed.

Archer lifted his head and gave a sharp whistle.

Talia leaped in surprise, then laughed at herself. God, she'd better get a grip. What kind of astronaut was she anyway?

"Just calling Ringer." A hawk circled above them, then dove straight down. Talia squealed and ducked but Archer just swore and stuck out his arm where the hawk landed with amazing smoothness. "Always the showboat."

Talia's eyes widened. "Ringer?" She looked quickly around to make sure no one from the kennels was watching.

Archer sighed in disgust. "Now maybe you see what I have to deal with."

If she hadn't been so shocked, she'd have laughed. She imagined there was little Archer tolerated in the way of having his chain jerked, so she rather enjoyed the idea that this little . . . thing . . . had so clearly wrapped him around his, well, claw. Maybe she would find time to get to know the beast better.

It occurred to her then that maybe she was simply another stray Archer had adopted. And while she was reassured by the idea that the man had a heart, she wasn't sure she liked the idea of being a rescue project.

Baleweg met them on the porch. "We must go," he said, his blue eyes projecting a calm and serenity she didn't remotely feel.

"I just need to pack a few things."

"The court will provide what you need," Baleweg assured her.

"But . . . I'd feel more comfortable in my own clothes. At least let me take my own toothbrush."

"Toothbrush?" Archer asked.

Talia just looked at him. "What do you call it?"

"I don't know. What is it?"

"A little brush on a stick you clean your teeth with."

"Oh."

She rolled her eyes. "Well, I'm sorry, but it's our only defense against tooth decay. How do you keep your teeth from rotting out of your head?"

"They're sealed," he said, as if she were dense. "You just rinse with—"

"Children," Baleweg called. "Really."

Talia sighed, knowing it was the stress making her snap at him, but unable to reel it in. "Well, I don't care what you all do in the future, I want my own toothbrush— You do have running water, right?"

Archer nodded and shot her an infuriating grin.

She refused to back down. "And I want a book. Or two. And my nightgown."

Both men simply stared at her. Finally, her shoulders slumped. "It's not like I'm asking to take my teddy bear. You got to bring Ringer with you."

Archer's expression softened then and he kissed her quickly on the forehead. "Get what you think you need, but make it quick. And nothing you can't carry on your back."

She stepped back and smoothed her hair,

pretending a level of nonchalance she really didn't feel. "Thank you."

She turned to find Baleweg staring at them both and had the grace to blush. She'd forgotten that he was unaware of how things had changed between her and Devin last night. Or, considering the light in his eyes, perhaps not. Had he checked up on her last night, only to find her bed—and Devin's hammock—empty?

Well, she refused to be embarrassed. She was a grown woman who could make her own choices. Her cheeks reddened anyway. Dammit.

Baleweg merely smiled at them both, then looked directly at Talia. "I believe you've already found all you will need."

Chapter 15

Archer smiled when Talia came back outside a few minutes later, a bulging backpack over her shoulder . . . and Beatrice's godawful fishing bonnet on her head. He said nothing because he understood why she'd taken it. They might have eradicated tooth decay in his time, but people still clung to their teddy bears. The hat was her teddy . . . of sorts.

She came down the steps, her expression all but daring him to comment. Instead he pulled something out of his back pocket and extended it toward her. "Here."

"What is it?"

"The picture of your mother. I thought you might like to carry it with you. I should have thought to give it to you earlier."

She unfolded the silky paper and looked at the image on it. Her eyes were glassy when she looked back at him. "With everything that's been going on . . . all the memories . . . I'd forgotten, too. Thank you."

He could only nod, feeling moisture gathering in his eyes, as well.

"Shall we?" Baleweg said gently. With a hand to Talia's shoulder he guided them to her truck.

Talia stopped. "Wait. We're . . . driving there?"

Baleweg smiled. "No. But it would look rather odd if we all departed and took no visible means of transport. And we cannot wait for a taxi to take us away from here."

"Right. Of course." Talia took a deep breath and Devin found himself taking her hand in his.

He liked how it felt, how she so willingly wove her fingers through his. She was terrified and yet she held her head up. Oddly, though he'd intended to support her, she was the one teaching him about strength. "We're going to drive into the city and park in a hotel lot," he explained. "It won't be questioned that way."

"Just really expensive. Do you have any idea what they charge for parking?" Talia laughed suddenly. "Listen to me. I have the fate of a future kingdom resting on my shoulders and I'm worried about valet parking."

Archer leaned down and kissed her temple. "My shoulders are pretty broad, too, you know." He was surprised at how eager he was to share her burden. Devin Archer, the guy who worked alone, lived alone, and liked it that way. Then she glanced up at him when he opened the door for her and—wham. It was just there. No explaining it.

Her lips twitched in that smile of hers he liked best, the slightly crooked, self-mocking one. "You might be carrying me on those shoulders soon, so be careful what you offer, big guy."

Archer leaned in and kissed her. Hard. He couldn't help it. Only Baleweg's noisy throat-clearing stopped it.

"Maybe I shouldn't drive," she said.

Archer smiled. "If you want us to get there in one piece, you will. Neither of us knows how to operate this kind of vehicle."

"Oh. Right. Of course. Okay." She turned away

and clutched the steering wheel. "I'll drive. I'll be just fine."

Archer closed the door and crossed around to the other side. She'd be okay, he told himself for the thousandth time. She damn well had to be.

Over the next hour, she drove while they did their best to explain the inner workings of court, at least as well as they knew them. Neither he nor Baleweg was a royal insider, both being more an outcast . . . each in their own, individual way. But while Archer might not know all the nuances of court procedures, he did know most of the players, having worked for many on private matters.

"Parliament has a separate building alongside the palace proper. All the politicos have their offices there, but they are in and out of the castle often. None of them reside within the castle however—only the queen and her royal staff and guard. And there are seemingly hundreds of them. I've only met with her once and you go through what seem like endless channels to get to her. Her security is good, but not perfect. I imagine she'll want to spend time alone with you, but otherwise I'll be with you as much as possible."

"Okay."

Talia had spent most of the hour nodding wordlessly. Archer was worried, unsure how much she was retaining. She seemed to be paying attention, but heaven only knew what her thoughts were.

He did know she was terrified and wished like hell he could have some time alone with her, to do something, anything, to lessen that fear. But he knew the best thing was to just get there and let her start dealing with it. She'd handle the transition better than she thought she would. It wasn't all that different in the future. Not in the most basic ways. His concerns centered more about her handling the surreal pressures of life in a royal court. She lived out in the countryside, holed up with a bunch of misfit animals and wonky old people, for God's sake. Then he smiled. Actually, the comparison was closer than he'd thought.

Talia wound her way deeper into the city and parked in the largest hotel lot she could find, tucking the ticket in the visor flap before steering them into a distant spot on the roof level of the lot, as Baleweg instructed, far away from the other cars.

She turned off the ignition and turned to face both of them. "I appreciate all you've told me, but there is one thing you still haven't covered."

Archer could see she was striving to sound cool and in control and most people probably would think she was. He knew her well enough to realize she was hanging on by a thread. He reached over to take her hand and found it cold and lifeless to the touch.

"You are worried about what you will be expected to do for the queen," Baleweg said calmly.

Talia nodded. "I realize I can't stay here, that I have to go and at least try. But what will happen to me if I can't . . . do anything?"

Archer wasn't sure how to answer her. If Catriona and the baby died and Chamberlain—and, via him, the Dark One, Emrys—took over . . . He stopped there. He'd been so arrogant, certain they would find a way, he'd never honestly asked himself what would happen if they failed. He looked to Baleweg. "Surely if her skills proved inadequate Chamberlain would see that and have no use for her. Emrys would surely move on to other amusements if Chamberlain took over the throne."

Talia slowly slid her hand from his. It was as if a piece of that unswerving trust she'd had in him had dimmed slightly. Dammit, he never failed. And he wouldn't fail in this. Not if it meant failing her.

Baleweg looked to Talia, then Archer. "Don't give up on her so quickly, young Archer. Fate will open paths we cannot see as yet."

"Meaning what?" Archer all but shouted. He was only slightly mollified when he felt Talia slide her hand back in his. He held on tightly, suddenly uncertain about his role in all this. "I'm not about to go thrusting her off into Dalwyn's court for them to do with as they please. I want some reassurances she'll be released safely if she can't help."

"Fate offers no such reassurances." He lifted a finger when Archer began to argue further. "I can assure you that not going back will certainly put her in more danger." He opened his door and climbed out. Ringer, a black cat now, hopped out beside him. "Come now, it is time."

"Wait just a damn minute!"

"Waiting time is over. I sense that things are deteriorating rapidly at home and we must go if you hope to have any edge over Chamberlain."

Archer swore under his breath and turned to Talia. "Come on." She looked a little hollow, so he instinctively shot her a grin and a wink. "Now I get to show you my town."

Talia swallowed hard, but a smile made a tentative appearance. "Can't wait."

He got out, but his smile faded as he came face-to-face with Baleweg. "If I say she comes back, she comes back. No questions. I want your promise that you'll bring her back here if either one of us gives the word."

Baleweg held his steady gaze with infuriating calm. "It will all go as it must, young Archer." He lifted a hand to stall Archer's outburst. "Now *you* must trust me."

Archer grated his teeth as he pushed past him and went to open Talia's door.

She was already standing beside the truck, crushing her ugly bonnet in her hands. She looked vulnerable and frail, although he knew her to be anything but. As her paid protector, he had to project confidence, to make this seem a harmless little adventure. But when he looked into her huge gray eyes, he realized it was a daunting task.

Then she smiled, as if reading his tension, and perhaps she had. It should bother him, that she understood him so easily. And it did, but in a not-so-unpleasant way. He'd never had anyone look at him as she did. Not ever. They were both misfits. Maybe that was all it was, one outcast bonding to another.

But he didn't think so.

Baleweg rounded the vehicle and came to stand beside them. He looked to Talia. "I will create a door. You must hold Archer's hand and step through at the same time."

Talia nodded, then looked to Archer. He squeezed her hand and held on tightly. With his free hand he slapped his thigh. "Come on, Ringer." The cat leaped into his arms. He looked at Baleweg. "Let's do it."

Baleweg nodded, then turned his back to them. Rather than watch the old man do his thing, Archer kept his eyes on Talia. If he hadn't been so worried about her, he'd have smiled when her eyes bugged at the sight of the triangle.

Her grip tightened painfully, but he didn't mind. When Baleweg motioned to them, she looked up at him and he dropped an impulsive hard kiss on her lips. "Hold tight to me, Tali."

"I will."

And just like that, they stepped into the future. Together.

Talia blinked, then swung around to look at the rapidly closing spot of wavering air. She fought the urge to yank free and dive back through it. But Archer squeezed her hand, diverting her attention. Then it was too late. The door, or window or whatever the hell it was, was gone.

She was still standing on top of a building, but this one wasn't a parking garage. It was heavily vegetated with tropical growth, lush and beautiful. The sky above was a blinding blue and the air amazingly fresh for what appeared to be a sprawling city. But she had no time to process the endless vista of shimmery buildings with cloud-high spires, the spaces between and around them dotted with air traffic that looked a little like airplanes and a lot like flying minivans with no wheels.

"Thank God," Archer said, drawing her attention to him. He let go of her hand and knelt to gather up an astonishing array of *Star Wars*–like weaponry. It all disappeared into unseen places and pockets sewn into his clothes. It should have frightened her, how much more relaxed he seemed now that he was loaded down with enough armament to defend a small country. He wore it well, almost casually. *He is a mercenary, Talia.* She hadn't forgotten, really. She'd just never had such a . . . visual reminder of what and who he really was. It should have put her off, or at least made her feel somewhat more alone, being faced with the fact that the one person she thought she knew well in this time was also still a stranger to her.

But if she had to know only one person in this strange new world, better the guy with all the ammo and a working knowledge of how to use it, right?

"Pretty good aim, mate," Archer said to Baleweg. "We didn't even have to catch a transport this time."

Baleweg stepped in then, looking a bit weary, his eyes not so vivid, his skin a bit pale. "Home is always easiest to find," he said, fatigue clear in his resonant voice. "I trust your vehicle is still secured down below. You will see Talia safely to the queen."

"You really won't be going with us?" Talia asked.

Baleweg shook his head. "My place is not in court, Talia. Too many vultures. There is little or nothing I can do for the queen in any case. And you and I have done all we can together."

"But what if we need you? Your . . . other skills?"

"I will know it, never fear that. But the less attention drawn to your already remarkable return, the better. Archer will be in the best position to protect you."

"But—"

He shushed her gently. "Talia, were I to attend you with the queen, it is likely Emrys will find the combination irresistible. It will only make what you have to do harder, and he would rather enjoy that, as well."

"Then you mean he'll be at court? Directly? But what if—?"

Baleweg silenced her with a brief touch. "I will be here," he said, brushing her head. "And here," he added, motioning to her heart. "And you will be with me always. Trust in Archer. More importantly, trust in yourself."

Before she could respond, he turned to Archer. "There is one offer I would like to make, however. Allow me to watch over your other companion while you escort Talia and watch over her."

Ringer, who was now a small brown rabbit, seemed to understand the offer and quickly changed into a cat again and wove his way around Baleweg's ankles.

Talia didn't miss the surprise and hurt on Archer's face, even though he quickly masked it.

"Yeah, sure," he said. "Last place I need him getting into trouble is at court."

Talia took Archer's hand and rubbed his arm. He looked so surprised at the gesture that she almost dropped her hands away, but he quickly covered her hand with his.

"He'll be okay here," Talia told him, knowing it was true because Ringer had decided to transmit his comfort to her. "But it doesn't mean he's leaving you."

Archer rolled his eyes as if that were not remotely what he'd been worried about, but Talia swallowed a smile, because she knew that was exactly what he'd feared. He was used to thinking himself fully independent. It would take some time to get used to the fact that maybe he'd changed a little during his stay with her.

As if making a huge concession, Ringer deigned to waltz over and rub against Archer's legs. He leaned down and scooped the cat up. "Listen, mate, don't give him a hard time. He could send you off to God knows where and I'm not about to chase you across the centuries." Ringer purred and butted his head against Archer's chin, earning a scratch between the ears and a grin.

Talia felt a momentary pang at the connection, the bond they shared. She'd never been able to do that, to reach out at such a personal level, to give her whole heart like that. She gave little pieces of it to all the animals she'd helped, to the people in her life, too. But never all of it to one. She envied Archer that he could, even though he'd probably deny it.

Ringer leaped down and wandered off to explore

the rooftop. Archer stared after him for a moment, then turned back to Baleweg. "Thank you for what you've done. For Ringer. For Talia. For me."

The old man shook his head. "I've done what I could. You will know where to find me when the time comes." He looked to them both. "If that is what you wish."

Baleweg took Talia's hand and she felt that odd energy again, only far, far stronger than before. Perhaps he'd also regained some of his "armament" now that he was back in his own time.

"You will feel things far more acutely now that you are home," he said, as if reading her mind. And perhaps he could. Indeed, now that she'd seen, with the triangle door, just how far-reaching his level of skill truly was, she wouldn't doubt it. "You have the skills to channel it effectively," he went on. "Respond only to what you must. Follow your heart. And welcome home."

Home. She didn't feel as if she were home. She didn't know what she felt. But she wanted to reassure Baleweg. He'd done so much for her, given her the knowledge of her mother that she'd longed for ever since she could remember. "I'll do my best." On impulse, she leaned in and hugged him. "Thank you for helping me, teaching me. And for being a friend to my mother. And me."

He gave her an awkward pat on the back before quickly breaking apart. Talia wasn't insulted, more curious. The hug seemed to have startled the old man. He looked at her differently, although she couldn't explain how. It was as if he knew something now that he'd not known before.

She found herself automatically reaching out in her mind for some connection to his feelings, only to pull back immediately, shocked by how naturally she'd attempted it. Never once in all the time with him had she even considered trying, and if she had, it would have certainly been a very deliberate thing. Not that it mattered. Baleweg's mind was completely his to control and she'd never get in no matter how skilled she was.

Archer extended a hand to Baleweg. "Thanks, mate. We'll be back."

Baleweg took Archer's hand, held it in both of his, then let go, looking more relaxed. "I will see you when the time is right."

Archer looked at his hand, then shook it a bit before nodding. "Right."

Talia hid a smile, glad to know she wasn't the only one who felt that tingly sensation when touched by Baleweg.

"We're off," Archer said, then stopped. "Wait a minute. What day is this?"

"As many days have passed here as have passed while we were gone. I cannot move back in the life you have lived."

Talia swallowed hard, suddenly wishing she could stay in Baleweg's rooftop paradise a bit longer. Say good-bye to Ringer or have a muffin and some tea or something. "Yeah. Okay." She lifted her hand in a little wave. "Bye."

Baleweg nodded, an almost secret smile on his face. Then Archer was pulling her with him. She gave one last fleeting glance, then followed Archer to the small door that led inside, pausing a moment when she passed an opening in the foliage. She could see the entire city that lay below. The city she'd been conceived in, that her mother had been born in. She trembled as she saw buildings made out of materials that shimmered with an almost ethereal glow in the sunlight. They were built in shapes and sizes that seemed to defy science and the laws of structure and balance. Nevertheless, there was an ancient feel to the city. Interspersed with the shimmery and futuristic were stone buildings that likely had been ancient during her real lifetime. It was oddly reassuring, to realize that some things lasted seemingly forever. She relaxed a bit, feeling as if she still had one foot in the past, while stepping into the future. She felt a stirring of excitement at the thought of exploring this new, strange land.

That was the ticket, she thought suddenly. She'd pretend she was on a trip abroad. A visit to her homeland. She was merely in a different country, seeing where her mother had been born, searching for her roots. So what if it happened to also be, oh, a hundred and fifty, two hundred years in the future?

She trembled. Yeah. Right. She looked down to the street a number of stories below. The people bustled along just as they did at home. Their clothing didn't look all that different to her; the people looked normal, too. No Klingons or Ewoks meandering about. *Boy, that was huge relief.* This was still Earth, her home, where she was on holiday in Wales. She could handle this.

She took a deep breath and wondered again at how fresh the air was despite the heavy traffic and the density of buildings and people. Maybe that was why she felt so dizzy. The air was too good. Either that or it was jet lag. Could you get jet lag traveling through time? And just how many time zones had she passed through anyway?

Archer tugged on her hand just then and she followed him, feeling more than a little dazed. One thing was certain. "We're not in Kansas anymore, Toto," she murmured.

"Oh, good," Archer said, "it's been fixed."

Before she could ask, they were inside what she thought was an elevator, but it shot them to the ground in a tube similar to the ones that zipped from the drive-in window to the bank teller and back. Only people-sized. She popped out on a loud city street, head still spinning.

"Hey, it's still here and in one piece."

"Great," she said, having no idea what he was talking about. She was goggling at just how tall the buildings looked from here on the ground.

"Hop in. No entry hatches on this model, sorry."

She looked back to him. He was standing by his car, or whatever you called it. Sleek and some sort of translucent green color, it was a sporty little . . . thing. And it just sat there. About two feet off the ground. She looked under it. Nothing but air.

She stood upright and told herself that after everything else she'd already dealt with, why not? She held on to the side of the . . . whatever, and it dipped and rocked, sort of like a boat. Or a waterbed.

Archer scooped her up and dropped her gently into the passenger seat. "It takes some getting used to. But you'll like it a hell of a lot better than those bone-rattling contraptions you pilot."

And then he was inside and the thing hummed to life, and before she could catch her breath, they were moving.

Really, really fast.

Shit. Shit, shit, shit.

She clung to the sides as the wind whipped her hair straight out behind her head. Her stomach hovered somewhere in the vicinity of her throat.

The city streets passed in a blur. And then they shot out the other side, away from the crowded streets and buildings into a startlingly green countryside.

And before her sprawled the most magnificent castle she'd ever seen. "Welcome to Emerald City,

Dorothy," she murmured beneath her breath. It wasn't Oz, but it was every bit the magical fairy tale that any little girl could have ever dreamed of.

Only she was fairly certain she wasn't dreaming.

And she wasn't a little girl anymore, although she had an increasingly strengthening desire to curl up into a little ball and cry for her mummy.

A mummy who had once lived in yonder glistening castle, she realized faintly.

And had fled it in fear for her life.

Just what in the hell had she gotten herself into?

Chapter 16

*A*rcher said a prayer of thanks beneath his breath. He'd tempted every Transport Agent in the monarchy with his warp-speed drive here, but he had no idea who might know of Talia's presence and felt it was best to get her under castle guard as quickly as possible.

As he sped toward the large gate in the outer wall that surrounded the castle he only hoped he wasn't delivering her to a worse fate. He chanced a quick glance in her direction, wishing the trip had allowed them to talk, but all his concentration had been on maneuvering them out of the city undetected. She looked pale and more than a little anxious. His fingers twitched on the controls as he debated swinging them around and heading straight back to Baleweg. But then the castle gate was opening and he knew there would be no turning back now.

He was guided by the royal guard toward what looked like a solid wall. An invisible seam opened in the middle as he closed in, sliding soundlessly shut behind them after his transport had passed through. They were in a dimly lit tunnel that extended into darkness ahead. He'd come this route before, but last time there hadn't been a solid wall of guards lining the edges of the platform. He was relieved to see Catriona was well prepared for his return with her precious cargo, but as a guard stepped quickly forward, he nonetheless kept the security field up around his vehicle.

"I wish a direct audience with the queen," he said. Not that he doubted they knew exactly why he was here, and with whom.

The guard nodded. "We will escort Ms. Trahaern inside."

"You will escort both of us inside."

The guard's impassive expression didn't alter one whit. "I am instructed only to bring her."

"Then call in and get different instructions. We both go in, or she stays here behind the shield." Archer knew, as well as the guard, that the shield would not hold up under their collective weaponry, but he also knew Catriona would not be happy if Talia's life were in any way jeopardized in what should be a routine, if highly secure, transfer.

The guard acted exactly as Archer predicted. He pulled the mouthpiece wire down from his earpiece and spoke into it. Archer turned to Talia. She hadn't moved. In fact, he wasn't sure she was breathing. "You okay?"

She looked at him and made a valiant effort at a dry smile. "Define *okay*."

He smiled. "That's the way."

"What's happening?"

He took her hand, wishing he'd been able to touch her the entire time, relieved to have contact again. "We're just getting clearance to go inside."

She gripped his hand hard enough to shut down all blood supply. He didn't mind. "Don't worry, Catriona won't want to argue about this, she'll want you in and under her direct supervision as soon as possible."

Talia seemed to relax a little, but she was still pale

and probably a bit unnerved at all the sudden changes.

"I'm sorry for all this, Tali," he said abruptly.

"What do you mean?"

"Bringing you here. Maybe I shouldn't have. Maybe there was another way."

"I tried to tell myself that, too." She looked at him, gripped his hand even more tightly. "But if you hadn't come to get me, someone else would have."

Archer had thought the same thing, had woken up in a panicky sweat several times, dreaming that very same scenario.

"I'm glad it was you," she said quietly.

"Yeah." Then the guard was standing before them again. Archer merely lifted a brow.

The guard's expression might have reflected just a bit of irritation as he nodded tightly. "Follow me."

Archer grinned and shut down the shield. "Right, mate." He turned to Talia. "Don't get out until I'm on your side."

A phalanx of guards surrounded him the instant he leaped from the car and followed as he moved around to her side. Another cadre approached Talia. Archer timed his move to slide in front of them and plant himself directly beside her, effectively blocking them all out. "Stand back. Don't crowd her. She's unused to this."

Archer smiled when Talia stiffened and immediately began clambering out. "Don't make me sound like a helpless idiot," she whispered fiercely.

"Me? I'd never do that," Archer said, taking her hand.

Talia snorted, then leaned back in and scooped up her backpack. He wondered if she'd go so far as to put that hideous hat on, but decided he'd slay the first man who so much as raised an eyebrow in her direction if she did. But she left it squashed inside the front pocket and strapped the bag on her back.

She eyed the guards nervously as they stepped in and ran a full body scan over both of them, and her pack, but her back was ramrod-straight. Archer smiled again, proud of her and for once pleased with her natural regal bearing. It would only serve her well in this circumstance. Maybe later he'd have the chance to unbend that bearing a little. *Not the time to be thinking of that, mate.* But that didn't stop his body from pondering it a while longer.

"Stay directly by my side. If you feel anything unusual or alarming, squeeze my hand and stop immediately." He looked at her. "Ready?"

"Oh, yeah." She smiled weakly. "I was born ready."

He squeezed her hand, when what he wanted to do was pull her into his arms and deliver a lengthy, mind-blowing kiss. But neither of them could afford clouded thinking. A shame, that. He'd save it for later. And he intended there to be a later.

Archer nodded to the troops. "Lead on."

They were surrounded four deep by the red and black suited men. Archer should have felt secure, but those damn hairs were lifting on his neck again. He kept keen eyes trained all along the tunnel and corridors, looking for the source of it. Likely there was surveillance of some kind. He'd felt it on his previous visit. But this was something more. It felt . . . menacing. He wondered where Chamberlain was and if any of the royal guard were in his private employ. Probably. Archer would insist that only the queen's private guard be in charge of Talia's security. They were handpicked by Catriona and most came from families that had been loyal to the Dalwyns for generations.

As they went deeper into the castle, the guards

peeled off, until they reached the queen's private sector. Much to Archer's relief, by the time they stood in front of the massive double doors that led to the queen's quarters, their chaperones were entirely composed of the queen's personal guard. Black suited with gold trim and eminently serious, they silently ushered them both in, motioned for them to be seated in plush, ornate chairs in a small antechamber, then dismissed themselves. Two remained inside the doors. Two more were positioned beside a large door on the opposite wall. Archer knew the remaining ones were stationed just outside.

So far he was pleased, at least as pleased as he could be. He had no doubt that Chamberlain was already well aware of Talia's arrival. Had probably been somehow watching delivery through the passageways personally. But his instincts had calmed somewhat now that they were in the queen's private chambers.

Before he could say a word to Talia, the doors on the opposite wall slid soundlessly open. A small woman with dark hair pulled back in a no-nonsense knot, also dressed in the black and gold uniform of the queen's private staff, stepped out and crossed the sumptuous rug to where they were seated. Archer had encountered her before. She was the queen's personal assistant.

She stopped before them, hands clasped in front, professional smile perfectly in place. "Welcome," she said to Talia, who nodded, and glanced surreptitiously about at the magnificent surroundings.

Then the assistant turned to Archer and her smile abruptly disappeared. "You will be seen immediately." The smile returned as she looked to Talia. "Please wait here."

Confused, Archer looked at Talia, then back at

the woman. "Excuse me?" He'd assumed Talia would be all but rushed to the queen's side, urged to perform her magic at once. In fact, Archer had been formulating plans to remain as close to her as possible, since he expected they would try to make him leave.

Perhaps that's what this was about. The queen was going to thank him, pay him off, and have him escorted out. Well, she'd be rethinking that scenario shortly. He stood, intentionally using his towering height to his advantage. "Ms. Trahaern does not leave my side until I have personally delivered her to the queen."

"Yes, well." The assistant pursed her perfectly painted lips. "I believe that is what the queen wishes to discuss with you."

Archer planted his hands on his hips. "Is there a problem?"

She folded her arms, no longer the pleasant professional. "Did you honestly think you'd get away with this . . . this sham?"

Archer opened his mouth to ask what the hell she was talking about, when Talia spoke. "I think I can explain."

They both looked at her.

Talia raised an eyebrow. "I'm not mute or deaf." She stood. "I think I understand the confusion. You were, perhaps, expecting someone older."

Archer's expression cleared. Of course. He'd forgotten they were expecting Eleri. And the queen was completely unaware, as far as he knew, that he'd traveled through time and collected her daughter instead. Talia was the spitting image of her mother, but younger than Eleri had been when she'd disappeared, much less the age she'd be now. He laughed. "You honestly thought I'd hired an imposter?"

"There is a large fortune at stake. Some men—"

Archer's expression hardened. "I'm not 'some men.' I was hired to bring back the royal healer. I have done so. If there is any explaining to do, we will do so to the queen. Together. Now, either escort us both to her immediately or I will return Ms. Trahaern to where I found her and you can get someone else for the job."

The assistant's eyes widened, but otherwise her professional demeanor held firm. She folded her hands once again in front of her. "I shall be right back."

"You have one minute or we're gone."

She turned then, her smile brittle, but her eyes fierce. "You will go when and where the queen allows you to go." She nodded toward the guards.

Archer's respect climbed a notch—a tiny one—for the fiery little woman, but his grin didn't reveal that. "Sweetheart, you've never seen me in action."

She flushed, and retreated.

He turned to find Talia studying the room. Only when she rubbed at her arms did he realize she wasn't quite as cool and collected as she pretended to be.

He sat next to her. "Quite the place, huh?"

"It's . . . amazing." She looked up at hand-painted domed ceiling far above them. "It feels so old and historic and yet it's modern and hi-tech, all at the same time." She looked at the doors that had whooshed silently shut behind the assistant.

Archer understood her awe. "The castle was built on the foundations of one that was old even in your time. Over the centuries it has been the site of countless battles, the last of which occurred during the Insurrection. The aftermath resulted in the split of the United Kingdom into three separate lands, ruled by three separate monarchs."

"How long ago was that?"

Archer shrugged. "Long before I was born. Probably a hand more than a hundred years now." He sat back in his chair. "Llanfair is the capital of the Welsh kingdom and the seat of the monarchy. The House of Dalwyn has been in power since shortly after the uprising. Queen Catriona is the sixth Dalwyn to rule."

Talia opened her mouth to speak, but apparently thought better of it.

Archer, who was feeling proud of himself for having put together that much factual history of his adopted homeland, realized then that she had no idea what year she was in.

"It's twenty-two-thirty-five." She blanched and he wished he'd kept silent.

She looked at him and smiled. "It's okay. I mean, you had to deal with this same thing, right? When you came to my . . . my time." She tucked her hair nervously behind her ears. "You handled it fairly well. So it shouldn't be too hard for me."

"I think the learning curve is a bit steeper on your end." He shifted so he faced her directly. "Don't think you have to be perfect here, Talia. Once we explain the situation, the queen will understand what you are dealing with. She's young, but with a wisdom far beyond her years."

"How young?"

"Twenty-five."

"And she rules the whole country?"

Archer nodded. "Every last bit of it. Her father, King Cynan, whom your mother served, was assassinated three years ago. Catriona ascended the throne very young, but she's held the place together well enough, until . . . well, until she grew ill."

"I can't even imagine," Talia whispered. "All that and she's pregnant, too."

Archer nodded, not knowing what else to say, already wishing he hadn't said as much as he had.

"What about the father? Is she married? Is there a king, or whatever they call a queen's husband. Prince regent or something? I was never a royal watcher."

"She wasn't married. She's never spoken about the father."

"I guess that's normal, even in my time." She looked at him. "Do people still get married?" She hadn't put any emphasis on the question, until her cheeks pinked a bit and she rushed to add, "I mean, I was just thinking that my mother wasn't married either and that made me wonder if—Never mind."

Under normal circumstances, when a woman he'd been intimate with brought up the M word around him, no matter how seemingly casual the reference, Archer immediately began making his bon voyage plans. But when Talia had mentioned it, his internal alarms hadn't made a sound.

The doors slid open before he could think about that, much less answer Talia. The assistant hurried over to them. "Follow me. Quickly."

Archer took his time standing. "Now she's in a hurry."

But Talia leaped to her feet, then smoothed her hair while taking a deep breath. She darted a look at him and murmured, "Thanks for standing up for me."

"I promised, didn't I?" He winked at her and placed his hand on the small of her back, beneath her bulging backpack. "What do you have in there anyway?" he asked quietly as they crossed the room to the door.

"Just . . . stuff."

"Some things never change, I guess." Archer

smiled and waited for her to look up at him. She smiled then, too.

He took her hand, not caring who was watching them or what message the connection sent. He squeezed. "You'll do fine in there, Tali."

He felt the fine tremors, but she stood tall, chin lifted. "God, I hope so."

Archer swallowed a grin. She had every bit as much presence as Catriona. Should be an interesting match.

The doors whooshed open in front of them and the assistant stepped aside, revealing a vast sea of carpeting decorated in the royal seal of black and gold. Enormous gold lions adorned either side. The assistant motioned them to precede her.

He heard Talia sing something under her breath that sounded like "Follow the Yellow Brick Road," before stepping cautiously into the room.

Two very tall, very erect guards stepped forward. Their flamboyant black and gold uniforms were of an extreme design that would have looked almost comical if it hadn't been for their intense manner and bearing.

"This way, please," they said in deep-throated unison.

"Not exactly Munchkins from the Lollipop Guild, are they?" Talia murmured.

Archer leaned closer. "What are you talking about?"

Whatever she might have said was lost as they traversed the long room and stopped in front of what Archer knew to be the door to the queen's bedroom. The guards stepped back, and with what seemed like a flourish, the door, though much smaller than the ones they'd just passed through, slid silently open. The room was dimly lit, and the bed on the opposite side was deep in shadow.

"Step forward where I might see you," the queen commanded, sounding far older than her years. Yet Archer heard the underlying fatigue. She sounded weaker than she had at their last meeting. He looked to Talia, wondering if she was picking up on anything. The tension in the room seemed to pervade even his senses.

Talia stepped in front of him, her face cast in shadows. She squeezed his hand one last time, then let go. He marveled at their silent communication, at how easily they'd fallen into that type of partnership.

Partnership.

Did he truly view the two of them that way? He who worked alone? He didn't waste time wondering. Instead he watched with a sense of pride as she stepped to the middle of the room.

"Stop there."

Talia faltered, but quickly regained her composure. She stood in a pool of light that came from a recessed lamp in the ceiling far above them. Archer stayed just outside the circle, close enough to signal his presence to anyone who cared to question it.

His attention was jerked toward the bed, lost in the shadows, as a gasp from the queen filled the chamber.

Chapter 17

*E*leri." The queen's shocked whisper filled the small chamber. "I couldn't imagine it, but you look too much like her to be an imposter. How can it be?"

"I'm not Eleri." Talia began to step forward. She couldn't see the queen and it was more than a little unnerving.

"Come no closer."

She froze. Archer hadn't been kidding when he said the queen was mature for her age. Catriona's voice alone scared the bejesus out of her. "Okay."

"Explain yourself."

Talia decided that she would have to stand up and not be intimidated. "I'm Eleri's daughter. My name is Talia."

There was total silence.

Talia forged ahead. "I understand she served your father before she left your kingdom under threat to her life."

"And you are only now coming forward? I find that suspicious in the extreme."

"I didn't know about her past until recently."

"Where is your mother now?"

"She was killed in an accident when I was a child." Since the moment Talia had stepped into the room she'd had to work at resisting making a connection with the queen. She fought against the urge, mainly for the sake of self-preservation. Until she understood more about where she was and what was really going on, she wasn't going to make herself vulnerable in any way, and that included inviting an assault of any kind against herself.

"You say your mother never told you of her position in this court?"

Talia shook her head. "She told me many tales as a child, tales I grew up believing were nothing more than bedtime stories. Only now I realize she was telling me where she was from. She died before she could tell me the whole truth. I suppose I wasn't old enough to understand."

"You have an accent. American?"

"Yes. I've lived in the U.S. all my life."

Again silence. This time Talia took the initiative. It helped her focus against the increasing demand to reach out. The need all but hummed inside her. "I was never trained as a healer. I'm an empath, but that is as much as I know."

The fight to keep from reaching out suddenly took on mammoth proportions. Talia had to use all of her focus to keep the feelings out. Which made no sense. Why such a strong bond with someone she'd never met? Then she realized. She was born to serve the royal family. The daughter of the royal healer. For the first time she felt a tiny shred of hope. Maybe there was a real connection after all!

"You have no healing powers?"

"I—I haven't had much time to explore the extent of my . . . gift."

"And yet you came willingly."

"Yes, ma'am. Your Highness, I mean."

There was a long, very uncomfortable pause. "I see," she said at length.

Talia didn't have a clue what that meant. This entire meeting was nerve-racking.

"You have given me much to think on," the queen said, sounding dismissive. Then abruptly, she asked, "How old are you?"

"Twenty-eight," Talia replied, caught off guard. When the silence grew long, she finally said, "I know you were counting on my mum to help you. I don't know if I can do anything. I wasn't able to learn much from Baleweg—"

"The Old One?" The queen seemed stunned. "You actually found him? Eleri was rumored to have a strong affection for him. My father searched far and wide for him after her disappearance. How did you find him, Mr. Archer?" she demanded.

Archer stepped into the pool of light beside Talia. "Trade secret."

"I do not find your arrogance amusing. Explain how you found him. And where, exactly, she hid herself and her daughter. Obviously you were not the only one to uncover Eleri's secret, so either you tell me or I will summon the High Parliamentarian directly. I believe he was likely the one responsible for commanding the actions of both Mr. Anteri and Mr. Dideon. Am I not correct?"

Archer swore. "What do you know of that?"

There was a pause and Talia was surprised to hear the queen answer his question. "My sources tell me Chamberlain was actively working against your cause and had sent agents of his own to thwart you. But where, when, and how they planned to do so, I was unable to determine."

"Did you question him? Or Dideon? Anteri?"

There was a frosty pause that made it clear the

queen was not happy being interrogated, yet she responded again. "I did not. Not directly. I have no tangible proof of his mutiny and I do not wish to force a confrontation until I am certain of a swift victory."

"So you knew nothing about Talia?"

There was a brief pause. "No," she answered, her voice strangely tight. There was a pause, then her tone hardened once again. "I was only aware that his agents had been sent to halt your efforts and had returned unsuccessful. We hadn't learned more than that when you arrived. Now explain to me how you located the Old One."

Archer blew out a sigh. "In my research, I discovered Baleweg was the last one to have contact with Eleri."

"This was not a secret. He has been the subject of many investigations, but no one has ever found him."

"He made himself available to me."

"Why now? He must have known when others looked for him in years past."

"He knew Eleri's daughter was in danger. He only came forward to aid her."

Another pause, and the temperature in the room seemed to drop twenty degrees.

Talia tried not to fidget. She was certain the queen was not thrilled to hear that Baleweg's allegiance was to her mother first and not his queen.

Then the queen asked, or rather demanded, "Where is the Old One now?"

Archer smiled. "You sorely underestimate me if you think I will give you that information. Or that he would remain in that location if I did. He isn't given to suffering the predatory nature of court. Besides, there is nothing more he can do."

There was an impatient sigh.

Now Archer's expression hardened, as well. "I did my job. Your part of the bargain was to ask no questions."

"A part I am now regretting. But you are right. I am, however, interested in finding out what you know of Anteri's and Dideon's activities. You have the Old One. Who is helping Chamberlain?"

Archer paused, then said, "There is one other like Baleweg. Someone with . . . peculiar powers like his. Perhaps even stronger. He is the one helping Chamberlain."

"The Dark One," she murmured. "I never really believed—" She broke off. "How did you circumvent them?"

"Wait a minute. You knew of him?" Archer's temper visibly spiked. "Didn't you think this information might have aided me?"

"His existence was as much a myth to me as the Old One was. I had no idea either was involved in this. In what manner did he aid Chamberlain?"

"He is the one who helped get the agents in to monitor Talia."

"Then he already knew of her existence?"

Archer nodded. "Chamberlain was simply having her monitored. Baleweg thinks he intended to use her skills against you somehow. When we showed up, the stakes changed. That is when he sent Anteri. I was able to prevent him from completing his mission and we brought Talia here immediately afterward."

The queen fell silent for a moment, then said, "There is much we must discuss about this before you leave."

"I will be more than glad to discuss it with you, as I intend to continue to be responsible for Talia until it is known whether or not she can help you."

"Impossible."

Archer smiled coldly. "Nothing is impossible, Your Highness."

"You doubt I can keep her safe?"

"I didn't say that. Considering the pressure the court is under, the divisiveness that even now threatens to split Parliament, and your failing health, I'd think you'd gladly take me up on the personal service I am offering. In addition to your personal guard, of course."

Talia slid her hand into Archer's. He tried to ease his hand away, signaling to her that this was not wise, despite the fact that they'd entered the chamber with hands held. They'd been in darkness then. But Talia figured she held some sway here, and she intended to use it now. "I wish him to stay."

"I see." And there was no doubt, even in those two little words, that she did, indeed, see. Talia saw a great deal, too. Or heard it. The fatigue in the queen's voice had increased in the last several exchanges. She sounded younger . . . and vulnerable. Talia wondered what her regal bearing had cost her these past minutes. She felt her own guard slipping and the tentative tentacles of her mind beginning to reach out. Only the queen's resumed speech snapped her focus back into place.

"I will want to talk with you, Archer, and with you, Miss Trahaern, at length. But at the moment I need my rest. I will have Marletta show you to your quarters." There was a pause, then she added, "I am assuming one suite of rooms will be sufficient for your needs?"

Archer smiled, but Talia felt her cheeks heat, despite the fact that she'd been the one to bring their relationship out into the open. But she didn't ask for two rooms, either.

"Yes, Your Highness," he said. "That will be quite suitable."

The queen's assistant materialized behind them then and touched Talia's shoulder. "Follow me."

Although the experience had been nerve-racking, now that it was over, Talia felt as if she hadn't done enough, that she'd somehow let the queen down. Maybe she should have reached out. Maybe that was what a royal healer did. Followed her instincts. And she'd failed before she'd even begun. She'd protected herself, when she was born to protect the queen first.

Baleweg thought her mother would have eventually brought her back here, to serve the House of Dalwyn, that this was what she'd have wanted. Talia thought so, too. Otherwise why tell her all those stories? Was it too late now? She took a calming breath and tried to still her racing thoughts so she could reach out, but Marletta was there, talking.

"The queen must rest now."

"Wait." The connection was right there. All she had to do was reach for it. She turned and stepped toward the queen, only to encounter a shield. Not an invisible wall, so much as air too thick for her to walk through.

"I must insist," Marletta said firmly.

Talia turned to find the queen's assistant pocketing a small device. She very firmly took Talia by the shoulder, a grip that was immediately, if gently broken by Archer.

"No one touches her but me."

In an efficient tone that brooked no argument, the assistant merely said, "We must leave now. The queen is asleep. I daresay this has been an overly taxing day for her." She was already ushering them toward the door.

Talia wanted to ask how in the hell she could tell

what the queen was doing, buried in the shadows as she was, but the personal guard had surrounded them, separating them from Marletta, who was leading the throng out of the room and through a doorway she hadn't seen before. A large mural in the antechamber where she and Archer had waited literally shifted to painted air, then after they passed through, turned solid again as Talia saw when she looked over her shoulder.

"State of the art," Archer whispered with a wink.

"Very funny." But Talia gulped nonetheless. Unbelievable. She tried to focus on where they were going, on the scenes painted on the walls, wondering how many concealed additional pathways and how many were just paintings.

They stopped in front of a rather large, elaborate one and Talia felt her cheeks flame yet again. "I see the queen has a sense of humor after all," she muttered under her breath.

The painting on the wall in front of them was a stunning rendering in oil, or what appeared to be oil anyway. The subject matter, however, was . . . explicit. A man and woman, both nude, both fully and quite graphically entwined, lay stretched out on a carpet of flowers. Delicate little fairies floated above, dropping red and white petals on the lovers. Talia couldn't tear her eyes away from the way the woman's slender back arched and the muscles in the man's shoulders bunched as he—

"I like the queen's taste," Archer said, then made a small *ooph* sound when Talia dug her elbow into his ribs.

"You would," she said.

"Your palms are sweating."

She scowled and tried to slide her hand out of his, but he wouldn't let her.

He leaned down to her ear and whispered to her

as the painting in front of them turned transparent.
"I wanted to make love to you in exactly the same
kind of bower. Maybe the queen can read minds,
hmm?"

Talia's only response was a tight swallow . . . and
continued sweaty palms, as the queen's assistant motioned them to follow her. "You will be safe here for
the night. I will have a full supper sent to you
shortly. Tomorrow the queen will send a summons.
At that time you will have a full guard escort. Do not
leave with anyone other than the queen's personal
guard. Until then, please enjoy your accommoda-
tions."

Archer smiled at her. "And if we need anything?"

The small woman turned with a smile of her own.
"You won't."

Archer stepped through the screen, pulling Talia
with him. They both turned in time to see the
queen's guard take up stations along the passageway.

Archer nodded in approval, then the screen
turned solid and they were inside their chamber.

Prison, actually. Talia felt a sense of claustropho-
bia, of being sealed inside a tomb or something.
Until she turned around at Archer's urging.

"Look at this," he said. "Nice setup."

Talia's mouth dropped open. It was like something from a sultan's fantasy. Silk draped the walls
and the carpeting was so thick it almost swallowed
her sandals. The ceiling was a recessed dome,
painted with scenes that Talia only glanced at, but
already knew were likely produced by the same artist
who had done the handiwork in the passageway. She
looked back to the room, which was dominated by a
huge fireplace, and fronted by a sumptuous, wide
lounge upholstered in opulent jewel-toned fabric
and edged with thick, gold-colored fringe.

"It's . . . different."

Archer laughed. "Do you think the queen is trying to tell us something?"

Talia tried to laugh, but it came out as a sort of rasp. "Gee, I can't wait to see the bedroom."

Archer grabbed her hand and tugged her to one of two doors, framed in gold, on the far wall.

"I was joking," she managed, but he was already halfway there. "Archer!"

He looked over his shoulder. "Aren't you curious?"

She stalled. She was curious, but she didn't think she wanted to tell him that. She was still reeling from everything else she'd witnessed today.

"Come on. Dinner will probably be here shortly. If there is a bathroom behind that other door, you can wash up as soon as we're done exploring, okay?"

Now she did laugh. "We're not at Club Med, you know."

"Club what?"

"Never mind." She lifted her free hand. "Lead on, MacDuff."

"And people say Aussies make no sense."

She was smiling at his back when he opened the door and swept her through in front of him. Her smile froze on her face. *Oh. My. God* was her first and only thought.

Archer crowded closer and nudged her farther into the room so he could see. He whistled his appreciation. "You know, I never understood why people threw money away on decorators. I'm rethinking my position on that."

"I bet," Talia said dryly. She slid her hand from his and stepped farther into the room. If the front room had been pure sex, this room was downright pornography. "Well, the queen accomplished one thing," she said, looking over the sea of silk and pillows that only someone who thought about sex twenty-four hours a day might describe as a bed.

"And that is?"

His voice was disturbingly close, right behind her left ear. But he didn't touch her. In some ways, that was even more torturous. "She's taken my mind off my worries."

Archer chuckled and the husky sound sent ripples of pleasure over her skin. "There is only one thing you're supposed to do in this room. And it's not worrying."

Talia slid out of his way and circled the massive bed to look at the various lounges that encircled the large room. Each one was structured in an . . . unusual shape. "What in God's name are you supposed to do on these?" She looked up to find Archer's grin so broad it made his cleft almost slice his chin in half. "Never mind," she said firmly. "I don't want to know. And I don't want to know how you know, either. Sex can't have changed that much in a couple hundred years, and if by some miracle it has, I don't think I want to know about that either."

Archer shrugged and moved off to examine some of the lounges. "If you say so."

Talia made a face at his back, but then the painting on the wall just beyond the lounge in front of her caught her eye. The same pair of lovers that starred in the painting in the hallway were performing an encore. On a piece of furniture much like the one positioned in front of her. "So," she murmured. "That's how you use that."

She ignored Archer's low laugh. But that didn't stop her from moving on to the next lounge and the next painting. "Wow." And on to the next one. "Jesus." And the next one. "Dear God, how does she do that?" By the last one her knees were decidedly weak and her panties unabashedly soaked.

Archer cleared his throat, making her start. She quickly turned around and attempted a self-deprecating smile. "I've heard of circuit training, but these two—" She gestured toward the walls in general, then gave up any pretense of being cool about this, and closed her eyes and covered her face with her hands.

The next thing she felt was Archer's fingers prying her hands free, then lifting her chin. "Look at me."

She did, warily.

"When they bring dinner, I'll have them move us."

It was the last thing she'd expected from him.

"The queen has had her little joke and I can honestly say I appreciate her sense of humor," he went on. "But you have enough to deal with, without—"

Talia shut him up with a kiss. When she finally let him up for air, she was already unbuttoning his shirt. "Dinner can wait."

Chapter 18

*A*rcher's muscles bunched in his shoulders as Talia arched beneath him. The silk draped across the bed felt slick against his skin . . . and looked damn erotic against hers. Her hips slid easily up to his and he leaned down to take her mouth again as he pushed deep into her. "Talia," he groaned. "Dear God."

"I know," she whispered, then moaned as he moved harder and faster. She grabbed his shoulders and hung on, moving with his every thrust. "Devin. Please."

"I will, Tali. I will." And he did. And that was the way it went, for hours. Their bodies communicated with very little need for words.

Finally, their bodies still twitching from their most recent release, Talia slid off Archer and the divan, down onto the carpet, her face serene, sated . . . and smug. She stretched, smiling even as she winced.

Archer slid onto the thick carpet beside her. "Too rough?" He pulled her limp body to his, draping her lazily across his chest and legs, unwilling to be even an inch away from her without touching her.

Her head lolled toward his, her eyes luminous. "No. I just discovered some muscles I didn't know I had."

"Maybe we need . . . what did you call it? Circuit training? Maybe we need to train more often." The suggestion alone made her shudder with pleasure against him. He grinned and pulled her closer.

She kissed his chin. "Most definitely." Then she leaned down and pressed her lips to his heart.

Archer felt his eyes burn and there was absolutely no reason for it. Except his heart felt as if it were going to explode and that sweet little kiss she'd just delivered might have been the one to push it over the edge. She gave herself to him so generously, so completely, he wanted to please her as fully in return. "Are you hungry?" he managed.

She tipped her chin onto his chest and looked at him, the most wicked grin on her face. "Ravenous."

Archer had to laugh.

She smacked his chest, but laughed along with him as she pushed herself upright. "Where are my clothes?"

Archer rolled to his knees just behind her. He reached past her and yanked a silk drape off one of the lounges. "Here, use this."

"I believe we already have," she said dryly.

"My, we are the wicked ones, aren't we?" He pulled another swath of silk off the lounge, then tugged her unwillingly to her feet and wrapped it around her. "I'd as soon keep you nude, but I imagine dinner has long since been delivered to the next room and I have no idea if the guard is within, or without."

Talia's cheeks reddened. "You really think they were out there? The whole time?"

Archer laughed again. "What happened to my wicked vixen?"

"I enjoy some things, but I'm not into exhibitionism."

"You're into a lot of things you had no idea you were into."

She tried to look affronted, but failed miserably. "I'm not normally like this."

He grinned. "Define *normal*."

She narrowed her gaze, but there was a teasing light in her eyes. "Great. You'll think of me as some kind of sex fiend forever."

And right then Archer realized just how deeply he'd placed his heart in jeopardy. One word and he'd known. *Forever*.

Because the idea that someday he wouldn't be with her was incomprehensible at that moment. How had that happened? Clearing his suddenly tight throat, he tried to cover the nervousness with a laugh. "No teasing," he said, then winked. "And no worries on those screams, either. I doubt sound travels beyond these walls."

She tried to smack him again, but he grabbed her hand and impulsively kissed her palm. "I'll see if we're clear while you make use of the bathroom. Forgiven?"

She nodded, but instead of the kiss he expected, she nipped his lower lip instead. He pulled back, surprised, but she merely imitated his expression, then strolled to the connecting bathroom door. Allowing the silk sarong he'd fashioned to loosen and slowly slide over her skin to pool on the floor behind her as she left.

"Dinner is already cold, you know," he warned. "I don't care if it sits."

Her response was a laugh as she closed the door between them.

He was on his feet and halfway to the bathroom, thinking a nice joint shower would be just the thing, then stopped when he realized why he was following her. It wasn't because he felt the need to make love again already. It was because . . . well, he missed her when she was gone. Silly and ridiculous, since he'd been having her for hours now and she'd only been gone for a few seconds. But there it was. Staring him in the face.

That and the word *forever.*

He managed to find his trousers and pulled them on, then wandered out to the main room. No one was there, but a huge dinner service had been set up in front of a still-crackling fire. He was pleased to see the dishes were heated, as well. "Thanks, Catriona," he murmured. "For more than I can say." He slid open one lid and his stomach contracted on a huge growl. He snagged a sugared carrot and wandered aimlessly about the room while waiting for Talia.

Now that his head was clearer, he wondered at Catriona's choice of rooms. Had it just been an amusing little joke? Or was it a calculated move? And if so, what did it mean? He'd lost himself quickly to Talia's needs, so quickly he hadn't stopped to think that perhaps they hadn't been alone since entering this chamber. He shifted his attention to the walls, to the shadows and nooks . . . but of course there would be no obvious surveillance, just as there had been none in the passageways. And yet, he'd felt watched there.

He hadn't here, but was that because he'd been so wrapped up in Talia that his instincts hadn't kicked in? He didn't think so. But the thought that someone might have witnessed such a private act between them infuriated him. Had they made a recording and planned to use it to coerce him to do their bidding?

He was stalking toward the screen entrance when Talia entered the room from the other door wearing a silk robe the color of rubies. It was dazzling against her skin and the contrast with her dark hair robbed him of all thought.

She stopped in the golden doorway. "What's wrong?"

"Nothing." He shook his head. "Nothing at all. You look . . . amazing. The food is still warm." He crossed back toward the table. No point in ruining what had been an incredible evening. He definitely didn't want to alarm Talia. Despite her openness with him, her reaction to the idea that the guards might have overheard so much as a moan indicated how mortified she'd be if she thought someone had actually recorded them.

He realized then the real gift she'd given him this night. Trusting him with a part of herself that she wasn't even comfortable admitting she had. Except to him. With him she was not only comfortable with her sexuality, she was downright playful with it. Only with him.

And he had another epiphany just then. He realized that he wanted to be the only man sharing that part of her. Which meant . . . ?

"Are you okay? You look . . . ill." She hurried over to him and felt his forehead. "You feel okay? Maybe we'd better eat."

"Yeah." He cleared his throat. "Probably. I'm starving."

Talia looked at the small black domes. "How do you open these?"

He smiled and tried to shove all his concerns aside. There was nothing to be done tonight except enjoy their meal. And make damn certain they were under the silk covers when they went to bed. He moved his hands over the sensor and one of the tops slid back. He showed Talia how to do it and let her do the others.

"Neat trick." She leaned down. "It smells incredible. And I even recognize most of it."

"Food hasn't changed much, I don't think."

"Yeah, well, I don't take anything for granted."

Archer caught her eye just then. "Neither do I," he said, imbuing the words with far more meaning than she could know. "Not anymore."

She paused then, her smile caught halfway between a grin and one of confusion. He almost wished she'd reach out to him then, connect with him, so she'd know what he was feeling. Then he wouldn't have to decide whether to speak of this huge thing he felt squeezing his heart. He wouldn't have to take the risk of saying words he'd sworn since childhood never to say to anyone again. It was one thing to feel it—and that alone was so amazing he still hadn't fully comprehended it. But sharing it was something else entirely. And despite his feelings right now, he still wasn't sure he ever could.

He broke eye contact and began serving up their plates. Far too much to think about. Far too much yet to be done.

They were still sampling from the vast array of chafing dishes when Talia innocently rendered his planned retreat totally ineffective with a single volley. "You know a great deal about me. I mean, about my past," she began. "I hardly know anything about you. I'd like to."

He stilled, the ladle of gravy poised above his plate. He covered his sudden alarm with a grin. "I'd say you know a great deal about me," he said,

She smiled, but there was that look in her eye, that determination he'd seen when she worked with a newly arrived orphan. He understood their panic now. Taking that step, handing over that trust, wasn't easy. He'd handed her a great deal more than he'd even known he had to offer. But this . . . this was territory he was extremely uncomfortable with.

"You've never really spoken of your family."

He clenched his fork so tightly he was surprised

the heavy sterling didn't bend. So here he was, close enough to someone to care what they thought, scared enough to want to lie and avoid the whole issue. "No, I haven't," he said tightly, keeping his attention on his plate. *Please, let it go, Tali, just let it go.* He begged silently, without shame, because he knew he couldn't lie to her.

Of course, she didn't let it go. But not in the way he'd expected. And that was his final undoing. She fell silent, until he found himself looking up at her. She'd dropped her gaze to her plate. Her voice, when she spoke, was quiet. "I'm guessing neither of us had an idyllic childhood." She pushed her food around. "I missed my mum for a long, long time."

It wasn't calculated. And she was letting him off the hook, not trying to weasel more information out of him. So why he opened his mouth and said, "I didn't miss mine," he had no idea.

She looked up then and he met her eyes squarely. And what he saw wasn't pity, or even morbid curiosity. What he saw was understanding. From someone who knew what it was to be abandoned, to be left behind, to be unwanted. And suddenly it wasn't a hard decision to make. He only hoped she wouldn't be so turned off by his past that she distanced herself from him altogether. That was the risk he'd spent a lifetime avoiding.

If he never allowed anyone to get close, he never risked losing them. Of course, his whole life he'd believed he didn't need anyone close, thereby avoiding the whole issue. He hadn't counted on meeting someone who challenged that notion. Someone so important to him that he knew if he didn't share the past that had shaped the man he'd become, then whatever closeness they achieved would be built on a hollow foundation. And nothing worthwhile was built on a hollow foundation. If he expected her to accept him, she had to know all about him.

"Right," he said under his breath. So why was he so bloody petrified? He put his fork down. "My mother had a tough go of things." He picked his fork up again. "She, uh, she was on her own at an early age. A mining town in Queensland. Not a great place for a woman alone. But she made a living." He stirred at his food, then put his fork down again.

Talia reached over and took his hand in hers. "You don't have to—"

He looked her directly in the eyes. "Yes. I do."

She stilled, then she nodded, lacing her fingers through his. "I'm guessing you didn't know your father, either, is that it?"

"Aye. My mum, she learned to survive. She was a good businesswoman. Managed to carve out a life there."

Talia smiled. "So you come by your talents honestly?"

His grip on her hand tightened unwillingly. He made a conscious effort to relax. "I've always said that." He'd said it a bit harshly and maybe he hadn't been as understanding of his mother as he'd always told himself he was. "Hopefully I've a bit of my dad in me, as well."

Talia's eyebrows lifted. "What bit is that? I've always wondered what part of me is like my dad, for that matter like my mom, too. But it's too much torture to spend time on it."

"Agreed." He took a deep breath. "Well, there's no way around it, so here's the thing. My mum's business was selling her body. And she'd made it quite a commodity."

"Oh, Archer, I'm sorry, I didn't mean to—"

"It's okay." And oddly, it was. As terrifying as it was, it felt good to get it out. "Anyway, getting pregnant wasn't part of her business plan. She tried to get rid of me." He grinned briefly. "But I was a stubborn blodger, even before I was born."

Talia smiled, but her eyes were sad. "What happened to you?"

"Well, being the businesswoman that she was, she fed and housed me, more or less as an investment. One that took five years to mature before she cashed in on it."

"Oh, Devin!" Talia covered her mouth in horror.

He quickly reached for her hand and pulled it away. "No, not that way. But she had no intention of continuing my care and feeding, either. Cramped her already cramped lifestyle. Australia is a land colonized by convicts, but since your time much has happened there. When contact with other people . . . and by that I mean people not of this planet . . . was made, a certain ages-old trade sprang up once again." He paused, then spit out the rest in one long breath. "A slave trade. I think she got her money's worth and I got a firsthand lesson in the law of supply and demand. It's held me in good stead in this life. But I'd like to think I'd do things different. That's the bit of my dad I hope I got. Or maybe it's the part that's all me."

"She sold you into slavery?" She wasn't just horrified now, she was pissed. Archer rather liked that reaction.

"You were only a little boy!" She looked down at the hand that held hers, then turned them over. "Those lines. The scars." She traced the thin, silvery lines that circled his wrists.

He knew, as she did now, that they also marked his ankles. Her eyes drifted to his neck, and he knew what she saw there, as well. There were other reminders, too. He hated the idea that he might repulse her now.

"I thought—" She stopped and swallowed. "I know you lead a fairly rough life, and I noticed the scars but I thought they were the battle wounds that came with a tough business." She looked back at him, her eyes round and glassy. "I never imagined—Never would have thought— Oh, Devin."

It wasn't repulsion he saw there. It was pain. Maybe he shouldn't have told her. She felt things too keenly. "I didn't mean to hurt you by telling you this."

"Hurt me? Hurt me! My God, Devin, do you really think me so self-involved?"

He squeezed her hand. "No, of course not. I just hate seeing you suffer." He looked away for a moment, then back. "I've never told anyone about my past. It's something I've never cared to explain, much less attempt to trade on. I've always felt it best to leave it where it is. Over."

"I don't blame you." Talia held his gaze. "You have a very balanced attitude about this. I don't think I would. I'd have probably ended up twisted with hatred or worse."

"No, you wouldn't have. You're a survivor like me."

"You have more faith in me than I do, then," she said. "What happened to her, do you know?" She immediately shook her head. "I'm sorry, I had no right to ask that. You asked to leave it in the past and I—"

"It's okay. It was a long time before I was able to find out what happened to her. I managed to escape from bondage when I was eleven. I've been on my own ever since. I was nineteen when I finally found out what happened to her. As it happens, she died when I was about eight or so. Her business was profitable, but rough. As far as carrying any anger over it, I look at it this way: at least I survived. I understood that she wasn't cut out to be a mother. It was probably better she gave me up." And he was very careful not to expect unconditional love ever again.

"It's not like she gave you up for adoption. She sold you!"

He shrugged. It was all he could do. "People do what they have to do. I've learned not to expect anything from anyone. Then I'm never disappointed."

"That's a harsh lesson for a five-year-old."

"Well, you don't get to pick when you learn things, easy or hard. You learned some rather harsh ones yourself at a tender age."

She nodded, but shuddered. "True. But at least I knew I was loved. I still believe there is good in people. But I understand why you lost faith. I can't imagine what you went through."

"And I'd rather you didn't." He looked intently at her and she nodded, realizing what he was asking her. That was one area he'd as soon she never probed. "It wasn't pretty and it changed me forever. But I'm not ashamed of it."

"I should hope not. You could hardly be blamed."

"Not everyone would be so forgiving. There is a definite stigma in coming from my particular past. But no, I don't waste time with blame. It's a lost cause. In the long run, what I lived through as a child shaped me into who I am today." He looked at their joined hands and suddenly he felt tongue-tied. "I . . . I wanted you to know." He looked up at her, his breath trapped in his chest. "If it changes anything, I'll understand."

She looked at him in that way she had that made him feel stripped naked. Only it wasn't so uncomfortable now. In fact, he felt such a sense of relief he was almost shaky with it.

She smiled. "Oh, it changes things. But only for the good." She lifted his hands and pressed a kiss to both of his wrists. "Thank you for telling me. For trusting me."

Before he could make an idiot of himself and begin to blubber, or do something equally unmanly, her face split into a wide grin.

Surprised by the sudden change, he asked, "What's funny?"

She shook her head. "Well, not funny. Ironic. It occurs to me that I've been torturing myself over having a torrid affair with a man who sells his skills to the highest bidden, and now you've got me championing your career path. Pretty tricky piece of work there."

He smiled. "Talia—"

She lifted her free hand, stopping him. "I'd be lying if I said I was a hundred-percent comfortable with what you do, but not because I'm passing any moral judgment. I meant what I said. You've nothing to be ashamed of, not then, not now." She looked at him intently, those gray eyes of hers filled with so much emotion. "I guess I hate the fact that you have to continue to put your life on the line to survive."

"I've done all right." He smiled, trying to soothe her, all the while stunned by the fact that she cared so deeply for him. "And I chose the business I'm in because I'm good at it. No one is making me do it. But it's nice to know that someone's worrying about me." He stood and pulled her up beside him so that they were face-to-face. "No one has ever worried about me, save the people who hire me. But I think they're mostly concerned about their investment."

He smiled, but it faded as he drew his thumb across her lip, a lip that quivered beneath his touch. "I don't like for you to worry about me, Tali, but it does mean a great deal to me that you do. A great deal." He leaned in and kissed her. It was that or go the rest of the distance and tell her he was falling in love with her.

Which he'd realized now he could never do. Not because he didn't want to. He'd come a long way these past several hours. It was all but bursting inside him now that he'd made peace with the idea. But baring his soul to her had served to remind him of something he'd forgotten in his rush to explain himself. She was a sensitive woman who needed security and a life that wouldn't test that sensitivity to an extreme. She also deserved a man who would be there for her. Not a man who gallivanted about the universe with little but luck to serve as a shield between life and death. And a thin shield it was, but he'd rather she didn't know that.

No. Having even a piece of her heart was a treasure worth more than any amount of money. To put even that small piece in jeopardy of breaking was something he would never do. If he was ever to be proud of something, it would be that one selfless act.

And pride was a lonely, hollow victory. But it was victory enough if it meant keeping her heart intact and whole. Whole so that she could offer it to the right man. And that man wasn't going to be him.

Chapter 19

alia woke up early. At least it felt early. There were no windows or clocks in their bedchamber and she discovered her watch no longer ran.

The dull gonging sound that had roused her repeated itself and Archer stirred. She smoothed her hand over his back, thinking how wonderful it had been to sleep with his large warm body next to hers. Entwined with hers.

Her smile dimmed as her fingers encountered the not-so-smooth patches of skin scattered across his back. She now knew they were from his childhood. A fierce, protective anger washed through her. How dare they do that to a child? She continued watching his back rise and fall as he slept, amazed at how strong her feelings for him were. As much as she'd grown to count on his steady presence, she couldn't deny this need she had to be there for him, too. He chose that moment to stretch and groan a little.

"I think we're being summoned," she whispered in his ear. But it was only when she went to shove the covers off them that he truly awoke and pulled them right back over them again. "You can't be cold," she said. "Your body is like a furnace."

He rolled over and she was surprised by just how alert his eyes were, considering his mumbling response just moments ago. She supposed deep sleep wasn't something he indulged in, not if he wanted to live to sleep again. "I'm not sure how to answer a gong."

He looked confused, then the deep sound vibrated the walls again. "Wait here. Do not leave this bed." His tone was surprisingly fierce.

"What's wrong?"

"Nothing. Just don't leave the bed, okay?" He was already rolling to his side and reaching to the floor for his trousers, which he slid on as he walked to the door.

Back in bodyguard mode, she thought, trying not to worry. Instead she thought about last night, the way he'd tucked her beneath the covers, stroked her hair until she'd fallen asleep. He was a man of surprising integrity and a deeply ingrained sense of pride. She had no doubt that he cared for her. But he was also doing his job, keeping her safe. When this was over and done, she had no doubt he'd go on to his next job . . . and she'd go back home. The memories would be enough. Because they had to be.

Archer came back in the room just then and scooped her robe off the floor. "Here, put this on." He all but enveloped her as she came out of the bed and slid the robe on her arms. He was belting it before she was completely finished. She laughed. "What's up?"

He looked into her eyes. "The queen's guard is here. Catriona wants to see us. Now."

Talia's heart stopped for a second. How was it she'd forgotten, even for a second, why she was here in the first place? Then she was moving. "Okay, just let me find my clothes."

Archer grabbed her backpack from one of the lounges. "Here. I assume you have some clothes in there, right?"

"Crumpled beyond repair, so I hope the queen isn't a stickler for dress."

"Right now I think the queen will be perfectly happy with speed."

Talia tried not to let Archer's urgency faze her. She rarely, if ever, saw him like this. He wasn't one to jump to do another's bidding. But the more she tried to focus, the more tangled her fingers became. The zipper on her pack refused to budge and her robe kept slipping off her shoulder; her hair was in her eyes and she finally ground her teeth in a silent scream of frustration.

And Archer was there, taking the pack from her. "Hey, hey, no worries. We'll get it done. I'm sorry I came back in a rush. I should have realized—"

Somehow, hearing how nervous he was calmed her somewhat. "It's okay. If you can get this zipper open, though, I'd be eternally grateful." He flashed that grin of his and she felt her heart finally slow to a more manageable level.

"I'll hold you to that," he said.

"Please do," she said, feeling steadier now.

She slid out a rolled-up cotton T-shirt dress and shook it out. The wrinkles weren't too bad, but for an audience with the queen . . . "I don't exactly have a ball gown in my wardrobe." She'd faced her yesterday just as casually dressed, but somehow this situation felt more formal.

"You'll be fine," Archer said, hustling her into the bathroom and closing it behind them. He availed himself of a razor that, along with a full array of other products, lined the shelf above the double sinks.

"Guess they haven't made shaving obsolete, huh?"

Archer just grinned at her. "They have. I prefer this."

She was glad. There was something very sexy about

watching a man shave. "Do we have time for a shower?"

Now his grin was downright wicked, but he shook his head. "Not this morning, sweetheart. Later."

"I'll hold you to that," she said, smiling, then dressed quickly before stepping next to Archer at the mirror. She made a face at her own reflection.

Archer pulled her face to his and kissed her. "You're beautiful."

She wasn't. Mirrors didn't lie. But she felt much better anyway. She rubbed the shaving cream from her nose and dug out her toothpaste and brush from her pack.

Archer leaned back against the sink and watched in fascination. She felt a little exposed, but she'd watched him shave. "You're really going to enjoy this," she said with a laugh, pulling the floss out.

He folded his arms, remaining silent. But the look on his face . . . It felt so natural, being with him here like this, as if they ran through these little morning routines together every day. She had her mouth open and the words right on the tip of her tongue, so casual, as if she'd told him she loved him a hundred times before. At the very last second she snapped her mouth shut and turned away, shocked that she'd almost said them out loud. That she'd thought them at all. She tossed everything back in her bag, ran a brush through her hair, and turned back to him, pasting a smile on her face. "Ready."

"In under ten minutes. A true goddess."

She kissed him soundly on the mouth. "Flattery will get you everywhere." He grabbed her, making her squeal and swat at his roving hands. "Later." She turned into his arms. "Much later."

His smile faded and he leaned in and gave her a kiss so sweet her heart melted. He leaned his fore-head against hers. "I'll try to be with you all the time,

Tali. If for any reason we have to separate, when you attend to the queen, know I'll be as close as I can be." He paused, then pressed his fingers against her heart. "And I'll always be here."

She blinked hard against the sudden rush of tears. All she could do was nod and press her hand over his fingers. "Thanks," she finally managed. "Let's go."

Fingers linked, they followed the guard through the screen and were immediately swallowed by an even larger cadre of black-and-gold-suited men. They were escorted swiftly through a maze of corridors that were unfamiliar to Talia. She tried not to worry about what would be expected of her today. She'd take it as it came and do the best she could. What else could she do? The pep talk did little to help. The constant pressure of Archer's hand in hers did far more. She decided then that the queen would have to put up a good argument for separating the two of them.

She needed him. She didn't want to stop needing him. Dangerous, she knew, but right now she could have cared less. She would handle whatever she had to handle just as she had since she was six years old. But they would damn well have to accept Archer's presence beside her as she handled it.

He tugged her hand and winked as the guards pulled up. "No worries?"

"I'm trying."

Then the painted screen before them became transparent and they were ushered through. Just as quickly, the guards seemed to melt back through the screen, leaving them standing alone in the middle of an empty room with stone walls.

Talia's grip on his hand tightened. "Where are we?"

Before he could answer, the wall in front of them began to slide to the left. Archer immediately pulled

Talia behind him, his hand going to the small of his back for a weapon.

A small, square box lowered and hovered at the entrance to a small chamber. The monitor on the front flickered to life and the queen's voice filled the room, even though the tiny screen itself remained dark. "Mr. Archer, it is urgent that I speak with you. Miss Trahaern, I thought you might like to use the time to explore the room behind this wall. It was your mother's chamber, used by her during her service to the crown, and by all royal healers before her. As no one was left to take her place, my father had this room sealed after the search for her was abandoned. His orders were to only open it when the royal healer returned, and it has remained sealed for all the years since your mother's disappearance. I have no idea what lies inside but I ask that you do not remove anything without discussing it with me first. This is not an entirely unselfish act as I fervently hope you will find something within the room that will help me and my people. If you do, please alert the guards and you will be brought to me immediately." There was a pause and her voice was less strident as she added, "I wish I could offer you more specific tutelage, but regretfully this is all there is."

Talia had lost her breath. "Th-thank you," she managed, wishing she had the words to express her gratitude for this opportunity.

"Mr. Archer, the guards will escort you to me." The hum of the communicator shut off abruptly and it whizzed directly upward into a ceiling compartment, leaving them unable to argue against their imminent separation.

Talia turned to him. "Go. I'll be okay."

Archer's eyes widened. "You think so, do you?

You wouldn't know Chamberlain if you bumped into him, much less anyone working for him."

Talia placed her hand on his arm. "I want this time alone with my mother's things. Can you understand? Surely the queen will leave some of her personal guard."

She didn't want him to feel that she needed him every second, though in truth, she didn't want him to leave. Not because she feared for her safety, but because she wanted to share this time with him. It was special to her and so was he. But it was best if she remained on her own as much as possible. Wouldn't she have to soon enough anyway?

"I understand," he said.

She saw the quick flash of hurt come and go in his eyes. She hated the spurt of hope that gave her. Not that she wanted to hurt him, but knowing that she could— She stopped thinking altogether when Archer slid a small, harmless-looking piece of black plastic from a side pocket in his trousers and pressed it in her palm. "Slide this gauge from left to right to adjust the power. Aim like so." He lifted her arm. "And press here." He pressed his finger over hers and a white hot-beam shot out of the little instrument, making it vibrate in her hands and sending her stumbling back against him. It also left a nasty-looking hole in the stone wall across from them.

"My God," she murmured, looking down at the not-so-harmless piece of plastic.

"Don't let it out of your reach. Keep it on you at all times." He turned her face to his. "Promise me."

She merely nodded, still stunned by what she'd just done. "Won't the queen be a little miffed at the damage?"

"I imagine the queen has more important things on her mind. The guards didn't come running, which assures me this room is soundproof and probably quite secure." He looked away, sighed, then looked back at her. "I also imagine there is some kind of surveillance here, as there probably is everywhere inside the castle. Keep that in mind."

Talia nodded, not really surprised. Then as the ramifications sank in, she gasped. "You don't mean . . . Last night . . ." She realized then why he'd kept her covered after dinner. He must have realized it then.

"Talia, I'm sorry, if I'd thought— And I'm not certain anyhow, but it's wise to be cautious."

She felt her outrage and mortification lessen somewhat in the face of his obvious misery. "It's okay." She pressed her hand to his chest. "Really." She pasted a grin on her face. "At least we gave them quite a show, eh?"

He pulled her into his arms and kissed her soundly. "I've never met anyone like you, Talia Trahaern." He held her close and she thought he murmured something else, but it was muffled against her hair. Then he set her back and reluctantly let her go. "Don't leave here until I return. If you get in a bind, scream for the guards first, then use that." He nodded to the weapon still in her hand.

"Promise."

The door slid open then and a small squad of guards came in and silently surrounded Archer. They didn't even blink at the scorch mark on the wall. She surreptitiously scanned the ceilings and walls, certain now that Archer was right and they were being observed somehow.

Archer kept his gaze solidly on hers and backed out of the room. Then the wall screen solidified and he was gone.

For the first time in what felt like a very long while she was alone. Well, alone with whoever was watching. She turned back toward her mother's chamber and tried to keep her cool. Not an easy job seeing that she was on her own in a place and time of which she had no real knowledge . . . and was now faced with her mother's real past and identity.

She carefully made sure the power gauge was all the way to the left and slid the little zapper thing into the side pocket of her dress. Then she squared her shoulders, took a deep breath, and walked up to the wall. *What was she supposed to say? Open sesame?*

That turned out to be unnecessary. The wall dissolved in front of her . . . allowing her to walk into her mother's workroom. Fear and wonder, edged with grief, formed a tight ball in her stomach as she took the first tentative step inside.

She didn't even know where to begin. The room smelled dank, the air somewhat stale, though a faint herbal scent lingered. Had Catriona really left the room sealed as her father had wished? Considering her illness, Talia would think she'd have left no stone unturned. But as she moved farther into the room, she felt the unassailable sensation of emptiness, disuse, abandonment. She rubbed at her arms, wondering if the feeling was real or a fabrication of her mind.

Not that it mattered. She took stock of the room's contents. A long counterlike table ran down one side of the small room and there were several stools tucked under it. The countertop was lined with compartments and various bottles, all of which appeared to be empty upon a cursory inspection. Two rows of shelves were braced above the countertop, each with more bottles and containers, also empty. A large desk was positioned in the corner and a chair sat in the opposite corner. She ran her finger along the counter as she came further into the room and noticed there wasn't any dust. "When they seal a room, they really seal it," she murmured. Still, it seemed odd that there was nothing in any of the containers. If they'd just evaporated or turned to dust, wouldn't the rest of the room be dusty, too? It did explain the stale scent. The room had been airless for years.

She walked over to the chair and sat in it. Immediately a pool of light from some unknown source above winked on, bathing her in a soft white beam. "Well, isn't that neato." She leaned back and the chair actually felt as if it were morphing. She started to jump out of it, but stopped when she realized that it was merely changing to fit her body. "Oh, I want one of these."

She sat there for a moment and tears gathered in her eyes as she tried to picture her mother here in this very room. She blinked back the tears and looked around. The desk had a plain black surface and she'd bet there was nothing in the drawers, either. She recalled the queen's admonishment not to take anything with her. "What in the hell would I take?"

With a sigh, she stood and walked over to the desk anyway, settling into the chair behind it. It didn't do that neat morph thing, but it was comfortable nonetheless. She opened the center drawer and it was empty as expected. How did the queen expect her to learn anything in here? Maybe the king had taken everything out when her mother hadn't been found and sealed the room without telling anyone he'd emptied it first. And the queen hadn't known.

She leaned back and tried to stave off a wave of disappointment. Try as she might, there was no sense of her mother, or anyone else, in this sterile room.

She absently slid open a side drawer, thinking she should summon the guard and try and catch up to

Archer. A small black box rested in the bottom of the deep drawer. Talia forgot about the guard and pulled it out.

She set it on the desktop and turned it all around, but it appeared to be a solid cube with no lid or opening of any kind. "Perfect." She picked it up and examined it more closely. "It's a Rubik's Cube nightmare."

She put it down and searched the other drawers. Empty. She slid open the top one again and ran her hand back inside the long, flat drawer. Still nothing.

She leaned back and stared into the shiny black surface, trying to see past her reflection to what lay inside. Surely it held something. She looked at her reflection, thought about the picture of her mother, tried to imagine her holding this very cube, and seeing her own reflection, one that looked so similar to the one Talia saw now. "Mum," she whispered, reaching . . . for what, she didn't know.

Then slowly, so slowly she thought she was imagining it, the cube glowed to life. Stunned, she sat back, but said nothing and held the cube gingerly, hoping—praying—it wouldn't go dark again. Carefully she studied it; each side reflected a picture much like a video screen.

She realized each side was part of the room she sat in, only in the cube screen, the jars and bottles lining the counter were no longer empty. She gasped and turned it to show the wall of shelves. Crammed full of books. Then she looked at the desk and she did drop the cube then, which clattered harmlessly to the desk surface, but thankfully remained alive. The desk in the cube screen was cluttered with an enormous array of books, papers, and all sorts of odd items. But it was the person sitting behind the desk that had caught her full attention. It was her!

How did she make the scene in the cube come to

real life? she wondered. Maybe the empty shelves and counter were an illusion meant to protect the healer's craft. So it would appear empty to all but the healer who occupied it. Ingenious.

"Or maybe it's all a hallucination." But at this point she was willing to believe anything was indeed possible. She turned the cube over and over, wondering how to make the room match the vision in the cube.

"Why can't anything be easy?" she muttered, turning the cube in her hands once again. "I am Talia Trahaern, the royal healer," she intoned, then made a face. "And I sound ridiculous." She looked at herself sitting behind the cluttered desk in the cube, then swept her hand over the surface. Nothing was there. "Dammit."

Then the person inside the cube spoke and she froze, unable to do so much as blink. Because it wasn't her own voice that spoke to her. It was her mother's.

"I am sealing this record," she said, the lilting Welsh accent so pure in her voice Talia's eyes instantly burned with tears. "There is trouble afoot and I can't be certain even this sanctuary won't be breached."

Talia's breath caught and she found herself stroking the tiny image of her mother.

"This will only open again for me, Cynan." There was a pause and Talia watched her mother's hand disappear beneath the desk. "Or the one who follows me."

Tears streamed unheeded down Talia's face. "Oh, Mummy." Talia swallowed against the tight lump in her throat. Had her mother been stroking her burgeoning belly as she said those words? Talia knew she had.

"But I don't know how to open it, Mum," she said on a choked whisper.

Cynan. There had been such warmth in her voice when she'd said the king's name. Just Cynan. Not His Royal Highness or any other title of honor. Perhaps they'd become close during her attendance to him. She supposed her mother's role would have made her a valued guide and aide to the king.

"Time is of the essence. Record, seal," her mother said. Then the cube went black.

"No!" Talia scooped it up and turned it over and over. "Don't go! Come back!" She peered frantically into it. "I am Talia Trahaern," she said, desperation in her voice. "I am the royal healer." But the cube remained a cold, solid black, making Talia wonder for one hysterical moment if she indeed had been hallucinating the whole thing.

But she hadn't. And once again, she hadn't been able to say good-bye to her mother.

She stared into the cube, reaching out with everything she had, but all she saw was her reflection once again.

Now what? Feeling drained and emotionally exhausted, Talia wiped at her face and sniffed back fresh tears as she again looked about the empty chamber. "Maybe I'm not a healer," she whispered, finally giving voice to her greatest fear. Maybe her mother hadn't known it when she carried her, but had figured it out after. Could something have happened because she was born in the past? Perhaps that was why her mother hadn't told her, never trained her.

"And perhaps I'm losing what is left of my mind."

She looked at the cube. Maybe she should take it to the queen, see if there was a way to view her mother's message again. She stood and walked toward the antechamber, but the instant she passed through the doorway, the cube vanished. She gasped and whirled around, only to find it perched on the desktop. "Okay," she said shakily. So it wasn't leaving the room.

But she was. She put the cube back in the drawer and walked from the room to the antechamber. "Guard," she called loudly. "I'm ready to leave."

As the wall in front of her turned translucent, she took one last look behind her. The wall was already materializing, closing the room from her view.

"Good-bye, Mummy," she whispered. And she did feel a sense of peace then, and was grateful for this one last connection with the only family she'd ever had. "I love you."

Chapter 20

*A*rcher had a bad feeling about this meeting. He assured himself that the queen had Talia under surveillance and wouldn't let anyone harm her. Guards had remained on duty all along the passageway. She'd be fine.

He admitted that what was really bugging him wasn't so much relinquishing his role of protector as not being there when she went through her mother's things. He understood that it was a private moment for her. He simply wanted to share all her moments, private and otherwise.

The guards stopped and he was ushered into another room. Marletta awaited him on the other side. "Her Royal Highness is extremely fatigued. Please keep that in mind during the course of your meeting."

Archer nodded, wanting to hurry so he could return to Talia.

She ushered him through another hidden wall to a short passageway, then through a small door that led into the same room he and Talia had been in yesterday. Only this time there was no darkness. The room wasn't brightly lit, but he could see Catriona clearly.

The queen was abed, as before. He was startled to see that she looked considerably more fragile. Her youth was far more apparent beneath sallow skin and limp hair. Her thinness made her swollen belly look oddly misshapen in contrast. Her eyes, however, were still sharp and quite focused. "Thank you, Marletta. Did you receive the results?"

The assistant looked surprised by the question and darted a look at Archer, as if the matter were personal and she was surprised the queen had mentioned it in front of him. She nodded. "Yes, Your Highness."

There was a long pause and Archer could feel the tension in the room grow.

"And are they as I assumed?"

Marletta made no eye contact with him this time, in fact she seemed to stand more rigidly apart from him. "Your Highness—" She stepped forward and whispered, "Catriona, really, don't you—"

"Yes or no?" The imperious tone left no room for equivocation.

Marletta regained her composure. "Yes. They are what you assumed."

The queen showed no visible response to the news, but her voice was very tight when she responded. "Thank you, Marletta. Tell Tibbus I appreciate his swiftness." She paused to clear her throat. "Please leave us now."

Archer thought her assistant was going to argue, but she merely tightened her mouth and nodded, then left quietly through the door they'd entered yesterday.

"Mr. Archer, I must have more information from you."

He faced her squarely. "I have told you all I can."

"Perhaps and perhaps not. I would like to speak with Baleweg."

"As I said yesterday, he's not comfortable at

court. It would draw undue attention to him and that wouldn't be wise for Talia, or for you."

The queen considered this, then said, "I would ask something else of you, then."

"What would that be?"

"I want more information on the Dark One. To better help me understand just how powerful Chamberlain's sway might be. I need to know how far his assistance with Chamberlain reaches. I feel it likely extends beyond attempting to thwart our mission to return the healer to court."

Archer agreed she had a point, but said nothing.

"I understand the wisdom of keeping the Old One at a distance from this court, but in lieu of that, I would like you to go to him and request his help in this matter. Surely he knows more about his counterpart than he's revealed thus far."

"Why not do something about Chamberlain now? Remove him from parliament, strip him of his title and power."

"With or without the Dark One's assistance, Chamberlain is a danger to me. As I said before, I do not have the proof I require for a swift judgment in parliament. There would be severe political repercussions if I failed, and Chamberlain has a large enough following as it is."

"Loyalty that comes under penalty of threat—"

"—is still loyalty," the queen rejoined. "I will reward the Old One's assistance in whatever manner he wishes."

"It's been my experience that Baleweg is not motivated by reward."

"Ah, yes. His loyalty is to our departed royal healer." She paused a long moment, as if deliberating, then abruptly said, "As this has been a day for revelations, there is another matter I must discuss with you. Something that has nagged at me since meeting Miss Trahaern yesterday. It regards a story told so long ago I'm sure it's more myth than fact, but at the risk of appearing ridiculous, I ask anyway." She eyed him steadily. "I have no real understanding of what powers the Old One and the Dark One have mastered, but the myth stands that they can transcend time and move from place to place by the sheer power of their minds." She focused on him directly. "Do you know anything about that?"

For several moments Archer debated what to reveal but realized that there was no point in skirting the truth any longer. "I know that their powers are great. And yes, the manipulation of time is among their achievements. I don't know how they do it, or all the rules of nature that allow it to happen. But it does."

"Damn." Her quiet vehemence surprised him. "How stupidly arrogant and blind I have been." She suddenly gripped her head and it was clear she was in an extreme amount of pain. Archer went to step forward, but she stopped him immediately. "Come no closer." She took a moment to manage the pain, but Archer remained concerned. He understood her illness to be the sort that ravaged the body from the inside, not contagious in any way. Maybe she simply couldn't stand the fact that she must appear so weak in front of another. That he could understand.

"Should I call for Marletta?"

She shook her head. With her eyes still squeezed shut, she asked, "Is that where you found her? In another time?"

Archer saw no reason to hedge any longer. "Yes."

She opened her eyes, her expression severe, but the resentment was aimed at herself. "My father was certain Eleri had managed to leave this time. No one believed him, no one. Even after he married and I was born, he persisted in his belief. As I grew older, I joined those who thought my father was merely clinging to false hopes. I pitied him his weakness and thought him a fool."

She rubbed again at her head.

Archer hated feeling so helpless in the face of her obvious suffering. She was worsening by the moment. "You should let Talia see you. Maybe she learned something from her mother's room today—"

The queen lifted her hand. "That will not come to pass."

She sounded so certain, so final. He wasn't the type who gave up and he knew all about fighting for his life. He'd always thought of the queen the same way. "How can you be so certain? Why did you have me track her down in the first place?"

She looked sharply at him. "Call it the last, desperate act of a dying woman. I had no other hope, nothing to lose. Frankly, I never thought you'd find her mother and of course I had no idea there was a daughter." She stopped again, her attention shifting, as if she were grappling with some other, insurmountable situation. "I still can't believe it," she said, almost under her breath. "I should have believed him. Perhaps if we'd had more faith in him, he'd have had the support necessary to find her sooner," she said, her voice filled with quiet despair. "My mother was so bitter . . . so bitter. And I let that bitterness color my perception of—" She broke off and dipped her head. "If only I'd trusted him, understood more clearly what I know now. Things could have been so different."

Archer had never paid any real attention to the royal family. Everyone had known that Cynan and his daughter were somewhat reserved around each other, but he thought that all royals were naturally stiff and formal. "You do have faith in him," he said. "Maybe it just took being that desperate to realize it. Otherwise you would have never considered hiring me, to try again when everyone else except your father had accepted failure."

She looked to him, surprised.

"I don't claim to know anything about you, or him. But I imagine he understood your skepticism," Archer continued. "And yet I suspect he would be fiercely proud of you. Everything you've done for your kingdom, your people, would be considered an honor to him." Archer knew he'd far overstepped his bounds. But right now he wasn't talking to her as his queen, but as someone struggling with issues of life and death, love and hate. Those he understood well.

"I wouldn't have expected such insight into the heart from you," she said, finally looking at him. "You speak as if it comes from experience. Yet I know your past to be anything but heartwarming."

Archer recalled her allusion to his past on their first meeting. His gaze narrowed. "What do you know of that?"

"I prefer to know as much as possible about those I hire. Good business practice." A very slight smile curved her lips. "If it's any consolation, it took some digging." Her mouth smoothed and he could see her struggle against the pain. "So if your insight didn't come from your past, perhaps there is someone new you learned such wisdom from."

Archer thought of his heart and immediately pictured Talia. "Perhaps there is."

Her gaze narrowed then and he was pleased to see a certain sharpness return, even if he was the focus of it. "Talia?"

He saw no reason to deny it. After all, she knew

better than anyone where they'd spent the night. "Yes."

"I must admit I am surprised once again. I hadn't placed such importance on your liaison. You haven't known each other long." Her mouth twisted into a dry smile. "But then I should be used to the suddenness of love." The smile vanished, a frown suddenly replacing it as if another thought had just occurred to her. "You have plans, then?"

He was surprised by the question and her apparent disapproval of the possibility. Odd that she didn't mind him having wild sex with Talia in her own castle, but was unhappy thinking it might be more than that. However, now was not the time for arguing about his worthiness or lack thereof. Especially given his answer. "There are no plans. Talia's only commitment when she came here was to help you and your unborn child. It remains that way."

"How very mature, your love for her. I don't think I could be quite so generous." Her gaze drifted to her stomach and she covered it almost protectively with her hands.

Archer realized how distinctly different she was now in contrast to the day she'd hired him. It was clear now that this baby meant a great deal more to her than insurance that the House of Dalwyn would continue their rule.

"Surely if she's come this far, you should let her try. You said yourself you had nothing to lose."

The queen didn't look at him. She just kept rubbing her hands over her stomach.

Archer felt something primal shift within him as he watched her stroke her unborn child. He had always valued the preciousness of life, or he wouldn't have fought so hard to keep his intact. But this touched him in some deeper place. The vulnerability of the child within her called to a part of him he'd thought long buried. And despite the fact that he better than anyone knew that not everyone shared the value he placed on it, he couldn't look at the queen's face at this moment and not believe that she felt the same way.

"Please," he said as gently as he knew how. "Let me get Talia. Let her try."

She was silent for so long that Archer finally wondered if he shouldn't simply make a quiet retreat, find Talia, and bring her back here to try and do whatever could be done. He couldn't accept that Catriona wouldn't at least try.

Then a smile slowly curved the young queen's lips. There was such heartbreaking sadness in it that he couldn't look away. And yet, when she looked at him, what he saw in the depths of that unimaginable sadness and pain . . . was hope.

She reached to her side and pressed a small device that lay on her bed. "Bring Talia Trahaern to me."

Archer's heart began to pound. She was going to fight! But even as he tightened his fist in silent victory, he worried about Talia. It had been one thing to offer Talia's help when he was thinking only of the dying woman in front of him. But now that the queen was calling for her, Archer's concerns shifted to what Talia would be put through and damned himself for being so anxious to put her there.

Still, he knew that if she were here, she'd be pushing the same issues, doing whatever she could to help and damn the toll it took on herself. That was who she was. There was always the hope for a miracle.

"Allow me to escort her," he said, thinking at least

he could prepare Talia somewhat, warn her, comfort her.

The queen was once again staring at her hands rubbing her stomach. "She is already on her way." She looked up at him, her expression now almost beatific. "Finally, I think I have found a solution."

Chapter 21

Talia left the healer's chamber in the company of six personal royal guards. She wondered where Archer was.

The head guard stopped short just outside the room. "Your gazzer, please."

She almost ran into him. "My—what?"

The guard sent a pointed look to her side pocket. He extended his hand. "Please."

"Oh." She fumbled in her pocket and handed Archer's zapper thing to the guard, who promptly handed it to another one next to him, who in turn headed off down a different passageway. "It's Archer's," she added, not wanting them to dispose of something that wasn't hers. He'd be mad enough when he discovered she'd given it up without a fight, though frankly she was relieved not to have the deadly thing in her pocket. She wasn't cut out to be armed and dangerous. In fact, she was surprised Archer had been allowed to remain armed inside the castle. Maybe the queen felt better with him guarding her as well as her own guards.

"It is being returned to him now. Follow me, please."

She fell into step behind him. "Is he still with the queen?"

"The queen wishes a private consultation with you."

Talia nodded, but her knees felt a bit wobbly. Consultation? Was she expected to be a full-fledged healer now that she'd spent an hour or two with her mother's things? She hoped not. Tears threatened again and she pushed them away. She'd gotten to see her mother, hear her voice. She had new memories now. She'd cling to them.

She stopped suddenly as a shocking wave of pain assaulted her. Instinctively she threw up a mental block against it, but it still left her breathless and leaning weakly against the wall. Her head throbbed. *Where had that come from? And who?*

"Are you all right, Miss Trahaern?"

Two of the guards stopped beside her. One turned to bark orders at another but Talia quickly intervened. "No, that's okay. I'm okay." That was a lie, but a necessary one. "Let's continue. Please."

The guard paused, looking to his commander, who finally nodded tersely.

Talia was given no time to analyze what had just happened to her, however, and less time to fully recover.

They stopped moments later and the guard motioned for her to move in front of him. A large painting of two golden lions graced the wall in front of him. "You will be admitted now."

Talia nodded, then blew out a shaky breath. The screen turned transparent and she stepped into a dimly lit room. She took a moment to try and adjust her eyes. It was lighter in here than yesterday, but darker than the hallway.

"Come closer."

Talia started, then peered through the gloom toward the towering four-poster bed that dominated

the far end of the room. She looked quickly around
for Archer, but he wasn't there. Talia could see the
queen resting on the bed. Actually, she looked more
like a child from this distance, her small form hardly
taking up any space at all.

As she moved closer, the first thing she noticed
was the mound under the blanket that was her
stomach. Talia felt her own stomach grip tightly. *Dear
Lord, what had she honestly thought, coming here?* This was
no game. She had no skills to help this poor
woman. And what if she died, and God help her, the
baby, too, while Talia was with her? Her steps faltered.

"Closer, please." Her voice was well modulated,
and quite beautiful, but much weaker and not nearly
as imperious as it had been the night before.

Talia took a steadying breath and stepped closer.
The instant her gaze landed on Catriona's face, it
was as if her body had stepped beyond itself. She
froze as her mind leaped forward without her even
attempting it. She'd been so busy worrying that she
hadn't put up any guards at all. The connection was
swift and more powerful than anything she'd ever
felt in her life.

And she knew immediately who she'd connected
with in the passageway. *Intense and overwhelming pain.*
Talia's knees buckled under the force of the pain,
but she held her ground. *No one must see. Must stay strong.
For the kingdom. For my child.* Talia gripped her stomach,
feeling movement where she knew there was none.
Such a sweet sensation of fullness. *Joy, such indescribable
joy, feeling him move inside me.* Talia's throat closed over.
*Fear, deep abiding fear of the world I'm bringing him into. Just let
him live, please God, just let him live.* Tears burned in her
eyes. *Give him my strength and he'll be okay. Strength, must have
strength.* Talia locked her knees and focused her own
strength, wanting nothing more than to send it to

that unborn child. Oh, but the pain, the squeezing, wrenching pain. *Now that I've found her. Just a little longer . . .* Found who?

Talia wrenched herself back. Her skin was so damp her dress clung to her. She felt as if she'd just run a dozen miles. Her breath came in short gasps and she pressed one hand over her stomach, another over her galloping heart.

"Talia?"

She jumped. Realizing she must look like a loon, standing there panting and swaying, she tried hard to regain her outward focus, but the experience had been overwhelming. So overwhelming that she was afraid to even look at the queen again.

"Don't be afraid of our connection," Catriona said softly.

Talia kept her gaze fixed on the foot of the bed. "I'm—I'm sorry," she managed hoarsely. "I wasn't even trying to—"

"Don't be sorry. I had wondered about it yesterday when there was no apparent connection. You must have developed a great deal of control over your gift."

The queen sounded somewhat stronger. Talia shivered as she realized what she'd done. She knew that during a connection with an animal in pain, taking on that pain lessened the animal's suffering. At least for the duration of the connection. Unfortunately, when the connection ended, so did the respite for the animal. Nothing else would be changed. She was not a healer.

Talia thought of the suffering of the woman before her and was almost overwhelmed again by what she'd just experienced during their connection. She'd had no idea the queen was in such constant agony. Despite her fragile appearance, she managed to give such regal authority to her every word. Talia felt humbled and wished there was something more she could do for her.

"Have no fear, Talia, you just soothed a goodly number of my remaining fears."

Talia worked to steady her breath before she finally faced Catriona once again. This time she stayed within herself, but her legs shook and her fingers trembled with the effort. "I think you did just the opposite to me," she said with a shaky smile.

Catriona smiled then, and Talia was startled by the beauty that lay beneath the illness-ravaged face. She was so thin, too thin to be facing impending motherhood. Talia looked toward her stomach, reliving that miraculous moment when she'd felt the pressure of a child in her own belly.

"How far along are you?" she blurted, then stopped as the queen's words echoed in her ears. *You just soothed a goodly number of my remaining fears.* Did the queen really think that because she had taken on a measure of her pain, however temporarily, she was truly a real healer?

"Twenty-nine weeks," the queen answered.

Talia's attention returned to the queen's stomach. *Twenty-nine. That was good, wasn't it?* Even in her time they managed to save babies who were born extremely early. Certainly they'd improved on that over time.

"I don't want to build up false hopes," Talia said, knowing she had to get this out now. "I have no natural healing abilities like my mother did. I know you said it's hereditary, so I don't know why I don't, but I don't. As an empath, I can take on your pain, but that won't heal you. Surely there are doctors who could—"

The queen was shaking her head. "They exhausted their skills early on. The only method left to me now has only a small possibility of working and would certainly end my baby's chance at survival. I can't do that." She rubbed her stomach, then smiled at Talia. "Please stop worrying. I am not expecting to survive this. I only want to ensure that he does."

Talia was more confused than ever. "How do you think I can help the baby?"

"Not in the way I'd hoped when I first sent Archer after you." She motioned to a large chair positioned near the bed. "Please, sit. I'll have Marletta bring some tea."

Talia sank gratefully into the chair, but waved off the offer of tea. "No, thank you." She looked up to find the queen studying her with disconcerting frankness.

"You really do bear an amazing resemblance to your mother."

"Thank you."

"Of course I never knew your mother but my father kept images of her close by for the remainder of his life."

That information made Talia pause. "I found some sort of cube today, in my mother's chamber. Apparently she locked the contents of the room under some sort of spell or illusion. There was a message in it, though. She said she had the key to open it, or, failing that, the next healer would. But I don't know how. I tried. The cube cannot be taken from the room, either. I'm sorry."

Catriona waved away her concern. "I am sorry there wasn't more for you to look through, for your own sake. But there is little to be done for it now."

Talia paused, then said, "My mother . . . she mentioned your father's name . . ."

The queen's gaze sharpened. "Yes? Explain yourself."

Talia straightened, reminded again whose presence she was in. "It was nothing, really. Just the way she said his name. I got the feeling they were close. I imagine my mother's role was a trusted one, so that makes sense. I guess I was just warmed by the idea that she seemed close to your family. I know it wasn't easy for her to leave."

The queen's focus intensified. "You know why she left, do you not?"

"She was pregnant with me. Baleweg told me it cost her a great deal to turn her back on her obligations and leave, but there had been threats against her and she was afraid for my life if she didn't."

The queen closed her eyes and Talia started to rise, automatically opening herself up to find out what was wrong.

"Don't," Catriona said, her eyes remaining shut. "It's all right. I'm just . . . a little overwhelmed. I already had the proof but . . . I suppose I had to hear it from you."

Confused, Talia had pulled back before connecting with her. She had no idea what the queen was talking about. "Hear what from me?"

"Did you not wonder at the depth of our connection? You do know that empaths only connect with those they care deeply about, or are connected to in some way."

"Yes, I know that. I assumed it was because you are a royal, and I am destined from birth to . . . to serve you somehow."

Catriona shook her head. "Many rules apply between royal and healer, but that is not what forged the bond you felt today. Empathy is not exclusive to healers. In fact, it is a somewhat common ability. At least in this time, if not in yours—the one in which you were raised."

Talia opened her mouth, then shut it again. So she knew.

The queen smiled lightly. "Yes, I am aware that

the Old One helped to hide your mother in the distant past. Again I wish to tell you of my gratitude that you so willingly came to my rescue. I would like to think I'd have made such a selfless gesture, but I am learning that I am a far more petty and closed-minded person than I thought myself to be."

Talia had no idea what to say to that.

"As you have also discovered," she went on, "you are not a healer. That is not the source of our connection."

"I don't understand."

"Did your mother marry after leaving this time?"

"No, she never did."

"Did you wonder who your father was? Did you perhaps come back in hopes of discovering who he was?"

"I have wondered, of course, but no, actually, I never thought of looking for him here." She was somewhat surprised about that, given what she and Devin had talked about the night before. But it had never even occurred to her. "Do you know who he is? Is he—?" She couldn't get the words past a suddenly tight throat.

But Catriona was already shaking her head. "He is no longer living."

Her breath caught. "Then you know who he was?"

"Oh, yes. Tell me this. Do you have a birthmark? Anywhere on you, the shape of a small crescent moon?"

Talia shrank back in her seat, mortified beyond belief. "You *were* watching!"

Catriona looked confused, then actually laughed. It ended on a wrenching cough that had Talia leaping from her seat.

The queen managed to wave her away. "It's all right," she rasped. "Sit, sit." She took a moment to recover her breath. "I assume you mean that you think the room you shared with Mr. Archer last night was monitored. It is, as are all rooms in this castle save my chamber and the healer's. But trust that no one was watching you last night."

Talia let out a relieved laugh of her own. "Thank God." Then she sat up again. "Then how did you know—?"

The queen lifted her hand and drew her gown off her shoulder. There, above her right breast, was a small crescent moon. She smiled at Talia. "It's hereditary. From our father."

Talia's mouth open and shut several times, but nothing came out as the reality of what she was insinuating came crashing over her. *Dear God.* It couldn't be.

King Cynan was her father. Her father was a king. All those fairy tales her mother had told her about a brave king who would treasure a little girl who could talk to animals . . . she'd never once guessed.

"We are sisters, Talia," Catriona said. "Half sisters, but sisters to be certain. And that is why you will never be a healer. Had any other fathered you, you would have retained your mother's skills. But royal blood can never mix with a healer's blood. It ends the line."

Talia sat back limply in the chair, her skin cold and clammy. Her mother had left because she'd been carrying the king's child. Her! She couldn't grasp it all, it was too much. "Why didn't she tell me?" Though Talia realized now that in her own way, she had. "And wouldn't she have known I wouldn't have her skills?"

"I can't say, though I would imagine she did know. At least my father would certainly have told her, had he known." She stopped and frowned.

"What?"

"Maybe he never knew about you. It's possible

she also realized that if she gave birth to you here, once it became apparent that you didn't have her skills . . . people would know of their relationship."

"So she left to protect me and your—our—father."

"I don't know. We'll never know."

Talia was still trying to take all this in. "But you knew. How long have you known?"

"I never even knew of your existence until yesterday, though now I am amazed I never put it together."

"What do you mean?"

"My father spent his whole life searching for your mother. He made it out to be his royal duty to his healer, but my mother soon suspected it was more. He never gave up looking, not really. He was convinced she'd traveled through time and it was largely through my mother's behind-the-scene efforts that he was not taken seriously. Though my father denied the affair, she was quite jealous and her bitterness colored everything she did.

"I'm ashamed to say that I allowed it to color my perception of my father, as well. Not that I knew of the love affair, I only knew my mother held some deep-seated resentment toward him and it filtered down to me. I was the recipient of her diaries upon her death and the details were all there. It was a well-guarded secret. No one ever knew. And naturally I never told anyone." She fell silent, her focus drifting inward. "All those years," she said softly. "Wasted. I should have trusted him, or at least given him a chance." Catriona looked back at her. "Now that I think back on it, I'm sure my father never knew. If he had known Eleri carried his child, nothing would have stopped him from doing whatever it took to find her, even if it meant destroying his kingdom to do it." She shook her head. "I know my mother never knew. No one knew Eleri was leaving

until it was too late. I was stunned when you told me
who you were."

Talia knew exactly how she felt.

"I will admit my first reaction was suspicion," she
went on. "You were being somewhat evasive and it all
seemed too neat a package. I'll apologize to you now,
but when I saw you and Archer had grown . . . well,
close, I put you in that room for the sole reason of
obtaining a pure sample of your DNA. I had it tested
while you were in your mother's room." She talked
over Talia's gasp. "I know it seems rather calculated,
but there is a great deal at stake here and I'd do far
more than that to ensure that I'm not being drawn
into a trap."

"Trap?"

"If you had indeed figured out that you had
Dalwyn blood in your veins, then it was reasonable
to suspect you might be in cahoots with Chamberlain to take over the throne."

Talia's jaw dropped. "You've got to be kidding."

"I had to be cautious. The only curious thing was
that you did not use your empathic skills to connect
with me, probe me for your own gain. In fact, you
seemed to fight against it."

"I was protecting myself. I didn't know what I was
walking into."

"You also seemed rather earnest, if uncertain,
about helping me. You could have been faking that,
but I didn't think so. I observed you in the passageways and the antechamber with Archer, watched as
you prepared yourself to enter your mother's room.
Your demeanor is not that of a predator. Then,
when you arrived today and the connection was in-
stantaneous, I knew all I had to know. You truly had
no idea, did you?"

Talia shook her head, amazed at the intrigues and

assignations that had been swirling around her, all without her knowledge or suspicion. "Archer was right," she muttered. "I'm not cut out to survive at court."

"You will learn."

Talia's head jerked up. "Surely you don't still think I want to take what is not—"

Catriona's expression smoothed, but her eyes were lit with an inner light. Talia recognized it. It was hope. "I know you didn't come here planning to be part of the royal family, but here you are anyway. And seeing that you are here, you must take your rightful place in it."

If Talia had thought herself panicked over the burden of healing this young woman, she was completely overwhelmed now. "You can't be serious."

Catriona frowned. "Surely when you returned, assuming you were the royal healer, you intended to stay here? Your position has merely undertaken an extreme transformation." She smiled. "No need to look so horrified. I assure you I will set everything up before I die."

Talia leaped to her feet. "How can you say that? And how can you talk about your own death so cavalierly? I am not royalty, despite what my DNA says. I am not cut out to run anything more than my animal shelter back home in Connecticut, year two thousand and one." She paced. "Please don't think me ungrateful, but I came here planning to do whatever I could to help you, then go back home."

"This is your home." A touch of the imperious returned to her tone. "This is where you belong." Her tone softened as she touched her stomach. "We are your family. Your only family."

Family. What about her mother's family? There was only one person she knew that her mother had been close to. Baleweg. But she'd asked him about her father and believed even now he hadn't known. Or he'd have known she wasn't a healer. But someone had known, someone had suspected. Or had Eleri merely been paranoid to think someone would try to find her and kill her or her half-royal child? Then a part of what Catriona had told her of her own mother, about her bitterness, came back to her and she looked to the queen, a sick feeling in her stomach. "Are you sure your mother never knew about me? Or suspected?"

The queen stilled. "Why do you ask?"

"Because someone knew. Someone tried to kill my mother here. It's why she left. And she was concerned later; that's why she moved us around so much." She gasped as she put the rest together. "And whoever knew must have used the Dark One's powers to have her followed. Baleweg honored her request to be left alone and I believe him. Which leaves Emrys as the only other one who could have followed her through time." She thought about the car crash that had claimed her mother's life. "And perhaps killed her."

"And you think my mother was behind this?" Catriona's face grew even paler.

"Who else would have hated Eleri enough? Was your mother in Cynan's life before my mother left?"

The queen nodded. "They weren't romantically linked then, but soon after." She paused and rubbed at her belly.

Talia, despite the series of shocks she had been subjected to, felt immediately contrite. "I'm sorry, I shouldn't be questioning this now. You had nothing to do with that and no one can possibly know for sure. It's all in the past."

The queen wasn't listening to her. "You think your mother was murdered?"

"I never did before. I'm—This is all just too much to deal with. I'm imagining things."

"Your mother didn't think so. You say she moved you often." The queen fell silent. "Maybe my mother did suspect. As much as I hate to say this, she would be the type to do whatever necessary to ensure that Eleri never came back, especially with a child carrying royal blood." She seemed to slump down in the bed and Talia hurried to her side, but stopped short of touching her when the queen shifted away. "My God," Catriona whispered brokenly. "The Dark One . . . he must have known. And when the time was right, he made sure Chamberlain knew."

Talia took her hand then, steeled against the rage of pain but allowed it to invade her anyway, giving the queen any respite she could as she dealt with the blow of her mother's apparent vengeance. "Baleweg says the Dark One doesn't care about the throne or Chamberlain. It's all just a game to him. He enjoys toying with lives, Baleweg's specifically. It was Baleweg's connection to my mother that likely drew him into this in the first place."

Catriona looked up to her then and Talia was shocked by the fierce light she saw in her sister's eyes. "Well, he won't toy with my life!" She pulled free from Talia's grasp then and struggled to sit taller in her bed. She waved away Talia's hand.

"Your Highness—"

"That is your title too now, you know. And we will thwart them all because of it. Or you will."

Talia opened her mouth, then snapped it shut again as she felt the blood rushing from her head. She sat heavily in the chair next to the bed. "I . . . I can't— I'm not—"

"You are. And you will. At least until my son is of age to take over. My son. Your nephew."

Talia's gaze followed Catriona's to her distended stomach and terror filled her at what the queen was suggesting.

"You will raise my son, protect him. You will raise him as the next ruler of this country, to continue the legacy of the House of Dalwyn. A legacy you are now a part of."

Talia began to shake, but she couldn't look away from the mound of blankets that covered the next king. "I don't know anything about how to be ruler. And I know even less of being a mother."

"You say you run an animal shelter. Your maternal instincts are there."

"I hardly think that's the same thing."

The queen's expression sharpened, as well. "It's more training than I have." She held Talia's gaze with her own steely one. "You are the only one who carries the blood of my son and my father . . . and me, inside you. Don't you see, Talia? You are the only one."

Talia shot to her feet. "You don't even know me! How can you trust me with something like this?"

"You're my sister. You are a Dalwyn, Talia. Perhaps not purely, but what is not Dalwyn is Trahaern, the most trusted servant to a Dalwyn. How can I not trust you?" She held out her hand once again. "I must trust you."

Talia stumbled back behind the chair. "I need to— I need to think. I can't think."

Catriona lay there pale and wasting, and yet the fierce light of determination remained as powerful as ever in her eyes. Talia saw the strength then, the strength of a woman who had somehow managed, despite her youth and failing health, to rule a country. Talia was in awe of her. And completely terrified that this same woman would place all her hopes and dreams on Talia's so eminently unqualified shoulders.

Suddenly the queen's assistant was beside her again. She hadn't even seen her approach.

"Marletta, see Talia back to her room."

"But—"

"You can do this, Talia," the queen said, fatigue clear in her voice now, as was the pain. "We will speak of it again later. For now I must have rest."

Talia felt as if her world were spinning and indeed it was as Marletta helped her from the room.

Chapter 22

*A*rcher sprawled on one of the lounges, his demeanor deceptively casual as he watched guards oversee the clearing of the supper service that had awaited them upon Talia's return from seeing the queen. He was deeply worried about her and still trying to absorb the bombshell she'd dropped.

All dozen of them, from the apparent involvement of Emrys and Catriona's late mother, Her Royal Highness Gwendolen, in Eleri's death, to Talia's royal blood tie to Catriona, to the stunning request of the queen that Talia take her place and raise her child. He could hardly take it all in. He had no idea how Talia could be handling all this.

She was pacing in front of the fireplace, her food mostly untouched. Once the guards and palace personnel had finished and left, he rose and caught her in mid-stride, rubbing the shoulders she held so rigidly. "What can I do to help you? Tell me and I'll do it." He'd never felt so helpless, or so angry. Angry at Catriona for the horrifically unfair position she'd placed Talia in. Had he had any idea that was the fight she'd intended when she rang for Talia . . .

Talia turned to him, lifted her hands, then

dropped them to her sides again. "I have no idea. This is all way too much for me to deal with. I . . . I didn't come here thinking—" She broke off with a harsh laugh. "Obviously I didn't come here thinking, period." She paced again.

Archer grinned, trying to lighten the mood. "I always thought you carried yourself like a royal. I guess I had it right all along. Do I have to address you as 'Your Majesty' now?"

Talia made a face at him. "Very funny."

Archer held on to his smile, but it cost him. Not only was he dealing with the astonishing turn Talia's life had taken, but also the devastating death of his last remaining fantasies of somehow making things work with her. He understood now why the queen had been so concerned about his feelings for Talia. In fact, he was surprised she hadn't tried to separate them. Likely she realized Talia needed him now to steady her. And despite the fact that he felt wholly helpless to do anything for her, he wasn't above wanting to nurture that need.

She sank down onto one of the lounges. "I have a sister," she whispered. She'd alternately worried about the burden the queen had placed on her slender shoulders . . . and remained astonished by the fact that she had family living.

Archer took her hand as he sank down next to her. She looked up at him, her eyes luminous despite the worry and fear. "I honestly can't believe it."

"It's a gift. No matter what happens, Tali, you can believe in that. You have family now."

Her face crumpled. "A family that is going to die. Leaving me with a child I can't possibly be a mother to."

They'd already gone over this. There was nothing

left that he could say to convince her. Not that he honestly wanted to. The idea of leaving her in this pit of political vipers made his stomach knot. He simply couldn't see her raising a royal, either. Not that she wasn't capable of mothering him, but this wasn't the life he'd envisioned for her.

For them?

He shut that vision right down. Instead he tipped her face to his and kissed her. He felt her relax and sink into him a bit. "Maybe we should let this go for the night. You're going to have to talk a great deal more with Catriona before any decisions are made. Which can't happen tonight. So why not leave off and come to bed with me."

When he stood and pulled her with him, she whispered, "Thank you," a smile rising to her lips.

He wondered how it was possible for a heart to both swell and break at the same time. He squeezed her hand and led her silently to the bedroom. She came easily into his arms, as if she'd been born to fit there. But even as she gave herself over to him and allowed him to take care of her, making him feel as if he were the only one that could . . . he knew she'd been born for another role entirely. One that had no place for him.

❧

The following morning Archer summoned the guard before the queen could summon Talia. She'd tossed and turned all night and was paler than he'd ever seen her this morning. He hadn't forgotten the mission Catriona had asked of him the morning before and made a decision. "I need to speak with the queen as early as she is able. Tell her it is about the matter we discussed yesterday."

A communication monitor lowered in the main

room a half hour later. The screen once again remained dark, but the queen's voice emanated from it, her voice clearly weak. "I have meetings with several Parliamentarians and a long session with a host of physicians this morning, Mr. Archer. This had better be important."

"Physicians?"

There was a pause and Archer could feel the chill of the royal frost, but she did finally respond. "Pain management and a progress report on my son."

Archer bowed his head, uneasy with her unexpected confidence. But at least she spoke of her child now with the absolute confidence of one who expected his existence to continue. He only wished she had more of that optimism for herself. He was the sort who was unwilling to give up, but then he'd never faced the enemy she was dealing with.

"I need to go into the city," he said. "To obtain the information you requested."

"That can be arranged. You wish to go this morning?"

"Yes. And I want to take Talia with me."

"Absolutely not." Her tone wasn't nearly as weak as it had been the moment before.

"She needs to get out of here for a bit."

"She needs to remain under my protection. I assume she told you."

"Yes. Just as I assume this matter is still private knowledge."

There was a long pause, then, "Regardless, she is in danger and until you can get me the information I require, I must insist she stay here."

"Then it is impossible for me to get you that information. Because I refuse to leave her here."

"You do not think I can maintain her safety?"

"You do not think I can?"

"I have far greater numbers to watch over her."

"Many of whom you cannot trust. You know you can trust me. Your guard has performed well so far, but if even one person knows of Talia's real connection to you, she will be in danger."

There was another long pause. Archer knew he had a strong bargaining position. Catriona urgently needed to know what Emrys's role was. Was it more than a game to him? Only Baleweg could give them the answer.

Archer tried another tack, gentling his tone. "Talia is overwhelmed, Your Highness. If she can leave the castle even for several hours, she will have a chance to get her bearings and put things in perspective. We will be with Baleweg. You know he is committed to her safety. If he feels she is threatened in any way, we will return here at once. And he is best equipped to determine the danger she is in."

This time the pause was shorter and Archer sensed that he'd gained ground. Finally there was an audible sigh and he released the breath he'd been holding.

"I insist on sending a guard escort to and from the Old One's residence."

"Not if you expect him to be there when I arrive."

The queen swore and didn't bother to lower her voice. Archer smiled. He'd won.

"I do not like the position you have put me in, Mr. Archer. More stress I do not need."

"Neither does Talia and she's far more unaccustomed to dealing with it."

The frost returned. More like a deep freeze. "This is an extremely undesirable situation and I will not forget or forgive if anything goes awry."

"Dock my pay." Archer swore he heard a surprised snort. He fought his own smile. For the first time, he felt there truly was a family bond between Catriona and Talia. The queen had her sister's sense of humor.

"I just might," she said. "I want you back here no later than midday."

"Thank you, Your Highness."

"Do not test me, Mr. Archer." The monitor shut off and whizzed into the recessed area in the ceiling.

"What was that all about?"

Archer turned to find Talia standing in the doorway, looking delightfully rumpled. "Did you finally get some sleep?"

"Yes." She yawned hugely, blushing as she covered her mouth. "Sorry."

Archer grinned and went to her. He pulled her into his arms, wanting nothing more than to tumble her back into bed. But he knew he was on borrowed time. "I got you a present."

She smiled, surprised. "You did?"

"We're off to see Baleweg."

"*We* are? Me, too?"

"You, too. I need to ask him some questions, information the queen asked me to get yesterday."

"I never asked you what happened during your meeting," she said. "I can't believe I forgot."

"You've had one or two other things to deal with." He could have kicked himself as shadows crossed her lovely face once again. He leaned in and kissed her soundly. "But for the next couple of hours, no worries about all that."

"I can't believe Catriona is letting me go."

"I have good bargaining skills."

Talia looked over her shoulder at him. "I just bet you do."

"Hurry and dress. I'd join you, but we'd never get out of here."

"A shame that," she said, imitating his accent.

"I can remedy it later."

"Yes," she said, sashaying into the bathroom. "You can."

૨ે

Archer noticed that Talia enjoyed the ride into the city far more than she had enjoyed the ride out of it. Her head was tilted back and she reveled in the feel of the air rushing over her skin.

Archer also noticed the queen had sent a guard out, although they were trying hard to look inconspicuous. He let them trail him until they were well into the city proper. Then he turned to Talia and said, "Hold on tight, sweetheart, these streets get a bit tricky." It took him longer to lose them than he'd thought it would, but he managed it all the same. He looked to Talia, whose eyes were a little buggy, but she had handled it well, all in all. He parked in an alley, then put the shield up as soon as he helped Talia over the side. "Let's hope he didn't take off."

Talia looked at him in surprise. "Doesn't he know we're coming?"

"Do you really think there is anything Baleweg doesn't know?"

They knocked at his door, but no one answered.

Talia looked crestfallen. "So what now? Do we go back?"

"Ah, well, look there." He jogged down the hall to the tall window, then motioned to Talia with a wide grin on his face before turning back to open the window. "There's a good mate."

Talia reached him just as he pushed up the sash to allow Ringer to flutter in. "He's gorgeous," she said, watching as the small snow owl landed on Archer's arm. "How can you tell it's him?"

"Other than the fact that most owls don't land on

my arm, you mean?" He laughed at her pointed look. "I can just tell. It's in the eyes." He reached up and stroked the owl. "We're mates."

He looked back at her in time to catch the wistful look on her face. It fled a moment later as her expression shifted to a wide smile. "Baleweg!"

Archer turned to find the old man standing on the other side of the window. "Go to the door, I'll meet you there," Baleweg told them.

Moments later he was ushering them into his small kitchen where he had tea brewing. "I'd ask what brings you here, but I fear I already know." He looked to Archer. "The queen wishes to know more about Emrys."

"Yes." Archer squeezed Talia's hand beneath the table. "We think he was instrumental in Eleri's death."

Baleweg's expression reflected little. "In what manner do you believe him to be involved?"

Talia cleared her throat. "We think Catriona's mother used his skills to hunt my mother down. That's why we moved so much. We think her death wasn't an accident."

"And her rationale for wanting Eleri dead?" Baleweg's already pale skin went whiter as he raised his hand to stall her response. "No, you needn't say it." He turned to Talia. "Cynan was your father."

It wasn't a question. Talia nodded, her eyes glassy. "Catriona is my half sister."

"I had no idea," Baleweg said, almost to himself. He bowed his head and Talia moved closer to him.

"It's not your fault. You were honoring her promise."

He shook his head. "Always too lost in my studies. I should have paid more attention. I knew when she died, but in my grief I was worried only about not

betraying her trust. I never thought to question—"
He broke off and his shoulders shook slightly.

Talia leaned forward. "Baleweg—"

He looked to her, his brilliant blue eyes filled with pain. "I wasn't aware her death was anything but accidental. I should never have been involved in her life to begin with. I was always so careful to remain apart. I should have never befriended her."

"Why? She valued your friendship, you have to know that."

But he didn't hear her. "I hoped our brief time as friends had gone undetected. If I'd had any sense of it . . ." His shoulders shook again and his face seemed to crumple. "I didn't sense it."

Talia's eyes welled with tears, too. "It's not your fault. I don't care what your skills were, you're human and you can't be expected to know everything."

Temper flashed through the pain. "I should have known this!"

"How? How could you have? Emrys didn't have anything to do with my mother before she left, did he?"

"No. And your mother wasn't the focus of this, not then and not now. Nor are you. You're merely pawns in a game that has gone on far longer than it should have." He moved away from her. "It was me. It has always been me."

Archer sat forward. "You said before that Emrys likes to toy with you. Are you saying his dealings with Gwendolen so long ago, and now with Talia, the queen, and Chamberlain, are all part of some game he's been playing?"

"Yes." Baleweg rose and went to the counter, slowly preparing another cup of tea.

"Why?" Archer and Talia demanded simultaneously.

"What is his connection to you?" Archer demanded. "Why the games at all?"

Baleweg took another moment before turning to face them. "I was his mentor, of sorts."

Talia's mouth dropped open. "You taught him?"

A faint smile ghosted his lips. "You find that so hard to believe?"

"No. I mean, I'm not surprised that you could teach him. But you said he was . . . evil. He couldn't have learned that from you."

Baleweg shook his head. "Not evil. Not in the sense you mean. Soulless maybe." He sighed, as if struggling to find the words. "He lacks morality, or a sense of it. As I said before, his powers expanded easily and quite far, very quickly and with frighteningly little effort. He enjoyed stretching those powers, applying them to amusements that had little to do with learning and more to do with entertaining himself. He doesn't see himself as being on the same plane as mere mortals. He sees himself as above all that."

"What happened between you?"

Baleweg's expression shuttered then. "I felt he should focus on finding out the extent of knowledge that was out there for him to obtain." He fell silent for a long moment, then sighed again and said, "What I didn't realize, at least until it was too late, was that by pushing him to discover just how far-reaching his abilities were, I was enabling, enhancing even, his natural proclivity for the rest." He looked to them. "I learned that you can reach to the farthest boundaries of the mind's ability and discover wondrous amazing things. But you cannot learn to have a soul if you were never born with one." He sat down heavily across from them. "My greatest failing was not realizing that until it was too late."

Archer took Talia's hand and held it tightly. "How long ago did you two part ways?"

"A great deal longer than you could possibly comprehend."

Talia shivered then, or maybe it was Archer.

"I take it the parting wasn't amicable?" Talia asked quietly.

Baleweg shook his head. "He enjoyed mocking me, mocking my dedication to the educational aspect of the skills we possessed."

"How did you hook up with him in the first place?" Archer asked. "How could you know he had the same abilities you did?"

Baleweg looked down at his hands. So quietly they almost couldn't hear him, he said, "He was born of me."

"He's your son?" Talia asked in a stunned whisper.

Baleweg looked to her. "No. More a . . . scientific experiment." He sat heavily. "I suppose I must tell you the whole of it." He folded his hands and closed his eyes. "A very long time ago I was consultant to a king. It was another time, another place. Distant from here, from all you know. I was young then, naïve about the powers of the mind, but I was obsessed with learning more. And perhaps I was a bit reckless in how I went about doing so. I agreed to some rather . . . questionable studies in return for the funding of my own interests. Emrys was the result of those studies. The geneticists named him. It's a Welsh form of Ambrosius." He opened his eyes then. "It means *immortal*."

Talia clutched at Archer's hand. "So what exactly is he?"

"In your time, I believe he's called a clone."

Talia slumped back in her seat. "Born of you. Literally."

Baleweg nodded. "Only enhanced, biologically, supposedly to emphasize my strengths and minimize human weaknesses. Things didn't go as planned." He shook his head. "But then, they rarely do."

Archer tried to digest it all. Baleweg's hermit-like existence and his aversion to all things royal made far more sense now. "So he helped Gwendolen because he knew of your affection for Eleri?"

Baleweg nodded and turned to Talia. "I didn't have a great deal of contact with her, but I came to feel a great deal for her anyway. She was impossible to deny. She had such energy, such desire to learn. I admit, I was lonely. Starved for such stimulating interaction." He seemed to sink into himself. "Emrys had left me alone for some time at that point, pursuing his own pleasures, if you can call them that. I thought him bored with my simple life and pursuit of knowledge." He shook his head. "I suppose no matter how much I learn, I can still be a fool."

Archer stood. "Okay, so we all screw up. I don't think anyone blames you, Baleweg, but people's lives are at stake, lives your—whatever you want to call him—is presently amused with. So why don't you tell us what we can do to stop him?"

Baleweg said nothing, turning to Talia instead. "There is so much more for you to deal with than we knew. I'm sorry I couldn't have prepared you better. Had I known of your father I would have understood your lack of healing abilities. We never spoke of such things. Our time together was spent in learning." He smiled then and a glimmer of strength returned to his eyes. "I do know that she was overjoyed to discover herself with child, despite her fears for her safety, and therefore yours. Our kingdom was in chaos at that time and anyone close to the king was in peril. Parliament was a den of snakes and the threat of a takeover was very real. Naturally, I assumed her fears were political in nature, but once I successfully helped her to safety, I retreated heavily into my studies with no interest at all in the state of the monarchy." He reached for Talia's hand. "Forgive an old man his broken heart."

"Oh, Baleweg, I don't blame you."

But it was clear he still blamed himself. "So what is to happen now? What are the queen's plans?"

"She wants me to raise her son," Talia said quietly. "She's going to die and leave him to my care." She raised her eyes to Baleweg's. "The future king."

Baleweg's expression gave away nothing of what he might be feeling. "You will heed her wishes, then?"

Talia opened her mouth, then shut it again and lifted her shoulders. "I'm . . . I have no idea what to do, or what I can do. I didn't come here planning to stay."

Baleweg touched her arm lightly, sending his comforting tingle humming down the entire length of it. "Do not worry about this now. There is much yet to come."

Archer's gaze narrowed as he stepped closer. "What do you mean? Do you know something we don't?"

Now Baleweg smiled, though it did not reach his eyes. "I think I can safely say that is the case most of the time."

Archer swore. "This is not a joke."

Baleweg's smile vanished. "I do not believe I have treated it as one."

Archer paced the room. "If you plan to help, the first thing you can do is tell me what Emrys looks like, so at least I can warn the queen."

"A description of his appearance will mean nothing to you, or to the queen, as he can change it rather well."

"He's a shifter?" Talia asked, then looked to Archer. "I didn't know they existed in human form."

"They don't," he said shortly. "At least not that I am aware of."

Baleweg shook his head. "They don't. He is merely quite skilled in the art of deception. He understands how the human mind perceives threat and is amazingly adept at . . . shall we say, blending in."

"Okay, okay," Archer said, impatience clear in his voice as he paced the room. "So this whole thing, his game, is about hurting you. He helped Gwendolen find Eleri to hurt you. And now he has drawn her daughter into this little drama of Chamberlain's hoping to hurt you by hurting her? Can you stop him?"

"I would be willing to try, but as I said, his powers far surpass mine. I know little of his activities and will not unless he intentionally reveals himself to me. I can feel the disturbances, but beyond that, I have little power where he is concerned."

"If he realizes that I'm not a healer, will he leave the queen and the baby alone now? Will he abandon his game with Chamberlain and just come after me?"

Baleweg shook his head. "I have no way of knowing. If he's amused by playing chess with royal lives, he might very well continue. Or if he thinks he can find a way to torment you through them, and therefore torment me . . . he is capable of anything."

"Surely you must have some theory on what he will try next?" Archer asked.

Baleweg shook his head. "His mind works in a way that is far different than mine. Quite literally, I could not imagine what he might have planned."

"Then you must come back with us," Talia said, grabbing at his hand. "Help us from within the castle. Surely you'd know if he was there, if he was planning something?"

"Oh, he's planning something. But I would not be able to stop it."

Archer slapped the table, startling Talia, but Baleweg didn't even flinch. "Then what would you have us do? Sit and do nothing until he strikes?"

Baleweg calmly shook his head. "I would have you leave Talia here. With me."

Talia looked first at Archer, then at Baleweg. "Why? What would that do?"

Archer went to stand behind Talia. "I won't leave her unprotected. Why don't you come with us?"

"Because Emrys would like nothing better than to draw me to a place he knows I detest. I can do nothing to protect or help the queen, but I can help Talia. But only from here, where my strength is most powerful. Now that I understand the gist of his game, I realize it would be best if Talia and I remain close together until I determine a way to confront him." He stopped Archer's argument before he could speak. "Even with your protection, were you to take her back to the queen, he could—and would— find a way to take Talia and use her as a pawn against me. She must remain here."

"Then you think Emrys is in the castle?"

Baleweg nodded. "Somehow. Somewhere." He looked to Archer. "It is quite possible that getting Talia out of there today saved her life. Although I doubt he would have made his move until the royal birth was imminent. He relishes melodrama."

"If Talia stays then I stay," Archer said.

"But I can't just leave Catriona," Talia cried. "She is my only family."

"If you truly want to help her," Baleweg said

calmly, "then you will remain here, for you own safety, which is what she'd want, and Archer will return to the castle to observe and stay close to her. He can alert us to anything that happens." He paused, then asked, "Does anyone else know of your bond to her?"

Talia shook her head. "No."

Archer laughed. "You know as well as I do that if anyone in the castle knows something, the information will find its way to Chamberlain."

"Then there is no need for further argument. She is at risk from both Emrys and Chamberlain now."

Talia felt her throat constrict again. "Then what do we do?"

Baleweg reached into the pockets of his voluminous robes and withdrew a small blue orb. He held it out to Archer. "You will carry this."

"What is it?" Archer said, studying it, but not taking it. "I thought you simply knew things without needing any gadgetry."

"I can sense a great deal. But I cannot absorb all disturbances and ferret out the source, especially with Emrys opposing me." He placed the orb in Archer's hand and closed his fingers over it. "This is something I've worked on, privately, for some time. I doubt Emrys has any idea of its existence. I have not yet been able to test it well, but I am fairly certain it will hold up to the demands we will place on it."

"Fairly certain?" Archer said, staring at the blue lump of glass.

Baleweg ignored his skepticism. "It functions as a focal point for the specific energy of the one who holds it, a projection unit if you will. If you hold it enclosed in your palm, I will feel the energy coming from you. I will then be able to direct my focus immediately to wherever you are. As long as you hold the orb, nothing can prevent that connection." He held Archer's gaze. "Nothing."

"Why can't you just do something from here, now?"

"Without knowing what his plans are, I have nothing to focus my efforts on. It is not a foolproof plan, Archer," he said, for the first time losing a bit of his patience. "Nothing in life is foolproof, as we have all so painfully learned. You want my help; I am offering it. No guarantees. But it is far better than nothing. Which is the only defense you have without me."

Archer swore beneath his breath.

"What if he simply kills her?" Talia asked.

Baleweg shook his head. "Chamberlain would not be so foolish as to have her murdered in her own bed. Else he could have accomplished that far earlier."

Talia shook her head. "I'm confused. If she can't leave her bed and he won't kill her there, just what harm can he impose other than to wait for her to die?"

"That may well be his plan. But I imagine Emrys has another. He has little patience for waiting out nature's course. He much prefers to have a hand in directing fate when and where he can. Do not underestimate him." Baleweg looked to Archer. "Chamberlain will not want to risk being connected to the queen's death. Emrys is ingenious. If he's still interested in toying with royal intrigue, and I assume he is, especially as Talia is now linked directly to them, he'll find a way to let Chamberlain into power without drawing suspicion to him. Accept nothing at face value." He moved to the door. "It would be best if you made a quick return to the castle."

"Wait a minute, what if this is the trick I'm supposed to be questioning?" Archer asked. "How do I know I can trust you? That you aren't somehow in on this?"

"Is that what you truly believe?"

"That's not an answer."

"You survive by listening to your instincts. Do your instincts tell you I am the one to mistrust?"

Archer wanted to say yes, just to see what the old man would do. But it was almost impossible to lie when looking into those spectral blue eyes of his. Finally, he shook his head.

"Continue to follow them, Devin. They will always serve you well."

Talia turned back to Archer. "You should go. The queen will see you, listen to you. She'll trust you to stay by her side. Tell her—tell her I'm here waiting and . . ." She took a deep breath. "And that I'll do whatever I can to take care of her son."

"Talia, you don't have to—"

She pressed a finger against his lips. "I barely know her, but she is my sister. I have instincts, too. And they're telling me to do whatever I can to help her. Whatever that might be."

Archer leaned down and kissed her. "It's far more than most would do."

"It's what you would do." He opened his mouth to deny it, but she wouldn't let him. "You're doing it for me."

That stopped him, but only for a second. He grinned. "Yeah, but that's because you can be a real pain in the ass when you don't get your way."

She smiled now, too. "Well, so can my sister."

"God help us all." He kissed her hard. "Don't leave this building until I return." He looked deeply into her eyes. "And I will be back for you."

"Be careful," she whispered.

"I believe we've already discussed how we're going

to express all this gratitude. And I'm holding you to it."

"Please do." She suddenly yanked him into a tight hug. "And hurry, Devin," she murmured against his ear. "Hurry back to me."

Chapter 23

*W*here is she?" Had the queen been at all capable, Archer was certain she'd have come after him physically. As it was, her heightened color was alarming enough.

"She's safe. Which is more than I can say for you."

"I want her returned to me immediately!"

Now Archer was angry. "You do not own her. She is not a prisoner here."

"She hasn't the first idea of the threat against her."

"Oh, I'd say she has a very real idea. It is you who need a briefing on the subject."

Rather than castigate him, the queen surprised him by slumping back against her pillows, rubbing at her belly. It was such a guileless gesture, done so naturally and without calculation that Archer's ire vanished. She was no longer only a ruler worrying about how to defend her kingdom against some invisible threat, she was also a woman with a child on the way, fearing for his health above her own.

He moved closer to her bedside. "I have information that I think will make you understand why Talia is better off outside the castle for the time being."

"I just want her kept safe." It was as much a warning as a plea.

Archer felt his heart soften. Damn, but he was

becoming a maudlin fool of late. "Her biggest concern is for you and your son. She is ready to do whatever is necessary to help you, but she cannot help you if her own safety is compromised, as well. If she is kept hidden, the balance of power is shifted to you. All your chips are not being held in one hand, as it were."

The queen looked far wearier than she ever had before. "Then brief me on what you know."

Archer nodded and pulled up a chair. At that moment, Marletta buzzed and entered the room without awaiting the queen's consent. She looked alarmed enough that the queen immediately asked, "What is the matter?"

Archer sprang to his feet and planted himself between Marletta and the queen.

"Pardon the intrusion, Your Highness, but there is someone to see you."

"Who is it?" This demand came from Archer. His instincts were on full alert and he slid his hand toward the pocket of his jacket that held the blue ball. His other hand moved toward his gazzer.

"It's . . . *him*, Your Highness," Marletta said with hushed urgency, clearly uncomfortable saying more with Archer so close.

"I'm not going anywhere," he said flatly, "so you might as well say what you've got to say."

"Yes, please, get on with it," the queen demanded, then winced and rubbed once again at her stomach.

Marletta moved to her bedside and leaned close. "It's him. *Him.*"

"I don't know what you're—" Then the queen gasped and covered her mouth. "No! Not now. Not after all this time."

"Yes." Marletta straightened. "He wishes to see you."

"Absolutely not." Both the queen and Archer spoke simultaneously.

Marletta looked between the two of them, but settled on the queen. "You want me to just . . . turn him away?" She moved closer, her professional demeanor slipping away entirely. "But Cat—"

The queen's gaze sharpened, cutting Marletta off soundlessly, but very effectively.

Archer had no idea what was going on, but he didn't think it had anything to do with the current parliamentarian threat or the Dark One. But that didn't mean a threat didn't exist. Whoever this person was, it was clear the queen was distressed by his arrival. She and her assistant looked for all the world like two girlfriends in a dither over a man. *Uh-oh*. His gaze shot to the queen who had both hands protectively covering her belly. He thought he had an idea who had come to call.

"I can't see him, Marletta. Not after all this time. Not after what happened."

Archer flexed his fingers, perfectly willing to see the little bastard who had abandoned the young queen.

"He knows," Marletta answered, apparently having completely forgotten Archer was in the room. "He knows about the baby."

"Well, of course he knows," the queen spat. "The whole world knows of my condition."

"But he's the only one who knows . . . well . . . " Marletta moved closer again. "He has a right."

"He most certainly does not." In the next instant the severe, regal mask crumpled, shocking Archer. He'd known, certainly, that she was a young woman. But he'd never seen her lose control and act like one.

"He left me, Marletta," she whispered. "When I needed him most." Tears tracked down her wan cheeks. But then she dashed them away. "And he is not going to just waltz back in here after all this time because he's changed his mind."

"I never changed my mind, Cat."

Marletta and the queen both gasped. Archer was already running. Three guards were already on him.

"How in the hell did you let him get by—?"

"Cat, don't let them—"

"You cannot be in here!" Marletta rushed the door, too.

"Stop it!" This came from Catriona. "Stop it right this instant!" She gasped and grabbed at her stomach and everyone froze. "You," she managed, nodding toward her guards. "Release him." They immediately did as she commanded.

Archer didn't hesitate, however, and crossed immediately to him, planting himself between the young intruder and the queen. "Don't move."

The young man complied. "I'm not here to hurt her. I've done enough of that already." He looked steadily into Archer's eyes, which earned the younger man a slight measure of respect. "I'm here to help her."

He was shorter than Archer, but built ruggedly. He was blond, with startling green eyes and a handsomely carved face. Archer could see how the queen might have lost her head over him.

"Prince Niall," Marletta said, stepping beside Archer. "You should have waited."

"Prince?" Archer said. *Very interesting.* He'd wondered if the queen had perhaps been impregnated by a commoner, thereby giving up her son's right to the throne if word ever got out. But young and perhaps foolish as she was, she was not stupid.

The young man nodded. "The second son of King Jorik. I've known Catriona since we were chil-

dren." The young man's expression hardened. But it
was the honest fear Archer saw in his eyes that held
him still. "I know she believes I abandoned her, but
I have not. We argued when she learned she was ill.
We had differing ideas on how she should care for
herself. But I never gave up on her. I have spent
these past months looking for a cure." His jaw tightened mutinously. "I will not let her die." He looked
past Archer's shoulder. "Or our son."

Niall looked to Archer. "Please allow me to pass.
There is much we must discuss. Stay in the room if
you must, but I must speak with her before it is too
late."

Archer turned to the queen. She nodded warily.
But she also didn't try and get Archer to leave, either, which calmed him. She was aware of the danger
and he silently applauded her resilience, even in the
face of this new, emotional twist. To that end, he remained near the door but within easy reach of the
young prince.

"I didn't leave you, Cat," Niall said softly as he
approached the bed. "I told you I was going for
help."

"Just as I told you there was no help. Where I
needed you was by my side."

"To sit by and watch you die?"

Catriona turned her head away and Archer went
to remove the young man, but Marletta held his
arm. "Please, give them some time." She tugged at
his arm and he bent down. "He brought help with
him. I think he has honestly found the miracle we
have prayed for."

Archer went on full alert. "Help? As in a doctor?
Or medicine? What?"

"I'm . . . I'm not sure he's a doctor."

"Where is he?" Archer was already pushing past

her, heading to the door. Had Chamberlain somehow gotten to the young prince? Had he totally mis-
read the situation?

He was stopped at the door by the queen's voice.
"Archer?"

"I'm going out to talk to the visitor your young
prince brought with him." His tone sent an unmis-
takable warning.

What he saw was the prince's hand grasped tightly
in the queen's hand. Tears still wet her cheeks, but
from the look in her eyes, he guessed that they were
tears of hope.

"Please show Dr. Denby in," she commanded.

"Your Highness, allow me to just—"

"It may already be too late, Archer. Please, I can't
waste time. If what Niall says is true, I still have a
chance."

Niall took her hand and kissed it. "We. *We* have a
chance, Cat."

"I must at least talk to him. Hear him out. Please,
Marletta, show him in. Archer, you can stay right
beside him the entire time."

Archer swore under his breath. He'd never seen
the queen so hopeful. And perhaps he was on instinct
overload after listening to all of Baleweg's mumbo
jumbo about dark forces and unknown powers.
Still, when the older man stepped into the room,
Archer moved to stand directly behind him . . . and
remained less than a hairsbreadth away.

"That's close enough," he said, when the man had
barely entered the room. Then he remembered the
shield Marletta had activated the first time he'd
brought Talia here. He turned to Marletta and motioned her close.

She smiled. "Already done." She opened her
hand slightly to reveal the activator.

Archer realized they'd effectively sealed Niall in with Catriona, but he honestly believed the young man to be exactly what he claimed to be. Any fool could see he was completely besotted. He'd have to be blind not to notice that the queen had similar feelings.

The doctor turned to him and put out his hand. "Good day, I'm Dr. Denby. Must you stand so close?"

Archer grinned and ignored the outstretched hand. "Hello. Make one false move and I'm your worst nightmare. And yes, I really must."

The doctor swallowed visibly, then smoothed his white hair. "Yes, well, I suppose you can't be too careful these days, hmm?"

"No, you can't."

The man's Adam's apple bobbed as he swallowed once again and nodded.

Archer looked closely into the older man's faded blue eyes, but he saw only what one would expect to see from a slightly rattled guest to the queen's private quarters.

The doctor turned to the queen and cleared his throat. "Your Highness." He bowed somewhat awkwardly. "Thank you for allowing my presence. I believe I can help you. In fact, I know I can."

The queen said nothing and remained regally still. Archer noted that she still held Niall's hand, rather tightly, but despite the fatigue and pain, she projected her most royal, controlled self.

"Tell me exactly what it is you think you can do for me."

He glanced nervously at Archer, then took a tentative step forward. Archer moved with him, despite the presence of the shield.

"I . . . I know of a new technique that can repair

the cell damage and reverse the corrosive decay that is ravaging your immune system."

Catriona's eyebrows lifted dubiously. "I assure you, Dr. Denby, that I've seen every specialist there is. Along with every quack. I have no doubt I have exhausted every possible solution available."

"But there is a method—"

"I've heard of several controversial methods of treatment, all of which place my unborn child in immediate jeopardy. I will not risk him, not even to save myself. If that is what you are here to offer, then you can save your time and mine."

"You are far enough along to deliver with some degree of hope for his survival, are you not?"

"I am not willing to induce labor early in order to give myself treatment." She raised her hand to still his rebuttal. "And I will be frank with you, Doctor. At this stage I do not think I'll survive the delivery to seek treatment afterward."

Niall looked at her, taking her hand in both of his. "Cat—"

Still the queen, she cut him off, but with honest emotion in her eyes. "Niall. I know this."

"The method I am talking about should not jeopardize your child," the doctor explained.

"How is it we have not heard of this procedure?" She turned to Niall. "Did you find him off-Earth? Because I've had my consultants look to every plausible advanced society and the only methods they had were extremely questionable."

"Cat, I know you're going to find this somewhat hard to believe, but I've seen it firsthand." He looked to the doctor and then to Cat. "He's from the future."

As soon as Niall said the words, Archer realized they'd all been set up. There was only one person who could have taken Niall to the future. And it wasn't Baleweg. But the realization came a split second too late.

The triangle had already opened beside Niall. And it was on the other side of the shield. The doctor smiled then, his blue eyes twinkling. A cold chill shot down Archer's spine. The disguise had thrown him, but he recognized those blue eyes now, just not the demonic light behind them. *Emrys!*

"Shut it down! Shut down the shield!" Archer shouted to Marletta, who was already punching at her device.

"I'm trying! The buttons are stuck!"

Archer had already palmed his gazzer and was diving toward the doctor, belatedly remembering to grab for the orb in his pocket.

The doctor walked right through the shield, but it held fast for Archer, his speed bouncing him off it, and knocking the blue stone from his hand. It rolled across the floor, far out of reach. There was no time to go after it. He could only hope he'd held it long enough to signal to Baleweg.

"Call the guards!" he commanded as he rolled to his feet.

Emrys turned and smiled at Archer. "Your worst nightmare?" he taunted, his voice sounding much, much younger, even though he still looked like the elderly doctor. He tipped back his head and laughed. "You haven't had yours yet. But you're about to."

And then it was as if the triangle were sucking them into it, with a force of its own. The Dark One lifted a hand toward Niall as the young man charged him, sending him flying back against the shield. "Don't waste your time. Join your lady love there. You're about to take a trip."

"But . . . but you showed me!" Niall demanded. "I went with you and I saw with my own eyes—"

"Yes, annoying detour. But there is nothing like proof to nudge the undecided. Now move, unless you want her dragged from her bed."

The bed, Niall, and Catriona all slid toward the triangle, which had opened to its full size. Archer shouted to Marletta who was still wrestling with the shield device even as he tried to see beyond them, into the triangle, for any clue to where they were heading.

"Guards, fire at the walls to the side of the shield." Archer knew better than to aim anything directly at the shield. It would boomerang off, putting everyone on this side at risk and doing nothing to penetrate. He dove for the floor and slid toward the nearest wall the shield reached to. "Now, now!"

The guards' collective force blasted the wall. Archer covered his head as bits of stone flew everywhere. "Everyone, again! This wall." Again they assaulted it and this time the fringe of the shield wavered. Yes! He wedged himself through the narrow gap.

Catriona was in Niall's arms now as the bed they were on was sucked into the triangle behind the Dark One. The triangle began to shrink, the queen and Niall on the other side. Along with a laughing Emrys.

"Good-bye, Archer. Tell the Old One nice try."

Archer squeezed harder, forcing his upper body through. All he needed was to free his legs.

The triangle continued to shrink.

And then his legs were through. "Ha!" He rolled to a crouch, aimed, and dove again. "Look out, asshole. Here I come." His body arrowed right into the heart of the small triangle . . . and made it to the other side.

Chapter 24

*I*t's happened."

Talia looked up from the flowers she'd been admiring in Baleweg's garden. She didn't have to ask what he meant. Her heart slammed in her chest. "Do we go back?"

Baleweg shook his head. "They aren't there."

"What?" Then she remembered what he'd said. *He won't kill her in her own bed.* She gasped. "You mean Emrys has somehow kidnapped Catriona? She'll never survive that. What about her guards? Marletta?" She covered her mouth. "Archer!"

Baleweg placed his hand on her shoulder. "I don't know what ruse he used to get to her. The energy flash from Archer was a brief one, ending almost as soon as it began."

"No!" Her heart shuddered. "You don't mean—"

His hold on her tightened. "I mean they're *all* gone. With Emrys. Somewhere. There is no energy source there at all." He withdrew another blue stone from the depths of his robe. "I felt a ripple in the time continuum." He looked to her. "I think he's taken them through time."

"But how did he get to them?"

Baleweg shook his head. "I couldn't know."

"You think he took both Catriona and Archer?"

Baleweg nodded. "It would explain the way the

energy ceased so quickly. I would sense Archer if he were still there."

"What about the orb? Can't you connect with him through that?"

"It was such a short flash that I don't believe he could have held it for long. It matters not, as the link would not hold up once the time continuum was crossed."

"But how can we be sure?" Talia had horrible images of Archer lying in the castle somewhere, in a pool of his own blood. Even at such a distance, surely she would have felt something if he was hurt. She knew he would fight to the death for Catriona, against anyone being wronged. She felt a rush of pride even as terror consumed her.

Only Baleweg's touch slowed her headlong flight into total panic. "You must calm yourself. They need you right now. Your skills may be our only hope."

She whipped her head around. "How can I possibly help? And how is that supposed to calm me down?"

Baleweg allowed a brief smile to crease the corners of his eyes. He framed her face with his hands and she stilled. "It is within you to reach out and touch them, connect with them." He looked at her steadily. "With their fear, and their pain. It is the only way, Talia. It is why I kept you apart."

"But if we'd been there—"

"You would be at Emrys's mercy right now, as I predicted. And I would be left with no way to locate any of you."

"Surely you could have found a way—"

Baleweg merely shook his head. "My vulnerability would have been too high. He'd have had far too much sway." He sighed wearily. "That may not change when we find them, but at least I will have the advantage of planning my attack."

He let her go and she took several stumbling steps backward. "But if *you* can't reach them, how can I—?"

"I have many skills, but you can't learn to be an empath any more than you can learn to be a healer. Only you have an ability to connect with these specific people."

"What of Emrys? If he can thwart you, surely he can—"

"He could. If he suspected. But he will not. He is toying with me, taking one who is close to you, your family, and therefore dear to me. He will enjoy thinking that I am being tortured with the knowledge that I can do nothing to save your sister's life, and that you will witness my failing. He will be overconfident, knowing the fate of her entire kingdom rests in his hands. He will never believe we can thwart him, or that we will even try. Instead he'll be gloating, thinking us resigned to the painful realities of this latest display of his power. That arrogance will be his downfall."

"What about Chamberlain? Where is he in all this?"

Baleweg shook his head. "He was merely a pawn in this game, led to think he controlled Emrys. Perhaps he'd thought to give Emrys a position of power in the court if he succeeded in his plans with the queen." Baleweg shook his head. "I doubt he ever knew just who he was dealing with. Not that it matters, as he will get what he wants from this anyway." He stroked Talia's arm again. "We cannot concern ourselves with Chamberlain or what he might be doing at this moment. We must focus on your sister. And her child."

The humming sensation raced up her arms and

tingled through her, allowing her to get a grip on the emotions rocketing through her. She took a steadying breath.

"So, Talia, are you willing to do what must be done?"

She didn't hesitate. "Of course I am."

"It will not be easy and will cost you much."

The trembling started again, but she worked hard to tamp down the rising panic. "I don't know if I can pull it off." She pulled her hands free and clasped her arms to her. "But I have to try. For . . . for Catriona and her baby. And . . . for Archer. He'd have done the same for me. He's already done the same for the queen."

Increased respect filled Baleweg's eyes as he nodded and smiled at her. "You are your mother's daughter, Talia. As well as your father's. They would be very proud of you."

She dashed away unshed tears. "Thank you." She took a deep breath. "Okay. What do I do?"

Baleweg took her by the hand and walked into the forest of tropical plants that crowded his rooftop garden. In the midst of the palm fronds there was a small stone pool, the water in it completely still. Next to the pool was a small blue mat. "Sit there."

Talia looked at him, but did as she was told.

"You have not made too many connections with humans."

"Only two, and they were right near me."

"Not only will they not be close, you must connect with them through time."

"Oh, my God, I didn't think about that. How will I—?"

"The strength of what they are feeling and what you feel for them will be enough. But you must cleanse your mind of all else. You must feel none of your own fears or concerns, so that you will be able to feel theirs." He nodded toward the pond. "I want you to stare at the water, at the smooth surface of it, and imagine your mind as smooth, as clear, as calm. Do not think of them, or the situation. It will only cause you to react and then your focus will shift back to your own concerns."

Talia nodded.

He laid a hand on her shoulder, drawing her attention up to him. "I must warn you. This can be extremely draining, especially for a novitiate."

Talia thought back to how stunned she'd felt after her brief connection to Archer. But it had been energizing rather than draining. Catriona had been different. Equally powerful, but there had been pain. She'd yanked herself out of it before she'd connected too deeply, but she remembered the hammering she'd taken even with that brief connection. And now, with Catriona and the baby most certainly facing imminent death— Her body balked, her mind tried to pull away. She'd spent too many years protecting herself from this. But she had no choice but to risk it this time.

It was that or let them die.

"I'll be okay," she told Baleweg. She wouldn't be, she knew that. Just as she knew it didn't matter. Not any longer. This was what she'd been born to do. She understood that now and for the first time embraced the gift she'd been given as just that. A gift. Hopefully, this time, it would be the gift of life.

Baleweg nodded. "Look to the pond."

"Wait. If— When I make the connection, then what? If I can't fix them, I can't . . . what is it I can do?"

He pressed the blue orb into her hand. "If you can locate them in that manner, I can connect through you and determine where in time they are. You must not let go of the orb or your connection. It will not be easy."

Her heart pounded as the magnitude of what she was going to try drummed through her. She couldn't let herself think about it. She couldn't allow herself to think about success or failure. She simply had to focus on the connection itself, nothing else. Just as Baleweg had taught her. She nodded and turned her thoughts to the pond.

Calm . . . smooth. Tranquility. Emptiness. Open, opening. Talia felt her breathing slow first, then her heart rate. She kept her focus on the pond, then finally let her eyes drift shut and turned her focus inward. It was as if she'd transcended to some other place. *Complete calm, tranquility. Open, opening. I am open.*

She struggled to maintain the calm. *Breathe in, breathe out.* As time stretched out to what felt like infinity, she continued to focus. *Empty, open, I am open.* Nothing was happening. She fought back the edge of panic, of frustration. She could not allow anything to interfere. She redoubled her efforts, sank even deeper into her own mind. She envisioned a flat plane that stretched onward beyond the horizon. She pictured herself flying over this plane, moving toward something, something intangible, something—

The shriek of sudden pain all but pierced her to the very soul. She jerked and almost lost it, but forced herself to reach out again.

When it came the second time, she thought she'd be prepared. But she wasn't. It felt as if it were her own voice, shrieking in agony. *Dear God, oh, dear God.* She felt her body tumbling now, the plane having turned into a steep incline. Down she went, down. Deeper. The pain howled through her, echoing so strongly she thought she might go mad with it. Her body jerked against it, instinctively trying to protect itself. It took everything she had to force herself to let go, to relax, to feel it, endure it. But oh, dear God, the pain. Her stomach felt as if it were being ripped from her. Over and over again it was as if something were trying to wrench itself free from the depths of her very being. She wrapped her arms protectively over her stomach, the blue orb digging into her palm. She was losing it, losing her hold. She couldn't endure this ripping, this pushing, this—

And then she realized, and with realization came hope, and some semblance of control. It was the baby! He was still alive. He was coming! Through the haze of pain she focused once again, holding herself tightly in her own arms as the agony washed through her again. *Ripping, squeezing, pushing.*

She took on the pain, even though that meant being unable to control it. Catriona was dying. If she could take this pain away, take on the labor of childbirth for her, perhaps she'd spare her enough energy to survive it. *Stay with it, Catriona, I'm with you. I'm with you.*

Again and again the pain tore through her. It was so immense that she writhed with it, unable to brace against it. She knew childbirth could be agony, but this . . . this was more than that. Catriona's illness had ravaged her so thoroughly that the rigors of giving birth were literally tearing her apart. And Talia couldn't separate the pain of one from the pain of another. Her body jerked and twisted as each wave ripped through her. How much longer could she hold on? She felt her grasp slip repeatedly but forced whatever focus she had left to the single-minded effort of maintaining the contact so her sister might live through this.

The baby forced its way lower. Lower still until

she felt she was being torn in two. The baby! *Yes, yes, almost there!* She bore down and felt a scream tear from somewhere deep inside her. Or inside Catriona. She no longer knew where she ended and Catriona began.

Air. No air, no air! Breathe! Can't breathe. Suddenly Talia felt an encroaching cold crawl toward her. It was terrifyingly black, deeper than any hole, sucking her in. *So cold. Breathe.* Talia fought to hold on, but the black threatened to consume her. A howling pain shrieked through her. Icy fingers clawed at her belly. *Dying.*

"NO!" Talia jerked out of it and found herself lying in a pool of sweat, trembling hard, unable to catch her breath. Her body lay twisted on the blue mat. It took her a moment to focus on the water, then Baleweg's face came into view.

"The baby is almost there," she gasped. "Catriona is dying." She gulped at the air. She was so cold, so cold. Sleep. It pulled at her, begging her to give in to it and leave the pain behind. "I tried to save him, save her. Take the pain. I don't know."

"Talia," Baleweg said gently. "Talia." He took her shoulders and very gently moved her into a sitting position.

Shaking. She couldn't stop it. Couldn't control anything. God, she was so cold.

"Talia."

She managed to turn her head, to focus on him. Her hands were numb, her lips numb. She nodded.

"You did it. You connected."

No, she hadn't done it. She hadn't maintained the connection long enough to ensure that Catriona and the baby had made it. She tried to tell him, but she couldn't manage it. Her teeth were chattering now.

Baleweg's expression changed, smoothed. "We need to connect again."

Her body instinctively recoiled. She shook her head, wildly, back and forth. To willingly go into that nightmare once more . . . no, no, she couldn't do it again. But she already knew she had to try, to make sure she got Catriona through. She might not be a healer, but if she could just relieve the pain long enough . . . Panic began to crawl through her, the sense of failure she'd fought for so many years clawing at her again.

Baleweg took her face into his hands and gently forced her to look at him. "You must do this if we're to save them. The pain Catriona is in is too intense for me to sort it all through. You can't connect with her. It must be someone else. This time I want you to open up to your own heart, search there, then reach out."

Talia couldn't seem to stop shaking. "I—I don't . . . un . . . understand. She . . . n n-n-needs m-me—" Her teeth were rattling they chattered so hard.

"If you connect with Catriona again . . . you might not make it. The toll on you is just as immense and yet made more so by the stress of the mental connection. We need the time more than she needs you to take on her pain. You've given her a great deal, and perhaps it's been enough. But if you try and lose, then we will never find them."

"Don't care," she managed. "I must—"

"She needs more than this to survive." He gently stroked her cheeks. "Love, Talia. Reach out for that. It is stronger than pain, stronger even than death. You have that connection within you, but you must be willing to surrender to it, and then risk giving it away."

Talia didn't understand. She cared for Catriona and Archer, and the baby. She already knew that. What did he mean, surrender her heart? She was willing to give her life. Wasn't that a greater risk?

"Talia."

"Y-yes. I don't—" She shook her head, frustrated by her inability to speak coherently. She tried hard to find some center of calm, even a tiny piece, that would let her gain some control back. But she was exhausted.

He wrapped his hand around hers. "You must believe. This time the journey is into your own heart. What you find there will allow you to reach out and connect. Trust yourself."

He stood behind her as she worked at breathing in and out normally. As her heart gradually slowed, the trembling and shaking finally stopped. Her fingers hurt and her legs were still numb, but her teeth stopped chattering. Her entire torso felt as if it had been run over by a truck. "Okay," she said as calmly as she could. "I'm ready."

Once again she focused on the pond, on the water. Always she had been afraid of the fear and pain she felt when she connected with a dying animal. Her experience just now had only confirmed what she'd always known. To put herself through that even once more would almost certainly destroy her. Baleweg was right; she had to shift her focus if she was going to finish helping them.

What she hadn't counted on was how much more terrifying it was to reach out and connect with someone's heart. Because in order to connect with it, she had to be willing to put her own heart on the line.

Trust your heart.

She understood now what Baleweg had been telling her, just as she realized that this was the greater risk. There was no physical pain strong enough to equal the devastation of reaching out for a heart with one's own, only to encounter nothingness. Death would be kinder.

Calm, peaceful. Smooth surfaces, deep, tranquil depths.

She stared at the water and imagined herself skimming smoothly over the smooth, glassy surface. But something was pulling at her, sucking her down. *No! Not this again. No.* But there was no pain in this cold embrace. It was worse. *Isolation. Such complete isolation. No feelings. Nothing. Shut off. Nothing gets in.* She slid deeper down, and deeper still. *Protection. Safe.* Her heart began to pound. *Deeper, past the protection. No safety here.* She began to shake. *Dark, so dark, almost black. Untouched. Unexplored depths.* Her teeth chattered. *So cold, so lost, so alone.* She couldn't go further, it would suck her in and she'd never find her way back. The pressure grew, in her chest, constricting her, making it hard to breathe. *Deeper, must go deeper. No safety. Risk. Keep going.* But the pressure only grew worse. Tears leaked from her eyes and her chest burned. God, it burned so badly. She wanted to gasp for air, rush to the surface, away from that black nothingness.

Nothingness.

And then she felt the fear. She began to pull back, away from the bottomless darkness, back to the safety of isolation. *No. Fight it! Trust. Trust her heart.* She plunged further, certain she was going to be crushed by the pressure. *So alone. So dark.*

The pressure increased until she screamed with the agony of it. She pushed, crying freely now. *Want.* She wanted so badly. Like she'd never wanted before. *Terror.* She'd never been so terrified. Trusting that want, fighting for that want. She'd gone so far now that she had no hope of a safe return. If she wanted, she couldn't be safe. Her heart pounded. *Heart. Her heart.*

It wasn't about just wanting. It was about giving. That was the risk.

And then she knew what she must do if she wanted to connect with Devin. She had to give her heart away.

Pushing downward, feeling claws of ice piercing her, reaching for her heart. She fought through them, forcing images of her heart, whole and strong, beating, beating. *Red. Burning, burning. Huge. Pulsing, full of life.* Impervious to cold, to ice, repelling the claws. Reaching out, so warm, so full, so strong. Offering . . . wide open.

I am opening my heart to you. To you, Devin Archer. Only to you.

And it hit her like a wall of flame, the heat of it searing her. Blasting the ice out of her soul, releasing the pressure on her lungs so she could breathe. Heat infused her, all of her, and the rush of pleasure that followed was so complete the blackness in front of her exploded into a shower of tiny, brilliant shards, dissolving into a glittering cloud.

She loved. She'd trusted her heart to the nothingness. And survived. It didn't matter whether the gift was returned or accepted, only that she'd trusted her heart enough to give it away. And it was the strength of that trust that had made the connection.

"Talia." A gentle hand to her shoulder. But she didn't want to come back. Never had she been in such a wonderful place. She never wanted to leave. So tired, she just wanted to stay here, floating.

"Talia." The gentle hand again. "You must wake."

She shook her head, stubbornly refusing. Too hard. Too tired. She'd never been this tired. And then it was too late. The pleasure was receding, leaving only fatigue so bone deep that she wept with the need to find refuge from it.

"You must open your eyes and listen to me."

She shook her head, but opened her eyes all the same. "Where—" The word came out with a hoarse rasp. Her throat was raw and her voice was gone. She looked around her, remembering, slowly, that she'd been on Baleweg's rooftop.

She was no longer by the pond, or outdoors. "Where—" Again she was forced to stop.

Baleweg swam into view, then a glass was pressed to her lips. "Sip. Take a sip. It will help."

She did. The liquid, cool and sweet, felt so good, but it was not enough. She felt . . . hollowed out.

Baleweg mopped her brow with a damp cloth. "You've been through an ordeal, Talia, one that would have killed anyone with less heart than you." He stroked her cheek. "Your mother would be proud of you. You've used your gift for its intended purpose. But it will take some time for you to recover from it."

Then she remembered, all of it, what she'd been trying to do. The intense pleasure she felt when she finally surrendered her heart, trusting in her own love enough to give it away. Then her eyes shot wide in alarm as the rest came rushing back. "The baby—!"

Baleweg pushed her back to the bed. She was in a bed.

"You made the connection, Talia. I know where they are. I must travel quickly."

"Are they . . . ?" She couldn't put it into words.

"I will do my best."

She tried again to sit. "I'm going." Her throat was so raw that it was excruciating to speak. Her head immediately reeled, forcing her back to the pillow even before Baleweg could do it for her.

"You can't. You are far too weak."

Tears of frustration leaked from her eyes.

"No tears." He leaned in and took her hands in

his. "You were everything you could have been. Everything you've always known you could be. Now it is time for you to heal. You must go easy on yourself."

"Can I . . . stay here?"

Baleweg smiled. "You are here." He motioned to the room and only then did she realize she was home, in her own bed. In Connecticut.

"No!"

He calmed her. "I cannot leave you alone in my time. There is no one to care for you and you are too unfamiliar with everything to care for yourself. Here you have help."

"But Emrys—"

"Will have to deal with me. You will be as safe here as anywhere. You are far too weak to travel with me."

She wanted to argue, but she knew he was right. Damn, but she hated this. *Archer*. How could she just sit back and not fight for him?

As if he understood her thoughts, Baleweg took her hand in his. "You've fought for them as valiantly as any soldier gone to war. You've done your part." His expression tightened, his eyes steely. "Now I must do mine. When it is done, I will make certain that you know."

"But Emrys . . . how will you—?"

"I can only promise that I will do whatever I must to finish this." He looked beyond her. "One way or the other."

She immediately thought of Archer, of never seeing him again, and the resulting pain was so swift it took her breath away. But she'd given her heart, taken the risk, and she didn't regret it. "You'll come back," she whispered. "Promise me, Baleweg. You have to promise me."

"All your questions will be answered in time. I must go now." He pressed her hand to her heart.

"Trust this. Do not forget." He straightened and closed his eyes. The triangle opened behind him. There was a flash of something as he stepped through, but her eyes were swimming and she couldn't make it out.

"Good-bye, Baleweg."

He nodded to her as the triangle slowly shrank, swallowing him up on the other side. And then it blinked away. And she was alone. In her own bedroom, staring at her own ceiling.

"I'm back in Kansas, Auntie Em," she whispered. Then she rolled into her pillow and sobbed.

Chapter 25

*A*rcher felt Catriona's hand go limp in his. "No, dammit! Stay with us. You've got a family to fight for now." Sweat ran from his brow even as his heart pounded in a primal thump of joy at the sound of the new prince testing out his remarkable lungs. He'd never witnessed anything so miraculous in his life.

But he had little time for awe. Right now their focus was on the baby's mother. He and Niall thought they'd lost her earlier when the contractions had moved so close together she seemed to be almost wrenched from her own body. And then there had been a sudden calm and she'd gained steady ground right up until the baby had pushed its way, squalling, into the world.

"And what a world it is, mate," he murmured as he watched Niall do his best to clean the babe with his shirt. Archer had cut the cord with, of all things, Beatrice's old fishing knife. He'd gotten used to carrying it concealed on his body and almost forgotten that he still had it on him. The sight of it had wrenched at his heart as he thought of Talia, but the knowledge that she was, hopefully, safe at home with Baleweg allowed him to focus on the more serious problem at hand. The babe appeared healthy enough, but Catriona's pulse was thready and Archer feared she'd lost consciousness.

"Cat!" Niall cradled his son and tapped at her cheek, kissed her lips, then her hands. "There's work left to do, Cat. I know you want to hold your son. Come on, love."

Archer had never felt so helpless. The miracle of birth was quickly overshadowed by the specter of death. He pushed to a stand and once again searched their cramped prison cell for any means of escape. Although he feared it was too late now. Too late for Catriona, and her son if they found no way to feed him.

The Dark One had traveled them back in time, very far back, not forward as Niall had hoped. They were still in the castle, only it was hardly more than a tumble of stones, an unoccupied ruin. The lower dungeon held them fast with no chance of escape. He thought of Talia again, terrified at the thought that Emrys had left them here to seek her out.

He swore under his breath at the memory of Emrys's delighted recitation of his grand game. Even now Chamberlain was implementing a worldwide manhunt for the queen and her kidnappers. However, he would be the one to return with her body, and now her son's . . . as well of those of her killers, all of whom were slain in the rescue. The murderers being Niall, the father of her bastard child, and Archer, the man who'd do anything for a price. All he had to do was wait for them to die and Emrys to deliver their corpses to him. The Dark One found the whole charade vastly amusing.

What worried Archer was what Emrys's motivation might be. He wasn't in this for whatever measly royal powers Chamberlain could bestow on him after he took over the Dalwyn throne. No, he had something else in mind for himself. Some other twisted little amusement. And Archer was desperately afraid it involved Talia. What other target did he have left if his real goal was to get at Baleweg?

Then another thought occurred to him. If Catriona and her son died, that left only Talia with Dalwyn blood in her. Royal blood, and therefore a claim to the throne. Would she know that? And if so, would she try and stop Chamberlain? Archer doubted that Chamberlain would believe the connection, although he supposed the DNA tests that proved it to Catriona could be used to prove it to the kingdom.

Would she do something so foolish as to risk herself for a family she no longer had? "Dammit, I should never have left her behind." Even as he said the words he realized that if she had come with him, she'd be stuck here, left to die, as well. He had never been one to pray, but he prayed now, prayed that Baleweg would have the sense to hide her somehow, anywhere where Emrys would leave her alone.

His heart constricted as he was forced to face the harsh and painful reality that there might be no such place. His only real hope was that Emrys because bored with this game and moved on to some other demented pursuit, forgetting all about Talia Trahaern.

"I'm losing her!"

Before Archer could cross the room, a triangle began to open in front of him. He flung himself toward Niall, the baby, and Catriona, fearing that Emrys had come back to speed things up a bit.

But it was Baleweg, pale and exhausted, who stumbled through the triangle.

Archer swung around just in time to catch him as he teetered forward. The buzz he usually felt when he touched the old man was barely a hum as he cradled him in his arms. "Baleweg."

"I made it, then?"

"Yes. Where is Talia?"

Baleweg looked at him. "In Connecticut. Resting. Healing."

Archer swore loudly. "No! Emrys has left us here; I'm certain he's off to find her."

Baleweg, even as weak as he was, shook his head. "No. He will come to me. This time he will see it finished."

"We must get Catriona and the baby out of here," Niall demanded, his son setting up a squall again. "We must get her to the future. I've seen proof that there is a cure."

Baleweg struggled to his feet. "The babe," he whispered in awe. "Then he's arrived." A smile briefly touched his lips. "Talia did it, then. She'll be so pleased."

"Did what?" Archer stood even as Niall remained crouched by Catriona's body. "What did she do?"

"She saved this young lad's life. And hopefully left the queen enough strength to save her own, as well." Baleweg turned his attention to Archer. "She also connected with you and through her connection I found you. Had it not been for her, all would have been lost."

Archer tried to assimilate everything Baleweg was saying, but his head was humming. "Healing. You said she was healing? Is she hurt? Emrys—!"

"Will be coming, have no doubt. What Talia did took an enormous toll on her." He looked Archer straight in the eye. "Taking on the queen's pain almost killed her. Reaching out to you again after that all but finished the job."

"How dare you allow her to—"

"You dove through time to save the queen and thwart Emrys with no thought to how giving your life might affect her. So don't sit in judgment of her because she did the same for you."

Niall was sobbing now. "We must do something! Oh, Cat, please hold on." He turned to them. "Please help us."

"I have traveled twice," Baleweg said. "And it has taken far more out of me than I thought it would. Emrys must have thrown up barriers to me somehow. I'm—I'm not sure I can sustain another window."

"Then why the hell did you come here!" Niall shrieked, no longer the stately future king, but a man wracked with terror over the very real possibility of seeing his family die in front of him.

A triangle opened then on the other side of the bars, and Emrys strode through, looking for all the world as if he'd been out strolling in the park. Archer's mouth dropped open. Emrys, sans his earlier disguise, looked like a much younger version of Baleweg. Darker of hair and thicker of build, as Baleweg likely had been in earlier days, but the facial structure, combined with their eerie blue eyes were exactly the same.

"Yes, Old One," he sneered, "why in hell did you make the trip? Surely you didn't think to thwart my little game." He laughed and it made Archer's skin crawl. "But oh, I was hoping you'd try."

Archer flung himself against the bars. "Where have you been!"

With barely more than a tiny flick of his finger he sent Archer flying back across the cell, almost landing on the dying body of the queen.

"I don't answer to you." He laughed loudly. "I don't answer to anyone. Grand scheme life has handed me, hmm?"

Baleweg made no move toward him. "Life could

have handed you a great deal more. And your contribution to it could have been limitless."

Emrys's smug grin slipped a bit. It was a tiny moment, but a telling one all the same.

"Ah, yes, you and your silly obsession with expanding one's mind. What is the point in that, I ask you, if you can't use it to entertain yourself? Whyever have this cursed talent if not for that?" His voice had risen and there was a distinct pulse ticking in his temple.

"It was a gift—"

Emrys all but flung himself at them. "Gift!" he shrieked. "Gift?" He laughed maniacally. "A gift he calls it. Well, it was a gift I never asked for!" His face was so purple with rage that Archer instinctively flinched.

Baleweg, on the other hand, seemed to grow calmer, even stronger, the more Emrys lost his composure. It was as if he were feeding off it. Archer swung his gaze back to Emrys, wondering if he understood what Baleweg was about, or even knew of this particular talent.

"A gift isn't to be asked for, but to be accepted gracefully," Baleweg said calmly. "But then, grace was never one of your attributes."

If Emrys had gone purple before, he all but went black in the face now as he choked on his own laughter.

"What would you know of attributes, dear genetic donator? You spew your supposed wisdom and life lessons and yet you had no compunction in selling your DNA to the highest bidder to create me! So let's not sling arrows, shall we?"

Baleweg continued to prod him, his skin slowly regaining color. "No one chooses the manner of his own creation, but you did have a choice once created. You chose to squander rather than utilize."

"By utilize I suppose you mean burying yourself in your work, all for the sake of . . . what? You found your amusements . . . I found mine."

When Emrys paced away once again, Baleweg shot a quick look to Archer and mouthed, "Ready them!"

It took a moment for Archer to understand what he was asking. But as he continued to bait Emrys, Baleweg shifted himself so that he created a human shield to the trio behind him. And to the tiny triangle that was beginning to open just behind them.

Archer carefully kept his gaze away from the three of them and on Emrys, ready to do whatever necessary to keep Emrys's attention on Baleweg or himself and off Niall, Catriona, and the baby. But just then the baby let out a particularly spectacular howl and brought Emrys's focus swinging about at exactly the moment that Baleweg had opened the triangle wide enough for them to escape.

"Now, now, now!" Archer shouted, diving for them and shoving Niall through the triangle even as he tried to scoop the queen's lifeless body into his arms.

"No."

Archer turned just in time to see Emrys walk through the cell bars as easily as he had walked through the shield.

"Go!" Baleweg demanded.

Archer threw himself into the triangle even as it began to waver and fade. But surely if he left now, Baleweg didn't stand a chance against Emrys. Torn, Archer stepped through the portal with the queen. Then Niall was there, along with a half-dozen uniformed personnel in what looked like a hospital room. The baby had been handed to one of the white coats and Niall was taking Catriona's unconscious body from Archer's arms.

"Go back," he said. "Help him." He grabbed Archer's arm as he turned. "Thank you. For everything. You gave me my family back."

Even as he let Archer go, the triangle had all but disappeared. Once again, Archer aimed, dove . . . and stayed in the cell where he'd been left to die. And would almost surely die now. But he didn't intend to go alone.

Baleweg was already on his knees, his expression revealing the pain being inflicted on him, even though Emrys was standing several feet away. "How dare you interfere with my game!" he shrieked. "I had plans for them, lovely plans. I could have toppled a monarchy."

Archer knew Emrys could easily have followed them with a triangle of his own, but he remained to face Baleweg. The Old One had been right all along. Ultimately, Emrys viewed this as a game between the two of them, and only them. Well, not if Archer had anything to say about it. "Leave him be," he demanded.

Emrys barely flicked his hand, but this time when Archer hit the wall he knocked his head and nearly passed out. It took several moments just to clear his vision, but he could see well enough to see Emrys send Baleweg, who had been trying to stand, back to his knees.

Archer knew he was weak and would take little of this abuse before it did irreparable harm. He clawed his way back to his feet even as Baleweg once again raised his head.

"This is not the way to solve anything," he rasped.

Emrys laughed and aimed at him again. Baleweg collapsed onto the floor and lay unmoving as Archer staggered to him. He didn't care what Emrys did to him, he wasn't going to let Baleweg take this abuse unshielded.

Even before he got there, Baleweg was stirring. "Don't," Archer commanded. He turned to Emrys.

"You think to thwart me?" Emrys shrieked. "I think not!" He drove Archer to his knees right where he stood, and held him trapped there, unable to move, unable to do anything to escape. His muscles felt as if they were turning to stone.

"I don't care what you do to me," Archer ground out. "Just leave him alone."

Emrys smirked. "How touching. Yet I have a hard time believing you've developed any real feelings for this one. Hard to care for one so remote."

He abruptly released Archer from his invisible bonds, but his body merely collapsed, unable to bear its own weight. "At least he has the one thing you don't," he rasped.

"And what might that be? A conscience?"

Archer tried to stand, but with the simple raising of Emrys's finger he felt a pressure that prevented him from moving. To look at Emrys you wouldn't know he was exerting such power. But the more time he spent torturing Archer, the more time Baleweg was given to recover. Could Archer be cunning enough to last long enough to allow Baleweg to save them? And how could he do it? Emrys was no doubt the stronger of the two by far. Archer had no illusions that they'd get away with opening a triangle right in front of Emrys again. And he'd only follow them anyway.

At the very least, the longer they kept him here, the less he could interfere with Catriona's possible medical intervention . . . and Talia's recovery in Connecticut.

Archer still didn't understand what had happened between Talia and her connection to both Catriona and himself. But he'd witnessed that time during childbirth when the queen seemed to have no pain and had delivered her child. Had Talia been instrumental in that? And if she'd taken on the queen's pain . . . dear God.

Emrys released him once again and turned to Baleweg. Archer felt as if he'd been crushed under a pile of stone, his body weak and sore. Physical force wasn't going to make things happen here and he wasn't going to hold out much longer.

So perhaps a different kind of battle had to be waged. "No," Archer said, drawing his attention once again and bracing himself for another round. "I wasn't referring to your conscience. What you lack is a heart."

Emrys's wrath faded as his eyes widened in amusement. "So sayeth the mercenary? The royal bounty hunter? What do you know of the heart, Devin Archer?" Emrys circled him as he lay on the floor. "Let me guess. Rutting about with that useless brat of the healer has made you think you understand love? How pathetic."

Archer used what was left of his energy to lunge at him, but it was a weak effort that Emrys stopped easily. It took all of his will to grunt, as his body collapsed again, rather than moan.

"Big heart," Emrys said, making a playful tsking sound. "Small brain. Now you see why I value the size of the latter over the former." He swung around to Baleweg. "Now what to do about your ever so untimely little trick?"

Archer slowly moved toward the wall and used it to bear his weight as he clawed to his feet.

"You can choose to do nothing," Baleweg said, sounding only marginally stronger. "Move on to other pursuits."

"When I'm having so much fun with this one?" Emrys laughed gaily, all signs of his earlier rage gone. "I don't think so." He paced through the bars, then back again. "I'm not very pleased with your meddling, Old One."

"I could say the same of you."

Emrys ignored him, tapping at his lips. "I just have to decide which I'd rather do. Move forward and thwart the hopes and dreams of an entire kingdom by making sure that wretched little screamer and his dear mummy don't survive . . ." He swung his malevolent gaze to Archer. "Or trot off to the quaint Connecticut countryside and deal a little blow to that weak organ you're so fond of touting." He strode off again. "No heart," he muttered. "As if I had a use for one."

Archer knew better than to charge him again, though it took considerable control not to say anything. Instead he looked over to Baleweg. "Are you okay?" He stumbled over to him.

Emrys did nothing to stop him. Archer didn't much care what Emrys thought at this point. Baleweg nodded, but up close Archer could see that his skin was pale and his eyes were bloodshot. "Let me take him on, so you can feed off his rage again."

Baleweg looked to him then and Archer helped him to stand. "Is that what you thought I was doing?"

"What else?"

Baleweg shook his head, but said nothing.

Archer leaned close as Emrys strode through the bars again. "Tell me."

"Yes," Emrys said. "Tell us both, why don't you?"

Baleweg seemed to stand taller. "What gives me strength is exactly what we've been discussing. Heart. Love. I fear I've shut myself off from it for far too long, all for the selfish desire of self-preservation. Although I dandied it up under the guise of seeking knowledge and learning." He shook his head. "I knew that if I let myself love anything, you'd merely come along and destroy it. What I didn't realize was that loving, even briefly, gives me a greater understanding of the world than any number of years of pursuing whatever skills might be found inside my mind." He frowned. "And yet, the one and only time I did allow myself to love, the tragedy didn't simply befall me." He eyed Emrys. "How pathetic," he said calmly, "that human life is the worthiest subject you can find for your own tiny amusements."

"Tiny? You consider human life so trivial?"

"No, but you do. And that makes you a tiny being. No matter how immense your skill, your power, you will forever be a man stunted by your lack of—"

"Compassion? Morality?" Emrys rolled his eyes. "Talk about pathetic."

"How could you be expected to master those qualities when you lack the very basis of it all?"

"Are we back to that heart thing again?" He smirked.

Baleweg took a small step forward. "Perhaps if I'd started with you, things would be different."

"Whatever do you mean?" He took a small step backward.

"Had I allowed my heart to open to you," Baleweg said softly. "It is to my shame that I allowed jealousy to color my feelings toward you."

"Oh, did you want to be my sweet papa?" Emrys said sarcastically.

"Hardly," Baleweg said, his voice cool.

"Oh, please, tell me how you really feel, old man."

"I was never your father. You are the son of an institution, unfortunately for us both. But I could have been a true mentor. However, I was taken aback at the ease with which you learned, how quickly your mind adapted to any and all sort of stimuli or applied thinking."

"And you think that if you'd given me a few hugs along the way, I'd be a better man for it now?" He puckered his lower lip. "How touching."

"It could have been. We would have been a team rather than adversaries. Imagine what we might have discovered."

"That's your problem right there."

They both turned in surprise when Archer spoke. "Yeah, mates, I'm still here." And he had had enough of this. He folded his arms, hoping his still-shaky legs wouldn't betray him. "Baleweg, you talk about heart, but your bottom line is that you still wanted Emrys here to be your lab pal, your partner in science and all things mind-expanding." He gestured to a bemused Emrys. "Like he said, a few hugs wouldn't have changed things. You'd have had to have felt a real bond with him." He looked to Emrys. "I'm not sure you can bond with someone who has no emotion save his own banal search for anything that will stave off boredom." He laughed when Emrys's mouth quirked. "Let the little brain continue, if you will. I understand how boredom might be a problem for someone like you. I mean, when a guy figures out how to walk through walls, it's hard to find someone to be an entertaining chap to a mate like that. It's easy to see how you'd think yourself above it all, and how that would lead a bloke like you to start thinking of other people as a game. Little pieces to be played with.

"Which leaves the only bloke you'd have a chance in hell of even passing a decent evening ale with as the guy who can hardly stand being in the same room with you." He shrugged. "Makes perfect sense that you'd want to tweak the chap a bit for his hard-headedness. And, since you stopped seeing people as humans long ago, I guess it makes sense that your attention-getting scams got larger and more elaborate as time went on." He looked to Baleweg. "Of course, your opting for the complete dull life package must have driven this blodger nuts. Gave him nothing to play off."

He turned back to Emrys, whose eyes had narrowed considerably.

"Until now," Archer continued. "You find his one weak link, the way to finally get his goat for good." He nodded a salute. "Pretty sharp. But now what? I mean, okay, you got him this time, you hurt him good, with the bonus of restructuring the entire future of a monarchy. I'm guessing that will be entertaining as all hell for, oh, what, an hour? A few days?" He shrugged. "So now what? How can you top that? I mean, he's not likely to give you another candidate, is he now?" He glared at them both. "Now you'll really have to go out and find a way to entertain yourself. Because we all know this was never about your having a good time, it was about your proving you could hurt him. And you have. So bingo, mate, you win the prize!" He laughed, knowing well it might be his last. "How does it feel to be the big winner?" He turned from them both, hoping like hell he was pulling this off. Yet he meant every word he was saying. "You ask me, you're both pathetic. You both lose. You deserve each other."

There was total silence and Archer waited for Emrys to kill him on the spot. But Emrys did nothing. Hope began to well inside him. He'd spouted off because he'd realized what was really going on here, the two of them in an age-old war of basic family dysfunction. Except they happened to have some pretty serious methods of wounding each other. Maybe, just maybe, his mouthing off was actually going to help.

Baleweg was the one to break the quiet. "In order to inflict pain on someone, or wish to," he said quietly, "one would have to care in the first place." He made a tsking sound. "Never thought of it that way."

"I don't care a whit about you," Emrys said petulantly.

Archer thought he sounded for all the world like an angst-ridden teenager annoyed with a stubborn parent. Probably a somewhat accurate summation.

"I never imagined you did. Though now I wonder." Baleweg cleared his throat. "Archer is quite right, however. I never gave you a spot of a chance and suppose I deserve everything I got in return. I only wish you hadn't involved others in your vendetta against me."

"I wasn't getting back at you!" Emrys suddenly exploded. "I never wanted you in the first place!"

Baleweg very quietly said, "Didn't you, then?" When Emrys didn't move or speak, he moved closer. "I am, as Archer said, the only person who could ever truly understand you. It would make perfect sense."

Emrys abruptly let out a long-suffering sigh. "Well, you've certainly taken all the fun out of this little adventure." He whirled around as if to flounce off, but Baleweg reached out his hand and laid it on Emrys's arm. Blue sparks shot around the room and bounced off the walls, and Archer ducked as they whizzed by.

"Where are you off to?" Baleweg asked.

"Why on earth would you care?" He sneered. "Archer says, Archer says. Well, he of little brain is not all-knowing. I have many grand adventures planned and none of them concern you. I will be perfectly happy to never see you again. I've tired immensely of our little game of cat and mouse. You'll not be seeing me again for quite some time, though I daresay that won't bother you as you go back to your yawningly dull little existence."

"It is rather dull, isn't it."

Emrys said nothing, but neither did he move away. And Archer knew he wouldn't. He was finally getting what he'd always wanted. Baleweg's full attention.

Baleweg took his time, fulfilling the role of the reluctant parent all too well. If the situation hadn't been so serious, Archer would have been amused as he watched the war wage behind those blue eyes.

Finally Baleweg sighed, as long-suffering a sound as Emrys had made earlier. Quite grudgingly, he asked, "I don't suppose you'd like some company on your next adventure?"

Emrys's eyes, an exact copy of Baleweg's, narrowed. "What manner of trick would this be?"

"No trick. Perhaps I am tired of living a shrouded existence. Perhaps I should try to spice things up a bit. See how the other side lives."

Emrys laughed. "I seriously doubt my pursuits would be of any interest to you."

Baleweg merely raised his brows. Challenge issued . . . and accepted. "Why don't we find out? Then perhaps you can try on one of my rather tedious little adventures of the mind."

Emrys examined his nails and Archer felt himself relax. Emrys was well and truly caught now. His interest was piqued. He was indeed nothing more than a very spoiled child, albeit one with dangerous powers, who'd been doing anything and everything to get the attention of the only person in his life who could possibly understand him. Baleweg, a man with pent-up jealousies who had hidden himself away instead of confronting them, burying his head in the sands of his studies . . . and thereby provoking Emrys on and on. It was a vicious circle, the cycle of which might never have been broken if they hadn't been finally forced to confront one another. Archer only wished they could have done so without putting an entire kingdom at risk.

Not that he thought it would all be resolved so easily. But, at the very least, Baleweg could watch over the devil rather than leaving him to his own devices. And perhaps the old man would learn that there was more to knowledge than what could be found inside his own head.

"I suppose we could try," Emrys said finally. "But one little squeal from you, old man, and phht, I'm gone."

"We'll see what the future holds." Baleweg turned to Archer, then looked back to Emrys. "Would you mind if I spoke to young Archer here in private?"

Emrys huffed, but opened a triangle behind him. Archer moved forward, alarmed that perhaps this had all been an elaborate charade. He wouldn't put it past Emrys.

"I'll be back," Emrys said, then sneered. "And don't worry, hunter. I hate Connecticut in any time."

Archer felt like collapsing with relief. He was surprised to find a very stern Baleweg when he turned around. "Don't give me that look. I just saved your arse, old man."

"And set me on a course I'm not so certain I like."

Archer shrugged. "I didn't force you to make that offer."

Baleweg said something that actually sounded like a curse under his breath.

Archer would have grinned, but he had other concerns on his mind. "Do you think he meant it? He'll leave Talia alone?"

Baleweg nodded.

She was safe. He leaned his head back against the wall. Thank God. So he had no right to feel cheated. No right to feel sorry for himself. This was what he'd wanted for her all along. A safe return home for them all.

Safe. He remembered then what Baleweg had started to tell him earlier. "You meant Talia was the one who gave you strength against Emrys, didn't you?"

Baleweg nodded.

"But didn't you say she was almost killed trying to help Catriona and helping you find us?"

"But she is a woman with an immense heart. I told her she had done her best, that it was my turn to fight. I should have known she wouldn't be able to stand back and do nothing."

Archer grabbed his robes. "Is she okay?"

Baleweg smoothly released himself from Archer's grip. "I imagine she is very, very weak. But yes, I think she's okay."

"You *think*?"

"You could go find out for yourself."

That stopped him. "Don't bother playing match-maker. Talia is back where she belongs. I'm sure she'll meet someone who can keep her safe and warm."

"You can walk away so easily? It is you that she loves."

His heart stopped.

"Her connection with Catriona may well have saved that baby's and the young queen's life. But I couldn't connect with you through all that. It was her connection with you that did it. She had to surrender her heart to do it."

He felt as if Emrys had sent him into the wall again, headfirst this time. "She did?"

Baleweg nodded. "I promised her that her questions would be answered."

Archer slumped back then. He should have felt an

overwhelming joy and relief that there was even a slim chance he'd see her again. But how on earth could he ever walk away from her if he knew that she felt for him what he felt for her?

"All that talk about heart. Now it's your turn to tell her. You owe her that much."

He was right. She was home, in Connecticut with no idea what had happened to them all. He owed her a proper good-bye, even if it killed him.

"And, of course, I assume you'll want Ringer back."

In all the tumult, Archer had actually forgotten about his little mate. "Where is he? You didn't leave him—"

"I left him in very good hands." Baleweg smiled.

Archer swallowed hard. "Talia has him?"

He nodded.

"What, you didn't think I'd go back so you put an insurance policy in place? What if I decide to just leave him with her?" He didn't say he'd already thought about that anyway. Ringer had never been happier than when he'd been in Connecticut. With her.

And he couldn't deny he had ever been, either. Dammit.

"Okay. I'll go back. But just so she knows what happened and to say a proper good-bye."

Baleweg said nothing, merely gave him that wise look he'd grown to . . . Okay, so he didn't mind it as much these days.

"What about the queen? What if Talia wants to go back to court?"

"I'll arrange whatever you wish."

Archer fell silent then. "I can't believe I saw a life come into this world today."

Baleweg merely nodded. "A miracle every time."

"Do you think they made it?"

"I'm sure they did all they could."

"Could we go and find out? So I can tell Talia?"

Baleweg smiled. "I'm sure we can work that out."

"What about you and Emrys? Do you think the two of you will work things out?"

Baleweg's smile vanished. "I'm not certain. Perhaps I can redirect his . . . energies." He didn't bother trying to hide his irritation. "I am set in my ways and this new direction I've chosen might prove to be an ill fit." He sighed in the face of Archer's knowing grin. "Perhaps we were both on a path to destruction. In our own separate ways. Perhaps your wisdom in showing me this will be a blessing for us both."

Archer nodded, ignoring the skepticism clear in his voice. "I just hope you don't live to regret it. He's . . . something."

"Yes. He is that." Baleweg cleared his throat and smoothed his robes. "Now I believe it is time for you to embark on your new direction."

The triangle opened before them.

Chapter 26

*T*alia had no idea how long she had slept. The sun was streaming through the dormer windows when she finally opened her eyes. She felt as if she'd been hit by a truck.

She groaned as she rolled to her back. However long she'd slept, it hadn't been long enough. She looked at the clock. *God, it was late.* She had to get up and feed and water the animals. She went to stretch, but her fingers cramped. She looked down and saw the blue ball still clutched tightly in her fist.

Oh! Tears immediately sprang to her eyes as it all rushed back with painful, heart-wrenching clarity. She squeezed her eyes shut, wanting to go back to several seconds ago when she hadn't remembered. But it was too late.

The images came pounding at her, assaulting her, and she was too weak to shut them off. Archer making love to her in that unbelievable bedroom. Catriona telling her that they were sisters. Connecting with her, feeling the baby despite all that horrendous pain.

Connecting with Archer.

Baleweg holding her hand and telling her not to forget. As if she could. Reaching for him, hoping that through him, she could help Archer and Catriona. That final connection snapping, the last thing she remembered before she'd lost consciousness.

Maybe it had all been some sort of nightmare. A dream that she'd finally awoken from. It was certainly fantastical enough.

The luminous blue orb in her hand said otherwise.

As did the snowy owl perched at the foot of her bed.

At the sound of her scream, which had been more a hoarse croak, the owl merely turned his head and stared at her with big, dark eyes. Archer was right. It was there in the eyes. "Ringer?"

The owl bobbed its head.

"Oh, God. You're still in Oz, Dorothy."

Ringer lifted his wings, shook them out, and settled down again.

"How did you get here?" Then she remembered. The flash when Baleweg had backed through the triangle. "Little sneak." Her voice was very rough, her throat even rougher. She needed to take a warm shower. An aspirin or ten wouldn't hurt, either. But that meant leaving this bed, and she was pretty sure that wasn't happening yet.

"How are you at making tea?"

Ringer merely blinked.

"That's what I thought." Talia looked toward the window, then at her clock. Stella and the girls were likely already at work. She laid her head back on her pillow. God, she really was home. It was almost impossible to imagine going back to her regular routine, her normal life.

But it wasn't completely over. Baleweg had promised he'd come back and tell her what had happened. Her heart clutched as she thought of Catriona and the baby. And Archer. Whom she'd never see again. No. She wasn't ready to handle that yet.

But she was grateful for Ringer's presence. He was her only link. And she'd cling to that link without apology.

She heard the slam of a truck door. Stella. And her thoughts drifted back outside. She wondered what they'd say when they realized she was home. Then she remembered something else. Her truck was still at the hotel downtown. Well, that was the least of her problems at the moment. She was sure Stella would give her a lift into town to pick it up. How she'd explain being back without it, or Archer or Baleweg . . . much less the weakened condition she was in . . . she had no idea. She groaned, unwilling to think about it.

Thoughts of Archer crept back in, along with worries about whether or not Baleweg was able to get to Catriona in time. Certainly if the worst had happened, she'd have felt it when she reached out that last time, but she'd been so weak, it had taken all she'd had just to find Baleweg. It was only because of his strong mind that the link had been made at all.

And then the idea hit her that she could try again to connect with them. At best it would give her some idea of Baleweg's success. She tried to sit up, but the wave of nausea and little twinkly lights blinking in front of her eyes drove her right back onto her pillow.

That was out of the question. At least for now. She stared at the ceiling, letting the totality of the experience finally filter in. Not the specific feelings, but the overall effect it had had on her. She marveled that she'd done it, but also shrank away from the toll it had taken. She didn't think any amount of training or discipline would make that an easier ordeal. She'd done the wise thing in choosing the career path that she had. Veterinary medicine would have destroyed her for certain.

A strange peace settled over her then. And she realized it was the last of the guilt leaving her. She hadn't let them down, or herself. She wasn't a healer. Not in her time, or in her mother's. And yet, as an empath, she had made a difference, she had saved lives. Many of them. Perhaps even Catriona's and the baby's.

The baby.

Her stomach clutched and her head throbbed anew. Baleweg had promised he'd let her know. She clung to that. If . . . if Catriona hadn't survived the birth, then what was to be done with her son? Talia was his only living relative. Well, if you could call living several hundred years before his birth a living relative.

The headache pummeling her worsened and she had to let the whole train of thought go. There was nothing she could do at this point but wait. And worry.

No worries. She heard Archer's voice so clearly in her mind, her gaze shot to the door, half expecting him to be standing there. Seeing it empty only underscored just how empty she felt without him. Her heart ached. They hadn't even said good-bye to one another. "Please just be okay," she whispered.

Ringer bobbed his head again.

Talia tried to smile, tried to take that as a positive sign. Who knew, maybe the little shifter could feel things, too. In the end, the smile wobbled as tears tracked down her cheeks anyway. It was over. She was home. "Alone."

Ringer hopped off her footboard and pecked at her toe, making her yelp. "Hey! Okay. Not alone. Jeez."

He stretched his long wings, shook them, then refolded them. His owlish stare was unwavering.

"Of course," she said softly. "He'll come back for

you." Then she shut her eyes tightly. "But what will he do about me?" Could she stand seeing him again, only to watch him walk away? No.

Yes. Yes, if it meant seeing for herself that he was healthy and whole. Yes, if it meant being held by him, kissed by him, one more time. Even if it was a good-bye kiss. She needed that. They deserved at least that.

&

When Talia awoke the next time, it was with the knowledge that she'd been dreaming. Dreaming of Archer and their time together. She looked about the room, but didn't see Ringer. It was very late, shadows were deep. Her stomach growled loudly. Surely that was a good sign.

But where was Ringer?

She didn't like the spurt of panic that shot through her. There was a desperate feel to it, as if Ringer were her only insurance and without him . . . No, no, she couldn't do this to herself. She'd already pinned far too much to Ringer's presence. She was going to have to get on with her life. Alone.

Just then a black furry thing leaped up and landed on her chest. She shrieked and batted at it, sending it flying toward her feet. Only when it rolled and landed on its feet, staring back at her with yellow eyes that were somehow familiar, did she realize. "Jesus, Ringer." She blew out a deep breath. "We're going to have to talk about this."

She sank back on her pillow, willing her heart to settle down. When it did, she realized she felt a tiny bit better. Not great by any stretch, but not as shaky. Maybe if she took things very slowly, she could make it to the bathroom. And if that went well, downstairs for some warm tea and toast. Actually, what she wanted was a huge steak and an ice-cold beer. But since her stomach recoiled violently even at the thought, she figured she'd have to settle for toast.

She very carefully rolled to a sitting position. And that was as far as she got for a good five minutes. That was how long it took for the cold sweats to go away. She considered calling the phone in the kennel office and asking Stella for help. But she wasn't up to explaining anything.

What would she say? What *could* she say? The whole thing had been an amazing adventure. But adventures were only fun for a while. She admitted then that she was thankful to be home. This was where she belonged. She wasn't the type to live for adventure. Not like Archer.

"Well, that was depressing."

She already knew that they weren't destined to be together, but she really didn't want further proof at the moment, thank you. So she blessedly shut down the whole avenue of thought and put all her concentration on what was of utmost importance to her right now. Getting to the bathroom.

❧

A week passed and Talia had almost regained her full strength. She still tired easily, but she was back at work, glad to be around Stella. Everyone at the Lodge had sent over get-well cards filled with notes on all kinds of herbal and holistic remedies, along with a casserole they'd made in cooking class and some handmade tissue-paper flowers. She'd been so touched she'd cried for an hour. But she cried easily these days. She blamed it on her illness, but she knew it was more than that.

Archer's absence from her life was still like a living thing inside her. It wasn't going away, it wasn't dulling with time. And it didn't help that Stella looked at her with such sorrow in her eyes.

Talia had had to fabricate a huge story about her
sudden return, a return that had left her truck in the
city. She had ended up telling them that they hadn't
had such a wonderful time and she'd come down
with a bug and taken a taxi home. Stella had been
crushed that their romance hadn't worked out.
She'd been so certain, she told Talia. Talia had finally all but begged her to not mention it anymore.
So now she just got those looks instead. Not much of
an improvement, but at least she didn't have to talk
about him.

She stood on the front porch and waved good-bye
as Stella and Tugger, along with one of her part-
timers, left for the day. They'd brought her truck
back for her, saving her the drive, which she still
wasn't really up to.

Talia scanned the area for Ringer. She could always tell it was him, whatever form he took. The eyes
were always the giveaway. Fortunately he seemed to
understand she was the only one he could reveal his
true nature to. She had lived in mortal fear the first
week or so that he'd change in front of Stella or one
of her other workers.

There was no sign of him at the moment, so she
went inside, fixed a cup of Miss Helen's Revitalizing
Rutabaga and Rosehip Tea, which was actually quite
good, then found herself wandering down to the
kennels. Stella had taken in a rescue during her brief
absence and Talia had found herself taking over full
care for the little guy. Something about him had
tugged at her right from the first . . . and she'd
given in to it rather than throwing up her usual barriers. This morning was the first time the pup had
shown the beginnings of trust. She smiled now just
thinking about it.

She let herself in quietly and stopped several feet

away, not wanting him to see her, just wanting to
observe. He was a shy one, usually staying in the back
of his run when anyone walked by. But she'd observed that he was somewhat more confident with the
other dogs, even defending his area with a swagger
and occasional growl or yip. Since he was all of ten
pounds, this was amusing—as well as being a very
good sign. His will hadn't been totally beaten into
submission.

Her heart tugged when she thought about the
connections she'd made with him, the pain he was
still recovering from. Any other time she'd have
stepped back, protected herself. But she simply
couldn't with this one. Or maybe she just didn't
want to.

Her persistence and patience had paid off this
morning. He hadn't slunk back when she approached. He hadn't come closer, but he hadn't
run. Right now he was wrestling a knotted piece of
denim into submission. Another good sign. *Work out
those frustrations, little guy.* Talia smiled. He'd take some
time, but he'd make it. They both would. She felt
her eyes burn as she came to the decision she'd
known she'd been approaching all week.

It was time. Talia Trahaern was going to adopt her
first pet. "You and me, tough guy," she said softly,
thrilled and not a little apprehensive about her decision. It was the right one, she knew. She'd learned
that giving her heart might be scary, but the rewards
were so great it was worth the risk. She stepped closer
to the pup, wishing she could scoop him up right
now and pour out some of the love she had building
up like a wave inside her.

The pup looked up from his rag with wary
eyes. But he didn't move. "Yeah, that's it." She
stayed where she was, just letting him get used to

smelling her. "I guess I should figure out what to name you."

"Fella goes on walkabout for a week and he's replaced by a dog."

Talia's heart came to a complete stop. Her stomach leaped up to take its place. And the room might have actually tilted. Certainly she was hearing things. He couldn't be— She whirled around. "Devin!"

Grinning, bold as life. "In the flesh."

All her fantasies of what she'd do, how she'd act, what she'd say, how she'd protect herself, her heart, if he ever came back, were rendered useless. She had already launched herself into his arms. And thanked God when he wrapped his arms tightly around her.

"I can't believe it. It's really you," she said, breathless.

His eyes squeezed shut. He said nothing, just held her, very tightly. Talia clung to him, still reeling from the shock of seeing him again. And was thankful beyond words that he needed to hold her as much as she needed to hold him. They'd sort the rest out later. Just as soon as they could let each other go.

Finally he shifted her back enough so he could look at her. Surprisingly, there were tears in his eyes. She laughed, because there were tears in hers, too.

"You're okay." They both spoke at the same time, then both laughed and nodded.

"Baleweg told me what you did, Tali. You scared me to death."

"Saved your life," she shot back, but her grin disappeared. "What . . . what happened? Baleweg promised he'd let me know, but I'd begun to think the worst."

"Did you?" There was worry and concern in his eyes. "That's the part I hated the most. But there were things we had to do and I wanted to answer all your questions when I did come. I hated leaving you here, not knowing. I'd hoped maybe you just . . . knew. I've spent every moment of every day thinking about you, hoping you were somehow connecting to that."

"I . . . I wanted to. At first I couldn't. Then, as I got stronger again . . . well, I guess I was just . . . I was afraid of what I'd feel." She pulled the blue orb from her pocket and laughed self-consciously. "I carry this around all the time; it makes me feel closer to you." She finally shrugged and looked away. "Baleweg promised and I figured if he never came back, that would be my answer."

He pulled her back to face him. "Tali, I'm sorry we worried you."

"It's okay, you're here now." She steeled herself. "So, please, tell me. I have to know. What happened? Catriona?" She swallowed hard. "The baby?"

"She's going to be okay. You should know that much, it was you who got her through childbirth." He stroked her face. "You have a nephew, Talia. You saved his life, and your sister's."

"She's okay?" Talia grabbed his shoulders. "But how?" She felt as if her whole being had been lit up from the inside. "I have a nephew?" she whispered in awe.

"Trevor is a right fine little man. We're mates. Only fair since I helped pull the little battler into this world." His eyes reflected his own awe. "It's a miracle, Tali, seeing a child be born."

"Trevor." Talia stilled. "Oh, my God." She had a nephew. She hugged Archer tightly with the sheer thrill of it. "And you were there!"

He hugged her back just as tightly. "We were both there, Talia. We were both there."

She pulled back. "Is Baleweg okay?"

"There's much to tell you. He and Emrys—"

"Emrys! What did he do? I tried to connect, tried to help—"

"You did, Talia. He's . . . well, I can't describe the odd bond that ties the two, they are so different. And yet, seeing them in the same room . . ." He shuddered. "It was the oddest thing. Emrys is younger but the spitting image of the old man when you look at him, especially the eyes."

"But, you can't mean . . . surely you did something to make certain he—"

"I did my best to make them see they were set to destroy one another and I think they understood that. Emrys is more like a spoiled child who was trying to get attention and Baleweg was the father figure who didn't have the first idea how to provide that attention. They're . . . working on it." He didn't look any more convincing than he sounded.

Talia was more than a little dubious. "They're working on it. Together."

Archer shrugged. "At least he can keep tabs on him this way. I can't tell you more than that."

She shuddered. "I'm not sure I want to know."

Archer nodded, clearly feeling the same.

"So, where is he now?"

"Last I heard, he's stayed at court. He personally escorted Niall, Catriona, and the baby."

"Niall?"

"Long story. He's a Nordic prince, the father of the baby, and he's the one who found the cure for Catriona. Actually, believe it or not, it was Emrys who led him to it."

She stopped dead. "Emrys?"

"Not with the intention of actually helping, mind you. He'd only done it to lure Niall into his plan to get close enough to the queen to take her."

She opened her mouth, at least a dozen different

questions on her tongue, then stopped and held up her hand. "I'm sure you'll explain all this to me, but right now I'm having a hard enough time imagining Baleweg willingly going to court." Talia put her hand on his arm. "Just tell me Emrys is not with him because no matter what—"

"Not to worry there. They've reached a certain . . . understanding. Emrys isn't too fond of the wee screaming ones at any rate." Archer pulled her back into his arms. "Baleweg has handled it. Trust in him, Tal."

She nodded, but was not completely convinced. "So," she said at length. "Baleweg is at court." She shook her head, pushing out the worry and letting the much-needed joy swell inside her.

"Pain in the ass he is, too. Stubborn, autocratic, thinks he knows everything about—" He broke off as Talia started laughing. "What?"

"Takes one to know one," she said, beaming up at him.

Archer opened his mouth, then closed it.

Talia just kept grinning. She didn't think she'd ever be able to stop. She couldn't even speak. The joy of simply standing here, staring at him, listening to him, was overwhelming. No matter what happened next, right now everything was perfect in her world. *He was okay. They were all okay.*

Archer looked concerned. "Sweetheart, don't take this the wrong way, but you look as if a band of fairies could knock you over. Maybe I should get you to the house."

"But—"

"No buts. I promise I'll tell you every single detail of what happened."

"I just wanted to tell you. About Ringer."

"Ah, yes, about that. Baleweg's idea. I know you mustn't have been too—"

She shushed him with a kiss. "It was the best present he could have given me. A living, breathing connection to you. Proof that I didn't dream the whole thing up." She smiled. "He does take some getting used to. But I guess you could say we're mates."

Archer scooped her up in his arms and whirled her about. "Well, all is fine in my world, then. The family of Devin Archer is now whole and complete."

Talia laughed, not minding that her head was spinning. Then his words sank in. "What exactly do you mean?"

He let her feet slide to the ground and looked into her eyes. "I mean what I said. My family is complete." His expression sobered. Except for the passion in his dark eyes. She felt the thrill of it down to her toes. "I know I took too long in coming back and I regret the worry I caused you. But I didn't want to come until I could—" He broke off, then blurted, "I knew I'd botch this."

She didn't know what to say, or even what he meant.

"You know, this isn't at all how I planned this."

She was so touched by his obvious distress but she couldn't help the dry smile that curved her lips. "You? Planned?"

He pretended to look offended. "I'll have you know I've spent long hours planning this very moment."

Her mouth tilted up, but she knew she was going to cry.

"Oh, no, we'll have none of that. Wait, wait."

She sniffed through her smile. "What is it I'm waiting for?"

He scooped her up again, carried her outside, and almost tripped over something. Swearing colorfully, he maintained his hold on her and barely got his balance back.

She looked down. "What is that?" Just outside the kennel door was her backpack, another larger one, three duffel bags, and several oddly shaped cases. "I, um, packed. Just a few things."

Talia did cry then, even as she laughed outright at the color that crept into his cheeks. "Just some stuff, huh?"

"Yeah." He dried her tears with his fingertip. "Do you think you're feeling well enough for a short walk?"

Right at that moment, Talia was fairly certain she could fly if she put her mind to it. She nodded.

Archer let her slide to her feet. "Wait just one moment." He turned and dug into her pack, then came back with Beatrice's hat in his hands. "Here." He plopped it on her head. "I've actually dreamt of you wearing that horrible thing." He hoisted another pack on his back, took her hand, then said, "What the hell," and scooped her back into his arms.

"Devin—"

"Yeah, yeah, you can walk. I just want to hold you." He looked down at her. "Okay?"

"Okay." She realized then they hadn't even kissed yet. And it was suddenly a yawning, gaping need inside her. But he'd "planned" and she was going to let him call the shots.

"Almost there."

Talia had a pretty good idea where they were going, but she still found herself holding her breath until they got there. She let it out when Archer stopped by the flat rock. Their rock.

He let her slide to her feet once again. "Okay, now turn around."

"What?"

He motioned with his hand. "Turn around. Don't peek."

He was actually nervous. She smiled, touched.
"Really, you don't have to—"

"Tali, please."

She raised her hands, totally charmed. "Okay,
okay." She turned around, but listened un-
ashamedly. Zippers whizzed open, things rustled,
something broke, Archer swore, another zipper
whizzed, more rustling, more swearing. And she
thought her heart might just burst with how much
she loved him. "I didn't know kangaroos could do
that," she said. "Do all Aussies swear so creatively?"

"We're creative in all kinds of ways, sweetheart. I
thought you knew that about me by now."

Talia felt the heat climb inside her. And then his
hands were covering her eyes and the heat spiked
clear through the top of her head.

"Okay," he said next to her ear. "You can turn
around, but don't open your eyes. Promise me."

"I promise." He turned her around, and into his
arms. Then his lips were on hers and her eyes stayed
shut anyway. It was better, so much better than all
her fevered dreams and wistful remembrances. And
once wasn't nearly enough.

"You make me want things I've never wanted,
Tali," he murmured against her mouth.

She opened her eyes, but looked only at his. "I
know what you mean. I was all set to live alone, me
and my animals. Animals I gave away to someone
else to love. I can't settle for that anymore. You
taught me that."

He looked honestly shocked. "I did?"

She nodded. "You taught me that I have a lot
more to give if I am willing to risk my heart."

He was trembling. "I didn't even know I had one.
Not really. My whole life has been focused on security. Making sure I had enough, that I'd never want

for anything ever again. And that I'd never depend on anyone else to give it to me. And then I met you, and I needed you. In ways that had nothing to do with independence or material wealth." He took her hand, kissed her palm, and placed it on his heart. "You gave me back this. And I want to share it with you."

Tears sprang to her eyes again.

"You once asked me if people still get married in my time. The answer is yes, they do, if that is how they wish to show their commitment to one another. I never, ever, believed in that romantic type of love, much less any kind of commitment. But I've already committed my heart to you, Talia. And I find that I want the rest." He shifted and turned so she could see what he had set up.

There was a silk blanket, suspiciously woven in the royal colors, and a bottle of champagne with two glasses. But it was the petals, the hundreds of petals, that caught her attention. Some were blackened and crushed from their arduous journey—perhaps those touched her the most.

"My romantic bower," she whispered.

"You deserve more, and I want to give it to you."

She turned back to him. "I want only one thing from you. I want your love."

"I do love you, Talia. That I most certainly do."

"Then the answer is yes."

Archer tipped his head back and shouted to the skies, then once again swept her up in his arms. "She loves me! Did you hear that?" His words echoed across the pond.

"I'm fairly certain they heard you all the way to the Lodge."

He spun her about, then stopped. "Say it, Tali. I need to hear you say it."

"I love you, Devin Archer. I love you with my whole heart."

A loud purring intruded and they turned to find Ringer, in sleek, black cat mode, luxuriating among the rose petals.

"Thinks I did all this for him, most likely."

He'd tried to sound irritated, but Talia saw the love and the relief in his eyes as he looked at his other life companion.

"I won't tell him if you won't."

Archer looked back to her. "Let me give him the boot."

She traced a hand over his face. "You do know how much what you did means to me."

"I just wanted to—"

"I know," she said, reaching up to kiss him. "You need the romance as much as I do." His face reddened adorably, but he didn't deny it and she kissed him again. "Now, about all that other stuff you packed, does that mean—?"

"Yeah. I'm home." He looked down into her eyes, and winked even though his eyes were glassy. "*Our home.* I quite like the sound of that."

She held his face in her hands and kissed him long and hard. "Me, too."

"I'm thinking that, at the moment, *our bed* has an even sweeter ring."

She grinned. "I'm thinking I agree with you."

"See? We're starting this marriage out on the right foot, then."

"Don't get too used to it," she warned, still smiling.

"Oh, I plan to get used to a lot of things. Mostly, I plan to get used to seeing you smiling up at me like that and knowing I am at least partly responsible for it."

"Oh, Devin." Her heart melted completely.

He winked and swung her up the path, toward home, toward their future.

Behind them, Ringer stretched out among the petals and smiled.

Epilogue

*H*e truly is a miracle." Talia looked down, mesmerized by the perfect little hand clinging to
her finger.

"We think so."

Talia sent a quick smile toward Catriona, who was
herself smiling up at her husband, Niall.

Archer propped his chin on her shoulder and
toyed with Trevor's other hand. "Not a bad-looking
sort."

"He's the finest-looking young man in the land."

Talia swallowed a laugh. Baleweg had become a
man transformed since the rescue. "Well, you're a
bit biased, being his godfather and all."

Baleweg sniffed, but his eyes glowed as he turned
his attentions to his godson. He'd been coming to
terms with the life he'd spent distancing himself
from everyone. He and Emrys were working on it,
but it wasn't easy. Still, he was sticking it out. And
the little future king was doing a great deal in teaching the Old One how to reach out with his heart.

Talia slid her finger from her nephew's fierce
grip and moved back next to Archer. "They're all so
happy."

Catriona, who was still recovering, but already re-
markably healthy-looking, sat ensconced in a plush
lounge with Trevor in her lap, her husband perched

next to her. "Yes, we are." She leaned over to kiss Niall.

Talia thought again about the amazing, tumultuous adventure that had brought them to this moment. Emrys was basically behaving himself, Chamberlain was in exile, and the queen had regained a firm hold on the monarchy. Baleweg worried anyway, but when he looked into his godson's eyes, one would never have known.

"I'm glad he's here," Talia whispered to Archer. "It's good for all of them." She looked to Archer and squeezed his hand. "I meant what I said. If you want—"

"My life is with you. At our home. In Connecticut. Occasional holidays to court to see our favorite nephew will be more than enough." He turned her face to his. "I love you. And I have never been more content."

Talia settled back against him. Archer had embraced his move back in time with all the gusto he embraced everything else in life. He seemed quite happy and settled out in the country.

He had surprised her by taking on the task of winning over the Lodge residents with equal fortitude. She grinned. Not an easy task, despite the fact that he was now her fiancé. In two short months, he'd already taken on the job of adding another Furry Friends Day, which he ran himself. He'd told her just last week that the Colonel had begun sharing war stories with him. And Miss Helen had been caught staring at his backside with more than a little admiration.

And then there was his recent discovery of the stock market, which no longer existed in his time. She'd already driven him into New York City to walk Wall Street and watch the frenzied trading firsthand at the Stock Exchange. He'd already made some investments and, not surprisingly she supposed, they were thriving. The whole enterprise captivated his business mind. And she was perfectly happy with it, as it allowed him to be home with her more often than not and got them both into the city on occasion, too.

He wanted driving lessons next. She didn't even want to think about that. She still had a wedding to plan.

Catriona and Niall had tried to convince them to have their wedding here at the castle, but they'd wanted to begin their life together where they intended to share it. She wished her sister and brother-in-law could attend, but understood they couldn't leave. They were hoping, however, to convince Baleweg to come. If he could take a break from playing doting godfather, that is.

"Have you asked him yet?" she whispered to Archer.

He shook his head. "Don't want him getting too swelled a head just yet. He's already been in a royal wedding. Now he's a royal godfather. Being my best man . . . well, there'll be no living with him after that."

She swatted him on the arm, then slid her hand around his waist, leaning on his shoulder as they watched Niall and Catriona nuzzle and coo at their son.

"I'm not so sure we can top the royal wedding," she said.

Archer wasn't listening. He was watching Trevor and his parents. "So, you think we might have ourselves one of those?"

She looked up to find him grinning at her, hope twinkling clearly in his eyes. *How have I come to find this?* She'd never even contemplated being a mother. Had never even thought to be married. Now, everything seemed possible. *You make me want things I never knew I could want.* His words rang truer every day.

"I'm still getting used to dealing with Ringer and Rascal." Her little puppy was no longer so little. Ringer had steered clear at first, but eventually he'd revealed himself to the fluffy mutt and they'd forged an unlikely bond. In fact, she probably owed most of Rascal's rehabilitation to Ringer. Rascal seemed to understand his ever-changing friend, and from that he had learned that not all humans were the same, despite their similar appearance.

"Rascal isn't exactly the coddling type," Archer said.

Talia laughed. Rascal was still more standoffish with his humans than she'd like, but they were getting there. "Since when did you want a pet you could cuddle? Because Ringer is about the least cuddly pet I've ever met."

"Ringer isn't a pet. He's a mate. Family." He squeezed her. "So is Rascal." He winked. "I suppose."

The teasing light faded from his eyes and he stood silent for a moment. Her soon-to-be husband was such an incongruous mix of arrogance, confidence, and boyish uncertainty. He was so sure of himself, except when he wanted something and wasn't sure she'd go along. He so wanted to please her, but he was equally determined to get what he wanted. He'd quickly discovered that asking her in bed, just after making breathless love to her, was a successful approach. But he honestly couldn't do anything unless he really thought it was okay with her. It bothered him endlessly if he thought she'd just given in to him. Then he was so charmingly insecure she couldn't help doing whatever she could to work things out.

"I wasn't actually joking," he said finally. "Earlier I meant."

"About?"

"Having one. Of those, I mean," he added, nodding toward Trevor. "Of our own." He leaned down and kissed her neck. "You and me."

She let him kiss her neck, her heart already a melted pool at her feet. "We're still planning the wedding, and you're talking kids?"

He turned her around then, and looked quite seriously into her eyes. "I'm not saying right away. We have a lot of adjusting to do, with one another. I know that. I just wanted to, you know, feel you out. On the subject. In general."

He really was quite adorable. She stepped in closer. "Well, on the subject, in general, I'm thinking, oh, I don't know. Four? Five?"

He looked confused, then his eyes popped wide. "Five?" He swallowed hard. "Now wait a minute, I mean, maybe we should—"

Talia laughed and pulled him tight against her, kissing him quiet. She could see another round of negotiations in their future. "This should be interesting," she murmured against his lips.

Then he took charge of the kiss, making her squirm against him and forget completely that they weren't alone. He grinned against her mouth. "I was just thinking the very same thing."

About the Author

Nationally bestselling author, Donna Kauffman, has often wondered what the future world will be like. The demands of a busy husband, three growing boys, two rowdy terriers, two noisy baby parrots, and a house that looks like a tornado site often have her wishing one of those handy triangles would open up in front of her. She's not picky, even a window to modern-day Hawaii would be just fine. But as that is unlikely to happen, she's just as happy to take a break from her everyday insanity to enjoy notes and posts from her readers. Please feel free to visit her website at *www.donnakauffman.com* and drop her a lifeline.

Dear Readers:

I've wanted to revisit the inspiring western high-lands of Scotland ever since I wrote *The Legend Mackinnon.* Finally, I'm getting the chance to do just that with my next romance, *The Charm Stone,* set on a tiny island off the coast of Skye, and coming soon from Bantam Books.

Meet my hero, Connal MacNeil, clan leader of the MacNeils, who has been waiting in Black's Tower for the return of his clan's charm stone and the prosperity it promises to bestow. The problem is . . . he has been waiting for three hundred years! His patience has just about run out completely, to say the least, when he meets our heroine Josie, who finds the stone when it washes up on her beach . . . in South Carolina! Charm stones have a long and colorful heritage in both Scottish and Celtic history as bearers of good fortune, and so Josie decides to return this stone to the original family owners. She never imagines this will lead her to a devilishly handsome ghost, hundreds of years old, who is demanding not only the charm stone she has in her possession . . . but also that she bear the next MacNeil clan chief!

I was inspired to write this story when I read an article about the actual MacNeil clan. For a pound note a year and a bottle of whisky, the current clan chief signed a 1,000-year lease with Historic Scotland to ensure continued renovations of the clan seat, Kisimul, on the island of Barra. Legend has it that Kisimul has been a MacNeil stronghold since the eleventh century, which really blew me away. As I kept digging into the history behind this, a story began to take shape. Wouldn't it be interesting if my heroine ended up in Scotland in possession of the MacNeil stone . . . only to discover that the bearer of the charm stone is destined to belong to the last clan chief . . . who lived three hundred years before her?

I hope you'll pick up a copy of *The Charm Stone* and read Josie and Connal's love story.

Best wishes,
Donna Kauffman